Bloodstone

by

Helen C. Johannes

Bloodstone

Cover Art by *Rae Monet, Inc. Design*

The Wild Rose Press, Inc.
PO Box 708
Adams Basin, NY 14410-0708
Visit us at www.thewildrosepress.com

Publishing History
First Faery Rose Edition, 2013
Print ISBN 978-1-62830-055-0
Digital ISBN 978-1-62830-056-7

Published in the United States of America

Dedication

To my critique partner Joe
who spurred me on to finish this book.
To Mary Ellen
who read this first
and helped find the weak spots.
To my WisRWA friends who kept encouraging me
throughout the process.
To my husband
who's been behind me all the way.

List of Characters and Places in *Bloodstone*

Ayliss – Durren's sister

Brandelmore – Master of Nolar, a Landowner controlling the region and town

Burl – Gem trader

Durren Drakkonwehr – Dragon Keeper and heir to the Sword of Drakkonwehr

Errek Eolan – Durren's best friend and second in command

Freth – Cook at the White Boar Inn

Gareth – Stableboy and servant at the White Boar Inn

Kiros – Legendary hero who set the Stone Dam at Herrok-Eneth

Koronolan – Legendary hero who brought down the Last Dragon

Krad – Beast-men who infest the Wehrland

Leah – Gareth's mother

Mirianna – Daughter of Tolbert, determined to accompany him to Ar-Deneth

Nell – Serving maid at the White Boar Inn

Owender – Historian and chronicler of *The History of the People*

Pumble – Partner of Rees

Rees – Guide provided to Tolbert by the Master of Nolar

Shadow Man – Gem hunter, provider of bloodstone

Syryk – Mage seeking the Dragon Chant to raise and control the Last Dragon

Tolbert – Gem-cutter commissioned to make jewelry for the Master's wedding

Ulerroth – Innkeeper and gem trader of the White Boar Inn in Ar-Deneth

Ar-Deneth – Town at the western edge of the Wehrland

Beggeth – Place of banishment for enemies of the People, a stronghold of black magic

Drakkonwehr – Dragon Keep, a fortress to guard the Last Dragon's resting place

Herrok-Eneth – Stone Dam keeping creatures of Beggeth out of the Wehrland

Nolar – Prosperous town and region east of the Wehrland, controlled by a rich Master

Wehrland – Mountainous no-man's land separating the People from Beggeth

Chapter One

Mirianna peered through her lashes at blue sky decorated with wisps of bright clouds.

Morning? But how…?

A quick inventory of her senses told her she lay on broken plates of rock. Spikes of meadow grass leaned over her shoulder. Distant treetops speared the sky, ringing a clearing that sloped down and away from the lichen-studded stone under her fingertips.

The last she remembered, she'd been riding her horse through the night and searching for her father. Alone. Lost in the no-man's land that was the Wehrland, while branches lashed her face and snatched at her cloak. Running from…*something…*

Led by…*someone?*

Twin glimmers of yellow-green, luminescent *eyes* hovered on the edge of her consciousness and vanished when she tried to bring them into focus. The effort awakened a torrent of complaints from every muscle and joint in her body. Mirianna groaned.

Had she fallen? She moved each of her limbs in turn. Finding them stiff but uninjured, she struggled to sit up, and a damp cloth dropped from her head into her lap. She stared at it while everything else pitched and rocked.

"Would you like some tea? It's willow bark. Good for aches."

Mirianna carefully raised her gaze. A boy about thirteen knelt beside her. He wore a cloth wrapped around his forehead, and his tunic, ripped over one shoulder, was russet with dried blood. All she could think of to say was, "You—you're hurt."

Color rose on his pale cheeks. "I'm on the mend. You're the one who fainted." With a crooked grin, he proffered a bowl. "Drink this. It'll make you feel better. I should know."

He'd coaxed a smile from her, and he looked harmless, so Mirianna held out her hand. When he made no move to pass her the tea, she leaned toward him and took the bowl from his grasp. His gaze, which ought to have followed her movement, remained fixed on a point somewhere near her chin.

The blind boy.

Apprehension thrilled along her nerves. *The boy couldn't possibly be alone. He hadn't been alone before...*

Memories followed in a stomach-tightening rush, tumbling over one another, strange events made even stranger by this ungodly wilderness. A voice in the night, sounding from nowhere and...everywhere, terrifying her and yet somehow stopping her horse from bolting. A presence haunting her room at the inn, invading her dreams with vivid, erotic suggestions. A touch—*a dream!*—that wasn't so much a touch but a desire made...*tangible*. Mirianna quivered. Her breasts swelled, and the burgeoning nipples prickled against the fabric of her bodice.

Where was the boy's master? Where was the Shadow Man?

Her fingers clenched, sloshing warm liquid onto

her hand. She sucked in a breath, placed the bowl on the ground, and twisted her body to find the answer.

"So," said the voice that made her stomach break into shards of sensation, "you *do* remember."

Mirianna forced a swallow. The Shadow Man stood so close she could smell boot leather and wool, could see black-encased thigh and calf muscles that looked as solid as the rock on which she sat. *Looked* solid, because underneath the black hood, gloves and all-concealing clothing had to be nothing at all but darkness.

"I—I remember you told us the way to Ar-Deneth." Resisting the inclination of her gaze to rise, she turned away, making a show of reaching for the tea and sipping it. *Don't look at him!* Instead, she scanned the clearing for signs of her father. *Be safe, Papa. Please be safe!*

"Did you make it to Ar-Deneth?" The boy leaned forward with hands on knees. "I served at the inn until a few days ago. Did you stay there?"

"Yes." Mirianna managed a wan smile until she remembered he couldn't see it. She touched the back of his hand instead. "It was a very nice place."

"Gareth," the Shadow Man said, "check the pack mare. See if her leg is fit."

A look of disappointment crossed the boy's features, but he stood without hesitation. Staff in hand, he felt his way down the hillside toward four horses tethered below. Mirianna noticed her own gelding among them.

She sipped the tea, swilled it, and sipped again, forcing herself to linger over the cooling liquid. The Shadow Man's brusque order to the boy told her he stood so close, she could almost feel the imprint of his lower legs cradling her spine. She wished he would speak or leave before the brackish tea made her vomit or her strung-tight nerves made her bolt.

"Why didn't you stay in Ar-Deneth?" he demanded. "Why did you have to come back?"

His voice, though low, ripped at the shreds of her control. Not because it accused. She'd expected that. Just as she'd expected anger. And menace. What set her nerve endings vibrating was something that underlay all the rest, something she should have expected because she'd heard it before, only she hadn't recognized it then. Nor could she quite name it now, except it bore elements of frustration. And anguish.

She set the bowl aside. "Please understand, I wouldn't have come, but we—my father—needed more bloodstone. Ulerroth said—the innkeeper said you were the only one who—"

"There were three men with you. Where are they?"

His tone brought Mirianna's chin up, but she held her gaze fixed on the empty tea bowl. She was not going to cry. Her father was safe…somewhere. He'd been ahead of her when they escaped the ambush. "I—the clearing was full of Krad. We got separated."

"Krad!" The Shadow Man strode to the lip of the hillside and planted one boot on a rock.

He stood half turned away and far enough the jangling of her nerves faded to a hum. Emboldened, Mirianna let her gaze rise. The morning sun shone full on his back, showing her the sheen of wear on the black hood, tunic and breeches that concealed every inch of his flesh but hid none of the contours. On his raised thigh she detected a tear that had been carefully

4

mended. His gloves and boots bore the creases and scuffs of long use. Even his belt showed faintly green where the dye had faded. A sword, the broken blade extending no more than two hands' span from the hilt, stuck out from his belt like a common thief's dagger.

Was this the being who had invaded her dreams and turned them so disturbingly sensual? Was this the wraith who two nights ago had spirited the blind boy from their sight? Was this the possessor of a voice that had shaken her to the core? In the full day's sun, he looked no more than a man, taller than some, leaner and more fit than most. Chagrinned by her fears, Mirianna rocked to her knees and made ready to rise.

He turned at the rustle of her movement. Her gaze went automatically to his face. But there was no face to be seen. Only a shapeless drape of black cloth filled his hood where eyes and nose and mouth should be.

Mirianna sat as if turned to stone. Horror cooled her blood, and the hair rose on every part of her body. *It's his look. One look from him—at him—and men go mad. Or die. By the Dragon, let me not die!*

Somehow, she summoned the power to close her eyes. She knew she'd succeeded only when she opened them again and the Shadow Man no longer filled her vision. Every nerve, however, thrummed with his presence, and she knew he stood not more than three paces behind her and to the left. She knew, too, he faced the forest's edge, his right hand gripping the scrolled hilt of the weapon in his belt. She knew all this, and more, because somehow he'd let her know it so she might never again forget who and what he was. *Don't worry. I won't forget again.*

She turned slowly, like one waking from a dream,

and saw what had captured his attention, three riders emerging from the trees. "Papa!" she choked, and stumbled to her feet to meet him.

Tolbert slid out of the saddle and wrapped his arms around his daughter. "Mirianna, lamb, I thought I'd lost you."

Mirianna pressed her face into his neck. She clung for a moment, then leaned back and let him look at her. "I'm fine, Papa. Honestly, I am. But you—" She plucked a cedar twig from his hair. Creases etched his cheeks, and a distinct grayness underlay his usual color. He looked every one of his years, and more. "You need to eat."

Tolbert chuckled, but the sound broke into a cough. When he recovered breath, he hugged her again and kissed her gently on the cheek. "So, lamb, do you. So do we all, now."

"Perhaps we can share your fire."

In the joy of finding her father, Mirianna had forgotten Rees and Pumble, the two men the Master of Nolar had given her father as escort. And even that dark *being* which stood somewhere behind her and drew Rees's stony glare. The Master of Nolar's man still sat his horse, and his hand hovered near his bow. Beside him, Pumble stood, sweating, his fingers twitching over the hilt of his sword. She turned slowly in her father's arms.

"I said," Rees repeated, "perhaps we can share your fire, *this* time...Shadow."

The Shadow Man stood at the rock ledge, his body as motionless as a bat captured by the sun. His hand rested on the hilt of the sword in his belt, and between his gloved fingers something glinted red. His hood revealed only a drape of cloth where his face should be, yet she knew underneath every inch of that which passed for face was turned on Rees, and the air between them stretched to a brittle thinness.

"Do with it as you please," he said at last. "The boy and I were just about to leave."

"Wait!" Tolbert put Mirianna aside. "I need—"

"Bloodstone?" The black hood swiveled. Her father stiffened under the weight of the invisible regard. "There is no more bloodstone, old man. Go home, while you still can."

Tolbert shook his head violently. "But Ulerroth—"

"Ulerroth is a fool," said the voice that vibrated along Mirianna's nerves. "And so are you, if you stay another day in the Wehrland."

A stallion's shrill scream punctuated his words.

The Shadow Man spun. Below the rock ledge, the tethered horses milled, huffing. The blind boy clung to the pack mare's halter, his face a pasty white. "Sir, I think I smell—"

"Krad!" Rees coughed, recoiling from a wave of stench that stole Mirianna's breath.

"They must have followed us!" Pumble wheezed.

"Fools!" The Shadow Man's faceless gaze raked from Rees to Mirianna. "I should damn you all to Beggeth, but the Krad will see to that soon enough." He turned. "Gareth, free the horses!"

"Wait!" Tolbert said as an unearthly, high-pitched clamor erupted from the woods below. "What about us? What do we do?"

Only the hood rotated, cocking with exaggerated deliberation. "Why, you die, old man."

Her father blanched. His grip on Mirianna's arms

7

faltered.

She saw the Shadow Man turn, saw the muscles of his thighs bunch as he prepared to leap down the hillside, saw, in the corner of her eye, shapes gathering along the tree line below, horrible shapes she'd seen only hours before rushing at her from a darkened clearing. With a shudder, she broke from her father's grasp.

"Please!" She reached out to the black sleeve. "Help us!"

He recoiled at her touch like one snake-bitten. The sudden, sharp focus of his regard staggered her, but she backed no more than a step. No matter how he terrified her, he'd helped her once. She'd been led to him again, and not, her instincts told her, without reason.

"Please," she repeated. "Help us. I—we'll do anything."

"Anything?"

His voice was a whisper that caressed flesh.

Mirianna's stomach quivered. Her breasts tingled. Her mouth grew even drier.

Without thinking, she slid her tongue along her lips. Vaguely, she wondered what she'd done. And why time seemed suspended, as if everyone but she and the Shadow Man had been cast in stone and all sound arrested.

All sound except the taut, guttural repeat of his question.

"Anything?"

If she were sane, she would seize the opportunity to clarify, to explain, to negotiate her reply.

But even as she watched herself stand on the rock ledge and confront a shadow, she knew the question spoke not to her head but to her heart, and her heart answered in the only way it could, plainly and without hesitation.

"Yes," she breathed, "anything."

Chapter Two

Ten days earlier…

The stone glinted, a red-black clot amid the usual sand-and-pebble slurry in the panning dish. The man peering at it through the eyeholes of his face-covering sucked in a breath.

At least fifty-five grains, said the Voice in his head. *Enough to be quit of this place.*

Only if it proves true. He closed his eyes, mastering his breathing, until his hands steadied and his concentration focused. Then, with deliberate care, he tilted the dish. Water dribbled out, leaving only quartz chips, flecked granite, and sand particles clustered around the thumbnail-size stone.

With a gloved fingertip, he nudged the stone from its sandy nest and rolled it into the center of the dish. *Perfectly oval.* He blew out a breath, fluttering his face covering. *Color and shape, good.* There was but one more test. His gut knew the stone was true, but his gut had fallen for an illusion before, and he had to be sure.

Pinching the stone between thumb and forefinger, the man picked it up. Blood hummed in his ears, but his hands were steady as he set the dish aside on a flat rock. He placed the stone in the center of his gloved palm and pushed out of his mind all thoughts of what a find like this could mean. This was the Wehrland after all; nothing was ever as it seemed. With another breath, he stretched out his arm and opened his hand and its contents to the sun.

When only the black glove warmed, his muscles tensed. *This is taking far too long. It's not—*

The stone flared into translucence, transforming his palm into a pool of deep, glossy red. "Bloodstone," he breathed.

"Let Ulerroth find the flaw in this," he announced to the gray horse grazing on the opposite bank. The animal's ears flicked, but it did not raise its head.

Before he could close his fingers, could tuck the stone safely away, spears of scarlet light burst from the bloodstone, slashing red across the solid black of his tunic and sleeves. Without thinking, he stared at it. Into it. And the world shifted, wrenched itself inside out, and went dark...

He saw himself crouched, as always, in a rock-hewn tunnel lit by a distant torch while smoke oozed from crevices around a massive oaken door. Tendrils spiraled upward, feeding a thick yellow haze overhead. He coughed. Sweat dripped from his hair, stinging his eyes. The sound of rushing footsteps brought him swiveling to his feet, shield up, heart pounding. His fingers gripped the hilt of the ancient double-edged Sword of Drakkonwehr, where the large bloodstone embedded in the intersection of hand guard, blade, and hilt glowed softly, a dark, deep red...

In the meadow, in the late afternoon sun and fresh mountain air, the man snapped shut his fist, sealing the stone inside, quenching its fire, stopping the nightmare before it began. Again. If only he'd moved faster to secure the gem.

He inhaled a cleansing breath, clearing lightheaded

specks from his vision, before he focused his thoughts on the stone, hot in his gloved palm. "Some fool will pay a pretty price to dangle this between his whore's breasts." His fingers tightened at the image, but he forced them to relax. He would trade with Ulerroth, as usual. Nothing else.

I'm beyond such needs. He stared at the trampled moss between his boots. *I have to be...by now.*

Your dream woman would disagree, said the Voice in his head. *Or don't you remember her in the daylight?*

He did, all too vividly. She was not the *form* of woman that usually filled his dreams when *this* body— this cloaked and hooded *shell*—grew hungry, but one particular woman whose face had begun taking form a scant two months ago as soon as he entered the Wehrland. That his mind had conjured a complete stranger disturbed him as much as the vision itself.

All the more reason to leave as soon as possible, said the Voice in his head.

On the bank above, his horse shook its bridle and huffed.

"Steady, Ghost." Rising from his crouch, he followed the animal's pricked-ear gaze. At the edge of the upland clearing, a stone's throw away, a large, yellow-gray shape slipped through mottled shadows. "It's only that she-lion again."

He dropped the gem into a pouch at his waist. Climbing to the top of the bank, he watched faint movements of foliage as a Wehrland lion traversed part way around the clearing's edge. When it reached a spot upstream of the man, it paused in a pool of sunlight and stood, black-tipped tail twitching, and rubbed its cheek against a sapling.

The man snorted. "Don't think you're fooling me, she-cat. I've been watching your every move, too." Two mornings ago he'd first noticed the huge feline lying on a sun-drenched outcrop overlooking the stream he was panning. It had done nothing then, nothing but watch him collect garnets, gold dust, and jet. He'd seen it in the afternoon, too, a flash of yellow-gray glimpsed between bushes. And at night, the scream and the sudden flare of cat's eyes—too close—while Ghost plunged at the end of his tether. He'd brought the horse nearer and slept with his knife beside his hand. Today, the animal had followed him here.

Being stalked irritated him. Almost as much as traveling this far into the Wehrland for a handful of gems.

"Go fill your belly elsewhere," the man said, stooping for a rock to throw.

The big cat dropped into a crouch. Flattening its ears, it stared.

The man froze in mid-reach. His mind told him something else had startled the lion. His senses, reporting over the sudden roar of his blood, told him the animal's gaze was fixed on something beyond him. Under his hood and face-covering, the back of his neck prickled and he listened.

Bees still hummed in the clover near his boots, but the meadowlarks had ceased their calling. His hand moved stealthily toward the knife at his belt.

At the scrape of gravel, he spun. The Krad was on him in a split second, a dark blur of matted fur. The man had only enough time to dodge the down-swing of the creature's flint blade, to pivot sideways and thrust his own knife upwards. His knuckles hit ribs, and he jerked the weapon back. The beast-man crashed into the panning dish, flipping it into the stream. A few stones followed the dish down the bank to the water's edge.

The man whirled, but the mountain meadow behind him was empty of anything more threatening than a quail flushed from a blackberry bush. He spun back to the creature lying in a heap on the stream bank. Its mouth was open and spittle clung to the furred chin. Under heavy brows, deep-set black eyes stared at nothing. The flint knife had broken, but the man still kicked the pieces away from fingers caked with dirt. One scratch, one nick from even a fragment of the poison-smeared blade was enough to kill, and even though the creature looked dead—

The stench hit him full in the face. "Filthy, stinking Krad!" Leaping to the stream, he plunged his gloved hand and knife into it and scrubbed away every trace of the beast-man's blood. He had been lucky. This was the first Krad he'd encountered since entering the Wehrland, and this one was alone. Grabbing his panning dish and gear, he mounted his horse. Where there was one Krad, there was sure to be a pack.

****

The town of Nolar, east of the Wehrland...

Mirianna dreamed the same dream again, just before morning. Her lover leaned over her, as he always did, with his strong shoulders blocking the light and his face nothing but a glimmer of eyes. Sometimes he touched her lips, but when she woke to the contact, it was her own fingers tracing the shape of her mouth, leaving her hungry and unsatisfied. Remembering the dream while she dressed, Mirianna sighed. Someday she would find the man of her dreams. Someday she would no longer have to endure furtive touches from the leering boys and men of Nolar, but would enjoy the stroke of one special man's fingers, hands, lips, and—

She jerked open her eyes and pressed her palms to burning cheeks. It wouldn't do if any of her father's customers found her daydreaming. Especially if her face looked as red as it felt. They already looked at her sideways even though she'd lived among them her whole life. Just because the tailor had once seen her "brandishing" a sword in her father's workshop, she'd had to close the shutters whenever a bejeweled blade tempted her to try its balance. The residents of Nolar apparently considered it improper for a gem-cutter's daughter to find the weapons as fascinating as the precious stones her father set into the hilts.

Mirianna pulled a comb through her hair. What would her good neighbors think if they knew it wasn't the weapons that drew her but the legends they figured in, the Deeds of Kiros, Koronolan and the Hero Mages, the Sword of Drakkonwehr? The stuff of dreams, they would tell her—just like her "lover"—and not fit to be part of a dutiful daughter's day.

She finished fastening her hair—which the butcher's wife insisted was "as thick with curls as a harlot's"—into what she hoped was a respectable knot and returned her attention to her morning chores. Tomorrow she would see about buying straw to stuff the mattresses afresh. That is, if the butcher liked the Nolar guild ring her father had made for him. And if he paid in something other than trade.

Sighing, she surveyed her father's worktable. There was but one reason a gem cutter and goldsmith of his skill should live so sparsely. The butcher would by now be saying, "Did I promise you beef, Tolbert? I'm so sorry, but it's old this time of year. I can let you have pork next week, if you don't mind waiting." Just as the weaver had said to him last month, in her presence, "My apprentice, you know, was taken ill, and I've had to do the work of two. I promised you a cloak of dyed wool, but all I have is this short cape. Will that do?"

Mirianna would have held out for what was due, but Tolbert, with his eager smile, had bobbed his head and accepted the cape. "Better to take what you can than to leave with empty hands," he told her when she remarked it would hardly keep him as warm as the formerly agreed upon cloak.

"Then, at least," she said, "ask for more than your work is worth. That way, you can bargain and still receive full value."

Tolbert's watery blue eyes widened. "Never!" He threw aside his mallet. "I have a reputation to uphold."

Mirianna had bent to kiss his head between scattered strands of graying hair. He was right, of course. He'd lived fifty-two years on the principle of personal integrity, and she with her meager twenty winters could hardly dispute his experiences. She only wished others in Nolar adhered to the same principle, or that he would occasionally listen to her about insisting on full payment. Perhaps then she could divert some of their income for living expenses before her father spent the coin on some unique gem or another handful of uncut stones.

She busied herself with his worktable, organizing his tools so each would be in its assigned place when he sat down to work. It was a task she performed at least three times a day. If she didn't, Tolbert would tear the cottage upside down looking for a chisel he'd laid down an hour before, in plain sight, on the opposite side of the table.

"Mirianna! Mirianna!"

It was her father's voice, breathless and...frantic? She spun to the half-open cottage door and gripped it.

Tolbert burst through the gate, his balding head glistening and as red as his cheeks under the wisps of gray beard clinging to them. He bustled through the door she opened for him, dropped two bundles on his worktable, and grabbed her hands.

"What news I have!" he cried, spinning her around with the energy of a twenty-year-old. "What wonderful news!"

Mirianna clung to his hands as they whirled past crockery, kicked over the broom, and landed with a thud on the bench beside the door. "Papa, Papa, what?"

"Flowers!" He gamboled to the worktable and grabbed one bundle. "Flowers for my lovely daughter's hair, for her hands, for our table!" Thrusting a bunch of peonies into her lap, he kissed her cheek and tucked one huge pink bloom behind her ear.

The blossom drooped. She caught it beside her cheek. The fragrance, heavy and sweet, welled up around her. She closed her eyes, momentarily drunk with it. "Papa...?" she whispered.

But he was already shaking out the other bundle. "A cloak!" He draped it across her knees with a flourish. "The finest in Nolar and the same color as your hair, lamb."

Mirianna stared at the cloak, at the fine, tight weave and rich, oak-brown color. She touched it, gingerly, and knew at once it was worth more coin than her father had seen in months. "Papa, where—?"

"I'll make you a turquoise clasp set in silver." Tolbert rummaged in the tiny drawers of a set of shelves standing on the wall side of his worktable. "I have the stones already. I've been saving them for years because, well…" He glanced at her and his already high color deepened. "Because they remind me of your mother's eyes, and yours, too, of course." He turned back to the tabletop. "Ah, here they are." He pulled on his apron, sat down, and sorted through his tools. "I made two clasps last month. Let's see, where did I put them?"

Mirianna laid the flowers carefully to one side on the bench. Gathering the cloak in her arms, she plucked a scattering of peony petals from it, and then draped it over the bench back. "Papa," she said, rising and placing her hands on his shoulders as he worked, "everything—the cloak, the flowers—is lovely, but…how did you get the coin to buy these?"

Tolbert lowered the gem he had been sizing. "Didn't I tell you?" He looked for a moment befuddled, then laughed. "Why, it's wonderful, child. The Master of Nolar has commissioned me to make all the jewelry for his betrothal and wedding! His manservant saw me delivering the butcher's ring and insisted I see Master Brandelmore immediately."

He unfastened a pouch from his belt and dropped it onto the table. "Look! He's advanced me coin to buy the gems."

The pouch had landed with a solid chink, and now it sat bowing out like a distended belly from its knotted neck. Mirianna was certain there was more coin within than her father had seen in his lifetime. Even if the

Master's fortress sat atop the bluff overlooking Nolar valley, and even if Master Brandelmore owned most of the vineyards and all of the forests for several leagues in all directions, this had to be coin he counted dear.

"Papa," she breathed, "there's so much."

"The Master of Nolar wants only the finest." He pushed the pouch aside. "He'll pay me the rest when I deliver the finished pieces."

"There'll be more?" Mirianna whispered.

Tolbert leaned an elbow on the table and combed fingers through his beard. "I'll see Burl for the emeralds, amber, and diamonds. He should have amethyst, too, but not the jet and bloodstone."

"Bloodstone! He'll give his bride that?"

"Said he wanted her bound to him in blood. The rich..." He waved his hand. "Too much at stake, I suppose."

Mirianna shivered. If she were Master Brandelmore's bride, she'd hardly be comforted to receive petrified drops of the legendary Last Dragon's blood as a sign of the marriage bond.

"I'll have to go to Ar-Deneth," Tolbert mused. "Perhaps I should go there to see Ulerroth first, before I see Burl. After all, the size and shape of the bloodstone will determine much about the companion gems."

"Ar-Deneth!" Mirianna gripped his shoulders again. "But that's across the Wehrland!"

Tolbert nodded absently. "It's the only source if you have to have bloodstone." He straightened and patted her hand without looking at her. "The two men the Master's giving me as escort will be here in the morning. Be a lamb and pack my things while I finish this."

She nodded, but the rest of her body stood frozen in place by the shock of his announcement. *This must be the fear my mother had for so many years. Now it's mine, and I don't know what I should do.*

Her father had traveled to Ar-Deneth several times. It was the last, when she was nine, she remembered most vividly, watching her mother's hollow eyes stare at the western horizon day after day. Tolbert was three months late that time. He'd started out twice and each time been driven back, first by marauding Krad, second by heavy snow. Finally, he'd joined a group of fur traders and forged his way across the mountainous no-man's land. Adelia thinned dramatically after that and, although she never spoke of it to her daughter, Mirianna was certain the memory of that fear hastened her mother's death a year later.

Now her father was about to embark on a similar journey, but one he hadn't taken in eleven years. Mirianna studied her father. His hands moved quickly, confidently from tool to gem to setting. His eye was still sharp, requiring his magnifying glass only for fine detail. But his shoulders had stooped so, she could see over the top of his head when they stood side by side. On the occasions he made the four-day trip to Burl's, he returned complaining of pains in his knees and back. One ankle swelled in hot weather, and he coughed at night if he forgot to drink the tea the town herbalist specially mixed for him.

"I'll pack," she said, "but I'm going with you."

Tolbert cocked his head as if trying to grasp her words. He laid down the clasp and turned, his forehead grooved into three curving furrows. "You—but that's the Wehrland."

She didn't want him to know she feared for him or he'd refuse her instantly. No, she must choose her words and make him believe her fears lay elsewhere. "You'll be gone for at least a month. What will I do here alone for that long? And if you're delayed? We have no relatives here. I'd be a woman alone."

Tolbert frowned. "Our neighbors will look after you. They've done so before."

"Yes, but that was for only a few days at a time. This could be months."

His frown deepened. "I hadn't thought of that. All the excitement..." He gestured to the bag of coins sitting in the center of the table.

Mirianna could see confusion in his eyes. One more subtle idea, carefully planted, would be enough. She lowered her gaze and smoothed wrinkles from her apron, letting her hands worry the edge of it. "Besides, the miller's apprentice has been looking at me lately, and—"

"That little weasel?"

She nodded, keeping her gaze averted. "He makes me uncomfortable when he...when he stares like that." He was no worse than the others, but her father didn't need to know that.

"That does it!" Tolbert slapped his hand on the table. "Wehrland or not, you'll just have to come." He turned back to his work with a dismissive wave. "Don't just stand there, girl. Hurry up and pack."

"Yes, Papa." She turned away quickly, hiding her smile.

Halfway up the ladder to the loft, her excitement waned. She'd convinced her father to take her, but just what was he taking her into? Even small children knew the Wehrland was a place from which not everyone returned. And those that did return, with her own ears she'd heard some swear they'd never enter it again. *Well, we'll be together at least, and I can watch out for him.*

****

At his campsite, the man stoked his fire, raising flames. He passed his knife three times through the fire's heart, making sure every trace of the beast-man burned away and the blade was purified, before laying it on a rock to cool. A branch burst in the ash, shooting a spiral of embers toward a sky streaked with twilight. He straightened and watched them catch the breeze, scatter like fireflies, and, one by one, wink out. An all-too-familiar urge to join them, to explode brilliantly and then...*dissipate* shook through his body. If only he hadn't survived that day, hadn't awakened to the horrible aftermath and the...*abomination* it had made of him.

He stared at his gloved hands, at the black fabric cuffing his wrists and extending up his arms, over his head, and down to his feet, concealing every inch of his flesh. *Dear Koronolan, even I can't bear to look!* Groaning, he sank down on a rock and cradled his head in his hands. "I should have let the creature kill me! Then I would be free."

You'd be dead, said the Voice in his head. *How is that being free?*

Be still! But the voice was right; he would never allow himself to die at the hands of a Krad. Not even now, after more than a dozen years of this...*existence*, doomed to hide himself from everyone, with only a damned, annoying voice in his head for company.

Talking to it—to whatever part of his splintered self had spawned it—kept him sane.

The horse whinnied. Eyes rimmed in white, the gray stallion shook its head and stamped.

Rising with an effort, the man followed the stallion's gaze to the edge of the clearing. The Wehrland lion sat in lengthening shadows, its eyes pinpoints of reflected firelight.

By Kiros, not the damned lion again! He bent to retrieve the knife lying on the rock, muttering, "Fresh-killed Krad not to your taste? Don't think you'll find a meal here."

A slight tilt of the she-cat's head made him freeze in mid-motion. Behind him the fire hissed and popped, but the feline gaze glowed now with a steady luminescence, a steady, unnerving, yellow-green luminescence. The man's skin prickled. He swallowed, but he had no power to pull his gaze away. No power at all...

"—I saved you, Durren—" said a voice, *not* in his head.

The man whirled, knife in hand. His stallion reared, squealing. Overhead, a night bird veered off with a sudden beat of wings.

"Who's there?" the man cried. But no shadow moved, no creature detached itself from the forest's edge, no form materialized from the gathering darkness.

"I'm hearing things." He slammed his knife into its sheath. "You've done it!" he shouted, swinging back to the lion. "You brought the Krad! You made me—"

The lion was gone.

The man stood, shivering as the breeze licked up his back. "I've had enough of the Wehrland." Striding to his horse, he weighed the gem pouch at his waist. "It's time to go to the valley and trade these cursed things." The bloodstone alone would fetch as much as the others combined. Together, there should be enough to buy supplies and go home.

Yes, home, said the Voice in his head, *where illusions won't call you by name... Durren.*

The name burned in his gut like the twist of a knife. He sucked in a breath, enduring, before he spoke, saying it out loud so there would be no mistake. "That name is dead." *If only the nightmares would leave it buried.* They might, if he could leave the Wehrland tonight and return to the caves, the tunnels, the deep silent blackness he longed for in the bowels of Drakkonwehr fortress.

But first he forced his fingers to unclench and comb through the stallion's mane, first they would have to go to Ar-Deneth. And he would have to deal with people. Well, it would have to be done. He shivered again and flung on his cloak.

****

In Ar-Deneth, the White Boar Inn, days later...

Gareth rolled away from the jostling hand. "Get up, boy," Ulerroth said, pulling him out of a dream. "I don't pay you to sleep."

The boy sat up and rubbed his eyes. It was dark, well, darker than usual for one who saw only shadows. He saw one now, the hulking form of the innkeeper illuminated by some little light, a lantern, he supposed, not the fire that usually glowed under the inn's kettles across the room. He yawned, wondering what had roused his master. Predawn guests usually cheered Ulerroth with the prospect of twice the coin, but his touch and tone had been brusque.

"What should I do, sir?" Gareth felt for the tunic he'd placed at his feet before lying down to sleep, found the hem and dragged the garment over his head.

"Go to the stable. We have a guest."

"At this hour?" the voice of Freth, the cook, shrilled from across the kitchen. "Can't he wait till morning to eat?"

Gareth found his staff beside the bed where he'd leaned it to mark the location of his shoes.

"Be quick about it, woman," Ulerroth said. "And be sure it's good."

Wood tumbled into the hearth pit. "Good!" Freth sputtered. "Who the demon is he, traipsing around at night this close to the Wehrland, a prince?"

Gareth tapped his staff to the door, found the latch, and lifted it. Warm, moist night air caressed his face. Behind him, his master spoke in a hushed voice.

"Not a prince, you idiot, but the Shadow Man."

Freth's sudden intake of breath startled Gareth. His hand slipped on the latch and the door closed, leaving him outside.

Alone.

Chapter Three

Gareth stood for a moment, calming his nerves and opening his senses. Being surrounded by darkness wasn't particularly frightening when the condition didn't improve with the sunrise. If anything, the shadows of day confused him with their changing shapes and sudden movements. Gareth preferred the night when he could maneuver with confidence.

At night there were fewer sounds and he could hear the echo of each tap of his staff. The echoes spoke to him of length and breadth and height. The breeze was like a living thing then, full of whispers about the shapes it slowed and parted for ,assages, walls, and posts. It brought, too, slight temperature changes, fragrances and odors.

There was an odor now, and a subtle warmth. Gareth hesitated. The odor was the expected one of a strange horse and its leather trappings. He could tell by the shuffle of hooves that the animal stood just within the stable doors.

But the warmth? There was no post or other obstacle here. The area was open between the stable and the kitchen, at least it had been when he last walked it after supper. Now he was distinctly aware of something diverting the breeze from his face.

The skin on the back of his neck prickled. Who was Ulerroth's guest that he arrived in the dead of night and was spoken of in hushed tones? What kind of man would take upon himself the name of Shadow but one who could stand undetected in the dark? Gareth swallowed. What if—what if the man stood there now, before him, watching and—

The warmth dissipated.

Gareth stood, gripping the head of his staff while the night breeze circled his forehead like a friendly cat. He breathed it, carefully, but there was only the smell of the horse now. Whatever he'd sensed before was gone.

The horse huffed.

He turned toward the sound, took a step, and concentrated again on the fickle breeze. It licked at the damp hair at his nape, teasing him with the promise of a chill. Nothing diverted it. He shook off his uncertainty and approached the horse, holding out his free hand. "Easy, my boy. It's only Gareth come to rub you down and settle you in for the night."

The horse shook its bridle, stamped, and thrust its muzzle into his outstretched palm.

Gareth smiled. He stroked the animal's head, then followed the ears to the crest and down to the withers. It was a tall animal, sixteen hands, and sturdy enough to carry armor, but the saddle it bore was a light one. He ran his hands along the rigging, finding a crupper and a chest harness in addition to a well-worn double girth, all signs of hard riding in uneven terrain.

"So," he said, unfastening the reins from a hook near the door, "your master's not a warrior, eh? The better for you." He led the horse into a vacant stall and closed the gate.

He heard a faint echo, that of a latch lifted and

closed again, but distant, as if the sound had bounced off rafters and beams. Gareth's hands froze on the saddle girth. Or not an echo at all, but the kitchen latch...admitting someone.

The breeze invaded the stall. It slithered under his tunic and licked at the moisture sheening his torso. *The Shadow Man* was *here. And he watched me.*

****

Mirianna turned her face into the breeze, letting it play with her hair. She, her father, and the two men of Nolar had entered the Wehrland two days ago, but she'd seen nothing unusual to mark their passage. Indeed, if her father hadn't announced it, she wouldn't have known. The upland meadows looked like all the other meadows they'd ridden through. The stands of pine, spruce and fir looked no denser. If anything, wildflowers grew here in greater profusion. Each time they rested the horses, she amused herself finding as many varieties as she could among the asters, daisies, and hawkweed.

Granite outcrops pushed up everywhere, sometimes soaring thirty or forty feet above their heads. And streams ran icy cold over rocks still raw from spring heaving and cracking. As they traversed a ridge, Tolbert gestured to five spear-pointed peaks visible in the distance.

"Legend says Koronolan and the Hero Mages forced the Last Dragon to earth here and turned him into stone. Those are reputed to be five of the spines on his back."

Mirianna surveyed the snow-dotted mountains. "I suppose that's why there's bloodstone here."

Her father swatted at a black-winged fly. "Where

else do you find dragon's blood but where he died?"

"Some folks say the dragon's not really dead, only sleeping," another voice said.

Shading her eyes from the noon sun, she turned toward Rees, the Master of Nolar's man riding at her gelding's tail. "Why's that?"

"The cracking. From season to season, from dark to day." The blond man used a stretch of flat terrain to urge his mount beside hers. "They say the Wehrland cracks when the dragon dreams. Someday—" He gestured with a sweep of his arm. "—he'll wake again and break free. He almost did once, you know."

"I haven't heard that story," Mirianna said.

He inclined his head. "I'd be pleased to tell it to you."

I'm sure you would. She turned away from his gaze. Why hadn't Master Brandelmore assigned them two like Pumble, whose pear shape bobbed in the saddle some thirty feet ahead? He smelled, but at least he didn't stare at her with that predatory gleam of teeth she'd grown so weary of encountering in Nolar. From cobbler to carpenter to herdsman, they'd all stared at the young woman who had nothing but an aged father and her own wiles to keep their lust at bay. Some, thus emboldened, had tried what Rees would no doubt attempt some night soon, maneuvering her into the darkness alone. A man who wore his tunic cut to conform to a muscled body and unlaced to mid-chest would expect her compliance, if not her invitation.

She sighed. There was always the knee, properly applied, or, if necessary, the silver and turquoise-handled knife her father had given her to wear at her waist. If that failed—she rubbed a hand over her thigh, feeling the faintest bulge under her riding skirt—there was always the slender dagger even her father knew nothing about.

Not smiling, she glanced once more at Rees. "Shouldn't we be stopping soon to eat?"

"Yes." Tolbert reined to a halt. "My stomach's been—"

His horse jerked sideways, spinning. Tolbert, hands clutching at air, tumbled off.

"Papa!" Mirianna flung herself out of the saddle even as her own horse blundered into Rees's mount.

"Grab the horses!" Rees shouted.

Mirianna registered the blur of Pumble galloping away, but she paid no heed. Her focus was on her father, his body sprawled between hummocks of moss.

"I'm fine, I'm fine," Tolbert wheezed when she threw herself to the ground at his side. He caught her hand, pulling himself up to sit despite her attempt to hold him down. "Just a tumble," he told Rees, who'd dropped to one knee at Mirianna's side.

"You certain?" Rees said.

Tolbert brushed off Mirianna's hands. "Yes, yes. Don't worry about me."

Rees stood. His gaze swept Tolbert from head to toe, and then surveyed the ridge line. "What in Beggeth spooked the horses?" he shouted to Pumble, who rode up holding the reins to Mirianna and her father's mounts.

"Not Krad," Pumble said. "It's too open."

"Lion?"

Pumble shrugged. "Could be just a bird in the brush."

Rees slapped crushed moss from his knee. "Bloody

Wehrland!" A moment later he turned and offered Mirianna his hand. "Can I give you a leg up?"

She shook her head at the gleam returning to his eyes. "Help my father." Ignoring Tolbert's protests, she brushed bits of greenery from his hair and clothing, checking once more for any sign of injury. Assured he was unhurt, she held his horse's bridle while Rees boosted him into the saddle.

"Mirianna," her father warned as she handed him the reins.

"What? I didn't say anything."

Tolbert scowled. "But you're thinking it."

That I'm glad I didn't stay behind and let you take this journey alone? That you're not the horseman you used to be? That maybe now you're just a little bit glad I'm here? Masking those thoughts from her eyes, she laid a hand on his knee, squeezed it, and smiled. "How do you know what I'm thinking, Papa?"

With more confidence than she felt, she grabbed her own horse's reins and swung into the saddle before Rees could open his hand for her foot.

Rees glanced from her face to her father's and back again. With lowered brows, he said, "We'll ride till we find a stream."

Mirianna nodded. Left unsaid was what they all understood: This was not a place to tarry in. She glanced about as they moved on, wondering what had spooked the horses. A small voice in the back of her head reminded her, *This is the Wehrland. Isn't that reason enough? No,* she wanted to reply, but she wasn't sure she should or could.

****

The cloaked and hooded man stood in the

balcony's shadows, noting the common room below was nearly empty now midnight had passed. It was always like this on the first evening after his arrival, everyone trying to catch a glimpse, hoping for something strange to happen. *But I never give them what they want, the fools.*

Approaching the rail, he slid gloved palms along it. There were only two farmers and one old man below. The farmers were struggling to stand while they complained the markers in their bead-casting game were shape-shifting, due, no doubt, to the presence of the Shadow Man. The old man lay curled up and snoring on the fireplace bench.

Ulerroth's voice boomed out as he crossed the common room to help the farmers gather their cloaks. And to gather his payment, the man thought, watching the innkeeper count the coin poured into his palm. With a merry laugh, the bulky innkeeper shuffled his charges to the door and let them out. He, too, checked the old sleeper, stepped back with a shake of his head, and returned to the door to bar it for the night.

"Gareth! Fetch a blanket," Ulerroth called as he secured shutters over the large window.

The man descended slowly, one step for each candle Ulerroth extinguished in the wheel above the main table. When darkness stretched over the bottom step, the man paused there.

The boy entered. The man watched him cross the room bearing a blanket. He looked about thirteen, with thin limbs and a squarish face. His crudely cut hair, the color of wet sand, stood out in tufts upon his head. He walked confidently to the bench where Ulerroth directed and covered the old sleeper. Smothering a huge yawn with the back of his hand, he returned to the kitchen.

The man frowned. This had to be the same boy he'd watched in the stable last night, the one who'd looked straight at him without seeing. Now, though, he walked without a staff. Still frowning, the man stepped to the common room floor.

"Ah, you've come down," Ulerroth said, wiping his hands on his apron. He hovered near a table on the fringe of the firelight. "Will you have dinner now?"

"If it pleases you." The man selected the chair with its back to the fire and sat in it.

"Gareth!" the innkeeper called, taking the chair opposite. "Bring food for our guest." Perspiration shone on the innkeeper's high, rounded forehead. "You've brought me business, as usual." He hefted a tankard left on the table, found ale in it, and drained it in one swallow.

"Do they spend much?"

The innkeeper wiped his drooping mustache on his sleeve. "Oh, plenty, my friend, plenty indeed."

"Even though I don't appear?"

Ulerroth's teeth flashed in the firelight. "All the better. They buy on hope. That's more than enough to keep them drinking."

The man leaned back. "They're fools."

The innkeeper dragged another tankard over, peered in it, and pushed it away. "There's always hope. What's a man without hope, anyway?"

"A man like me."

Ulerroth's gaze shot across the table. The man watched it try to penetrate the hood folded about his face, the face-covering underneath. For a brief, irrational moment, he was tempted to unveil, to show this brazen ale-pumper precisely what it was he so callously sold his customers the promise of. But Ulerroth, as if catching himself, looked down, away, everywhere else in the room.

He knows. Or else he's afraid of what might be...like everyone else.

"Freth!" The innkeeper stood, knocking his chair back on two legs. "What in Dragontime is keeping that food?" Damp circles darkened the innkeeper's armpits, and a trickle of sweat beside his ear glinted in the firelight.

Better to have fear and run and hide, Ulerroth, than to dream lunatic's dreams—the man's cheek twitched against the fabric covering it—*like mine.*

The kitchen door opened. The boy entered, bearing a tray. "Freth's gone to bed, sir."

"Here," Ulerroth said. "Set it here."

The man watched the boy approach, find the table's edge with his hip, then lower the tray to it. All the while, the boy's eyes looked at nothing.

I was right.

When the two men were alone again, the man said, "Your stableboy, I haven't seen him before."

Ulerroth re-settled his bulk in his chair. "He came with his mother last fall. Just before snow closed the pass."

The man picked up his spoon. "Your cook...is she—?"

"Gareth's mother? No." The innkeeper studied his hands. "Pretty woman, Leah. She used to cook, years ago, but found she made more upstairs." He gestured to the darkness above.

The man's fingers tightened around the spoon. Unbidden images filled his head, images he pushed away even as he pulled the bowl of stew closer. *Forget what was. That door is closed.*

"She did, too," Ulerroth continued in a wistful voice, "until one lucky trapper offered for her hand. I never expected her to say yes, but that was in those dark days right after Herrok-Eneth broke when we all thought the world was about to end. I guess she didn't want to be alone. She stayed up in the mountains after he died, till the Krad got too close. Not long after she and the boy got here, the winter fever took her." He stared at the fire for a moment, then shook off his reverie and pulled from beneath his apron a square of soft black cloth. "What do you have for me this trip?" he asked, smoothing the cloth flat.

The man unfastened the gem pouch from his belt and laid it on the table.

The innkeeper weighed it in his hands. "This all?"

"Some pouches of gold dust, too," he said, maneuvering a spoonful of stew between folds of cloth, "and a handful of garnets." He'd long ago mastered the art of eating hooded, but it didn't allow for looking up. Nonetheless, the weave of the cloth concealing his features was just loose enough for him to see through it almost as clearly as through the small holes positioned over his eyes. Without lifting his head, he watched Ulerroth open the gem pouch and pour its contents onto the cloth.

The innkeeper's breath hissed between his teeth. Rising, he broke a taper from the overhead wheel and lit it at the fire. He propped the candle in an empty tankard and surveyed the rainbow of gems glinting against the black fabric before he sat down again.

"Ah, bloodstone." His fingers made directly for the oversized gem. "Lovely, lovely," he murmured, holding it up to the candle flame.

The man watched a faint speck of red fire dance across the innkeeper's swarthy face. "There are five other, smaller ones."

"Good. Wonderful." Ulerroth picked up a large lapis and examined it. "The usual terms?"

He intended to say no, as usual, but flat out and early this time, before Ulerroth had a chance to misunderstand. For weeks, he'd rehearsed it, played the scene over and over in his mind. The amount of payment didn't trouble him. Ulerroth was as fair a man as any he'd dealt with over the years, and fairer than some. There would be plenty of coin, not that he had much use for it beyond what he spent in this place. Nor was he concerned for the cost of room and board for himself and his horse or the cost of supplies provided with credit from the gems. It was the other, the third part of Ulerroth's standing offer he had to refuse, but this traitorous body fought to keep the word from passing his lips, and it would continue to fight him every moment he stayed in this place.

The realization made the food taste like iron in his mouth. It was only that—he forced himself to chew and swallow another mouthful of stew—it was only that he was still so damnably human. *Even after all this time.*

"We'll settle tomorrow night?" the innkeeper said, sweeping the gems back into the pouch.

The man nodded. Tomorrow. He would burn until then. *Damn this body!*

****

"I'm not serving that—that Shadow *thing* again!" Freth said as she sloshed water into the hearth kettle. "Sitting there in the dark like some giant black-winged bat—" Gareth heard the shiver in her voice. "'Put the food there,' he says. 'Leave.' Well, glad I am to go, that's certain."

She plucked the carrot from Gareth's hands. "Scrub harder. They're not clean enough."

He nodded and picked up another carrot.

"He's been coming here for years," Nell, the serving girl, said from his left. "Always just past midsummer, too."

Gareth heard crunching and guessed she'd taken one of the carrots from his bunch.

"Well, you'd think Ulerroth could tell him just once that the place is full."

"He won't."

"Why? He's told it to others he didn't want staying here."

"He brings bloodstone. There's not many that do."

Freth pushed Gareth's hands from his pile of cleaned carrots. "That's enough, boy. Fetch more water."

"All right."

"And a handful of apples from the cellar."

Gareth nodded. He wiped his hands on his tunic and pushed away from the table.

"Bloodstones or not, he gives me the shivers. Why, I'll wager he sleeps hanging upside down from the rafters," Freth said as he tapped his way to the door. "You ever been up to his room?"

"Not while he's there. Although I hear," Nell added in a low voice, "Ulerroth's offered him some women desperate enough to go."

"Not for gold!"

"What else?"

Gareth stepped outside and closed the door on their whispering. The conversation made him flush, remembering moans and rhythmic creaks he'd heard more than once coming from the upstairs rooms. Ulerroth was not above renting rooms by the hour. Some nights all the rooms were full, and Gareth had to deliver trays of ale, bread, and cheese to the threshold of each. There was a smell that emanated from rooms so engaged, a musky smell like that of a dog in heat. The smell made Gareth's palms sweat even now, only remembering it.

****

The Master of Nolar waved his servants away. He sat unmoving while, with hushed whispers, his personal attendant hustled the others through wide oaken doors. He listened for the sound of the latch and then, after a shuffle of footsteps, the silence that told him he was finally alone. Even then, he sat for some minutes more, his eyes closed.

Anyone entering would have said he was meditating. Or dozing. They would have assumed the day-to-day pressures of mastering his realm took its toll on a man of forty winters, despite the well-muscled look of his patrician body. He allowed a faint curve of his lips. Others might think so, but they would be at least partially wrong.

The Master of Nolar opened his eyes and flexed his fingers. Managing this realm was a chore, but planning was much, much more demanding. He reached for a thong lying just under the lace collar of his tunic and tugged gently. From the space between his chest hair and his undertunic, he withdrew a leather pouch. He opened the pouch and placed the single item within, still warm from his body, in his hand.

In the candlelight, it shimmered like water filling his palm. Long as a finger, the faceted column rose like a pillar of ice from a jagged base to a chipped and cratered peak. He rubbed his thumb-tip gently back and forth across the broken base.

As he did, the column began to glow from within, first yellow, then purple, then blue. At a murmured word, all three colors appeared at once, each highlighting a facet of the column. With a minute turn of his wrist, the colors shifted facets, interchanging again with each additional movement. Repositioning the object between thumb and index finger, he raised it slowly to eye level. At another murmured word, the colors vanished.

He smiled at a faint, dark, human-like shape writhing within the column's core. "How kind of you, Master Brandelmore, to buy this piece of crystal and cut yourself handling it. I was beginning to wonder if I'd ever have a body again. So generous of you to shed just enough blood I could trade places with you. Pity you don't have the talent—or knowledge—to reverse the spell."

He leaned back in the chair and stroked the salt and pepper goatee covering his chin. He'd never grown one himself, but perhaps he should have. This one provided such an astonishing array of tactile stimulation, and he'd gone so long without any such stimulation. "And how convenient that you're about to be wed." He laughed. "How convenient, indeed."

With an absent flick of the wrist, the imposter palmed the crystal, shutting off its light. No, even planning wasn't that difficult when events fell so neatly into place. It was the waiting, the damned, interminable waiting. *And I've waited too long already!*

He unclenched his fingers and watched blood ooze from three small cuts the crystal column had made in his skin. The dark, deep red droplets shone like gems. His heartbeat quickened, slamming into the walls of his chest. *Soon. Very, very soon.*

Chapter Four

The man drew on his gloves and cuffed the sleeves of his tunic tightly over each wrist. He felt around the edge of each jointure, making sure no sliver of skin was exposed. When satisfied, he reached out in the darkness and located a folded piece of soft cloth. This he slid carefully over his head, centering it so the slit sat over his mouth and the two small holes opened over his eyes. Reaching out again, he touched folds of coarser cloth. Picking these up, he draped them over his head like a deep, muffling hood and fastened the ends to his tunic shoulders. Only then did he strike flint and light a candle.

The flare of light was like an intruder, sending its nosy glance into every corner of the room. It showed him the tabletop marred with indentations where previous occupants' knives had stood, tip embedded, hilt ready to the grasping hand. It showed him the fireplace with the missing mantel stone, the floor with its warped boards and dark, circular stains of spilled wine.

Or blood.

His thoughts seized the idea, eager for anything to divert his gaze from the dark-shrouded northeast corner of the room, and the bed he'd tried for hours to sleep in. Instead, he forced himself to wonder how many murders had been committed in this chamber. Ulerroth was not known to discriminate among his customers. Gem buyers, sellers, and thieves alike frequented Ar-Deneth and lodged at this very inn.

Tonight, however, he had the upstairs entirely to himself. It was not that he worried about thieves the way other men with gems or gold in their pouches did. Only a fool would try to rob him.

Only a fool who knew nothing about the Shadow Man, said the Voice in his head.

The Shadow Man! His fists clenched at the table's edge. *It always comes back to that, doesn't it?* He raised his hand and swung at the candlestick.

Light cart-wheeled around the room, flashing up, down, across his face-covering, and then...nothing but the heavy *thunk-thunk, thunk-thunk* of the candlestick rolling across the floor. He leaned against the tabletop, his breath echoing thunder in his ears. *Why the demon did I do that? Light, dark...nothing changes what I, what this body wants to do here.*

A scurrying sound penetrated his hood, and his attention snapped to his door, to the hall beyond it. The supposedly *empty* hall. His breath came light and quick as his senses identified the slow—*tentative?*—approach of footsteps. He could expect Ulerroth, disturbed by the candlestick's noise, but this tread was too soft. Much too soft.

Under the door, breaking the bar of faint light cast by the single hall torch, stretched a shadow—a slender shadow, cast by someone who tapped three times on his door and held her breath.

By Kiros, a woman!

"Go away!" he growled before his body—*this damned body*—could propel him toward the latch.

"Please, sir," she whispered through the thick wood, "don't let Ulerroth send you anyone else! My child's ill and I need...I need the coin."

"I don't want a woman," he said, panting as though he'd run half a league uphill, digging his fingers into the table's edge to keep them from reaching for the door and opening it.

Outside, she burst into a wail of despair.

"Damn it all to Beggeth!" He dug one hand into his coin pouch, seized a handful, and slung them at the gap under the door. "There! Now go! And tell Ulerroth to send no one else!"

There was a scrabbling noise, knees thumping floorboards, a faint "Thank you!" and then retreating footfalls. Only when he was sure she was gone did he unclench the fingers of his left hand from the table's edge. He groped for a chair and sat in it.

Gold. What fools people make of themselves for it. It never failed to amaze him that Ulerroth could find women desperate enough to risk their sanity, their very lives, to spread their legs in a darkened room for a man they did not dare see, a man they would know only as the shadow haunting their dreams, their nightmares.

And mine, too, even though I refuse. If only that could stop the dreams, the memories, but he'd had years to learn nothing would avail, and the sensations would gather, just as they were now, and sweep over him. He could pretend he was only imagining how hundreds of bodies had since used the bed in the corner, but that was a lie. This body, this damned body's own actions had infused this room with the one memory he forced himself yearly to confront.

She'd been young, pretty, and new at selling

herself. An altogether enticing package, even if she hadn't been a gift from his men that night. Still, he ought to have refused, but he'd been a slave to this body all those years ago, and she'd made him forget, for a few hours, what he shouldn't have forgotten, shouldn't have put off doing, because the delay had cost him.

Everything.

His stomach convulsed. He let it churn, accepting, even savoring, the waves of disgust surging through his body. *You deserve this. You knew how it would be, once again facing down temptation.* Like sweat, the taint would cling to his body until he could return to the pool to cleanse himself once more.

He rose abruptly, located another candle and struck flint. His gloved hands shook in the wavering new light. He stared at them, forcing them to still. *Are you afraid, flesh? You brought me here. I'll buy the supplies to feed and clothe you another year, but I'll be damned if I'll give in to these, these base animal urges!*

****

Mirianna emptied the waterskin. The dribble that leaked out barely covered the bottom of her cooking pot. Not enough for her father's nightly tea and certainly not enough for the morning meal. She'd have to go to the stream they'd camped beside to fetch more. Tossing the waterskin and another empty one over her arm, she walked quickly beyond the firelight.

Twenty feet through aspen saplings, Mirianna broke into a cleared area lit by a rising half moon. A dark ribbon of water snaked through the center of the hollow, glimmering here and there as it rippled over submerged rocks. She slip-slided down the ravine, her boots crunching on gravel thrown up by spring floods. The ground leveled out, and she stepped from rock to rock to the water's edge and knelt on the lip of a buried boulder.

She'd filled the first bag and was lowering the second into the stream when she heard the clatter of a falling stone. In the space of another heartbeat, she heard two more tumble down. Her breath locked in her throat. Someone—some *thing*—was behind her.

She ought to panic, to scream—if only she had breath—but some instinct, some deep knowledge held her still, silent. Then, as if impelled, she freed one hand from the waterskin and inched it toward the knife at her hip. Her other hand, immersed in snowmelt water, automatically contracted around the skin's mouth. She eased back on her haunches, shifting her weight to the balls of her feet.

Gravel showered into the stream.

Mirianna spun. The full waterskin, powered by the force of her rotation, flew ten feet and connected with a splat. Not waiting to see if the intruder fell, she bolted for the trees.

A sputtered string of curses halted her halfway up the ravine. Turning, she saw Rees clamber to his feet.

Starlight silvered the hair plastered to his head and glistened like a moon-in-miniature from the crystal disk he wore around his neck. Water dripped from the tunic sleeves he held out to her. "What in the name of Beggeth did you do that for?"

He'd startled her, but she didn't want to tell him that. Instead, "Maybe…maybe I thought you needed cooling off," slipped out of her mouth.

"It's not funny." Rees snatched up the water pouch.

"I could have been a Krad."

"I know." She drew a shaky breath and pointed to the waterskin he was refilling. "Wouldn't that have worked just as well if you were?"

Rees grunted. He tied off the pouch and reached for the one she'd already filled. "You shouldn't have come here alone."

"It wasn't far." Looking down, she noticed the knife still gripped in her hand. Her knees shook. She sank to a rock on the ravine's side and, with trembling fingers, sheathed the weapon.

Both waterskins slung over his shoulder, Rees climbed the slope. "It's my job to protect you. I wish you'd let me do it."

Mirianna glanced at the hand he held out to her, and then up at his moonlight-shaded face. His eyes resided in the darkness somewhere, and she could catch no glint of expression. Still, she could sense by the change in his tone that his mood had altered. *Cold water doesn't affect you for long, does it?*

Leaning away from his hand, she rose and started to climb the bank. "As long as you have those, you might as well carry them back to camp for me."

His hand caught hers just above the wrist. It was a wet hand. And cold.

Mirianna halted and rolled her eyes. *I should have climbed faster. Now we have to go through this foolishness.* Every one of her father's customers had looked at her with the same expression Rees wore, as though she were a gem they coveted, a lovely prize to be added to their collection. She was heartily tired of that look.

"Is that all you'd like me to do for you?" He

stepped closer on the slippery gravel. "I can think of a number of things we could do together...in the moonlight."

"Rees," she said, fixing him with a cool, steady gaze. "No."

His brows puckered. "No?"

She pulled her wrist free. "No." Catching up her skirt, she climbed the gravel bank.

She was nearly at the top when Rees caught her arm again. "Maybe I didn't say that right. Let me try again." Dropping the waterskins, he pulled her into an embrace. "You're a pretty woman. I like what I see." He leaned toward her and, closing his eyes, breathed deeply. "I like what I smell, too." His hand traveled down her back, found one rounded buttock, and squeezed.

"Rees!"

"Mmm," he murmured, nuzzling her cheek. "You feel good, too. But I bet you taste even better."

Mirianna braced her forearms on his soaked tunic and turned her face away. His clothing dampened hers, making her shiver. "Rees," she grunted, "I said no."

"That's what you said," he murmured, "but you know that's not what you mean."

Oh, for the love of the Dragon! He thinks I'm shivering for his sake! Imbued with sudden strength, she pushed.

Rees staggered, slipped on the gravel, and fell to one knee.

Mirianna didn't halt this time at his expulsion of curses. She scrambled over the ravine's edge and dashed into the aspen grove, running pell-mell until she saw firelight glowing between the saplings. At the edge of the trees, she slowed to a walk, smoothed her skirt, and listened for Rees's stumbling footfalls while her breath returned to normal. She heard him crashing through the underbrush as she strolled into the campsite.

"Where's Rees?" Pumble said from the fire's edge.

"Washing up." Suppressing a smile, she knelt and smoothed out her father's bedding.

Rees broke out of the aspen grove and stalked into the firelight. He flung the skins to the ground beside Mirianna. "Here's your water."

Pumble sat back on his haunches and gaped at him. "What'd you do, take a bath?"

"Shut up!" Rees marched around the fire pit and, seizing the smaller man by the collar, hauled him to his feet. "Go check the horses."

"Sh—sure. All right." Pumble backed out of Rees's grip and hurried into the darkness.

Tolbert, who'd been dozing against his saddle, woke with a snort. He peered across the fire at the tall blond man and blinked. "You're all wet. Is it raining?"

With a muttered curse, Rees snatched his spare tunic and stomped back into the aspens.

Mirianna swallowed her laughter. "No, Papa," she said, pouring water into her pot. "Here, I'll have your tea ready in a few minutes. Then we can all get some sleep."

Tolbert grunted. He shifted on the hard ground, rubbed his backside. "I thought I *was* sleeping."

****

Gareth balanced the tray with both hands as he counted the stairs. *Twelve...thirteen...fourteen.* He paused at the top, remembering which room Ulerroth had told him to knock at.

"Mind now, boy. The one at the end of the hall," his master had said for the third time as he placed the tray in Gareth's hands.

Ulerroth's hands were sweating. Gareth felt the moisture on the tray's edge. His master sounded harried. Not cross, but...uneasy. This morning his master, who usually greeted the morning with a ringing bellow of good cheer and a sound slap on Freth's backside—prompting, in turn, a sputtered tirade from the cook—had arisen late, called for Gareth with a hoarse voice, and broken his fast in hurried silence.

Now Gareth shifted the tray to one hand, turned left, and walked slowly down the hall. He trailed his fingers along the wall, noting doors. When he'd counted three, he halted. In this room was the man they called the Shadow. He'd served him twice, both times in Ulerroth's presence, but on neither occasion had the man spoken. *I'd think he didn't exist, except I can feel him...somewhere...in that room.*

Gareth shivered. His tray tilted. The tankard slid into the platter with a loud clunk.

There was an answering sound from within the room.

Two sounds, Gareth's mind told him even as he stood frozen at the door: the muffled sound of boots touching—not hitting—the floor and then the footfalls of someone moving, cat-like, across the room. For one suspended moment, Gareth waited for the whisper of a knife sliding from its sheath. When it didn't come, he unpeeled one hand from its death grip on the tray and, swallowing, tapped his knuckles on the door.

"I—it's Gareth. I—I've brought you bread and

cheese."

There was no answer for such a long time, the sweat that had bloomed under Gareth's armpits moments earlier trickled down his ribs. He wiped his upper lip and wondered if he'd only imagined the noises. *I could just leave the tray. He probably won't answer, anyway. I'll just knock again and—*

"Come."

Gareth started. The tankard skittered across the tray. He caught it with a shaking hand. Wishing fervently he were anywhere else but at the threshold of this room, he fumbled for the door latch. It gave easily, and he pushed the door wide open.

Most guests preferred to open the shutters for air, and Gareth was used to navigating by the familiar shadows the incoming light would reveal. This time, although it was early afternoon, the chamber was dark, as dark as the stable at night. Gareth swallowed and walked slowly across the floor, finding the table with his outstretched hand. He slid the tray onto it and transferred the platter and tankard to the tabletop. His ears strained for any sound, but it was difficult to hear over the rush of blood in his ears. Still, a faint scent of warm leather told him the room's inhabitant occupied the left near quarter of the room. Lowering the empty tray to his side, he turned in that direction. "Will that be all, sir?"

Again, nothing for so long he thought he'd been mistaken about the voice, the sounds. Then, "No."

The word sent a jolt through Gareth. He clutched the empty tray to his chest. "Wh—what can I do for you, sir?"

"Tell me what you see, boy."

It was a quiet voice, resonant yet muffled in some way. Gareth adjusted his face toward the sound, wondering at the unexpected question. "Nothing, sir."

"Nothing? Ever?"

Gareth shifted his stance. He lowered his head and skated a hand along the edge of the tray. "Well, I do see shadows, sir. And sometimes shapes, when the light is bright."

"It's nearly dark in here. Do you see me, my shape?"

"No, sir."

"You're facing me. How do you know where I am?"

A grin pulled at Gareth's lips. "Why, your voice, sir."

There was silence for another space of heartbeats. Gareth heard the sound of something, leather brushing wood? He cocked his head toward it, then started again at the man's voice. "I'm going to move. Count to ten, then point toward me."

"As you wish, sir," Gareth said, frowning. "But, why?"

"Just do as I say, boy."

Almost immediately, he heard the sounds of movement. First right, then back again left. Gareth turned slowly, following the faint scuffing, forgetting, for a moment, to count. When the sounds ceased, he realized he was supposed to point. "You're over there, sir."

"So I am. How did you find me?"

"I can hear you."

"I was being very quiet."

"I suppose so, sir, but I still heard you."

The man chuckled softly. "Then let's try once more. This time, go out in the corridor, close the door, and count to ten. Then come in and find me."

Gareth's frown deepened. This was a peculiar game, but the man, at least, seemed amused by it. "As you wish."

A long count of ten later, he opened the door, entered, and closed it behind him. His breathing had eased, and he listened for sounds that were not his own. Hearing nothing definite, he turned his face to all sides, letting the air's movement play against his cheek. There was a faint scent of wool in the air, wool and—he sniffed—leather. He turned toward it. A subtle heat warmed his cheek. He stepped closer. A whispering sound of inhalation tickled his ear. Confident now, Gareth advanced. "Here, sir," he said, stretching out his hand.

A gloved hand grasped his wrist, preventing his arm's full extension. It was not a wide hand, but the fingers were long, easily enclosing Gareth's bones in a grip that spoke of strength held in check. The leather that impressed itself lightly on his inner forearm was butter-smooth and, surprisingly, warm.

Heat rushed up Gareth's cheeks. *Why shouldn't it be warm? He's human, isn't he?* He remembered Freth's comments, forced a swallow, and wondered who was more right about the possessor of the grip that turned his arm aside and released it.

"How did you find me, boy?"

The question shook Gareth from his thoughts and he blurted, "Why, smell, sir." He flushed at the insulting sound of that and added, "I mean scents. And heat, too. That's how I knew you were in the stable yard two nights ago."

"You didn't challenge me."

Gareth lowered his chin. His cheeks burned. "I—I wasn't certain until I heard the kitchen latch."

He heard the man inhale deeply, and then let the breath out. His breathing, too, had a muffled quality. Gareth wondered if he wore something over his face.

"Go back to work, boy. Tell your master I'll see him later."

It was a cool dismissal, even curt. Gareth frowned. Had he somehow displeased the man? "Yes, sir," he murmured.

****

The man had watched the boy all evening. From a stool placed deep in the landing's shadows, he'd watched the boy come and go from the kitchen bearing trays of food, platters of cheese, tankards of ale, doing everything his master and the serving maid directed, and doing all of it promptly and efficiently. Shifting his gaze, the man surveyed the candlesticks arrayed on ledges along the walls and those fastened into the wheel over the common room. *One would hardly guess his world is as dark as mine; he moves so well in this one.*

But he could move in yours, too, the Voice in his head said. *As well or better than he does here.*

The man shifted on his stool. The idea disturbed him although it had been fomenting in his brain since, since first seeing the boy in the stable yard? Or after listening to his voice greet and soothe Ghost? He remembered the sound of that voice, soft, womanish almost, as it straddled the boundaries between child and man.

The man snorted. He looked away from the

dwindling crowd below and fixed his gaze on the triangle of deep shadow in which he sat. *This is my world. Here, on the edge of darkness. Alone. There's no room for another!*

Unless he were blind...

The man scowled. *The boy will die.*

Eventually. But so will Ghost. You're prepared to cope with that.

But Ghost isn't human.

No, the Voice admitted, *but you still are.*

The man's fists clenched, driving leather into skin, tendons, veins, until everything throbbed with the beat of his blood. *Damn this body! And damn you, Syryk!* Rocketing off the stool, he turned his back on the merriment below and swept down the corridor.

****

Mirianna smiled. Her lover leaned over her, his face in shadow, the sun outlining his shoulders and head. His hand cupped her breast and kneaded it gently. She sighed and arched toward the touch. His fingertip circled her nipple, teasing the nub until its ache sent ripples through the pit of her stomach. Her legs shifted restlessly beneath the weight of his body pressing her down, holding her hard against the grass—no, the ground—no, a blanket on the ground—

"See, now? I knew you wanted me."

Mirianna's eyelids jerked open. In the heartbeats required for full consciousness to rush into her body, she realized the shadowy form looming over her was not the faceless lover of her dreams, but Rees. And his fingers had worked the lacings of her bodice nearly open.

"Damn you! Get off!" she hissed, shoving at him.

His hand clamped over her mouth. "Easy, love," he murmured, straddling her. "I wasn't going to hurt you last night and I'm not going to hurt you now. I just want to show you how much we can give to each other on these long, lonely nights." He bent his head and touched his mouth to the hollow of her shoulder.

Bile rose in Mirianna's throat. Rees's thumb and fingertips dug into her cheekbones, holding her mouth pressed against his palm, preventing a scream. She knew her father slept too heavily for a muffled noise to wake. And Pumble—Rees would have set him on watch someplace too far away to interfere. She pushed once, ineffectually, at Rees's shoulders, then fumbled for her knife. A grinding feeling beneath her back told her the weapon had slipped under her body. Her thoughts flew to the dagger strapped to her thigh, but she knew at once it was unreachable under his enveloping legs. Frantic, she launched her fingers at his hair.

He deflected her hand with a forearm, shifted his weight, and pinned her wrist with his arm. "Relax," he murmured beneath her ear. "You'll like this."

"No!" Mirianna gasped into his hand. She thrashed from side to side, bared her lips, snapped her teeth at something, anything...and found the inner web of his hand.

Rees howled and jerked his hand back.

She gulped a breath, but the scream that echoed off the surrounding trees and shivered through every muscle in her body was not hers.

Rees's eyes showed white. His gaze darted around the clearing while his body remained unmoving, frozen in the act of recoil. For heartbeats, Mirianna heard nothing but the rasp of his breath. Then, ever so faintly, a hissing sounded.

Rees bolted to his feet. "Pumble!"

The shorter man burst into the clearing, his sword drawn. "What in Kraddom was that noise?" he panted, face moon white. "The horses are jumping all over the place."

Rees backed across the campsite, pausing once to glance at Tolbert's still sleeping form before reaching his own bedding. "Lion, I think." Snatching up the bow and quiver leaning against his saddle, he pivoted slowly while fitting an arrow to string, and his gaze raked the clearing's edge.

Mirianna sat where she'd lain, fingernails digging into her palms. The forest loomed on all sides, dark and unnaturally silent. Overhead, even the canopy of leaves didn't rustle. She heard no crickets, no night birds.

"Throw wood on the fire."

Rees's order startled Mirianna. When her head snapped in his direction, he jerked a nod at the fire pit. "Lots of brush. I want flames."

Her mouth dry as cottonwool, she crawled to the fire pit. Her arms shook so, half the twigs and branches she heaved toward the coals scattered around the rock ring. Those that landed true, crackled, popped, and roared up.

"More! I want more flame."

Mirianna threw larger handfuls on the coals. In moments, the flames strained at their rock perimeter as twigs curled and broke and leaves vanished in an explosion of heat and light. The flaring drove shadows out of the cleared space and behind the birches.

"Good," Rees murmured. "That ought to keep the

beasts at bay."

"—Not all of the beasts—"

Every hair on Mirianna's arms rose at the voice.

"Who—who's there?" Rees demanded, his back jammed against Pumble's, arrow drawn and bow raised.

"Dragon's blood!" Pumble wheezed. He yanked a charm out of his tunic collar, kissed it, and mouthed over it words Mirianna couldn't hear. Both men's faces shone in the flickering light as they circled slowly, defending the clearing against...what?

Though the roaring flames assaulted her body with heat, Mirianna shivered, cold to the core. What magic was this that spoke with a disembodied voice? That screamed like a woman in agony? A lion, as Rees said? She shuddered again and dragged her wayward knife into position at her hip. *Not all of the beasts,* the voice had said. What did that mean? That the fire wouldn't keep all the beasts in the Wehrland at bay? Which ones were invulnerable to it? The Krad? No, she'd heard the Krad were afraid of fire. What then? The lion? Teeth sank into her lower lip, she glanced toward her father who still slept, blissfully undisturbed, six feet away.

The distance was too far, much too far for a night and a place like this. Turning on her hands and knees, Mirianna crept toward him. Pebbles bit into her knees, but she ignored the stabs of pain. Her father was what mattered, her father and his safe—

A flare of yellow-green light on the fringe of her vision brought her to a halt inches from her goal. For a moment, she hesitated, thinking she'd imagined the image glimpsed yards away between a double-trunked birch, that it was a reflection of firelight off some object—a spider's web, perhaps, damp with dew—but something within told her it was not. Holding her breath, she stared.

The image returned, sharpened, solidified. *Glowed.* The eyes—for that was all she thought they could be— seized hers and delved into them, probing her thoughts, mind, heart until her consciousness was rendered blank. She stared, powerless to move or pull away but strangely unafraid while six words slowly filled the emptiness of her mind: *Remember, not all of the beasts.*

Heartbeats later, her mind was her own again. Her eyes focused and she found herself staring at Rees while he stared at her. She was awake and cold and filled with a strange whirling uncertainty that had at its core a deep, solid knowledge of...*something* that made her cringe away from him and burrow deeper into the warm arms surrounding her.

"There now, lamb," Tolbert's voice crooned in her ear. "You've just had a fright."

Mirianna's gaze darted across the faces ringed around her at the fire pit's edge. "Th—the lion—?"

"Gone." Tolbert sighed. "I didn't even get to see it."

I did. And it, it told me...something. She glanced furtively at Rees, who'd laid aside his bow and was bending to the pile of firewood.

"We'll keep the fire burning for the rest of the night." He fed chunks of wood into the flames. At each thrust of his arm, the slice of crystal dangling from his neck danced and sparkled. "That should keep it away."

Will it?

Mirianna tore her gaze from the glittering disk and studied the Master of Nolar's man. *Or is there something else here, something that's not afraid of fire?*

She gripped her father's arm and leaned into him, not arguing when he insisted she spend the rest of the night at his side. *It's where I belong. And where I should stay, for both of our sakes.*

Chapter Five

The man opened his eyes at the sound of the knock. He'd not been sleeping, merely lying on his bed in the stale darkness of the closeted room, fully clothed, waiting.

Waiting for what? said the Voice in his head. *A summons to act?*

There were only two paths available—flesh and soul—and both, he thought bitterly, were all but closed to him. Syryk's curse had sealed off the first. *And the second?* His interlaced fingers compressed each other. He'd slammed that door himself.

"I—uh—I have your dinner," Ulerroth said through the heavy wood. "You didn't come down, so I brought it up." The innkeeper coughed. A floorboard creaked. "Uh—are you feeling well?"

And if I wasn't? Would you do anything for me? Could you? Or would you thank everything that's holy for delivering you from such as I? Sitting up, he lowered his legs to the floor and stood. "Your consideration is touching, Ulerroth, but I'm quite well. Bring in your tray."

The door opened. The unsteady light of one candle spilled into the room. "I—uh—hope you don't mind the candle," the innkeeper said, wiping his forehead. "I wasn't sure..."

Sure of what? Me? After at least a dozen years,

you're still not sure of me? His lips compressed into a thin line. "If it makes you more comfortable, why should I mind?"

Be civil, the Voice in his head said. *The poor bastard doesn't know any more about you than you've told him. And you know how little that's been.*

Bending slightly at the waist, he gestured to the table. "Are you joining me tonight?"

The innkeeper set the tray on the table and emptied it of bowl, platter and tankard. "No, I—" He rocked on his heels, then mopped his face with his apron.

What's troubling you, friend? You're more uncomfortable around me than usual. All because I didn't come down to dinner? "Is there something else?"

"Last night—" Ulerroth's beefy hands kneaded the apron gripped in them. "I'm sorry. I—I thought…you seemed as though you wanted…some company…"

The man's fingers clenched the chair's back. Perspiration sheened his body, bonding his tunic to it. *So it's you, flesh. You're the demon in Ulerroth's nightmare.*

"It was my fault, I know," the innkeeper rushed on. "You've made it plain you weren't interested before, but the woman insisted, and I sent her up because you might've changed your mind, and—"

"I haven't—" the man said, forcing the words through gritted teeth, "—changed my mind." Refusing yet again took every bit of his willpower, but now he'd done so, he wanted nothing more than to sink into a chair and close his eyes to the consequences before his body realized what it was being denied. But there was no time. Already his loins had begun throbbing, and sweat glued the inner cloth of his hood to his face.

Go ahead, flesh! Remember how you once enjoyed yourself here! One night—one careless, insignificant night—spent within these walls, before he entered that tunnel he saw in his nightmare. Before the world collapsed, crushing under the weight of it everything he knew and everyone he loved and everything he once was, except for this damned, mindless flesh!

"I don't want a woman," he enunciated to the open-mouthed innkeeper. "I don't want any woman."

Ulerroth stared. His hand fumbled from moustache to ear to forehead and, finally, outward. "Then wh— what do you want?"

Everything! Nothing! Something! The words careened through his mind, clamoring at every wall, every closed door, every lock. *Nothing a whore could ever give me! Nothing at all...like...that. But something...something...*

He leaned forward heavily, hands spread on the table. He knew the only possible answer. He'd known it ever since he'd entered Ar-Deneth and stood in a dark stable yard, watching and listening. It merely required strength, and acceptance of the risks, to form the words.

Sweat drenched every patch of cloth contacting the man's body. Under the table, in the concealing shadow, he could feel his thigh muscle twitching. Soon, the dreams would come, and if Ulerroth so much as hinted at procuring a woman, he'd be lost again, this time maybe forever.

"There is something," he said hoarsely. "I want the boy."

For the space of heartbeats, the words hung in the air between them. Then Ulerroth's face flushed crimson. "I'll not—I'll not—Gareth's just a lad! You'll not use him to—to—!" He strode to the door and swung round again, fists clenched. "By all the hosts in the Wehrland, I'll not let you use that boy!"

The man closed his eyes. His gloved fingers gripped the edge of the table and squeezed until he felt each separate grain of wood imprint itself on his flesh. "Bite your tongue, you seven-times fool," he said in a voice whose softness threatened more than a bellow. "I wouldn't harm him any more than you would."

When he opened his eyes again, he saw the innkeeper standing a few feet away, face white despite the color blotching his cheeks. His mouth worked like that of a beached fish, but no sound emerged.

"How much do you really know about darkness, Ulerroth? You trade with me and fancy you're flirting with the realm of the damned. You hold me up to your friends and customers and make coin of the connection, but how much can you really know of Beggeth if you think I'd be capable of something as evil and twisted as coupling with a boy?"

He straightened, rising to his full height as fury filled him. Lifting his hands to his hood, he gripped the edges of it. "I could show you the handiwork of evil, and then, fool, you'd know the truth!"

"No! Don't!"

The plea penetrated his consciousness slowly, as something akin to a distant but jarring sound, like the cry of a dying kitten. For a moment, he blinked, disoriented. Then his gaze focused on two protectively raised, hairy arms and a cowering, apron-clad body.

Backed against the door like a cornered rabbit, Ulerroth whimpered, "I'm sorry! I didn't mean—you can have what you want, just don't—!"

What? Plunge you into hell? Are you afraid to join me there? But the moment, the mood, the fury was gone. The man forced his fingers to relax, to unwind from his hood, to release it. His limbs felt oddly drained, heavy as lead. Seeing the chair close at hand, he pulled it out and sank into it.

"I want the boy as my manservant," he said, finding the words as weighted as his extremities. "After all, Ulerroth, what better match could there be than a blind boy and a shadow?"

The innkeeper slowly unbent his bulk. The corners of his mouth twitched as if trying to form a grin and failing. "When—when you put it that way..."

The man heard the door open and snap closed. *Go, yes, and leave me be. You think you know what I've done, and so do I, but neither of us really knows anything. And I'm too tired to care.* He licked his gloved finger and thumb tips and snuffed out the candle. When the acrid smoke dissipated, he leaned forward on the table, rested his head in the crook of his folded arms, and slept.

****

Mirianna awakened slowly. Her head felt heavy, as if she hadn't slept, yet here she was, still rolled in her blankets and the sky already light. *I must get up and put the water on to boil.* Peeling off bedding with stiff fingers, she struggled to a sitting position.

"She's awake," a man's voice said.

She frowned. What was a stranger doing in the cottage at this hour? Did her father already have a customer? She rubbed sleep from her eyes and saw the cottage's loft now ringed with birch bark. Disoriented, she turned to look for her father and found him puttering by a fire.

"Ah," Tolbert said, smiling, "just in time for tea and porridge."

Tea and porridge. Mirianna closed her eyes as the mundane image brought her firmly into the present. "Why did you let me sleep?" She pushed free of the remaining bedding.

"Rees thought it was a good idea." Her father ladled out a bowlful of gray mush.

He would, she thought, then wondered why she thought so. Like bits of a dream, the events of the night shuttled through her mind. The memory of his hand on her breast brought her fingers rushing to her bodice, but, to her relief, the lacing was still intact. Even so, blood pounded in her throat. He'd gotten too close, and she'd been lucky—this time. She vowed to stay beside her father and make sure Rees had no further opportunity.

She combed fingers through her hair while Tolbert brought her a cup of tea and a bowl of porridge. The brightness of his eyes and a faint flush coloring his cheekbones made her gaze linger on his face as she sipped the herbal brew. Years of watching her father's animation over some new stone's color or a hummingbird's vibrant hues or the unexpected presence of a flower amid a swath of green told her he was bursting now with the same childlike enthusiasm. *Whatever fear there was last night, it's clear you never felt it, Papa. And I'm glad.*

"You won't believe what Pumble found this morning." He gestured across the fire pit toward the short man shouldering a sack. "It's the biggest lion track I've ever seen."

Pumble's fleshy cheeks colored, but he grinned. "Bigger than your hand, Miss," he said, spreading his fingers.

"It's right over here." Tolbert plucked the porridge dish from her hands before she could eat a spoonful and set it on the ground. "Come on." He pulled her to her feet. "You have to see this. It's simply incredible for size, and the print is so clear, you'd think it was cast." He paused. Wrinkles congregated on his forehead. "I wonder if the Master of Nolar would like a jeweled lion's paw. I could make a cast of this and show him."

Mirianna smiled, accustomed to the sudden turns of her father's thoughts. "Perhaps later, Papa—after you make the wedding jewels." She disengaged her fingers and patted his hand.

Her porridge stood wafting steam beside her bedding. By all rights, her stomach should be craving it despite the unappealing color, but no overriding desire to eat compelled her hand toward it. Instead, her head obeyed an impulse to turn toward the clearing's edge. "Where did you say the lion's print was?"

Tolbert had knelt and was busily drawing shapes in the sand for his new creation. "Hmm? Oh. Right behind that tree with the double trunk."

Mirianna crossed the clearing in the direction he indicated. When she reached the border of birches, she picked out two trunks, each the size of a man's arm, leaning away from a joined base. A whisper of air glided over her face as she approached. *Warm.*

"—Like a breath—" a voice murmured.

Whose breath? her mind responded to the voice as if she had known it would be there.

"—His—"

Ahh... Her eyelids closed and her lover materialized. Tall, strong-shouldered, the sun bursting from behind him, his touch seared with the heat of it. She reached out. Her hands found his arms and wrapped around them. *Let me see your face. Let me know who you are.*

Even as she pleaded, the image faded and she found herself clinging to the papery bark of the twin birches.

She flashed a guilty look toward the campsite, saw Pumble was gone, presumably loading the pack animals, and her father still knelt in the sand, hunched over his drawing. Rees was nowhere in sight. She exhaled, blowing air over her flushed face.

Early in the journey, she'd given the dream image Rees's face just to see what would happen. *How stupid, to think it could be him!* His visage had promptly melted, just as all the others she'd tried to envision there, all the others who'd presented themselves as possible lovers and husbands. The right man would impose his face upon those dreams and even—Mirianna flushed hotter at the thought—fulfill them.

But now wasn't the time to think about such fantasies. They belonged, quite properly, to the night. Now was the time to break her fast and begin the day's work. Pushing away from the birches, she glanced at their base and glimpsed something that made her stand stock still and stare.

Imprinted in a patch of dirty yellow sand was the large, irregular shape of a paw pad and four toe pads. A strange sensation rattled through the pit of her stomach. Mesmerized, she sank to her knees and spread her fingers, as Pumble had demonstrated, over the print.

The heel of her hand sank neatly into the depression at the rear of the paw pad. As if possessed of a will of their own, her fingers contracted until, positioned like claws, they settled into the toe pads.

Almost at once, something bonded her hand to the ground. Mirianna's heartbeat skipped, but her panic fled as quickly as it had arisen. This was not a grip, not a phantom hand, but a force that gently held her palm and fingers pressed to the earth. She was certain if she pulled hard enough, she could free herself, but at the moment she had no desire to do so.

In the filtered morning light, the sensations rising from what should be cool sandy earth were strangely warm, and dappled sunlight played over her arm. She raised her head as if impelled, and her gaze traveled between the two columns of gray-etched white bark. It crossed trampled grass and scuffed sand where a saddle had sat, touched the edge of a fire pit, and came to rest on a pile of rumpled bedding.

There was a woman there...on her hands and knees...a young woman with tousled hair and a frantic look...trying to protect something...someone...

Thousands of prickling sparks rushed over Mirianna's face, across her chest, and through her extremities. Her fingers dug into the sand like five unsheathed claws. *By the Dragon, I am seeing me as the lion saw me!* With a little cry, she jerked backwards.

"What's the matter?" Tolbert demanded, raising his head from his sand drawing.

"I—" She stared at her hand. Sand dribbled from the palm, but the fingers flexed at her command. "N-nothing, Papa." *What can I tell him, that I've had a vision?* She brushed her hand over her skirt and stood.

"Something in the sand pricked me."

"What in the name of Beggeth are you two doing?" Rees stood beside the fire pit with hands on hips, blond brows a straight line. "We've leagues to make today. We won't make a single one if you don't get packed."

Mirianna ducked her head. "Yes, of course." She hurried to her father and helped him to his feet.

Rees stood, watching her roll her bedding. She felt his gaze bore into her back, but he said nothing and she didn't turn. Finally, she heard the crunch of his boots crossing the clearing. She looked up as she rose with her bundle and saw Rees halt behind the double birches and stare at the ground.

A muscle worked in his cheek. Muttering, "Bloody Wehrland!" he lifted a booted foot and rammed it down with the force one would apply to a snake's head. Teeth bared, he ground the heel into the paw print.

Mirianna shivered. She turned with her bundle and hurried toward the horses and away from the man at the clearing's edge.

****

The Imposter of Nolar sat up in bed. His hand went immediately to the pouch dangling under his nightshirt. It was warm, warmer than lying against his skin would warrant. Frowning, he tugged it free of his clothing.

Something had disturbed his sleep, but he was certain it was nothing in the room or immediately outside it. And the morning light too faintly illuminated his bed curtains for it to be time for a master and gentleman to arise.

Stifling a yawn, he opened the pouch and withdrew the crystal. It responded to his murmured word with a sparkle of color. Holding the column horizontal on his palm, he watched colors shift and reform along the faceted planes. At another word, an image coalesced just beneath the surface.

The Imposter of Nolar studied the image. "So, the old man has his daughter with him, eh?" His fingers tugged at his goatee. "A small complication, Rees, but nothing you can't handle, if you remember that your loyalty is to the gems." He sighed. "Such a nubile thing, too. Dare I hope you'll keep your breeches fastened long enough to bring her back to me untouched?"

His loins tightened at the thought. He smiled and stroked his free hand along the ridge of his arousal. *Ah, the pleasures of the flesh. You're too kind, Brandelmore, to have returned me to such a delightful state. And your bride, mm. Just think, it'll still be you rutting between her legs, but I*—he chuckled—*I'll be the one to feel it.*

He laughed out loud and flopped back onto piled pillows. Raising the crystal to palm its glow, he started at a flare of yellow. It was only the briefest flash, like lightning in the summer sky, gone before the mind's eye releases its image. Even so, he sat straight up and, tightening his grip on the crystal, peered at the image still contained within it.

Moments later, he raised his head and rubbed a hand over his face. "Brandelmore, these eyes are faulty. They see things that aren't there." He palmed the crystal, replaced it in its pouch, and lay down again. Even if something had managed to survive the initial spell-blast, too much time had since passed. *They're all dead. Every last one of them. There's no one in the way.*

He smiled, closed his eyes, and drifted off to sleep contemplating that thought and all its possibilities.

****

"You know I promised your mother I'd keep you here and see to your care," Ulerroth was saying. "And I've done a fair job of it, wouldn't you say?"

Gareth nodded. His master had clapped a sweaty hand on his shoulder shortly after he'd arisen and now, while he ate, Ulerroth's fingers returned so often to knead bone and muscle, Gareth's neck and arm ached. Stuffing the last hunk of bread in his mouth, he slid out from Ulerroth's grasp and handed Freth his bowl. "Was good," he managed around bread jammed into his cheeks.

"Don't gulp." Freth grasped his hand and placed a cup in it.

He dipped a fingertip in the tea, found it warm but not hot, and downed it in one long swallow.

"I told you not to gulp." Freth snatched the empty cup from his hand. "You've the ears of a stump."

Gareth grinned. "But the nose of a hound. I can smell when you're baking." Swiping a handful of walnut meats from the table, he dodged most of the spoon applied to his backside.

"Both of you out of my kitchen!" Wooden bowls thumped together. "Give me peace or you'll not eat today!"

Still grinning, Gareth popped a nut meat into his mouth and followed his master's footsteps into the common room.

At once, Ulerroth turned and gripped him by both shoulders. "About what I said, boy, I've always been good to you."

His master's hands lay heavily on his bones, their touch communicating unease. Gareth swallowed the remains of the walnut meat and stuffed the others into a pouch at the base of his cuffed tunic sleeve. "Yes, sir, I know you have."

"I wouldn't stand in the way of your...advancing, if that's what you want. But I want you to know—" Ulerroth's fingers flexed. "—you don't have to agree to this."

Gareth frowned. His master seemed distracted, and the words he spoke sounded like riddles old Melfick told when he had a pint too much ale. He hunched his shoulders at Ulerroth's grip, but it only tightened. "Agree to what, sir? I don't understand."

He heard the hiss of the innkeeper's exhalation and sensed Ulerroth straightening. The thick fingers kneaded his bones again. "The Shadow Man wants you to serve him."

Was that all? Ulerroth was afraid to send him to do again what he'd already done? It was hardly worth sweating over. "All right. I'll bring up his tray again, as long as he wants me to."

His master's fingers dug into his shoulders, preventing his attempt to turn. "Gareth, boy, it's not that simple."

The heaviness of the words made a knot clench in Gareth's stomach. It was a large knot, much like the one that had intruded there when Ulerroth first told him his mother was dying. His knees shook. He swallowed. "What then, sir?"

Ulerroth sighed. "He wants to take you with him...as his manservant...when he leaves tomorrow."

The knot pushed against Gareth's throat. *He wants me? To go with him? Tomorrow? But he's barely met me. And you're all scared of him. I am too...sort of...although he hasn't done anything to me except, except I can feel him watching me sometimes.*

"Why—why me, sir?" he whispered.

The innkeeper's shoes scuffed on the floor. "Probably, boy, because you're blind." He cleared his throat, hesitated, then continued in a low voice, "You see, it's said that to look on him unveiled is to—is to be struck with such horror that you'll go mad. Or die."

Chapter Six

His saturated tunic clinging to his body, Gareth stood before the third door on the left, the one at the end of the corridor. Ulerroth had said, more than once, Gareth didn't have to accept the Shadow Man's proposal. *But if I don't—what then?* The possibility of harm coming to his master, Freth, and Nell made him shudder again.

Even so, the White Boar Inn of Ar-Deneth wasn't his real home, not the tiny cottage with the sun-hazed windows where fragmentary memories of the man he thought of as *father* dwelt. And Freth was hardly an adequate substitute for his mother. Most days, she ordered him around, scolded him for his mistakes, and otherwise ignored him. Ulerroth showed more patience, but Gareth suspected it had been prompted as much by the innkeeper's interest in his mother as by nature. Still, the man had remained kind after her death and fulfilled his promises to her.

Gareth's fists clenched and unclenched as memories flooded his mind. It hadn't been easy listening to the bed creaking in the room above his pallet and knowing it was his mother who lay on it under Ulerroth's bulk. It hadn't been easy delivering a tray to a musky-odored room, knowing within it his mother served a man who'd hired her body. It hadn't been easy knowing how she earned the coin that kept them alive while his own body stirred with new urges, his limbs lengthened, and hair sprouted where none had grown before. It hadn't been easy, but he could have endured, if only—

Tears welled in Gareth's eyes, burgeoning behind his lashes and oozing between them. They burned, but he let them come, let them fall in rivulets of warmth down his cheeks and drip from his chin. His mouth opened in a sob, but no sound passed his lips. *Mother, why did you bring me here...and die?* Overcome with misery, Gareth stuffed his fist into his mouth and sank into a heap on the floor.

****

Footsteps. I know I heard footsteps. The man listened to the silence, then opened his mouth wide and exhaled a yawn, one that culminated with a huge stretch of both arms over his head. His shoulders popped and he rotated them absently, enjoying the languid feel of rested muscles. *I haven't slept that well in—what is it—weeks?* He sat, thoughts purposely blank, and savored the rare joint quietude of mind and body.

All too soon, he became aware of a new sound, one he couldn't at first identify. He frowned, rising from the chair he had slept in. Morning sunlight, by the reflected quality of it, glimmered through the shutter slats. It allowed his gaze to locate the remains of his evening meal still spread on the table. *Ulerroth, it must be Ulerroth...but he would knock, wouldn't he?* His frown deepened. He checked the folds of cloth over his face, the fastenings of his cuffs, and the position of his hood, listening all the while.

It was breathing, yes, but irregular breathing. And not quite the short, bated pattern of someone about to commit a crime, he decided, relaxing his grip on his knife. No, this was more uneven, the inhalations huge, the exhalations jerky, ending with a faint wheeze.

Resting a gloved hand on the latch, he leaned closer, wondering first if the person was ill, then why a stranger's health should concern him. *By Kiros, why did he have to pick my door to be sick in front of!*

Scowling, he strode part way across the room, turned. The sound nagged at him like a thought just under the horizon of consciousness, near enough to glimpse, too far to apprehend. Something about it, though, made his stomach clench and his throat tighten. Irritated by the sensations, he stalked to the door and jerked back the latch.

The boy sat crumpled on the floor, his face blotchy, his fist jammed to his mouth. He blanched at the sudden swish of the opening door.

He's terrified. Frightened to death of me.

The man's stomach twisted like a rag in a washer-woman's hands. "Get up, boy."

The boy gulped down another sob. A brilliant flush swept up from his throat. Ducking his face into his sleeve, he wiped furiously. "Y-yes, sir."

"Come in."

He watched the boy take a position halfway to the table. Despite overhanging hair obscuring most of the boy's face, his cheeks and eyes were puffy. Again, the man's stomach clenched.

Are you feeling...sympathy? said the Voice in his head. *How pathetically novel.*

I'm angry, damn you! He fears me when he's the one who should least do so. When he's the one, the one I need.

So, tell him.

His lips compressed. "What has Ulerroth told you?"

The boy suppressed a sniffle. "That—that you want me to—to be your manservant."

"What else did he tell you...about me?"

A quiver rippled through the hair dangling over the boy's face. He swallowed. "That to look on you is to—is to..."

The man's cheek twitched under the cloth concealing it. "To go mad with horror?" he said through gritted teeth. "Or, more mercifully, die?" *Oh, you were clever, Syryk. Gifting me with the power to put my victims out of their misery, yet withholding from me, your victim, that very same gift. But you wanted me to suffer, didn't you? By all the demons in Beggeth, I know you did!*

He inhaled a steadying breath and forced his fingers to withdraw from the indentations their nails had dug into his palms. This was not the time to vent his bitterness. This was the time to move to ease it, and in the manner chance alone had provided. A sardonic smile tugged at his lips. *But you forgot one thing, mage. You forgot that Perrinor—old, blind Perrinor—was the only one to look into the Demon Master's face...and live to tell the tale.*

He focused on the boy. "You have no need to fear, though, do you? After all, you see only shapes, or so you told me."

A shiver rattled through him. What if he were wrong? What if the boy's vision were sharper than either of them guessed?

He'll die, and then you'll know, won't you?

The man shuddered. It was the first of the risks. Sweat trickled between the blades of his back. His fingers flexed within their leather skin. Sucking in his upper lip, he licked salt from it. *I have to do this. I have to know if it's possible.*

"Well? That is what you told me, isn't it?"

The boy nodded, slowly.

The man's pulse raced at his temples, making him light-headed. His mouth had gone dry, but he forced himself to salivate, to moisten his lips, and to swallow. Ignoring tremors in his wrists and elbows, he raised his hands to his shoulders. One hand tugged at the hood, drawing it fold by fold from his head until it lay like a collar around his neck. The other wrapped fingers in the hem of his face-covering. It hesitated, trembling, while he blew out a breath. The room was dim, but there was enough light to know for sure.

By all that's holy, I hope I'm right.

Closing his eyes, he withdrew the cloth. A whisper of breeze from between the shutter slats caressed his naked cheek. It was startlingly cool without the filter of his hood. He tried to inhale it, but his lungs seemed constrained, bound in some way, and wouldn't expand. With what breath he had, he said, "Look at me."

When he opened his eyes, the boy was slowly raising his head and turning toward the sound of his voice. Ghostly in the dimness, the boy's searching gaze touched him, flicked away, returned, held.

A ripple of panic surged through the man. "Do you see me?" he breathed.

The boy's brows furrowed. He blinked. "Your shadow, I think."

He forced a swallow. "Nothing more?"

The boy shook his head.

The man breathed. Exploding lights dotted his vision, but he ignored them, holding onto the table while his heart regained its rhythm. When his legs no longer quivered, he released the table and replaced the cloth over his face. "You're safe, Gareth."

The boy seemed to wilt. The man shoved a chair toward his fumbling hand, and the boy slumped into it. "I—I'm sorry, sir, but I—I just..."

"Rest, boy, and listen. I'll tell you what I require of you." *Your voice, your company, a human presence. Something... good...to keep me sane.*

****

Gareth performed his midday duties mechanically, his mind so full his head ached. Ulerroth kept his distance and even Freth didn't scold him for spilling milk when he bumped the pitcher against a chair back. Still, at the odd moments when one or the other's presence diverted his attention, it was because of an odor that insinuated itself into his nostrils. *They're afraid of me, too, now that I've been with him.*

He didn't want to leave Ar-Deneth, but he had the vague feeling he could no longer live here in the same manner he had all winter and spring. He was no longer simply Ulerroth's least servant, no longer the stranger's son, an insignificant blind boy who used a staff to tap his way about the fringes of village life. Now he was set even farther apart because he'd been where others could not go—and lived.

But I haven't seen him! Don't you people understand? I can't!

Gareth dumped his load of wood into the iron rack next to the common room fireplace and slumped down beside it. He rubbed his forehead, wishing the tightness behind it would go away. Outside the thrown-open shutters, cart wheels sloshed through a puddle and a mule brayed complaint. He heard the joiner's dog bark and, immediately after, the owner's shouted curse. It was familiar music, the sounds of everyday life in Ar-Deneth.

What will I hear up there in the Wehrland? In the place he calls Drakkonwehr?

Gareth hugged his legs and rocked back and forth. He didn't want to cry again. It was bad enough he'd done so once today. Worse that he'd been caught at it. He flushed and ground his chin into his knees. That would keep it from trembling. He wished he could do the same with his memory, but nothing he tried prevented the Shadow Man's words from filling his mind again...

"There is only one important rule," the Shadow Man was saying. "You must not touch me."

Gareth frowned. "Not touch you, sir? But sometimes—"

"Yes, I know. Sometimes you'll need my assistance." There'd been the sound of footsteps and the swish of heavy cloth. "Even so, you'll hold out your hand or speak, and then wait for me to touch you first. Is that clear?"

Gareth nodded, remembering the peculiar game of a day earlier. His hand had been caught then, prevented from contacting the body he knew stood only inches from it. Why? He could think of only one reason, and it made his stomach shrivel to half its size. "Is there—could I be hurt...?"

"There's danger, boy, in everything associated with

me," the Shadow Man said, startling him with his nearness. "Remember that, for your own sake, and I'll be able to protect you."

His tone had made the hair rise on Gareth's arms. Even now, hours later, his skin still prickled at the memory. He rubbed his arms, wondering why, toward midnight, he should be willing to ride into the Wehrland with a man called Shadow. The simple answer involved the safety of his friends. *The true answer,* he thought as the tightness in his forehead migrated to his chest, *is that there's nothing to hold me here except a mound of earth.* And even that was disappearing. He flexed his fingers, remembering the cool, fibrous feel of the vegetation rapidly reclaiming the winter-turned soil over his mother's grave.

Gareth's eyes stung. He squeezed them shut, holding the lashes scrunched so tightly colors behind the lids turned from yellow to orange. Then he stood and, blinking several times, shuffled out of the common room to finish what tasks he owed his former master.

****

The late afternoon sun warmed Mirianna's shoulders. It soaked into her hair and leaned heavily on her neck, making her nod. *I shouldn't sleep,* she told herself each time she twitched awake, but the rhythmic motion of her mount's gait lulled her eyes shut again. They'd been traveling the last hour over a level stretch of trail and it was all too easy to trust her mount's sense of direction. Even so, she was sure it wasn't a sudden change in slope or pace that this time brought her head up with a jerk. The gelding's pink nose still bobbed stoically behind the swishing tail of her father's chestnut. And his horse still trailed obediently behind the rump of Pumble's pack animal.

She frowned, wondering what could've made her start so. She half turned, saw the blazed face of Rees's mount and knew he still maintained the rear. The knowledge ought to have comforted her. Yesterday, it did. Now, however...

She stole a glance behind her. Rees's eyes were like slits under the ledge of his brows and he rotated his gaze from side to side, looking first far, then near, then far again. His expression was grim, as if at any moment he expected something to spring from the meadow grass or swoop at them from the sky.

The lion? The thought brought visions of the morning and the previous night's events, memories Mirianna had steadfastly spent the better part of the day ignoring. Now they rushed in on her like an invading army, bringing with them all their attendant mix of emotions. Had she really seen what she thought she had? Heard what she thought she'd heard? Or was it only a trick of the night embellished by the Wehrland's peculiar power to bend minds?

Here, with the sun beating down and the grass humming with the gentle music of grasshoppers and bees, it surely seemed no more than that. True, there had been a lion. They'd all seen the paw print. They'd all heard it scream. But speak? Mirianna puckered her lips. She had dreamt a waking dream, and there was no more magic in this land than in—

"Rees!" Pumble shouted.

Her gaze rushed to the head of their little line. She saw Pumble, one arm waving furiously, struggle to stay atop a madly plunging mount.

Rees spat out the grass stem he'd been chewing

and spurred his horse past her.

Startled by the sudden shake of his mount's head, Tolbert fumbled for the reins. "What, what's ado?" he said, turning a bewildered face to his daughter.

Mirianna urged her gelding beside her father's mount. "Pumble's seen something," she said as Tolbert smothered a yawn.

His eyes brightened. "Another lion, do you think?" He adjusted the wide brimmed hat he wore and straightened in the saddle. "That would be something, wouldn't it?"

"Yes," she murmured without enthusiasm. She watched Rees's horse rear, plunge sideways, and try to bolt. The Master of Nolar's man hauled it back, but the animal kicked wildly at something she couldn't see in the tall grass. Finally, he turned the horse aside and dismounted, handing the reins to Pumble who, still mounted, clung to the white-eyed pack animal and the tossing head of the horse he rode.

Tolbert urged his horse forward. "What is it? What have you found?"

"Stay back!" Rees held up both arms. "Don't bring those horses any closer!"

Mirianna reined to a halt beside her father and watched Rees return his attention to a depression in the thigh-high grass. He walked two careful steps toward it, halted long enough to cover his nose and mouth with his tunic, and resumed his progress, hunching now.

Mirianna exchanged puzzled glances with her father. Her horse raised its head. The gelding's ears flicked back and forth and it huffed. The pink nostrils flared. She felt it shift uneasily beneath her. Curious, she sniffed the gentle breeze.

Two smells assaulted her nose at once, the first clearly the smell of rotting flesh, the second unfamiliar but even more rank. Grimacing, she covered her nose as the gelding back-stepped. "What's that?"

Tolbert wrinkled his nose. "Smells like skunk."

"But worse," she said, recognizing traces of a urine odor. There was something else, too, something equally pungent. Stale sweat?

The gelding tossed its head. Her father's chestnut huffed and kicked a hind leg. Both horses chewed at their bits. Mirianna turned the horse upwind until she could breathe again. "What is it?" she called as Rees returned to Pumble's side.

He mounted and both men rode upwind of the depression. He breathed deeply, coughed, and breathed again. "Krad kill," he managed in a hoarse voice. "Bloody things leave their stench on everything they touch."

"It looked like deer. Was it?" Pumble said.

Rees nodded. "Two. The Krad ripped them apart. Left the rest to rot." He shuddered and brushed at his clothes as if something foul clung to them.

"How long ago?" Pumble said, his face pale under his tan.

"Not long enough." Rees scowled at the sun. "And closer to Ar-Deneth than I thought they'd be." He leveled a glare at Mirianna.

He thinks I brought the Krad. And maybe the lion, too.

The idea stunned her. She flushed hot at the memory of his groping hand and her helplessness against it, then cold at the implied connection. *I didn't summon the lion! It was just coincidence, nothing more!* But she said, "Are we close enough to Ar-Deneth to reach it if we ride through the night?"

Rees's eyes narrowed.

She averted her gaze from the latent heat rising again in his. *Please don't misunderstand why I said that. I'm not afraid of you. I'm just...afraid.*

"If I remember the trail correctly," Tolbert said, leaning forward and stroking his chin, "we can't be more than a day or two away. There's the Bear's Tooth." He pointed to a conical formation of yellow stone visible along the rock wall in the distance. "It's been some years, but I seem to remember that as a landmark before the trail bends southward."

Rees, attention diverted, squinted at the sandstone monument. His lips thinned, but he jerked a nod. "All night and half the day—if you're up to it."

"I don't know about the rest of you," Pumble said, mopping his face, "but the sooner I get out of the Wehrland, the happier I'll be."

"Yes, yes," Tolbert said, nodding. "But we'll have to return this way, you know."

Pumble shrugged. "Better to be halfway and know you made it, than go to sleep once more, wondering if you will."

"What about you?" Rees said.

"Me?" Mirianna's fingers worried the saddle horn. "Oh, I'm not tired. Let's go. Besides," she added, forcing a smile for her father's benefit, "we can rest when we get there."

"And in proper beds." Tolbert rubbed his lower back. "This sleeping on the ground, well, I guess I'm not as young as I used to be." He grinned sheepishly and squeezed his daughter's hand.

Had they been anywhere else, she would have savored his admission. Here, though, a subtle alteration in Rees's expression demanded all of her attention. It was in his eyes, but not only there. There was a movement of lips, too, so minute she could barely note the change, barely identify it. And it had begun with her father's mention of "bed."

Mirianna closed her eyes. *I'll have to keep my door bolted day and night.*

Chapter Seven

The man sat on a low, flat stone before a small fire. He stirred the flames with a stick, poking apart the glowing carcasses of deadfall he'd set aflame only an hour earlier.

Ghost, tethered with the pack horses, showed gray in a sputter of sparks, then vanished as the glare faded. A night hawk screeched somewhere to the west.

The man lifted his head and peered at the sky. Between long, blank shadows of cloud, he located the five-star formation of Kiros and noted its position. Two hours until the first faint bluing of dawn.

He returned his attention to the fire, spreading it still more, letting it die. It was only a small one, and he'd built it primarily for the boy.

An involuntary contraction of muscles pulled up one corner of his mouth. *What does a blind boy need with a fire?*

Hah! How very droll, said the Voice in his head. *But you know very well there are more uses for it than light.*

He rested the glowing tip of the stick on a stone. A wisp of smoke, pungent with burnt sap, curled up from it toward the dark tops of aspens and spruces sheltering three sides of his campsite.

When the smoke dissipated, he looked down at a tankard nested in stones at the edge of the fire. If there was warm water left, he should drink it even though he had no intention of sleeping. They were still too close to Ar-Deneth, and he wouldn't rest until they'd put another day between themselves and the main trail. As it was, the trail lay no more than a league to the south. Were he alone, he wouldn't have stopped here. He would have continued until midday, rested the horses until evening and embarked again, putting as many leagues as possible between himself and the eyes of the curious before he would yield to the luxury of sleep.

If he were alone.

He glanced toward the blanket-clad figure lying on the ground an arm's length to his left. The boy slept like one dead, his face a pasty half-moon in the fading firelight.

Take him back. It's not too late, the Voice in his head said. Again.

The man returned his gaze to the gray-red glow, remembering how the boy had blundered into roots, caught his hood on low branches, and finally tripped over the pack to fall, face down, in the moss. The man straightened slowly, until his elbows rose from his knees and his hands unclasped and the palms rubbed, back and forth, against the prickly weave of the fabric covering his thighs. *He'll survive...once we get to Drakkonwehr. He'll be safe there. We both will.*

There was a sound...far off. The man froze. In the moments that followed, he heard the nighthawk screeching now to the north as it dove and fed, dove and fed. Ghost, in the darkness, huffed and was silent. There was no wind to rustle the boughs, yet he had heard...what? A rattle of stone? No, not quite that. Something else, something like...voices?

The man bolted to his feet, whirling so quickly his cloak whipped at his boot tops.

Ghost, under the spruces, raised his muzzle and, ears pricked, sniffed the air.

"Men," the man muttered. "Fools!"

The stallion huffed again and stamped.

The man glided to the animal's side and slid a hand under the stallion's mane. There was just enough time to unfasten the tether and vanish into the night. When the intruders arrived, they would find only an untended, dying fire.

And a boy.

A shiver twitched along the man's back. His gaze shot to the shrouded figure barely visible near the circle of embers. He surged two steps forward, then halted at the sound of hooves striking stone. He looked, once, toward the break in the trees and the shadows moving into it. Then, turning on his heel, he swept into the cover of the spruces.

****

Mirianna halted her horse just behind Rees and Pumble, the two men's mounted figures silhouetted against the faint light of a dying fire. *Ah, a fire.* It would be wonderful to warm herself for a moment or two, if only to beat back the chill emanating from everything in this forsaken region.

Ahead in the narrow mouth of the clearing, Pumble leaned toward Rees. "See, I told you it was a campfire."

"Shut up and keep your eyes on those trees."

Even though the hissed retort wasn't aimed at her, its tone shredded Mirianna's remaining patience. She urged her gelding alongside Rees's mount. "That's a fine way to talk to him! You've been leading us in

Helen C. Johannes

circles for hours. At least Pumble has had sense enough to spot the fire."

"I don't know where we went wrong." Tolbert nudged his horse beside Pumble's. He pinched the bridge of his nose, and then dragged his hand over his face. "We should have found the fork by now."

Mirianna slapped spruce needles from her cloak and glared at Rees. She gestured toward the single blanket-wrapped figure visible near the fire pit. "Why don't you just admit we're lost and go ask that man for directions?"

Although it was too dark to see more than an occasional glimmer of Rees's eyes, she sensed the weight—and heat—of his stare. "Because," he said, speaking slowly, as if to a peevish child, "I'm not sure there's only one man."

Her heart thudded. This was the Wehrland, after all. "Well," she said, stiffening her chin, "there are four of us."

Rees snorted, but he cupped his hands around his mouth. "Hallo the camp!"

The shout echoed off the trees and faded. A horse, under the spruces, nickered. Mirianna's mount shook its bit and replied. But the man, barely visible in the fading emberlight, lay still.

Something heavy pressed in on Mirianna's chest, shorting her lungs of air. "He's dead," she breathed.

"Or faking," murmured Pumble.

"Or a dummy," Rees said. "Pumble, go and see."

"Me?" Pumble's face shone white. He licked his lips. Drawing his short sword, he rode slowly forward. At the edge of the firelight, he looked from side to side, then dismounted. He crept toward the ring of stones,

90

scooped up a handful of kindling, and flung it on the embers. Backing two quick steps, he barked, "Hallo the camp!"

The blanket-wrapped figure jolted upright. "Yes, sir! What am I to...?"

A boy's face, pale in the light of fresh flames, emerged from a fallen-back hood. Mirianna watched, breathless, while it looked not at Pumble, standing fully visible across the fire pit, but turned first one way, then the other, then cocked, as if listening.

Pumble glanced toward Rees. Sweat glistened on the short man's face. At Rees's jerked nod, Pumble shifted the grip on his sword and demanded, "Where's your master?"

The boy convulsed like a startled animal. "Who—who's there?" He scrabbled in the sand at his side for something Mirianna couldn't see.

Pumble bolted around the fire pit. Rees, beside her, raised his bow.

"Don't! He's only a boy!" Mirianna grabbed Rees's tunic sleeve, jarring the bowstring, tipping the arrow upward. Pumble, halfway around the fire pit, skidded to a halt and spun.

But it was not to her they looked. Nor was it her voice they'd heard, as echoes of something deeper reverberated from the aspens and spruces. "Hold!" it had said. Yes, she was sure of it. It had drowned her own plea even though she'd screamed it. "Hold," it had said, "if you would live!"

Rees's face, beside her, shimmered. His gaze scanned the trees even as he shook off her hand. "We mean no harm," he said, the bow still poised in his hands. "We're travelers...on our way to Ar-Deneth."

"We're lost," Tolbert said, huddling into his cloak. "And I'm not afraid to admit it."

Rees swung toward him, but the voice, quieter now, cut across his retort. "Sheathe your weapons and prove what you say."

The two Master of Nolar's men exchanged glances. Rees lowered his bow. With a flick of his hand, he returned the arrow to his quiver. Pumble straightened slowly and sheathed his sword. He backed away from the boy who hunched like a stone on the ground. Both men turned slowly, scanning the trees.

"There," Rees said. "We've done what you asked. Show yourself."

A low chuckle rumbled around the clearing. It was near, Mirianna thought, yet not near—at once behind her gelding's tail and, a heartbeat later, echoing from a wall of aspen trunks. It was deep, reverberant, and full, and the sound of it sent shivers into the well of her stomach—long, spiraling shivers that ended in sudden flares of blue light. For one breath-stealing moment, she thought the lion had returned, but the voice, speaking again, was somehow different. And definitely masculine.

"They don't know what they're asking, do they, Gareth?"

The boy's head twitched upright. His already pale face blanched. "N—no, sir."

"Pity."

The drawled syllables hung in the stillness, thrumming not in the ear but along Mirianna's nerves. Beside her, Rees stiffened. The odor of his sweat, hot and pungent, rushed at her nostrils, followed by something more subtle, yet chilling. *It's only the night.*

It's only the night, ran through her mind like an incantation. *It's only the night and the Wehrland.*

"If you're bound for Ar-Deneth—" The voice startled her with its sudden, precise closeness. "—you've come too far north."

Mirianna's gaze searched the shadows between spruce trunks. Beside her, Rees shifted in his saddle. She sensed him lean forward, and knew he, too, peered into the darkness after a voice no longer as large as the trees.

"You'll find a path to the right as you leave this clearing," the voice continued, the tone cool now, humorless. Even brusque. "Follow it about a league to a single large willow. The trail to Ar-Deneth runs past the tree."

The words hung in the following silence like the memory of sound in a vacant corridor. *There should be more,* Mirianna thought. *Shouldn't there?*

Confused, she looked toward Rees, but he was staring into the darkness, fingers still gripping his bow. Her gaze skittered to the boy who, standing now, hugged a stick to his chest with both hands. Not a stick, she realized, but a staff. *He's blind. No wonder—*

Tolbert coughed. The plaintive sound brought her attention to him, and to the dry cold that had long ago crept into her feet and turned them to stones in the stirrups. *I haven't made his tea. He'll cough for hours if I don't.* She glanced at the fire, saw how the flames had dwindled now the kindling was spent, and cleared her throat.

"Might we," she spoke to the wall of trees, "share your fire until dawn? We're cold and the trail will be easier to—"

A twig snapped at her side, the pop ricocheting through the clearing.

Mirianna jerked around. Her gelding sidestepped with a squeal. A shape darker than the shadows detached itself from them. The gelding shied from it, half rearing. The animal blundered into Rees's horse and staggered, throwing Mirianna sideways in the saddle. With a little gasp, she flailed at the saddle pommel, trying to right herself. Out of the corner of her eye, she saw a phantom shape sweep toward the animal's head, saw the gelding's eye roll and flash white. She caught a handful of mane just as the gelding coiled back on its haunches.

She expected the plunge. She didn't expect the sudden stop that flung her against the gelding's neck and drove the saddle pommel into her stomach. She clung there, feeling the gelding quiver beneath her while her breath sawed in and out. When she could close her mouth, Mirianna pushed herself up. The gelding back-stepped, whinnying.

"Whoa," said a voice. "Steady."

Mirianna blinked. Her horse had no head.

Dry mouthed, she stared at the blackness slicing across the animal's neck only inches above where her face had lain. Logic told her someone had thrown something—a cloak?—over her horse's head. But logic couldn't explain the shape now standing next to the gelding's missing head, a man-sized tower of blackness. If she could discern even a hint of nose or chin, she could take the shape for a hooded and cloaked man, but what should've been face staring up at her was as blank as a wall of unpolished jet. A trickle of cold sweat crawled down Mirianna's ribs.

"This is the Wehrland," said the voice, welling unmistakably from the blackness scant inches away. The head turned as if surveying her companions who seemed somehow frozen although she knew, logically, the whole incident occupied no more than seconds. "You'd do well to be out of it." With a sweeping gesture, the figure stepped away, and blackness slid like a magician's robe from her horse's head.

The gelding snorted and back-stepped. Mirianna snatched at the reins and pulled them tight. To her left, the figure still stood, barely visible against the wall of trees. Then, as suddenly as it had emerged, it blurred into the shadows.

The clearing erupted with sound. "Mirianna!" Tolbert trotted to her side. "Are you all right?"

"What in the name of the Dragon was that?" Rees rode up with his bow still clutched in his hand.

"I'm fine." Mirianna squeezed the hand her father stretched toward her. It was cold, but her own was colder. Freeing hers, she tucked it inside her cloak before its tremor gave away her lie. Deep within her stomach and heart and spine, her body still vibrated like a sounding board. Sensations rushed and tumbled one upon the other, making her flushed then chilled. She was frightened, terrified, yet—somehow—calm.

"I'm fine," she repeated, this time to Rees who was riding his horse in a circle around both her and Tolbert.

"Bloody Wehrland," he muttered, reining to a halt between them and the line of spruces.

"Hey!" shouted Pumble.

They turned at the note of panic in his voice.

"The boy!" He waved his sword frantically at the fire pit. "Where's the boy?"

Mirianna stared. In her mind's eye, she could see the boy as he'd last appeared, frozen and clutching his staff. Now, the place where he'd stood was vacant. "He's gone," she whispered.

"Dragon's blood!" Tolbert breathed.

"They were here," Rees snarled. "Someone was here. Look, there's the damned fire! Somebody had to build it."

"I don't care." Pumble tugged his charm from his tunic collar and backed away from the empty circle of light. "I know what I saw, and I'm leaving—now." He seized his horse's reins and mounted.

Rees hauled his horse across Pumble's path. "What in Beggeth do you call yourself? A coward? Look at you—running from a few shadows in the night."

Pumble sat with his amulet pressed to his lips. His face glistened like a full moon on rippling water. "When it comes to the Wehrland, yes."

"I think that's wise," Tolbert said. "We have directions. I suggest we use them."

"Do you think they're true?" Rees retorted. "Look at who—"

"They're true." Mirianna's voice carried around the clearing though she was sure she'd no more than mouthed the words that had bubbled, unbidden, to her lips. She flushed, startled by their certainty.

Rees swung toward her, his face livid. "Now, don't you start—"

"Even if they're not true," she blurted, "what have we got to lose?"

"Right." Pumble urged his horse around Rees's mount. "We were already lost."

"If this path goes downhill, it's going in the right

direction." Tolbert motioned to Mirianna to follow him out of the clearing.

Keeping her eyes fixed on the chestnut's tail, she heeled her horse, maneuvering it around Rees. His horse jerked its head up and, for an instant, she thought he would cut her off. Instead, he sat immobile as stone while, one by one, they passed him and rode out of the clearing.

After Pumble had located the trail, and her father assured himself it led downhill, she heard the slow thud of hooves as Rees rode silently into place behind her. She felt his gaze burning at her back, but she didn't turn. Nor did she speak. Heeling her horse, she followed her father down the path that, somehow, she was certain would lead them to Ar-Deneth.

****

Gareth rolled over and sat up slowly. The pressure on his shoulder had eased with the slow fade of voices, but he hadn't attempted to raise his face from the moss until the weight lifted completely. Now he ran a hand down his shin, feeling gingerly over a lump forming across it halfway to his ankle. There was a companion lump on his other shin. The mark of a tree root, he discovered as his hand explored the ground on which he sat.

The vapor of spruce pitch hung thick in the air. Needles pricked at his cheek when he shifted forward, and he brushed them away. He was in the trees now. He knew that well enough. What he didn't know was how long he'd lain there. It seemed like hours, yet it couldn't have been more than minutes since the intruders had awakened him, and even fewer since the Shadow Man had snatched him from the fire pit and flung him face down here.

A bit of breeze licked up his back. Gareth shivered. Under his cloak, his tunic stuck to his skin. He peeled the fabric away and shivered again. Shifting his weight, he tried to untangle his cloak and wrap it around his body.

"Are you hurt?"

Gareth turned toward the voice. The Shadow Man spoke from perhaps two arm-lengths away, standing, Gareth decided. "No, sir." He rolled to his hands and knees and started to rise.

"Here."

Something hard nudged his shoulder. Gareth grasped it, found familiar indentations in the wood under his fingertips, and recognized his staff. He clung to it for a moment, holding on with both hands, leaning on it like a child leans on his cottage door after a wild run home in the dark.

"Get up, boy, and saddle the horses."

Gareth raised his head. "Do you—do you think they'll be back?"

There was the clunk of tankard against pot, the delicate patter of sand grains drizzling from a lifted pack, then the Shadow Man's voice paces away. "I don't intend to wait and see."

The shivers that had retreated to Gareth's stomach and coiled there, broke over his body again. He was not home. He had no home. He was here in the dark, in the wild, terrifying place called the Wehrland, indentured to a shadow. He rose slowly, muscles he didn't know he possessed aching in protest. "Yes, sir."

****

The Imposter of Nolar woke with a start. He was

sweating, and his nightshirt had molded itself to his back. Flinging off the bedclothes, he sat up. His heart galloped in his chest, pumping like that of a man in the throes of coupling. Tightness in his loins told him he'd been dreaming of just such a pastime. With the gem cutter's daughter, no doubt. That randy cock, Rees, by practically mounting the girl, had planted in his mind the feel of her young body writhing beneath him.

For a moment, he wondered if he should have chosen Pumble as his medium. The Imposter of Nolar grimaced. That sack of gelatinous fat was too slow, too stupid for his purposes. Rees would have to do, for now.

A sensation of heat in the middle of his breastbone captured his attention. He tugged the pouch free of his nightshirt and shook the crystal into his hand. It lay in his palm like a coal, hot, dark, and glowing faintly orange at the ragged edges.

The Imposter of Nolar's skin crawled. With a wordless gasp, he flung the crystal to the bedding. He scrabbled against the carved headboard and crouched, back pressed to the wood, staring at the knot of blackness filling the column.

It isn't possible! He can't have survived! No one could have. He himself had survived, but it was the crystal that had saved him—the crystal column and his knowledge of it.

The Imposter of Nolar straightened, emboldened by the thought. The sons of Koronolan were only human, after all—pathetically, stupidly human. Even if the Dragonkeeper had survived the destruction of Drakkonwehr and the fall of Herrok-Eneth, the curse should have made his life a living hell.

The Imposter of Nolar smiled. Even the Demon Master of Beggeth couldn't have laid on a better curse. And he'd done it in a matter of seconds, too. In the seconds that mattered before Drakkonwehr and the pit erupted around them.

He peered at the crystal again as the glow went out of it. The darkness within dissipated, like a cloud of smoke caught by a breeze. It lay like a column of water on the bedding, its facets reflecting what little light seeped between the window shutters.

He spoke a word, and colors rippled from the ragged edges. He reached for it, found it cool to the touch, and slid it into his palm. *What did you see, Rees? What did you really see?*

If the Dragonkeeper were alive, that would alter things—but not too much. He still had the crystal and the Dragon Chant that ambitious little slut had stolen for him years ago. *The fool! If only she hadn't reached for the gems too soon.* Well, he would have new ones when Rees returned. And he would have Master Brandelmore's bride.

He smiled, picturing himself asking, "Well, my dear, would you like to ride the Dragon?" She could hardly refuse. No woman alive could resist spreading her legs for a chance to couple with the Beast. Even if it killed her.

Chapter Eight

Just before dawn, Pumble located the single willow and the trail running beside it. The group turned their weary horses westward and followed the path down into a valley and along a river—the River Ar, Tolbert said between coughs. As milky green as the glacier it sprang from, the Ar rushed headlong over rocks, chilling the riders with vapors still rising from its little falls, vapors the sun wouldn't burn away for hours yet in the narrow valley depths.

The cold—and the dampness—seeped into Mirianna's extremities, penetrating to the bone. She didn't complain because the frequent mental reminders to flex her fingers and curl her toes kept her from dwelling on the night's wealth of unanswered questions. The voice still lingered around the edges of her consciousness like a dimly remembered dream.

Or nightmare.

Mirianna shivered. The Wehrland had that effect on people, she told herself. Yet she hadn't been entirely frightened. The man—or whatever it was—had somehow stopped her horse from bolting. She was sure of that. And they'd received true directions. But the boy had vanished into thin air, and he'd stood only across the fire pit from Pumble. Had they seen what they thought, or not?

She shook her head, trying to clear a strange,

sudden brightness from her vision when she realized it was sunlight. She sat up straighter and blinked at the shafts of golden haze slanting into the canyon. Ahead, the Ar turned a slight bend and poured into a wider, gently rolling valley.

"There's Ar-Deneth!" Tolbert pointed toward a distant cluster of thatch and shake roofs. He rubbed his hands, blew on them, and rubbed them again. "I can't wait to taste a mug of Ulerroth's ale." He touched Mirianna's hand. "It's really the best, you know."

"I'll settle for a leg of mutton, hot, with gravy and dumplings," Pumble said as his hands conjured the dish in the air. "Lots and lots of dumplings." He looked at Mirianna and sighed. "I wouldn't even care if it was old goat."

She laughed, and then, throwing off her hood, laughed again. The Wehrland was behind them, the sun beat freely on their shoulders, and all the comforts of home—beds, hot food, chairs and tables—lay waiting in the village ahead. Grinning, she said, "I'll take anything hot."

"I want something with flesh." Rees materialized at her side. "Flesh and—" His gaze swept over her body. "—blood."

Mirianna's grin faded. *Not all of the beasts,* echoed from the back of her mind. Rees had been so silent these last hours she'd forgotten he rode behind her. Now his expression told her precisely what thoughts had occupied his mind while her figure had filled his sight. Suppressing a shiver, she looked at him coldly, and turned her gaze forward.

Pumble urged his mount into a trot. "You can have your women. Just don't charm the cook till she's made my mutton."

Tolbert heeled his chestnut. "And leave off the serving maid till she's poured my ale."

Rees brayed out a laugh. "Not if I get there first!" Flashing a wicked grin at Mirianna, he lashed his horse into a gallop.

Mirianna held her gelding in check. Scowling, she watched Rees speed past her father. His raucous laughter echoed over the hoof beats while Pumble whipped his horse and, for a few hundred yards, gave chase until Rees, still laughing, outdistanced him. Her eyes narrowed as she watched his shape grow small against the cluster of roofs. This was his territory, land where he felt secure. In the Wehrland, he'd been as frightened as she. More so, perhaps. Now he had nothing to fear.

A shiver rattled through her despite the sun, despite the prospect of hot food, beds, and people. Despite being out of the Wehrland.

****

Gareth ran his hands gently down the pack mare's front legs, inspecting each in turn. His palms lingered on the fetlock, cupped the right one, returned to the left. "It's hot." Lifting the foot, he laid it on his thigh. The mare nuzzled his hip, and he patted her shoulder before probing the hoof with his fingertips.

A shadow blocked the sun's generalized glow, a shadow separate from the bulk of the mare Gareth leaned against. "Well?"

"A stone...here, I think." Gareth drew his knife and, using his left index finger and thumb as a guide, slid the blade between the shoe and the hoof. Stone and steel scraped. His tongue curled over his upper lip as he backed off, angled the blade slightly, and probed again. It was a small pebble, the size of a dried pea. He caught an edge with the point of his blade and carefully pried the stone out.

Once free, it rolled between his fingers and bounced off the toe of his boot. *My boot.* One of a pair the Shadow Man had selected for him from Ulerroth's store of goods abandoned in rooms due to either the untimely death or hurried departure of the owner. The boots were large, and his ankles, unaccustomed to being leather-clad, were already rubbed raw, but Gareth didn't mind. They were boots, not rough-hewn wooden shoes or leggings held in place with thongs. They were boots such as those he'd helped remove from the feet of guests at the White Boar Inn, guests who had gold in their pouches and coin to give a helpful lad.

Sheathing his knife, he released the mare's hoof, then bent and dusted the tops of his boots. Before straightening, he felt once more of the mare's fetlock. "I'll put a poultice on it. She'll be good as new in the morning."

"The morning!" The Shadow Man's boots crushed pebbles and the sunlight returned, full and warm, as his master strode several steps away.

Gareth stood listening to the coo of a dove. A breeze flirted with his face, touching it lightly then retreating. It bore a heavy scent of clover, sweet and not far away. The mare snuffled and raised her head. He stroked her neck, enjoying the warmth of the sun radiating from her skin. It was calm and pleasant here, and the warmth soaked into his body and tugged at his eyelids. He leaned his cheek against the mare and yawned.

A human shape blocked the sunlight and Gareth started when it spoke. "We'll rest her till dusk. That's all we can afford."

"But—"

"This is the Wehrland, boy." The dark shape swelled, swirled, and vanished into the glare of the sun.

Gareth flinched from the sudden brightness. He heard his master stride across the uneven ground, heard the squeak of leather pack straps being tugged loose, and recognized in their sound the same impatience evident in the Shadow Man's voice. And the same something else, Gareth thought as he felt along the mare's withers for the fastenings of her burden. Not fear, but something akin to it that made his stomach ball into a tight, hard knot. Sweat bloomed under his armpits as he remembered the voices in the night, the intruders.

"We—we've gone too far already for them, those people last night, to follow us, haven't we?" he said, fumbling with a knot.

Nearby, a pack crunched to the ground. "If they went to Ar-Deneth."

And if they didn't? But the Shadow Man said no more. Gareth tugged at the mare's pack, freed a sack of grain and lowered it to the ground, asking instead, "There were—there were only four, weren't there?"

"Did you count their voices?"

"Not then, but...later, when I had a little time to think." Gareth unpacked another sack of grain. "There were just four, weren't there?"

The Shadow Man grunted, as if shifting a heavy load. "Yes."

Gareth unfastened another strap. Four was not a

large number. Too many to deal with at once, perhaps, but not as large a number as, say, forty. There were four, and they'd frightened him, especially the loud one who'd stayed back on his horse. The one who'd come in close—Gareth wrinkled his nose. He could still smell the odor attending that one. There had been a third who coughed. And the fourth...

He scowled, but the memory refused to change despite its impossibility. Lowering another bundle to the ground, he straightened slowly and laid his hand on the mare's withers. "One of them...one of them was a woman, wasn't it?"

For two full breaths, his master neither spoke nor moved. Then his boot crushed a pebble. "Yes."

Gareth listened to him stride away, presumably to tend to Ghost. He wanted to ask why a woman would be traveling in the Wehrland, but the terseness of his master's reply told him the Shadow Man wouldn't welcome the question. At least, not now. He trailed his fingers through the mare's mane and patted her shoulder. "Here now, lass, let's get your leg looked to."

****

The man watched the shadow of a cloud run across the rocky clearing. Clumps of grass waved their heads gently in the breeze. Below his perch, in a narrow but level patch of grass, earth, and sandstone, the two pack horses, Ghost, and the boy's dun-colored mount stood side by side, nose to tail, flicking away black-winged flies. Now and then, the mare lifted her bandaged foot or sniffed at it. Amid the gear, about ten feet away, the boy lay sleeping in the afternoon sun, a sack of grain for a pillow.

The man flung away the blade of grass he'd twisted

into knots and broke off a fresh one.

Admit it, the Voice in his head said. *It's not the horse going lame that's bothering you. It's the woman, isn't it?*

If it was a woman.

The she-cat in a woman's form? Don't be a fool. There was no magic in those four.

Those three, he amended. He let the twisted blade of grass slip through his gloved fingers. *I'm not sure about the female.*

So you ran, didn't you? Just like before. Just like always...when you're not sure.

Damn you! This is the Wehrland. It's not—

Drakkonwehr?

The man shuddered. He snapped his eyes shut, but the image of flames penetrated his eyelids anyway, leaping up hugely against the delicate skin. Yellow-orange, hungry and hot, they ate through the thin wall of memory and he saw, for the millionth time, the rock-hewn tunnel filled with sulfurous yellow smoke, the barred oak door, and the black granite pit...

Sweat dripped from his hair, stinging his eyes. He swiped his tunic sleeve across his face. In the light of the single wall torch, he saw—and dismissed—the smear of red on his hand. Better he should suffer than his men. After all, he was the damned fool who'd been tricked into fighting his way back into his own fortress. The Drakkonwehr guardsmen couldn't help being spell-struck, but if more came between him and the mage who'd entranced them, he'd willingly knock their heads. Too bad that broken turret stone had roused the gatehouse. He and Errek might have had time to—

What? Find Ayliss?

His gut clenched. He couldn't think about her—what she may have done—now. The handful of men he'd sent to assault the gate would distract the guardsmen for only so long. Better for Errek—for both of us—that we concentrate on the mage.

The sound of rushing footsteps brought him swiveling to his feet, shield up. His fingers tightened around the hilt of the ancient double-edged Sword of Drakkonwehr.

His best friend—and second in command—Errek Eolen rounded the corner. "I've bolted the tunnel door. I don't think the guards know we've made it down here."

He blew out the breath he'd been holding. The yellow haze stirred, stinging his eyes and nostrils. He dropped back into a crouch. "Get down. The tunnel's full of dragon's breath."

Bending his large frame, Errek shuffled closer. "Durren—the Sword—look! Does that mean the mage has raised the beast?"

The large bloodstone embedded in the intersection of hand guard, blade, and hilt glowed softly, a dark, deep red. It knows we're close. *A thrill shivered along his nerves, but he kept his voice level. "I haven't felt any tremors."*

Closing his eyes, he concentrated on the heavy, sulfurous air, gauging its movement—first toward the door, then away—until, in the enclosed space and the darkness of his mind's eye, he saw the tunnel walls expanding and contracting...like something long...leathery...and alive! *Forcing his eyes open, he shoved away from the wall and panted.*

"What did you see?" Errek's fingers dug into his

shoulder. *"Tell me—was it Ayliss?"*

"No." He sucked in hot air. *"I don't know where she is."* That was true enough. Despite the second sight his Drakkonwehr blood gave him, he could divine no more than that his sister was within the fortress. But I can guess, Ayliss. Damn you, I can guess!

"We have to find her."

"Later." He caught Errek's arm. *"The dragon's stirring. We have to stop the mage first."* He nodded toward the door. *"Think your axe'll open that?"*

"Three strokes—if there's no spell on the wood."

"There won't be." When the big man shot him a questioning look, he stifled a sigh. He hoped he wouldn't have to explain how his whole plan relied on the little he remembered of Owender's* History *of the People.* He wished—again—he'd paid more attention to the scrolls, but it had always been the Sword that drew his hand and his heart. Gripping it now, he recited, *"'True hearts and no fear, against a mage's power, hold dear.'"*

Errek rolled his eyes. "That's a child's rhyme. I'd rather depend on my axe."

He forced a grin. "All the same, Syryk can't harm us if we trust each other. Just don't let his illusions rattle you."

Errek snorted. "You know me better than that." He stood and raised the long-handled Eolian axe. "Are you coming?"

"Right behind you."

The oaken door gave with a shriek of splintered wood. Smoke billowed out, thick yellow smoke that burned their eyes and seared their throats. Five steps over the threshold, the smoke thinned. Two shadowy figures rushed toward them.

"I'll take the big one!" Errek yelled.

"Illusion!" He flung his sword against Errek's upraised axe handle. "Don't strike!"

Errek stared at him, sulfur-induced tears streaming down his face, but the haze lifted, and the figures vanished. At their feet, inches from the toes of their boots, ran the edge of a wide rocky pit. Waves of heat welled up out of it—heavy, palpable waves of dry, intense heat.

"Ah, Drakkonwehr," said a sibilant voice, "how you delight us with your company. Pity you've arrived at such an inopportune time."

The mage stood in the middle of the pit, his arms spread over a stone pedestal on which a large circle of polished onyx lay like a tabletop. In the center stood a spiral of amber and silver. Enclosed within the spiral stood not an orb, as he'd expected, but something much more dangerous—a perfectly faceted column of crystal thick as a sapling and longer than a hand. Only the ancients—Black Mages and Hero Mages both—had mastered the power of a crystal column. And this one was already pulsing with color—brown, green, red, yellow—first one then another surging to dominance. Transfixed, he watched the colors dance in a rhythm that invaded his hearing and found itself an echo in the beat of his blood.

"Come to see me raise the dragon, have you?" the sibilant voice said.

He tore his gaze from the hypnotic display and focused on the mage. The magician's teeth gleamed in a thin, pale face. He was neither tall nor as old as one with his skill—or audacity—should be. More illusions.

"No, Syryk. We've come to stop you." Gripping the Sword of Drakkonwehr and his shield, he leaped into the pit.

He landed heavily, the heat a physical force pressing against him from all sides. He breathed, but his lungs would not expand. Waves of hot air seared his face, and he staggered, momentarily disoriented.

"Durren," said a voice, softly, at his side.

"Ayliss," he gasped.

A young woman clad in white shimmered before him. Her amber hair was fastened into a circlet of braids. About her wrists, throat, and forehead hung finely wrought chains of silver set with oval stones that glowed a deep, dark glossy red against translucent skin.

"Ayliss, how—? Why?"

"You have to understand," she murmured. "Let me explain."

He staggered backwards, eluding her outstretched hand. "Illusion." Blinking, he stared past her shimmering image and tried to focus on the table. Somewhere in the heat-distorted beams of light he would find the mage and his column of power. He had to break it—that much he remembered clearly from Owender's History. Break the crystal and break the chant, and thereby break the spell.

An anguished cry of "Ayliss!" sounded from above.

"Illusion, Errek!" he screamed. "Don't touch her!"

But Errek, still on the rim of the pit, lowered his axe and his shield. "Ayliss," he said to the shimmering woman in white.

"Errek." She held out her hands to him.

111

"No!" He lunged toward Errek, but his boots stuck to the pit floor. His shield hit the rough-hewn rock first. His cheek smashed into the metal rim. The Sword of Drakkonwehr, clattering against the stone, shook free of his hand. He lay for a moment, dazed, until the floor's heat seared through his tunic and breeches. With a cry of pain, he staggered to his feet.

—Trust me. For once in your life, please—

"Ayliss?" He turned automatically to the voice he knew. But no one stood there. Nothing loomed behind him but stone and heat and emptiness.

Gall rose in his throat. He clenched his jaw against it. Don't be a fool! She's an illusion. Or worse.

"Why did you do it?" he snarled, unable to stop the words. "Was it the jewels? Or the power?" He shook his head, but the images before his eyes still wavered like wheat in a fickle wind.

On the far side of the pit, the woman in white was ascending a narrow staircase, approaching Errek with a look of love on her face. He blinked, stared at her outstretched hands and blinked again. An image flickered in and out of view, an image of something held in one slender hand—no!—one large, heavy-wristed hand.

"Errek!" he screamed. "It's the—"

"Ayliss," Errek said, and embraced her.

The hand moved—in a quick, thrusting motion.

A cry ripped from his throat. He seized his knife and flung it at the woman in white.

There was a moment when time seemed suspended, when the knife, rotating gracefully hilt over tip, floated through the air while nothing else could move. Even his hand couldn't complete its downward arc. Nor could

112

sound, rolling like thunder, form into more than slow reverberation. Only the woman in white could glide onward, shimmering, through Errek's embrace.

"Illusion, Drakkonwehr," purred the mage's voice in his ear. "How kind of you to fall for it."

Powerless, he could do nothing but stare in horror as the knife, continuing its uninterrupted motion, slid smoothly into Errek's tunic. It struck a spark from the chain mail covering his friend's chest, a tiny spark that winked out even as the blade penetrated with agonizing leisure, penetrated to the hilt. A fine spray of red droplets punctuated the impact, hazing into the air.

"No!" he cried as Errek's body, ever so slowly, rounded over the antler-handled hilt, now spotted with blood.

The big man staggered backward and his hand came up to his chest. "Durren—" Errek raised his head, a look of shock in his eyes. "Your knife—" And he crumpled, slowly, to the ground...

"No!"

The cry echoed off the trees like a hundred howls of pain. The horses below jerked up their heads and stamped. A pair of crows took squawking flight from a dead pine. The boy sat up, blinking like a startled field mouse.

"Sir? Are you—it's early yet, isn't it?"

The man stared down at the boy, concentrating, trying to bring him into focus, to return his vision to the place and time the boy's voice called him toward. *It's not the words. The words are nothing. It's his voice that drives out the demons and leaves me here. Quivering— yes—but here. Not...there.*

He straightened slowly and pressed his tunic

against his chest to blot the moisture there. "Yes, Gareth, it's much too early," he said gently. "Go back to sleep. I'll wake you when it's time."

With hands barely poking out of over-long tunic sleeves, the boy knuckled his eyes and yawned. "I must have been dreaming, I guess," he mumbled and lay down again. "Sorry, sir."

The man watched him snuggle into the hard ground. Even from this distance, he could see dirt smudging the boy's cheekbone and bits of twig and branch clinging to his sand-colored hair.

He sees nothing of the outside, not even his own. He belongs at Drakkonwehr...with me.

The man raised his hands and, turning them over, stared at the gloves covering them like a black second skin. Even here, even in this desolation, this wilderness, he wouldn't take them off. Not in daylight. Nor in moonlight. Only in the deepest shadow of night where he himself could see nothing.

Raising his head, he turned his face northward while the breeze fluttered the edge of his hood. Drakkonwehr lay in that direction, in the shadow of peaks he could not now see but knew their location as a magnet knows true north even without ever reaching it. They would be safe there, he and the boy—if only they could keep moving.

****

It was just after noon when Mirianna woke the first time. She'd been dreaming of the lion. Its voice—and the words of warning spoken with that voice—had made her rise, disheveled and groggy, to check the fastening on her door. Satisfied it was secure, she'd lain down again.

Some time later, when the sun had begun to slant between cracks in the closed shutters, she awakened a second time. She lay for a few moments, watching dust particles float through the streaks of light. She felt warm and as spineless as a cat luxuriating on the thick mattress. When she stretched, her breasts tingled with the movement of her shift across them, and with the memory of her lover's touch.

She sighed, filled with an ache to know the man whose sensual presence haunted her dreams. Nightly he visited her, sometimes more than once. Since the incident with Rees, her lover's touch had become more erotic, more intimate, the aura around him darker, more shadowed. Closing her eyes, she wondered vaguely if Rees's groping had propelled her past some barrier. Or if it had opened a wider crack in her unconscious mind, allowing visions to enter that had been otherwise kept at bay.

The idea disturbed her. To shake it off, she tried to return to the comfort of her lover's arms, but the colors faded to blue and purple and filled with shadows, loud voices, and shapes that snatched at her from all sides in some sort of tunnel where she could run only one way—down deeper into darkness—before she fell and woke with a start.

Sitting up in bed, she saw by the shadow of the shutter slats that it was late afternoon. She rubbed her arms to chase away lingering chills, and heard the hum of voices below. She recognized her father's immediately, but the second man wasn't Rees or Pumble. The innkeeper, she guessed, and rose with a sigh. Although her father had retired for a nap the same time as she, the lure of gems had undoubtedly drawn him from his rest.

She grimaced at her reflection in the glass—sun-darkened forehead and nose, wind-dried lips, and light purple shadows under her eyes. Well, if her appearance left her less than comparable with the beauties of Ar-Deneth, all the better. Rees had set his charm to work on the serving maid who welcomed them, a woman of forty if she was a day, but as ready as he with a bawdy joke and leer. Mirianna had no doubt the woman would tumble into his bed as soon as he offered. Perhaps she had already. *I hope so. The sooner he satisfies his urges, the better for me.*

Downstairs, late afternoon sun cast a long rectangle of light through the open window and across a small oaken table. Her father sat there, the sun glinting off his newly scrubbed forehead. The innkeeper, a burly man in apron and shoved-up sleeves, straddled a chair to his right. He was leaning forward, pointing at a stone lying on a black cloth while droplets of perspiration decorated his balding head.

"There you are." Mirianna crossed the room to lay her hands on her father's shoulders. "Have you found anything you like?"

Tolbert glanced up, then refocused his glass on the stone between his fingertips. "Lovely color, but see that thin line there?" He held the glass and let Mirianna peer through it.

"A flaw?" She slid into the vacant seat to his right.

"It'll shatter if I try to cut it."

Ulerroth shrugged when Tolbert handed him the stone. He dropped it into a pile off to the side. "I have more."

Tolbert pinched the bridge of his nose. He still

looked tired, but Mirianna said nothing. Her father blew a speck of dust from his glass. "Actually, I was counting on you to have bloodstone. The Master of Nolar insists on having it."

"Bloodstone!" Ulerroth's expression brightened. "Why didn't you say so?" He tugged a small pouch from beneath his apron. With one thick hand, he shoved the other gems to the side of the cloth, while the other hand threw the pouch into the center of it. "There," he said, leaning back on two legs of his chair, "feast your eyes on the treasure of the Wehrland."

With a glance at Ulerroth, then at Mirianna, Tolbert wiped his hands on his tunic and reached for the pouch. He unfastened the thong and carefully poured out its contents. Five small stones rolled out first—the smallest like a barley grain, the largest like a pea—and settled into a loose semi-circle. Into their center rolled a stone larger than all five together. Dull, nearly black, each was slightly oblong and wider at one end.

Mirianna leaned forward, almost bumping heads with her father as they peered at the stones. The gems could have passed for obsidian, but they were far too dull. Unpolished jet sprang to her lips, but the words went unsaid as the sunlight sinking into the stones revealed a growing rim of dark red around the edge of each. Her lips parted and she watched, speechless, while Tolbert picked up the stones one by one and gently placed them in the center of his palm. Almost instantly, the stones began to glow a deep, glossy blood-red. *Like the first drops of a fresh kill,* she thought, and shuddered. At once, spears of scarlet light broke in all directions, streaking her father's palm, fingers, the table, their faces.

"Dragon's blood!" Tolbert breathed.

Ulerroth snorted out a chuckle. "In the flesh, my friend." He leaned forward, throwing his shadow over Tolbert's hand. Like an oil lamp, blown out, darkens a room instantly, the stones, deprived of light, became nothing again—nothing but dull, blackish, droplet-shaped bits of rock.

Transfixed, Mirianna stared. She'd seen bloodstone before. Her father had made a piece or two from it when she was younger. She'd watched him polish the stone and shape the silver setting. She'd even touched it once, with her fingernail, when he wasn't looking, but she'd never seen such a display of its power. He'd kept it inside then and worked under the light of his candle and lamp. The stone she remembered had lain inert, more black than red, and she'd wondered why anyone would choose such an ugly thing as an adornment.

"Well," Ulerroth was saying, "will you be wanting these?"

"Oh, yes." Tolbert placed them one by one on the table.

With some difficulty, Mirianna withdrew her gaze from the stones and turned it on her father. He sat with his hands spread on the table, thumbs pointing at each other and seemed to be staring at the stones. But it wasn't just the stones he was seeing, she knew; it was the possible settings and arrangements. Each minute flutter of his eyelids or shift of the pupils told her another idea had been considered and either discarded or saved. While she watched, the furrows in his forehead deepened. Two vertical grooves, either side of his nose, lengthened and leaned toward each other.

"I can't do it," he said, straightening. "It's not

enough."

Ulerroth's expelled breath was like an explosion. "What do you mean?" He thrust out a huge hand. "That's all the bloodstone I have."

Tolbert shook his head. "It's enough for a bracelet. And a pendant perhaps but..." He waggled his head again and slid his hands along the table's edge. "The Master of Nolar was very insistent I use bloodstone in every piece. I have to have more."

The innkeeper rolled his eyes. "Understand me, my friend, when I say there's no more to be had. I've but one source for the gems and he was here yesterday. This was all he brought."

Tolbert's face brightened. "Yesterday? Well, then, perhaps I can persuade him to find me more." He picked up the largest stone and rolled it between thumb and fingertips. "Two or three more this size would be just right." He replaced the gem on the table and squinted at the sun-drenched window. "Where can I find him?"

Ulerroth grunted. He leaned forward and, with a thick index finger, deliberately repositioned all six stones. "You don't know what you're asking, my friend."

Tolbert scratched his chin. "If it's your fee you're concerned about, I can see that you—"

The innkeeper slapped the tabletop, jumbling the stones. "Don't be a fool, old man! This is no ordinary gem hunter."

Mirianna eased her elbow from the table and rubbed where the jolted edge had bitten into it. The table's vibrations echoed along her nerves the way Ulerroth's outburst echoed in the high-ceilinged room.

The innkeeper was a substantial man, capable of knocking heads if the order of his establishment was disturbed. Yet sweat glistened on his forehead and she noticed his gaze wouldn't settle, not even on the scattered stones.

"Well," Tolbert said, clearing his throat as he removed his hands from the table, "this gem hunter will take gold, won't he?"

Ulerroth wiped his face with his apron. He laughed, but the sound only made Mirianna shift in her chair. Something about his manner made her skin crawl. "Papa, perhaps we shouldn't—"

"Listen to her." Ulerroth leaned across the table. "Forget this gem hunter. He won't let you find him anyway. He—" He hesitated, as if noting their startled expressions, and grinned—a quick, humorless show of teeth. "He doesn't like people."

"But I must have the bloodstone. These simply aren't enough." Tolbert looked from her to Ulerroth. "The Master of Nolar insists."

The innkeeper shoved his chair back, thrust himself out of it and paced the mantel wall. "Look, I can't help you. The Shadow Man—"

"The Shadow Man?" Mirianna breathed. The name sent a shiver of sensation down her arms. In her mind, an image wavered, an image of blackness...a tower of blackness. And a voice as deep as the night.

"The Shadow Man?" Tolbert's eyes widened. "But I thought he was only a winter's tale."

"He is." Ulerroth paused to lean against the fireplace and wipe his face once more. "Except for once a year when he comes here to trade with me."

Chapter Nine

"But who—or what—is the Shadow Man?" Mirianna recovered enough to ask.

"No one knows." Tolbert scratched his cheek. "A being like the shadow of a man, if I remember the story correctly."

Mirianna swallowed. The memory of the faceless shape and voice enlarged, vivid in all of its darkness. "Go on," she breathed, knowing with an odd, prickling certainty her vision and the being they spoke of were one and the same.

Ulerroth gripped his chair and placed it before the table again. "Black Mage spawn," he said, sitting down heavily, "let loose, some say, when the last mage tried to raise the Dragon."

"People blame all sorts of the world's ills on that incident," Tolbert said. "You'd think, after all these years, they'd realize what's happened since has something more to do with their own actions."

The innkeeper merely nodded, his gaze focused on his hands, which cupped the table's edge. "Everyone agrees it was Durren Drakkonwehr and Errek Eolan who trapped the mage Syryk at the Dragonkeep."

"And none of them were ever seen again." Tolbert straightened in his chair as if that pronouncement ended the discussion.

Ulerroth, however, stretched out a hand and

fingered the bloodstones. "The Stone Dam that Kiros set in the high pass at Herrok-Eneth ages ago, to separate the good land from the evils of Beggeth, was destroyed that day, obliterated from the face of the mountain when it broke. The River Ar didn't flow for days. And smoke covered the sun. It was dry and hot and dark, even this far down the mountain, and the ground trembled. Then the Krad came, those ancient scourges of Beggeth, through the crack in the mountain where Herrok-Eneth fell. They overwhelmed what was left of the Dragonkeep and poured into the Wehrland, rampaging like they had in Shadowtime before the warrior Kiros first drove them out and sealed the pass against them."

Mirianna shivered, but not from cold or fear. She knew the Deeds of Kiros, knew well Owender's *History of the People*. What made bumps rise along the underside of her arms was the innkeeper's voice, the way its quiet awe propelled her backward to childhood, to hours spent listening to the storyteller in Nolar and absorbing the ancient chants and tales of Shadowtime, Dawntime, Dragontime, Dragon's End. She knew the tales, but she knew them as a child knows them—as tales to be fantasized about while testing the balance of a bejeweled weapon in her father's workshop. The deeds were too distant to be real, the places mere names that tasted oddly sweet on the lips. Only the Wehrland was real. Only the Wehrland and the strange being who had stolen the head of her horse—and given it back again.

The innkeeper's sigh brought her attention back to his bulk. His expression distant, he rolled the largest stone back and forth with a fingertip. She watched the red aura shift with each movement.

"In Shadowtime," he mused, "we had great warriors like Kiros. In Dragontime, we had Koronolan and the Hero Mages. At Dragon's End, Koronolan gave us his sons and their sons forever after them as Dragonkeepers. He gave them his own sword, the Sword of Drakkonwehr, to keep the beast sealed forever beneath Drakkonwehr fortress. Now that the last of the Drakkonwehrs is gone, and the Sword with him, what do we have?"

"Black Mage spawn, shadows, and other such unnatural creatures," another voice said before Ulerroth could answer his own question.

Rees leaned against the wall at the foot of the stairs, his hair tousled and his tunic entirely unlaced. He scratched absently at golden chest hair exposed between the loose thongs. He looked, Mirianna thought, like a cat who'd just feasted on quail. Or, much more likely, a man who'd just risen from a shared bed.

As if sensing the direction of her thoughts, Rees fixed her with a gaze that lingered too long on her breasts. "Now, I offered to tell you that story, remember?"

Mirianna flushed.

With an insolent grin, he pushed away from the wall and strolled to the table. Hooking a chair with one hand, he swung it into place beside her and straddled the seat. His thigh, thick and hard, pressed against the length of hers. She tried to pull away, but her father's knee on the other side kept her hemmed in. Rees dropped her a look from half-lidded eyes, then turned his grin on the two men.

"Now, what's this talk about unnatural creatures

and such?"

"The Shadow Man." Tolbert leaned forward. "He brings Ulerroth his bloodstone. He was here only yesterday, but he didn't bring enough. We have to hurry after him and ask him to find a few more pieces because—"

Rees held up a hand. "Did you say, the Shadow Man?" His brows lowered and, alongside her thigh, Mirianna felt his muscles tense. "Are you referring to that—that *thing* that drives men mad and steals women to couple with and kill?" His gaze slid to her. "Young women. Unmarried women. Women fond of going off alone."

Her face burned, as much from the gaze that flicked from her breasts to the V between her legs as from the implication in his words. Her fingers clenched in her skirt.

Ulerroth colored. He balled his huge hands into fists. "He does nothing of that while he's here. Nothing except—"

Rees's head snapped up like a hound scenting rabbit. "Except what? Take a woman?"

The innkeeper stared at his hands. "There's some that would go," he mumbled, "for gold."

Rees's mouth curled into a sneer. "For gold, eh? Small compensation for coupling with a fiend." He leaned toward Tolbert, his expression conspiratorial. "I hear he has to drug them."

Ulerroth slammed his hands on the table. His brows bristled like thunderclouds. "Nothing of the sort happens in this establishment! The Shadow Man does nothing wrong while he's here."

"Nothing wrong! What about those three men?

That happened right outside this very inn, didn't it?"

Ulerroth's color deepened. He avoided Rees's stare and tugged at his tunic collar. "Two," he said, his voice gruff. "There were only two. And the fools tried to rob him."

"They died, didn't they?"

"What of it? Any man with gold would have killed thieves who came at him in the night."

Rees snorted. "Would any man with gold have killed them without touching them?" He lounged back in his chair. "Everyone knows they were found dead with looks of horror frozen on their faces. And not a mark on them."

"You've been listening to tales." Ulerroth dashed an arm across his forehead. The dark arm hair came away wet. "That was years ago. You know how stories spread."

"I was listening to your serving maid, telling me about the fiend that was here only yesterday." Rees rotated his head and fixed his gaze on Mirianna. "And in your room, too." He leaned forward, a feral gleam in his eyes. The charm he wore swung free of the hair it had nested in and spun, glittering. "Tell me, how did you like sleeping in *his* bed?"

Panic stirred in the pit of Mirianna's stomach. She remembered all too vividly the weight of Rees's body grinding hers into the earth, the pressure of his arms pinning hers beside her head, the taste of his hand clamped over her mouth, the sensation of helplessness, terror, loss. Her skin crawled. She wanted to bolt, to overturn the table and run. Rees's eyes, and the pleasure evident in the widened pupils as they basked in the terror broadcast from hers, held her rooted to her chair.

"You bastard spawn of a Krad!" Ulerroth lunged across the table, seizing Rees by the tunic and toppling both of their chairs. "The Shadow Man comes, he trades, and he harms no one! I'll not have a dung beetle like you spreading lies about my establishment or any of my customers! Do you hear me?"

Rees shrugged out of Ulerroth's grip and made a show of straightening his tunic. "Lies, Ulerroth? How can they be lies when everyone in Ar-Deneth knows you do more business in one day the fiend's here than you do in a month without him."

A muscle under Ulerroth's moustache twitched. His fingers flexed at his sides, curling and uncurling. Color washed in waves across his face. "Get out!" He jabbed a finger at the stones scattered across the table. "Buy your gems and get out! All of you! Now!"

Mirianna stood up slowly. Her father, beside her, fumbled with his gold pouch. "I—tell me your price."

"That's right. Tell him your *price*, demon trader."

The innkeeper's fists bunched. Mirianna feared—hoped—he would smash Rees's face. Ulerroth had the bulk and sinew to give the cocksure Master of Nolar's man the beating he deserved, but the innkeeper slowly straightened. "I'd wish for a Krad to cut out your heart and eat it, but I'd hate to disappoint the beast." Seizing a handful of coins from Tolbert, he turned on his heel and stalked into the kitchen.

Rees brushed at the sleeves of his tunic as if to remove clinging dirt. "Demon trader! Brothel for unnatural creatures!" He shuddered. "Pick up your stones and pack. Meet me in the stable."

Vibrating with the emotions that still charged the

room, Mirianna could do no more than watch Rees mount the steps two at a time and disappear around the corner at the top. Part of her wanted to rage at him for his obnoxious accusations. Another part asked if it was wise to remain in a place frequented, if not by unnatural creatures, then by those with similar unsavory reputations. However much Ulerroth tried to minimize the charge, he had not, for all his anger, denied its truth. And Rees, despite his faults, was only looking out for their welfare, wasn't he? Even the appearance of consorting with evil could brand a person, and she and Tolbert, with no other family to shield them, had little enough protection from that. Rees was right, of course, but—

Beside her, a chair scraped. She turned and saw her father tie a thong around the opening of his gem pouch. Lifting the thong ends, he tried to fasten them behind his neck. With a sigh, she said, "Let me," and tied a double knot.

Tolbert responded with a wan smile and tucked the pouch inside his tunic where the precious stones would lie next to his skin. "Come on, lamb." He touched her hand. "We'd best pack." With a sigh, he left the common room in which they should have been spending days, not hours, and mounted the stairs.

Mirianna followed him to the landing and turned to her room. Inside, she drew up short, instantly aware of darkness shrouding the ceiling beams. Gloom draped over them in folds, insinuating itself like the heavy canopy of a bed into the lighter space below. Shadows lurked in the room's corners and stretched dark fingers around the legs of the chair, the table, even the bed.

She swallowed, but no saliva dampened her dry

throat. The gloom, the shadows had been there before, hadn't they? Or did they seem thicker, denser, more substantial now she knew who—or what—had inhabited this room?

She wished she'd opened the shutter. She could open it now, but the window lay farther across the room than her belongings. With every instinct screaming at her to avoid contact with even the smallest shadow, she inched her way across the chamber toward her pack. As she did, her attention riveted on stains spotting the floorboards. She'd seen the stains before, hadn't she? Or did she only now notice them because—because—

Because they might be blood?

Dizzy, Mirianna put out a hand to steady herself, touched the bedpost, and jerked back as though snake-bitten. *He* had lain here. *Here!* In the very mattress hollows Mirianna's body had settled so comfortably, under the very blankets her body had snuggled, the possessor of the voice whose reverberant tones still struck echoes within her body had spread his limbs. *He,* the dark, faceless being who prevented her horse from bolting, had intimately occupied this very space.

Sensation shuddered through her, a strange shivery…*flush* that penetrated deep into her woman's core and left it damp and throbbing. Her knees weakened, and she swayed forward, drawn by an inexplicable desire to lower herself inch by inch to the bed and lie upon it. That same strange desire directed her to raise her arms above her head and open her legs so that she lay, spread-eagled and quivering, while the velvet shadows of late afternoon descended like drapery and enveloped her. Powerless to do otherwise, she closed her eyes and completed the seal.

At once, her lover materialized. He leaned over her, his dark shape haloed by golden haze filtering between shutter slats. The mattress sank under his weight as he stretched full length beside her. The scent of sun-warmed wool and leather filled her nostrils, trailed faintly by something...sweet, she thought, like crushed white clover.

He sighed, and the warmth of his breath caressed her face. Mirianna closed her eyes with pleasure at the contact. They flew open again when his knee crossed hers and the corded thickness of his thigh slid upwards, bunching her skirt above it. His hip leaned into the curve of her bone, and she felt, even as the breath shuttled in and out of her lungs, the pressure of the hard, hot ridge of his manhood against her abdomen. Her body thrummed with sensation. Her nerve endings quivered, jarred by a movement more intimate—and erotic—than any he'd made before.

Let me see your face, she pleaded, searching the shadow that formed his head. *Let me know who you are.*

His movements stilled as if her unspoken words had reached him. For heartbeats, she sensed the scrutiny of his gaze as he lay unmoving, his weight securing her hips beneath his, his knee holding the secrets of her body unlocked and vulnerable. Finally, his hand rose to the fine bones at the base of her throat and lingered there a moment. Then his fingers, feather light, unlaced her bodice and laid it open.

Mirianna sucked in breath while blood pounded in her ears. Her nipples puckered under the gentle breath he blew over each one. Shifting slightly, he grazed a fingertip over each hardened nub.

Mirianna's world pitched and rocked. Her body

arched upward, leaning, straining toward the touch. Her arms rose of their own accord and reached for his shoulders. She yearned to pull him down to her, to beg him to ease the sweet pain coursing through her body with more than a whisper of contact. But as soon as her arms entered the plane of his shape, he vanished.

She bolted upright and blinked like an owl while the room swam around her. Through the lingering sensual fog, she heard, somewhere, the scrape of boots and the sound of men's voices. Her father? Pumble? *That's right, we're leaving, aren't we?*

Her hands rushed to straighten her dress and leaped away when they contacted only skin. Mortified, she looked down and saw her bodice gaping open. A delicate flush colored her breasts and the nipples stood out firm and pointed. She cast a frantic glance around the room. Two long shadows stretched out from the farthest corner and, fingerlike, gripped the side of the bed. Over the mattress, the tips curled like claws, extending narrow bands of blackness across the depression in which her body had only moments earlier rested.

Fine hairs on the back of Mirianna's neck stood straight up. The down on her arms and body rose in waves that began at her shoulders and rocked to an end at the base of her spine. One thought took on crystalline certainty in her mind. One horrible, terrifying thought: *He touched me! By the Dragon, that—that creature was here and he touched me!*

With a groan, she sprang from the bed. Her fingers fumbled with her clothing, jerking the lacings tight over breasts that seemed twice their normal size and prickled with every shift of fabric over sensitized nipples.

Shaking like an aspen leaf, she snatched up her belongings, hurled them into her pack, and broke from the room.

In the corridor, she ran headlong into Rees. He absorbed the brunt of the collision with a grunt and a backward step. She ricocheted off his chest, bounced against the wall, and would have fallen if he hadn't dropped his pack and caught her arm.

His slowly blooming smile told her terror still radiated from her expression. "Can't wait to get out of this place, can you?" He stepped into the space between their bodies. "I don't blame you. A sweet thing like you has to be careful where she sleeps." His free hand skated up her arm, slowing enough next to her breast for the outside of his thumb to graze its swell.

She flinched at the contact, but he only tightened his grip on her arm. "Don't worry. I'll protect you from anything that tries to crawl under your blankets."

Revulsion—sharp, acidic, and wholly unmistakable—squirted through Mirianna's veins. Her body reacted, propelling her hands into his chest with a force only muscles still charged with panic could deliver.

Rees staggered back two steps, a startled look on his face.

"By the Dragon, don't you—don't you ever touch me again!" With a wild look, she seized her pack and bolted for the stairs.

Halfway to the stable, her legs turned to mush. She stumbled to a trough and sank down on the edge, breathing hard while dots of color exploded on the fringe of her vision. Her ears roared, but even within that roar, she discerned another sound. Her fingers dug into the damp wood, curling like claws as her body recognized the voice before her mind could distinguish the words.

—Remember, not all of the beasts—

For a score of heartbeats, Mirianna did not breathe. When nothing further echoed in her mind, she gulped in a lungful of air. *Beasts!* She shoved a shaky hand through her hair. There was no shortage of beasts in the vicinity—Rees, the Krad, Pumble, Ulerroth. Even her father fit the description for wanting to buy stones collected by something monstrous.

And then there was the Shadow Man himself.

Mirianna gulped more air. Her body still quivered with the aftershocks of his touch. *His* touch. Somehow, in that room, his...essence...had invaded her dreams and he had become—

"No!" She sprang to her feet and backed away from the trough, shaking her head. It was too horrible to comprehend. She would not even consider the possibility that he had become—that he might have always been—that he was—

It had to be the room. Nothing more. Now she was out of it, she was free. Wasn't she?

Mirianna spun, raking the inn yard with a desperate glance. In the late afternoon sunshine, shadows lurked everywhere, long, dark shadows that seemed to slink toward her with the patience—and purpose—of a Wehrland lion stalking prey. Sinking her teeth into her lower lip, she turned and ran toward the stable.

****

By all the sons of Koronolan, she's breathtaking.

The first glimpse of the woman who came to him like quicksilver through the planes of his dream always

132

left the man breathless. It didn't matter if she appeared after an absence of days or merely hours, her beauty stole the very air of life, withholding it from him just long enough to fill it with her own lush scent. Lilacs, he thought, breathing deeply. Blue ones, not the cloying purple. And—he breathed again—musk. Just a hint of her own unique woman's scent.

His body stirred at the thought of her scent warm and slick on his fingers. Hardened at the thought of dark, honey-colored woman's hair moist against his palm. Stirred and hardened even though he knew why she came, and what visions of paradise she would offer him before she vanished—and he awoke throbbing with need. If only he could wake now, before...but he had no more will this time than he'd had a hundred times before.

Skin the color of milky quartz, hair as luminous and golden brown as polished lion-eye, eyes the twin blue stars in Kiros's belt, she glided toward him. A shimmering white gown flowed sensuously with the movements of her hips and thighs. Each step parted the gown over a length of alabaster thigh. His mouth went dry, and heat pooled in his groin as she closed the space between them. All the while she looked at him, and there was nothing between his eyes and hers, nothing but a hand's breadth of air.

He groaned, riven with an ache both pleasure and pain. Her breath drifted across his collarbone and the slowly closing space between their bodies. Then, somehow, his world cart-wheeled and, when he opened his eyes again, she was lying beneath him on a bed of golden furs, her arms stretched above her head, the white under-skin incandescent against the wild array of her hair. Her thighs, long, cool, and as smooth as polished limestone, twined themselves around the leg he'd parted them with. Her eyes, molten blue, fixed on his while she slowly rotated her hips. His breath caught in his throat. Blood hummed in his ears. He leaned into her, pressed himself hard against the bone cradling her femininity, yearning to hold her a moment longer, to hang onto the dream before it dissipated—again—and he was left with nothing but the memory. And the pain.

By Koronolan and Kiros, stay with me...please!

As if in answer to his unspoken plea, her gown parted at the touch of his fingers and, like water, slid from her breasts.

Desire rocked through him like a hammer's blow, stealing his breath at the sudden and unexpected gift. One part of his consciousness knew the dream had changed, and wondered why. The rest merely stared, drunk with the vision of breasts round and white and as delicately veined as marble. Their crowning aureoles and firm mauve peaks seemed to beg for the caress of his fingers. Stretching out a hand, he reverently touched a fingertip to first one nipple, then the other.

Instantly, a shudder convulsed her body. A look as of pain pulled her lips from her teeth. Her body arched upward and her breasts grazed his chest. Dizzy, he reached for her, hungry for her nakedness, hungry for the touch of skin to skin. His arms closed on nothing.

The man blinked toward the late afternoon sun, seeing it without comprehending. The sensual fog filling his brain left him stuporous, heavy with the blood engorging his groin and flushing his skin. He looked down, saw his boots and realized he'd dozed where he sat. The flat stone beneath him gnawed at the base of his spine. He told himself to concentrate on the dull ache, hoping if he kept his focus, it might ease the desolation already coiling like a viper around his heart.

The despair broad-sided him anyway, like a sword he should have seen but didn't, even though he knew it was raised against him. Every time she came to him—and vanished—it was the same. Except this time.

He bit back a groan. This time it was worse. Much worse, because she'd offered him more, and then stolen it all away.

He caught his lower lip between his teeth and hunched over folded arms, trying to hold the pain, his agony—everything—within. He tasted iron, and knew the warmth trickling down his chin wasn't sweat. The realization, and the blood, made him gag. His hands balled into fists, fists of leather and flesh.

Flesh that will never see the light of day!

A snarl curled his lips from his teeth. His jaws ground together, and the cords of his neck stood out.

There will be no woman—ever—who will look at you the way a woman looks at a man. You aren't a man. You're nothing but a shadow. A denizen of the night, doomed to kill her if she ever sees you...unveiled.

He stood and gasped for air. His chest seemed constricted, as if bound by too tight armor, and he could draw nothing in. Lightheaded, he wavered at the edge of the sandstone outcrop.

A subtle movement to his left brought his vision instantly into focus. Twenty strides away, where the level patch on which he stood tapered to a point, the she-cat lounged on a sun-drenched, lichen-covered rock and stared at him.

Chapter Ten

Sweat bloomed on the man's chest and broke out in beads on his upper lip. His lungs still burned, but he dared not fill them with more than shallow breaths. The lion was too close. Even though it seemed relaxed, lying with ankles crossed as daintily as any highborn lady, the feline's powerful hindquarters could propel it with such speed the animal would be on him before he could run ten steps.

The she-cat rolled slightly onto her shoulders, raising one huge forepaw. The action revealed a breast patch of snow-white fur, the color a startling contrast to the tawny of the animal's outer coat. Eyes still fixed on the man, she lowered her head, angled her chin against her chest, and began to groom herself.

The rasp of her tongue, dragging leisurely across her fur, sounded overloud in the man's ears. He stared, mesmerized by the slow, steady strokes and the unwavering gaze of hooded, yellow-green eyes. With difficulty, his thoughts formed the questions that had lingered like brooding embryos at the back of his mind since he'd first seen the cat.

Who are you? What do you want with me?

As if in response, the she-cat paused, a tip of tongue showing dark pink against the black line of her lip. Her mouth opened, the tongue curled, and she yawned, exposing all of her teeth. Lowering her head again, she returned to her grooming. The luminescent yellow-green eyes, though, maintained their unblinking regard.

A frisson of awareness traveled the length of the man's spine. The look, the actions, though catlike, gnawed at the edges of his memory. *I know you, don't I?*

The lion paused again. One black-tipped ear twitched a fly away. The luminescent gaze remained unwavering.

Under its steady bombardment, he wondered if the animal was staring not at him but somehow through him, through the protective layers of his clothing, through the web of his thoughts, through everything he had become...to something buried...

"—Do you know me? Or do you only think that you do?—"

The reply rooted the man's feet to the ground. The quivering had gone out of his legs, and his lungs no longer burned. Although a corner of his mind screamed warning, his muscles refused to mount any defense. A kind of languor had stolen into them, rendering him powerless to pull away, powerless to do anything but remember...

He was howling like an enraged beast, and crashing forward as the spell broke, falling and cutting his hands on the stone, feeling nothing, not the searing heat or the jagged edges. He was howling for Errek, for big, loyal, lovesick Errek who trusted him—killed by his hand. By his own bloody hand!

He stared at it, at the rivulets of dark, glossy red oozing from his fingers and palm and dripping, ever so slowly, into his tunic cuff.

Helen C. Johannes

Somewhere nearby, the mage chortled. "You dragon keepers are such a foolish lot."

Jaw clenched, his lips curled into a snarl. "I'll kill you, Syryk! By all the sons of Koronolan, I swear I'll kill you!" His knife was gone, but he still had his dagger and his shield. And, not far away, lay the ancient Sword of Drakkonwehr, the stone in the crosspiece shimmering blood red in the waves of heat rising around it.

With one lunge, he scooped it up.

His scream was involuntary, a reaction to the metal's scorching imprint on his raw flesh.

The Sword clattered to the floor, and the mage laughed again. "You really are amusing, Drakkonwehr, but so pathetically predictable."

His vision hazed. The pit took on an orange glow as the cords of his neck tightened. His hand burned, and the heat inside the pit seemed to intensify. He could barely breathe, barely think, barely feel anything except heat.

And hate.

He ripped off the right sleeve of his tunic and wound the cloth about his hand. Stooping, he seized the Sword of Drakkonwehr. He straightened while his hand shook with pain at the grip, and the cloth wrapped around it smoked.

Across the pit, the mage stood with arms widespread over the onyx table. He swayed gently, eyes closed, and chanted words never meant to be said aloud, words written only on a scroll stored deep in the bowels of Drakkonwehr, words that should have remained buried forever:

"Beggeth beggedon tyrannor mott.

Ominoth peurinon cauldor keth.

Beggeth rappanon drakkonnor tor.

Tyrannoth drakkon ominor et!"

The mage's voice reverberated from the surrounding stone, its sound low, hypnotic, inviting.

*Comforting, he thought with a vague sense of surprise as tendrils of spell wove themselves around his consciousness. Gossamer thin, like spider web, they laid down a layer of...*nothing...*so quickly, he wondered why he was standing in this pit watching a man with outstretched arms and closed eyes murmur sounds that made no sense.*

He wondered, too, why he should be watching an amber-haired woman beside the table until, with graceful movements, she slid the white cloak from her shoulders and let it fall into a shimmering heap about her ankles.

Awareness slammed into him like an axe blow, shattering the mind spell. Ayliss! *his mind messaged.*

Her emerald eyes locked with his. I'm going to ride the dragon. *The look on her face was hard, determined.* And nothing you can do will stop me because I've already given Syryk the Chant.

All around him the Chant echoed, weaving the Dragon Spell, keeping his body in thrall, suspended where he stood.

Ayliss, why?

You're not the only Drakkonwehr.

I'm the male heir.

And I'm the female heir. *She drew his mind to the necklace she wore, to the glowing black-red stone suspended between her breasts.* You were given the Sword, but that's not enough now, is it? You need these. And this. *She gestured to the multiple stones decorating her wrists and forehead, and to the crystal column, pulsing with red, black and green.*

She raised her chin, holding it high while her eyes flashed green fire. Koronolan couldn't ride the Dragon. No Drakkonwehr since has dared to try. But I will. I will!

The Dragon Chant vibrated around him, the volume building, each syllable a physical force that lapped like a rising tide against his body, his mind. He was drowning, suffocating, dying—along with the world he knew, the world Koronolan and every son after him had been charged to protect by guarding the one thing that could destroy it, the beast entombed in Drakkonwehr.

—Illusion, remember? Don't believe everything you see. Or hear—

He started, his mind flying to Ayliss. Her eyes glanced from him to the chanting mage and back again. Something flickered in the emerald depths. Fear? Uncertainty? A moment of doubt? Don't believe everything you see! *echoed in his mind.*

He wanted to believe she was an illusion, that none of this was true—her thievery, betrayal, greed—but his second sight told him she was flesh and blood this time, and his heart—well, his heart was a fool!

Liar! Traitor!

Her eyes closed as a wave of what seemed like pain contorted her features. When her lids lifted, her face had altered. The look she fixed on him was infinitely sad. And every line of it spoke of parting.

—I still trust you, Durren. Help me...if you can—

Her hand, cradling the stone between her breasts,

closed on it. The knuckles whitened and, as he watched, transfixed, blood squirted between her clenched fingers. In unison, the stones about her forehead and wrists melted. Streaks of black-red blood trickled down her face and arms. With a ghost of a smile gracing her lips, her eyelids drifted shut and she slid, as delicately as her cloak had, to the stone floor...

"Ayliss," the man whispered as the vision faded. Emotions roiled in his chest like waves in a storm, threatening to swamp him. He clenched his eyes shut and held his jaw firm against their surges. Even so, a glimmer of something squeezed between his defenses and nudged at him until, oddly dry-mouthed, he opened his eyes and looked toward the lion.

"Are you—?"

The lichen-covered rock was vacant.

The man spun, raking with wild, frantic glances the ledge, the trees above, the campsite below, the entire rock-studded clearing...but the lion had vanished.

Sweat drenched his tunic. The breeze, active in the lengthening shadows, crawled up his back. Shivers racked his body, long, violent shivers that started with the clack of his teeth and ended with spasms in his thighs. He stumbled to the rock and flung himself down beside it, pawing through the moss, lichen, gravel for some sign the vision had been real, that the lion was only that—a lion.

Near his knee, he spied a bit of cream-colored fuzz. He pounced on it, held it up to the lowering sun and rolled it through his gloved fingers. Tiny kernels within revealed it as the seed cotton of a meadow weed.

Fresh sweat oozed from his pores. Black dots danced on the fringes of his vision while he told himself the lack of fur wasn't a true sign. The ground was too rocky to leave prints, and a lion didn't shed every time it cleaned itself. Still, a sense of dread settled like a rock into the pit of his stomach.

If it isn't a lion, then it's magic, said the Voice in his head.

The man closed his eyes. *Not magic. The mages are dead. The last one died at Drakkonwehr.*

Errek was dead, too. And Ayliss. This...beast wasn't Ayliss, no matter how much he might wish she hadn't died, no matter how much he might wish she hadn't betrayed her Drakkonwehr heritage. These occurrences were only dreams, the consequences of refusing to sate the needs of his—no, he amended with a deliberate shiver—the needs of Durren Drakkonwehr's flesh at Ar-Deneth. The last Drakkonwehr was as good as dead, too. Destroyed along with the Stone Dam at Herrok-Eneth.

The man stared at his gloved hands and fabric-covered arms. This body was only Durren's shell, black-wrapped and hollow. Void of everything that made a man...a man. With a shudder, he curled his hands into fists. *Void of everything—everything but the damned memories!*

That was YOUR choice, the Voice in his head said.

And it's a choice I'll make again! Shaking off another chill, the man strode off the ledge and clambered down the hillside toward Ghost and the pack horses.

That might explain the untimely visit of your lovely fantasy woman, but what about the lion?

The man froze, his hand stretched toward the pack mare's lame leg. Sweat cooled along his spine, raising

142

the fine hairs there. The beast was far from ordinary, even for the Wehrland where strangeness abounded. What if—what if it were...magic?

No. Too many years had passed. The destruction had been complete. True, he'd survived, but that had been due to—his mouth twisted—Syryk's foresight. Still, if the mage had 'saved' him, couldn't the mage have saved...something else?

The question impelled the man to turn toward Ghost, to slide his fingers through the stallion's mane, walk past the gray muzzle that lipped his tunic sleeve, and continue to his saddle where it lay on the ground. Bending, he ripped open a pouch fastened to the back and thrust his hand inside.

A piece of metal presented itself to his palm, and his fingers curled automatically around its scrolled length. *Ah, yes.* Sparks dotted his vision, and he remembered to breathe. Chagrinned by his fear, he waited for the giddiness to pass, then withdrew the object from his saddlebag.

Late afternoon sunlight glowed golden from the curved metal shielding his thumb on one side and his knuckles on the other. Sunshine gleamed like water from a broad, flat pillar rising two hands' span from curving hand guards, and glinted once from the raw edge of the broken summit.

He sat back on his haunches, marveling at the balance of a sword that, even broken, still fit his hand like an extension of his arm and moved as though mere thought propelled it. It turned now, angling itself so the dull, black-red stone embedded in the crosspiece was fully exposed to his gaze.

As if compelled, he lifted his thumb and rubbed the

pad of it across the stone. "*Bluet drakkenoth, ominor ay rhoenon pek,*" slid from his tongue like a long forgotten childhood rhyme.

A chill raised the hairs on his body as he recognized the ancient sounds of Shadowspeech, the tongue of Kiros. Another chill prickled through him as the meaning of the words echoed in his mind: *Drop of dragon's blood, show me what there is to fear.*

He had only seconds to marvel at how the words, so long buried, came so easily to his tongue. Only seconds, before he heard the sounds of...whistling? He spun to his feet, taking in the whole of the campsite in the motion, observing now with panic what he should have noted before, the vacant space amid the sacks of grain. "Gareth," he breathed, pivoting once more, this time toward the sound.

He spotted the boy, his sandy head and rust-colored tunic bobbing along a deer path cut through the meadow below. Whistling, the boy tapped the way with his staff, two full water sacks weighing down one bony shoulder.

The man frowned. It wasn't the boy he had to fear, was it? No, it had to be the lion.

Sweat oozed from his temples and trickled down his face, gluing his hood to it. He licked his upper lip and searched the edge of the rocky clearing for telltale signs of movement.

"*Bluet drakkenoth, ominor ay rhoenon pek,*" he repeated, flexing his fingers on the broken sword's hilt. A force he hadn't felt in years drew his gaze inexorably back toward the boy—and fastened it on a patch of briars twenty strides below the path. There, in the center, a branch moved languorously to and fro, its rhythm entirely unrelated to that of the breeze.

"Gareth!" The man hurdled his saddle and charged down the slope.

He was running, sliding, falling when he saw the feline burst from a honeysuckle bush to his left. Ears laid back, body a tawny blur of limbs, the she-cat streaked toward the boy.

"No!" The man flailed out, fell, rolled over broken rock that gouged into his shoulder. The pain bit the edge off his panic. He rolled again, twisting this time so his boot soles rammed into a hummock. He shoved against the impact, catapulting himself upright and forward.

The boy stood where the man had last seen him, a startled look on his face, blind eyes oblivious to the huge cat rushing at him from the side. "Gareth! Get down!"

But the boy only turned away from the cat, his head cocked, as if listening.

To what? The man could hear nothing but the roar of his own blood, the rasp of his clothing sliding over muscles that pumped and strained to move faster. *Faster!* The cat made no sound, only loomed larger, a blur although everything in his perception had so slowed each footfall shuddered from gravel to boot sole, from heel to ankle, from knee to thigh. He took another stride, and the cat made two, each longer than the last, each a tawny flight of teeth and claws.

He couldn't possibly reach the boy before the cat launched itself in a bunching of sinew and muscle, mouth agape and paws spread. But, by Koronolan, he could land on the back of the beast and stab it through the heart!

In a moment when time seemed suspended, the boy turned, ever so slowly. His face registered alarm and his mouth opened. If there was sound, the man didn't hear it. He saw instead the cat's ears flatten, the eyes slit, and the black lips curl away from pink gums and bare yellow-white teeth. He flung himself forward, but the beast had already sprung.

Gareth, still turning, must have sensed the beast's shadow, for his arms flew up in a gesture of self-protection. Helplessly, the man watched the airborne feline wrench her body sideways and slam, shoulder first, into Gareth's upraised arms. Boy and cat—and something else, something large, dark, and looming behind the boy—crashed to the ground.

The Krad smell hit the man first, even as the cat and the beast-man rolled in a tangled blur away from the boy's crumpled body. A glint of sunlight on a flint blade brought the man lurching to the right, and he threw himself between another beast-man and the fallen boy. The Sword of Drakkonwehr, like an extension of his arm, arced downward, broken blade gleaming, and sliced the second Krad's flint knife in half. The Sword's upward arc rammed the hand guard deep against bone and sinew.

And time returned.

The impaled Krad slumped over the man's hand. Revolted, he braced his boot against the beast-man's body and jerked the Sword free. The creature sprawled back and lay still.

The man spun, but nothing moved in the meadow, nothing but the she-cat, less than ten strides away, separating herself from a dark, fur-covered, unmoving mass. With bloodied jaws, she stared at the man, her eyes fixed, yellow-green, and mesmerizing.

—I saved you, Durren. Again.—

There had been two beast-men, and he'd seen neither, though the Sword had shown him where to look. His stomach twisted.

Why?

As if in answer, the lion advanced a stride.

Halfway between his position and the lion's, the boy lay on his side in a patch of hawkweed and blue aster. A rip across the shoulder and upper arm of his tunic fluttered gently in the breeze. Blood darkened the rust-colored fabric in both places.

By Kiros, no!

The lion's snarl brought him up short. The beast had advanced and stood, teeth bared, at the boy's shoulder.

Sweat beaded under the man's hood and tunic. His fingers tightened on the broken Sword of Drakkonwehr. "Leave him alone. He's nothing to you."

The she-cat's tail slashed the air. She growled, a low, rumbling noise deep in her throat. Her head tilted and the yellow-green eyes fixed on the man.

He recognized the look, but the steady luminescence had already seized his gaze, and its languor spread rapidly through his body, immobilizing his limbs. He could do no more than watch, helplessly, while the beast straddled the boy with huge front paws and lay down beside his head. Eyes fixed on the man, she lowered her bloody muzzle to the boy's shoulder... and licked it.

Chapter Eleven

Gareth drifted. A warm, cozy darkness cradled him like his mother's arms. Her hand combed through his hair, tugging gently at knots and tangles. She hummed, and he felt the tune as a rumble of sound where his ear pressed to her chest. Heaving a sigh, he turned to snuggle closer.

Pain seared through his shoulder. Gareth's breath shuttled in and out of his lungs. The rapid motion roused an echoing burn just below his breast on the same side.

"Easy, now. Don't move too quickly."

He recognized the voice, yet he couldn't place it. The tone transmitted concern...and fear? He rose slowly to an elbow. "I-I'm all right." An ache at the side of his forehead escalated to a throb with the motion.

"I said, don't move too quickly, boy."

At the warning in the low, bitten-off words, Gareth's mind cleared, and he remembered with a rush where he was and with whom. He'd been attacked—by something—and the stench of it lingered in his nostrils. He would have ducked his face into his tunic sleeve, but his master spoke again.

"Listen, boy, and do exactly what I say. You're going to move very slowly and very carefully toward me on your hands and knees. Can you do that?"

Gareth flexed his shoulder. The pain made him grit

his teeth, but he could move the joint. Besides, his head ached more than enough to distract him. "I think so." He rolled forward and untangled his legs. His hands found moss and gravel. His knees rested shakily on rock. "That smell..."

"Krad. Dead ones."

He froze, skin crawling. At the White Boar Inn he'd heard more than once of the beast-men that infested the Wehrland. And of the poison coating their weapons. A man was as good as dead, old Melfick said, if a Krad blade drew even a drop of his blood. A fresh wave of fire seared through his injured shoulder, chest and forehead, and he moaned. He was doomed as surely as if they'd stabbed him through the heart. *Mother, I don't want to die!*

Rough hands seized him under the armpits and dragged him into a sitting position. "Don't be an idiot!" Gloved fingers probed his head. "These aren't Krad wounds." Two hands peeled back his tunic and skimmed across his shoulder and chest. "This is rocky ground. You were in the way and—and you were hurt...falling."

Gareth sniffled. The breeze cooled his damp cheeks. "Rocks?"

His master slid an arm under his shoulders and another under his knees. "Rocks," the Shadow Man said, standing.

Gareth's head lolled against his master's chest. A heartbeat thumped there, solid and reassuring. If his head didn't ache so, and if he weren't so utterly drained, he would've marveled more at the human sound and the human feel of arms like a father's bearing him to safety. Instead, he heaved a sigh and rested.

****

The man dug a small hole and emptied a bowl of bloody water into it. He waited while the liquid soaked into the soil, then wiped the bowl with a bit of moss and dropped the moss into the hole. With his foot, he covered the drain and tamped the earth back into place. Only then did he allow his body to straighten and accept the uncoiling of too tight muscles.

The first stars of night peeked through smoke still rising from the brush pyre the man had heaped around the two dead Krad. Had he been alone, he would've cleared camp immediately and left the bodies rot. But he wasn't alone, and he had to dispose of the stinking carcasses before they drew attention to this campsite. He looked upwind where, on a level shelf of rock, the boy slept within a circle of grain sacks, blankets tucked around his body, a fire throwing light on a face that looked too pale under a russet-wrapped forehead.

That had been the easy wound to dress. It was the claw marks that worried the man. The she-cat had licked them clean, but he still had laid on what poultices he could devise, hoping against hope the gashes wouldn't fester.

Thoughts of the lion made him scan the darkening meadow once more. The creature had disappeared while he tended the boy, but he wasn't fool enough to believe the beast had vanished entirely. There had been too much of a claiming nature in her behavior.

The man stared at the bowl in his hands as if trying to divine truth from its well. No matter how many times he reviewed the scene etched into his brain, he couldn't deny the she-cat had saved the boy's life. Nor could he deny such had been her intent. Nor could he deny what troubled him most—the beast's snarling refusal to let him touch the boy. Not until Gareth had revived and come to him of his own accord, did the beast back away.

Magic, the Voice in his head murmured.

Perhaps. The broken Sword of Drakkonwehr rested like a big-handled knife at his hip, held in place by his belt. He resisted the notion the weapon still belonged there. How could it—unless it suited some cosmic sense of irony that a hollow man should bear a fragment of a sword.

He climbed to a spot halfway between the campsite and the Krad pyre and stood looking at the glowing residue of death. The bloodstone in the Sword's crosspiece had shown him what to fear, and it was not the lion. He shivered as the breeze ghosted up his back. *Bloodstone or no, I still don't trust the beast.*

Good, said the Voice in his head. *Magic is never to be trusted.*

If it's magic, then from what source? The bloodstone would show him dragon spawn and mage spell. Indeed, any of the evils of Beggeth. What other source was there?

Koronolan and Kiros.

The man snorted. *They're dead. And I have the only Sword.*

Shadowspeech, then.

Unbidden memories flooded his mind. He stared into them, one part of him marveling at the power of the mere name, the other part frustrated he couldn't defend against it. The language of Kiros was a tongue long forgotten to all but those who dealt in the magic of a birthing world, a magic whose wellspring was the very energy of creation. Owender had use of it. There had been a few pathetic imitations of the Hero Mages and Black Mages who'd tried to wield a power too elemental for the mastery of a mere man. Finally, there had been the Drakkonwehrs, charged as Dragonkeepers with knowing the means to control the beast they guarded.

And Durren, poor Durren. The man regarded his gloved hands as if they belonged to a stranger. *He was the last of them. And he doomed them all, didn't he, when he let Herrok-Eneth fall.*

Perhaps, said the Voice in his head, *they're not all dead.*

The man's fists clenched. *If one of them didn't die, why did he wait so long to show himself to me? Why now? Why not after the smoke cleared all those years ago?*

In answer, his gaze was drawn to the blanket-wrapped figure lying amid grain sacks. *You didn't have him, then, did you?*

The man swallowed. First the lion, then the boy, the Krad, and the woman—both the one of last night and the one in the dreams. Today, he'd used the Sword for the first time since...since it had broken. A shiver raced down his spine. This had to be magic, but whose and why?

He hugged his arms about his body and searched the dark edge of forest again. Where there had been two Krad, the pack couldn't be far off. He glanced at the sleeping boy. Tomorrow they would ride, even if he had to hold the boy in the saddle himself. Drakkonwehr was the only safe place. Drakkonwehr could keep everything out. Even magic.

****

All afternoon Mirianna had dodged shadows. Now she sat her horse near the lone willow and shivered against growing dread. Listening with half an ear to the men, she watched Wehrland firs swallow the sun. Instantly, deep green under their boughs darkened to black. In the depths, shadows writhed toward each other like droplets of water determined to meld. Soon, the darkness massing across the meadow would advance with talons bared and seize them all.

She forced a swallow despite the panic fisted in her throat. These were merely fears, the product of a particularly vivid waking dream and Rees' insinuations. Nothing ill had happened in the Wehrland on their first passage, other than the lion's appearance. Why should anything befall them now? It was Ar-Deneth where evil lay, and they had left the place hours behind them. If only they weren't pursuing the bringer of that very evil.

"I must have more bloodstone," her father was insisting. "The Master specifically said he wanted bloodstone—"

"—in every piece," Rees finished with a roll of his eyes. "I know, old man, but I'll be damned if I'll waltz into a demon's lair in the dead of night."

"I'll be damned if I'll go anywhere but straight home." Pumble mopped his forehead with his sleeve. "I didn't get my mutton. With a good mutton dinner under his belt, a man can face just about—well, a lot of things. Now, I don't—"

"Shut up!" Rees backhanded Pumble's hat brim. "You'll do what I tell you."

Lower lip thrust out, Pumble jammed the hat into

place. "I'd be a lot more willing if you hadn't gotten us thrown out of Ar-Deneth."

"The man was a demon trader. In Nolar we hang demon traders."

"We're not in Nolar." Mirianna huddled into her cloak even though there was no chill in the air. "And I'm with Pumble. I think we should go straight home, Papa. If the...Shadow Man...is as unwilling to be found as Ulerroth suggested, there's no point in hunting for him."

Pumble sat up straighter in the saddle. "See, she knows what she's talking about."

"But, lamb." Tolbert reached out to grasp her hand on the saddle pommel. "I can't go back without the necessary gems."

"You have six. You can make do with them, can't you?" She closed both hands around his. "Put one in each piece. Master Brandelmore will never know the difference."

Tolbert withdrew his hand and straightened. "But I will."

Mirianna huffed out the breath she had been holding.

Across from her, Rees sat with one fist planted on his hip, the other gripping the reins. His brows formed a blond line across his forehead. He looked from Mirianna to her father, glowering all the while. "If it weren't the Master's express wish—" He dragged his horse into a snorting back step. "We'll go to the clearing where we last saw this...creature. But don't expect me to traipse all over this bloody region for a few colored stones! If I don't find a trail from there, we're heading back to Nolar in the morning."

"That's reasonable, don't you think, Papa?"

Tolbert frowned. "I suppose."

"Well, then, let's move." Rees laid his spurs to his horse's flanks. The animal sprang forward with a squeal.

Tolbert's chestnut jumped to follow.

Mirianna held her gelding back. She watched Pumble send a glance and a sigh toward the road heading east. When he looked at her, she offered a sympathetic smile. He shrugged and gestured for her to fall into line ahead of him. Steeling herself, she lifted the reins and rode toward gathering shadows.

****

They found the clearing just after twilight faded. It came upon them suddenly, opening out to the left. They turned toward it, and into a wall of stench.

"Krad!" Rees gasped. His horse reared.

Mirianna's gelding whinnied and back-stepped. Around them, the trees erupted with a shrill, high-pitched noise. The sound assaulted her senses, beating at her nerve endings with discordant waves, raising panic in her blood. The gelding fought her grip on the reins, half rearing and blundering to the left.

"Turn around!" Rees was screaming. "Run!"

Mirianna hauled at the gelding's mouth. The darkness in the clearing's entrance roiled with shadows, shapeless gyrating and snarling shadows. Some of them sprang from beneath the trees and rushed the gelding. She lashed at them with the long ends of the reins. Something snagged her cloak, ripped through it. She grabbed her knife and slashed out blindly. Yips, howls, and then she was free, somehow, and clinging to the back of her galloping horse while tree boughs whipped at her face.

Long after her cheeks had gone numb with the lashing, after she'd ridden for what seemed like leagues, the gelding finally slowed to a trot. Mirianna raised herself shakily from its neck and looked over her shoulder. Nothing lurked behind her but trees, stones, and a star-patched sky.

Drawing a ragged breath, she unlocked her fingers one hand at a time from the reins. She dragged her knuckles over her cloak, smearing the froth of the gelding's sweat into the wool. Between her legs, the horse's sides heaved, and she could hear the rasp of its breathing over the thunder of her own. She drew on the reins and slowed the gelding to a walk even though her entire body still vibrated with the need to continue running.

But where to? her logic asserted, reclaiming control now the immediate danger was past. She needed to slow down, listen, and locate the others. Her father was no doubt calling for her; if only she could stifle the roar in her ears long enough to hear his voice. Willing her heartbeat to slow, she pulled the gelding to a stop.

All around her night-birds shrilled and crickets chirped. The breeze sighing through the trees carried no sounds but the rustle and scrape of pine cones, branches and twigs. Mirianna forced a swallow. "Papa?"

It was a croak unworthy of a crow. Clearing her throat, she tried again. Only her echo returned, ghostly and plaintive.

She bit her lower lip, stilling its tremble, and tried to think. She was sure her father had been behind her at the mouth of the clearing. He should've turned first, when Rees shouted, and fled cleanly. Only Rees and she had been caught in the melee. Squeezing her eyes shut, she remembered Rees swearing, the sound of a struggle, and then his shouted "Come on!" His horse's shoes had struck sparks, and she'd ridden toward them, but then the gelding had clamped the bit between its teeth and she could do no more than hang on.

She opened her eyes and stared at the dark forest. "Papa?" she called again, louder. She stopped herself when panic frayed her voice. If her father hadn't answered by now, it would do no good to shriek like a marshwight. The gelding had simply carried her headlong through trees and meadows in a direction different than the others. When it was light enough, Rees would locate her trail and find her.

In the meantime, her horse needed to walk until it cooled down. After that, she would think about finding a suitable spot to wait out the night. She touched her heels to the gelding's sides.

The horse plodded several strides, then abruptly raised its head and huffed.

Mirianna watched the gelding's ears twist and prick. One large, dark eye rolled on a white rim. The animal huffed again and stamped. She tightened her grip on the reins—and her grip on her fears. It was probably nothing more than a night animal. If it were a Krad, she would smell it too, and she smelled nothing but the heavy fragrance of pine and spruce.

The horse shook its head, whistled, and back-stepped. Mirianna wound the reins another turn around her hands. The gelding champed at the bit, trying to tongue it forward, but she intended to keep the animal, and herself, under control this time. She leaned forward and peered into the darkness.

Her intent gaze separated the forest into shadows of blue and black. The black stood solidly, like sections of impenetrable wall. The blue shadow quivered like liquid, dissolving and reforming before her eyes. Lacing itself through the black, it wove a darkness of muted edges and velvet curves so quickly, Mirianna was only vaguely aware of the transformation. Just beyond her horse's feet, pale bits of rock gleamed from the forest floor like scattered fragments of a fallen moon. Stirred by the whisper of the breeze, shades of bough and grass danced among the stones in an ethereal ballet.

While she sat, transfixed, warmth ebbed into her limbs, along with a strange tranquility that felt as if it had been willed into her. Her eyes drifted shut with the infusion of languor. She opened them slowly, knowing in her heart what would be waiting when she chose to look.

You're here, her thoughts said to a disembodied pair of yellow-green, iridescent eyes.

Yes.

The she-cat's voice purred along Mirianna's nerve endings as if the word had been transmitted directly to them. *Come,* it said, and not a sliver of her logic raised a protest when she heeled the gelding and followed a glimmer of green deep into the Wehrland.

Chapter Twelve

The man saw her as he straightened from spreading the burned-out remains of the Krad pyre. He froze in the incomplete motion of a turn and stared while ash settled in a fine powder on his boots. He knew he didn't dream, yet she was here, the woman of his dreams. She stood at the edge of his camp, her hair a halo about her face in the first golden rays of sunrise, her body a slim, glowing column against the purple line of forest.

"By Kiros," he whispered. He closed his eyes, breathed, and opened them.

She stood as before, wrists crossed under her chin, hands clasping the edges of her cloak. Hands like the sculpted wings of a dove. He imagined their feather-light flutter on his shoulders, the hidden fingertips' delicate glide over his chest, the slow slide of her palm down his belly. The thought sucked the breath from his lungs.

He completed the motion of his turn and, dream-walking, climbed toward her. She rotated like a carved figurine at his approach, and her gaze settled on him with a heart-stopping gleam of blue. Her eyes were large and luminous, her skin as softly translucent as pearl. Her fragrance, heady as lilacs scented from a distance, wafted toward him on the faintest breeze. He drank it in like a man dying of thirst.

Each deliberate step brought him higher and nearer

until his body broke the incandescent plane of dawn. Rays of sunlight filtered through the edges of his hood and formed themselves like golden tracery around his shoulders and torso. He was aware of the glow only as it reflected in the pools of her eyes, a glorious halo around the lightless form of a man.

Lightless.

His boot struck a stone, and he stumbled. His gaze dropped with his hands, for balance, and he saw his shadow.

His *shadow* had wrapped itself snake-like around her ankles. While he straightened, it rose sinuously along the curves and hollows of her body—curves and hollows his hands had longed more than a dozen years to explore. And now his *shadow* had touched her first!

Cold fury arrowed to his temples. His hands balled into fists. But there was nothing to seize and pummel, nothing but a shape-shifting absence of light whose touch sucked the vitality from living things and left a pale echo in its place. He watched in impotent rage while this...*shade* of himself slithered across her face, taking first her mouth and then her eyes into its unholy possession.

When the shadow passed, the sunlight had faded. Gone was the luxurious golden glow of sunrise. Gone, too, was the dream, and the woman of it. In her place, bathed by mundane daily brightness, stood her ghost.

The merciless light revealed cheeks from which all color had washed, eye sockets lined with charcoal, hair disheveled and festooned with pine needles and broken twigs. Two uneven, raised scratches stood out garishly red on her forehead and trailed into her hairline. More needles and twigs decorated her cloak and clung to a long, jagged tear near the hem. Her eyes, bloodshot and dull, fixed him with the dazed stare of a sleeper shaken from a dream.

The transformation left the man equally disoriented. He'd expected—what had he expected? Something evil. Lustful. A conjurer's trick. Not something as wretched and bedraggled as a—as a lost kitten. His gaze swept her once more, this time taking in the exhausted horse standing head down behind her. *A woman. Nothing more than a mortal woman.*

A woman? the Voice in his head said. *Or THE woman?*

The man's hands paused in the act of unclenching.

She came to your camp the night before last. Lost then, too.

There had been three men with her. Where were they now? His gaze raked the clearing, but nothing moved in the brush except a doe watching with ears outstretched. He raised his hand to the Sword of Drakkonwehr stuck in his belt. Closing his fingers on the hilt, he rubbed his thumb over the stone embedded in the crosspiece. *"Bluet drakkenoth, ominor ay rhoenon pek,"* he whispered.

He risked a glance at the bloodstone, but no glow answered the incantation. No mage magic here. But someone—or something—had clearly left the woman in a trance-like state.

"Who are you?" He resisted an impulse to shake her. "How did you get here?"

Her pupils narrowed at the sound of his voice, and her gaze shifted until it landed on his torso.

He felt it like an inadvertent touch between strangers, one that lingered a second too long. For a heart-thudding moment, he imagined her hand flattened there at the apex of his ribs. *By Koronolan!*

When her gaze reached the fastenings of his hood, he watched a swallow work its way down her throat. The action left her lips slightly parted, the lower one shadowed mauve. He yearned to touch his finger to it, to probe its fullness for the dew hidden just inside—and entirely beyond his reach.

Her head lifted and she looked full into the black shroud where his face should have been.

He thought he knew how to endure this moment. He'd seen it all before: horror, shock, revulsion, panic. But the fear contorting her features twisted in his stomach like a Krad blade. With rising gall, he watched her eyes roll back in her head and her body crumple.

She lay at his feet like a discarded rag doll, her cloak open, her throat a white curve descending into the hollow formed by fragile collarbones. Below it, an expanse of delicately veined skin stretched from her shoulders to her bodice and disappeared into a deepening valley beneath the lacings.

Heat flushed his chest. His hands tingled. Yellow light flickered around the edges of his vision. "By all that's holy," he whispered.

Take her, the Voice in his head said. *She's a gift.*

He shuddered. Why shouldn't he take her back to Drakkonwehr? A woman, lost in the Wehrland—who would wonder if she simply disappeared? He saw her stretched out on a bed in a darkened room, her body illumined by a single candle flame. He saw his black-gloved hands reach out, cup her breasts, stroke down her belly. Blood rushed to his groin, and he felt himself grow hard. He reached, in the vision, to snuff out the candle flame, and saw her face—and the terror etched there.

"No! Not that way!"

Not THIS woman.

He came to himself with a disconcerting rush. The echo of his cry lingered along the trees when he realized he was still standing over the unconscious woman, that he had not, in fact, knelt and touched her. Weak with relief, he sank down on the nearest rock and passed a hand over his eyes. *Take your fantasies elsewhere, flesh. I finished with you in Ar-Deneth.*

"—Good—" said a voice he knew. And feared.

The she-lion sat on her haunches not fifteen strides away, her body as motionless as a statue but for the leisurely flick of her tail. Her fur gleamed golden in the morning light, and her eyes shone like twin suns.

"You brought her," he said hoarsely. "Why?"

Her stare held his gaze for heartbeat after heartbeat. When he'd almost forgotten his question, he felt her reply purr in his ear. "—Because you need her. And so do I...Durren—"

The name shot through his body like a lightning bolt. He stared at the huge cat as she turned and glided toward the trees. "Ayliss?" he whispered.

She gifted him with a momentary turn of her head, black-lined lips curled in an enigmatic feline smile. Then, like a ghost, she melted into the shadows.

****

Mirianna peered through her lashes at blue sky decorated with wisps of bright clouds.

Morning? But how...?

A quick inventory of her senses told her she lay on broken plates of rock. Spikes of meadow grass leaned over her shoulder. Distant treetops speared the sky, ringing a clearing that sloped down and away from the lichen-studded stone under her fingertips.

The last she remembered, she'd been riding her horse through the night and searching for her father. Alone. Lost in the no-man's land that was the Wehrland, while branches lashed her face and snatched at her cloak. Running from…*something*…

Led by…*someone?*

Twin glimmers of yellow-green, luminescent,… *eyes* hovered on the edge of her consciousness and vanished when she tried to bring them into focus. The effort awakened a torrent of complaints from every muscle and joint in her body. Mirianna groaned.

Had she fallen? She moved each of her limbs in turn. Finding them stiff but uninjured, she struggled to sit up, and a damp cloth dropped from her head into her lap. She stared at it while everything else pitched and rocked.

"Would you like some tea? It's willow bark. Good for aches."

Mirianna carefully raised her gaze. A boy about thirteen knelt beside her. He wore a cloth wrapped around his forehead, and his tunic, ripped over one shoulder, was russet with dried blood. All she could think of to say was, "You—you're hurt."

Color rose on his pale cheeks. "I'm on the mend. You're the one who fainted." With a crooked grin, he proffered a bowl. "Drink this. It'll make you feel better. I should know."

He'd coaxed a smile from her, and he looked harmless, so Mirianna held out her hand. When he made no move to pass her the tea, she leaned toward him and took the bowl from his grasp. His gaze, which ought to have followed her movement, remained fixed on a point somewhere near her chin.

The blind boy.

Apprehension thrilled along her nerves. *The boy couldn't possibly be alone. He hadn't been alone before…*

Memories followed in a stomach-tightening rush, tumbling over one another, strange events made even stranger by this ungodly wilderness. A voice in the night, sounding from nowhere and…everywhere, terrifying her and yet—somehow—stopping her horse from bolting. A presence haunting her room at the inn, invading her dreams with vivid, erotic suggestions. A touch—*a dream!*—that wasn't so much a touch but a desire made…*tangible*. Mirianna quivered. Her breasts swelled, and the burgeoning nipples prickled against the fabric of her bodice.

Where was the boy's master? Where was the Shadow Man?

Her fingers clenched, sloshing warm liquid onto her hand. She sucked in a breath, placed the bowl on the ground, and twisted her body to find the answer.

"So," said the voice that made her stomach break into shards of sensation, "you *do* remember."

Mirianna forced a swallow. The Shadow Man stood so close she could smell boot leather and wool, could see black-encased thigh and calf muscles that looked as solid as the rock on which she sat. *Looked* solid, because underneath the black hood, gloves and all-concealing clothing had to be nothing at all but darkness.

"I—I remember you told us the way to Ar-

Deneth." Resisting the inclination of her gaze to rise, she turned away, making a show of reaching for the tea and sipping it. *Don't look at him!* Instead, she scanned the clearing for signs of her father. *Be safe, Papa. Please be safe!*

"Did you make it to Ar-Deneth?" The boy leaned forward with hands on knees. "I served at the inn until a few days ago. Did you stay there?"

"Yes." Mirianna managed a wan smile until she remembered he couldn't see it. She touched the back of his hand instead. "It was a very nice place."

"Gareth," the Shadow Man said, "check the pack mare. See if her leg is fit."

A look of disappointment crossed the boy's features, but he stood without hesitation. Staff in hand, he felt his way down the hillside toward four horses tethered below. Her own gelding, Mirianna noticed, was one of them.

She sipped the tea, swilled it, and sipped again, forcing herself to linger over the cooling liquid. The Shadow Man's brusque order to the boy told her he stood so close, she could almost feel the imprint of his lower legs cradling her spine. She wished he would speak or leave before the brackish tea made her vomit or her strung-tight nerves made her bolt.

"Why didn't you stay in Ar-Deneth?" he demanded. "Why did you have to come back?"

His voice, though low, ripped at the shreds of her control. Not because it accused. She'd expected that. Just as she'd expected anger. And menace. What set her nerve endings vibrating was something that underlay all the rest, something she should have expected because she'd heard it before, only she hadn't recognized it then. Nor could she quite name it now, except it bore elements of frustration. And anguish.

She set the bowl aside. "Please understand, I wouldn't have come, but we—my father—needed more bloodstone. Ulerroth said—the innkeeper said you were the only one who—"

"There were three men with you. Where are they?"

His tone brought Mirianna's chin up, but she held her gaze fixed on the empty tea bowl. She was not going to cry. Her father was safe…somewhere. He'd been ahead of her when they escaped the ambush. "I—the clearing was full of Krad. We got separated."

"Krad!" The Shadow Man strode to the lip of the hillside and planted one boot on a rock.

He stood half turned away and far enough the jangling of her nerves faded to a hum. Emboldened, Mirianna let her gaze rise. The morning sun shone full on his back, showing her the sheen of wear on the black hood, tunic and breeches that concealed every inch of his flesh but hid none of the contours. On his raised thigh she detected a tear that had been carefully mended. His gloves and boots bore the creases and scuffs of long use. Even his belt showed faintly green where the dye had faded. A sword, the broken blade extending no more than two hands' span from the hilt, stuck out from his belt like a common thief's dagger.

Was this the being who'd invaded her dreams and turned them so disturbingly sensual? Was this the wraith who two nights ago had spirited the blind boy from their sight? Was this the possessor of a voice that had shaken her to the core? In the full day's sun, he looked no more than a man, taller than some, leaner and more fit than most. Chagrinned by her fears, Mirianna rocked to her knees and made ready to rise.

He turned at the rustle of her movement. Her gaze went automatically to his face. But there was no face to be seen. Only a shapeless drape of black cloth filled his hood where eyes and nose and mouth should be.

Mirianna sat as if turned to stone. Horror cooled her blood, and the hair rose on every part of her body. *It's his look. One look from him—at him—and men go mad. Or die. By the Dragon, let me not die!*

Somehow, she summoned the power to close her eyes. She knew she'd succeeded only when she opened them again and the Shadow Man no longer filled her vision. Every nerve, however, thrummed with his presence, and she knew he stood not more than three paces behind her and to the left. She knew, too, he faced the forest's edge, his right hand gripping the scrolled hilt of the weapon in his belt. She knew all this, and more, because—somehow—he'd let her know it so she might never again forget who and what he was. *Don't worry. I won't forget again.*

She turned slowly, like one waking from a dream, and saw what had captured his attention—three riders emerging from the trees.

"Papa!" she choked, and stumbled to her feet to meet him.

Chapter Thirteen

Tolbert slid out of the saddle and wrapped his arms around his daughter. "Mirianna, lamb, I thought I'd lost you."

Mirianna pressed her face into his neck. She clung for a moment, then leaned back and let him look at her. "I'm fine, Papa. Honestly, I am. But you—" She plucked a cedar twig from his hair. Creases etched his cheeks, and a distinct grayness underlay his usual color. He looked every one of his years, and more. "You need to eat."

Tolbert chuckled, but the sound broke into a cough. When he recovered breath, he hugged her again and kissed her gently on the cheek. "So, lamb, do you. So do we all, now."

"Perhaps we can share your fire."

In the joy of finding her father, Mirianna had forgotten Rees and Pumble, the two men the Master of Nolar had given her father as escort. And even that dark *being* which stood somewhere behind her and drew Rees's stony glare. The Master of Nolar's man still sat his horse, and his hand hovered near his bow. Beside him, Pumble stood, sweating, his fingers twitching over the hilt of his sword. She turned slowly in her father's arms.

"I said," Rees repeated, "perhaps we can share your fire, *this* time...Shadow."

The Shadow Man stood at the rock ledge, his body as motionless as a bat captured by the sun. His hand rested on the hilt of the sword in his belt, and between his gloved fingers something glinted red. His hood revealed only a drape of cloth where his face should be, yet she knew underneath every inch of that which passed for face was turned on Rees, and the air between them stretched to a brittle thinness.

"Do with it as you please," he said at last. "The boy and I were just about to leave."

"Wait!" Tolbert put Mirianna aside. "I need—"

"Bloodstone?" The black hood swiveled. Her father stiffened under the weight of the invisible regard. "There is no more bloodstone, old man. Go home, while you still can."

Tolbert shook his head violently. "But Ulerroth—"

"Ulerroth is a fool," said the voice that vibrated along Mirianna's nerves. "And so are you, if you stay another day in the Wehrland."

A stallion's shrill scream punctuated his words.

The Shadow Man spun. Below the rock ledge, the tethered horses milled, huffing. The blind boy clung to the pack mare's halter, his face a pasty white. "Sir, I think I smell—"

"Krad!" Rees coughed, recoiling from a wave of stench that stole Mirianna's breath.

"They must have followed us!" Pumble wheezed.

"Fools!" The Shadow Man's faceless gaze raked from Rees to Mirianna. "I should damn you all to Beggeth, but the Krad will see to that soon enough." He turned. "Gareth, free the horses!"

"Wait!" Tolbert said as an unearthly, high-pitched clamor erupted from the woods below. "What about us?

What do we do?"

Only the hood rotated, cocking with exaggerated deliberation. "Why, you die, old man."

Her father blanched. His grip on Mirianna's arms faltered.

She saw the Shadow Man turn, saw the muscles of his thighs bunch as he prepared to leap down the hillside, saw, in the corner of her eye, shapes gathering along the tree line below, horrible shapes she'd seen only hours before rushing at her from a darkened clearing. With a shudder, she broke from her father's grasp.

"Please!" She reached out to the black sleeve. "Help us!"

He recoiled at her touch like one snake-bitten. The sudden, sharp focus of his regard staggered her, but she backed no more than a step. No matter how he terrified her, he'd helped her once. She'd been led to him again, and not, her instincts told her, without reason.

"Please," she repeated. "Help us. I—we'll do anything."

"Anything?"

His voice was a whisper that caressed flesh. Mirianna's stomach quivered. Her breasts tingled. Her mouth grew even drier. Without thinking, she slid her tongue along her lips. Vaguely, she wondered what she'd done. And why time seemed suspended, as if everyone but she and the Shadow Man had been cast in stone and all sound arrested. All sound except the taut, guttural repeat of his question.

"*Anything?*"

If she were sane, she would seize the opportunity to clarify, to explain, to negotiate her reply. But even as she watched herself stand on the rock ledge and confront a shadow, she knew the question spoke not to her head but to her heart, and her heart answered in the only way it could, plainly and without hesitation. "Yes," she breathed, "anything."

Time returned with a mind-numbing rush of sound and motion.

Leaping from the rock ledge, the Shadow Man seized her arm. She flinched, but he held her fast. "If you would save yourselves, then feed the fire, woman. Make flame, lots of it." His shove propelled her toward the smoldering ring of stones. To Tolbert, he said, "Get the boy. Bring him to the fire."

"What are you doing?" Rees's horse reared, but he pulled it into a tight circle.

"Have you fought Krad?" the Shadow Man retorted.

Mirianna dumped an armload of kindling on the fire. Beyond the sudden whoosh of flame, she saw Rees's features redden.

"Then hold your tongue and do as I say." At the Shadow Man's whistle, the gray stallion clambered up the hill, nostrils flared. Seizing a handful of mane, he swung onto the horse's bare back and wheeled it around.

"Those dung-beasts aren't doing anything," Pumble whimpered, sweat running in rivulets from under his hat. "Why do they keep screaming like that? Why don't they charge?"

"Because they're trying to scare you, mutton-head!" Rees snapped, his foaming horse whirling in another circle. "You've got a plan, Shadow. What is it and how much time do we have?"

"Not much." He turned to Pumble. "Krad are afraid of fire. Pile brush into a fire ring. Keep the others within it." Nodding to Rees's bow, he said, "Bring down the leaders."

"And you?" Rees fit an arrow to string. "What will you do, Shadow?"

The hood faced Rees's sneer, then turned slightly. Mirianna risked a glance at the black shroud and found her attention magnetically drawn to the upper half. A chill rippled down her spine as she realized he'd summoned her gaze, and that his words, though ostensibly directed at Rees, flayed at her nerves.

"Why worry about me?" The Shadow Man's stallion back-stepped. "I'm only a phantom, mage spawn of Beggeth. What can my kind possibly do to one of their own?" With a touch of his heels, the stallion sprang away.

"That 'one of their own' part is exactly what I'm worried about," Rees muttered.

Me, too. Mirianna dumped another armful of kindling on the fire. *Me, too.*

****

What he needed, Durren thought, was a torch and a spear.

And a new head! What in Beggeth are you doing confronting Krad? You haven't fought a battle since—since the mage took Drakkonwehr! What in the name of Koronolan do you think you're going to accomplish with a broken sword and a knife? And for what? A woman sent by magic and—

Be still! Now was the time for action, not doubts. Or fantasies. Durren shook his head to dislodge an image of the woman's parted lips. She'd said *anything,* hadn't she? That was enough for now. Later, he could sort the ramifications of her promise.

Kneeing Ghost to a halt, he dismounted, seized a small aspen tree and hacked it off near the ground. An eye on the figures gyrating at the tree line, he stripped the branches, chopped off the top, split the tip, and jammed in the hilt of his knife, fastening it with his belt. That done, he hacked off another, smaller sapling and remounted, carrying both.

The clamor at the forest's edge rose in pitch. The sound shrilled in Durren's ears and set his teeth on edge, but he didn't waste a look. His instincts, roused from years of non-use, told him he had only seconds before the terrifying roar of a Krad charge. Holding the two saplings aloft, he galloped back to the campsite.

The fat man, the woman, and the old man rushed like ants to complete a ragged circle of brush around the rock ledge. Near one side, Gareth stood with a flaming brand in hand, ready to light the ring. Skidding to a halt near the boy, Durren stretched over the brush pile and touched the unstripped sapling to the torch. Its leaves caught with a whoosh.

Holding the sapling torch in his right hand, he leveled the makeshift spear like a lance with his left and braced it against his hip. Legs wrapped tight around the stallion's girth, he heeled Ghost toward the onrush of beast-men.

The ragged line of attack broke before the swish of his torch and the thrust of his lance. He wheeled Ghost, pursuing, jabbing, burning fur. Krad stench assaulted Durren's nostrils. Their howls tore at his eardrums, making him grit his teeth against the pain, but he knew he was safe as long as he stayed out of thrusting reach of their spears and knives. If these were men or other mage-driven creatures of Beggeth, his lack of armor would doom him. But Krad never threw their weapons.

The scattering beast-men did, however, fling up a shower of stones, sticks and clods of dirt. Durren grunted as a rock bounced off his rib cage. Another ricocheted off his shoulder. Ghost pivoted, avoiding all but a pelting of his hindquarters.

His torch nearly burned out, Durren dragged it across the beast-men's path, igniting brush. The main body of Krad shrieked. They milled. Some hopped up and down, shaking spears and knives. Others hurled more rocks. This time the missiles fell short.

Durren kneed Ghost to a halt. Between his legs, the stallion's heart pumped and his muscles quivered. The horse pawed the ground, shaking his head at the message of restraint. Durren sucked air through his hood. Smoke, scorched fur, and Krad stench burned the length of his throat, and sweat glued his tunic to his body, but his blood pulsed with a fervor he hadn't felt in years. His fingers flexed on the makeshift lance, liking the weight of it, the balance.

Once a warrior, always a warrior, said the Voice in his head.

"By Koronolan, yes!" Lifting the charred sapling like a spear, he heaved it toward a cluster of beast-men. The creatures fell over each other scattering. Durren threw back his head and laughed. Drawing the Sword of Drakkonwehr, he waved it over his head. "For Herrok-Eneth! For Drakkonwehr!" Laying his heels to the stallion, he charged the Krad line.

****

Mirianna huddled next to her father and the blind

boy. Around them, the brush ring roared at the sky like dragon flame. A wall of heat scorched her face. Sweat trickled down her back and between her breasts, and smoke, thick with ash, stung her eyes.

She and her father clutched bundles of kindling, ready to toss them at any part of the ring that faltered. Pumble paced the circle, sword at ready, guardian charm between his teeth, lips caressing it in constant invocation. The blind boy stood gripping his staff like a club.

Outside the circle, Rees shot arrow after arrow. Now and then, through the blur of heat and smoke, Mirianna could see the creatures scatter where his arrows struck home. To the left, when the smoke parted, she could see the Shadow Man swoop at the Krad like a demon on horseback.

The creatures' shrieks carried over the noise of the fire, ripping at Mirianna's nerves. She ground her teeth, trying to shut out the sound, to keep panic from closing her throat entirely. But the noise only intensified, rushing at her ears like the roar of the fire. *Stop!* she wanted to scream, if only to hear her own voice, to prove the clamor could be penetrated, but it was too late—someone was already screaming.

"Get it off! Get it off!"

Her mind registered Pumble scrabbling on the ground with a dark, writhing mass. It registered her father, his armful of sticks flying away from his body, his hands reaching for the beast-man's shaggy pelt. It registered a flash of sword, of knife, and the reverberation of the scream rising in her throat.

Mirianna pivoted to launch herself at her father, to stop him, but another dark mass hurdled a break in the fire ring.

The Krad landed in a crouch, a long, curved knife gripped in one paw. Yellow-rimmed eyes, set close under heavy brows, fixed on her. The creature snarled, exposing blackened teeth.

Screaming, "Krad!" Mirianna flung her armload of sticks at its face.

"Get down!" The boy swung his staff, whacking the Krad alongside the head and knocking the beast-man to its knees.

Mirianna scrambled behind the boy. "Hit it again!"

"High?"

"Low!"

The blow caught the Krad full in the face. The beast-man fell backward, blood gushing from its nose. The creature rolled, struggled into a crouch, and spat blood. It raised the knife and pivoted near the edge of the fire ring.

"Push it!" Mirianna grabbed the staff behind the boy's hands and swung the blunt end toward the beast-man. "Now!"

Driven by the force of their double lunge, the staff rammed the Krad full in the chest. The beast-man keeled into the flames, landing with a crash on the burning brush. The creature yowled, rolled backward out of the flames, and scrambled to its feet only to crumple, an arrow protruding from its smoking hide.

Rees trotted up and jerked the arrow free. Casting Mirianna a look she couldn't read through the smoke, he restrung it and rode off. Behind her, the boy said, "Did we get it? Is it dead?"

Nearby, Pumble mopped his face on his sleeve. His sword ran with blood. Beside him, her father stood panting, cheeks ashen. At their feet lay a dead Krad. Neither man looked injured. Heaving a sigh dangerously like a sob, Mirianna slid her hand over the boy's and squeezed it. "Yes, it's dead. That was amazing...what you did."

He grinned and his face flushed. "We—we did it together."

Outside the fire ring, the clamor faded. Mirianna shook her head, wondering if it was only a trick of the blood still roaring in her ears, but when the smoke thinned, she saw the beast-men running toward the trees.

"They're leaving," Tolbert said, a dazed look on his face.

Pumble kissed his charm, pressed it to his chest, and kissed it again. "Just in time, too." He sheathed his sword with a flourish. "Or we would have slaughtered them. Right, Rees?"

An unsmiling Rees looked down from his mount. "Shut up, slug-brain, and get out here. We have horses to catch."

Pumble's lower lip quivered, but he hid it behind another vigorous mopping of his face, this time with the hem of his tunic. Drawing his sword again, he used it to poke open a path through the smoldering ring.

Mirianna took the boy's arm and led him out of the circle.

"Can you—" he said as she released him. "Do you see my master? Is he all right?"

"Speak of the Demon," muttered Rees, "and here he comes."

Mirianna followed the direction of his nod. Smoke hung across the clearing like a blanket of blue fog. The air reeked with Krad scent and scorched vegetation. Here and there, wispy tendrils swirled from smoldering brush, obscuring the ground, concealing its solidity. The Shadow Man emerged from the haze first, his head and shoulders a sharp black silhouette, the horse beneath him an insubstantial gray wraith. He glided toward them like an apparition, soundlessly.

Like a dream, Mirianna thought, mesmerized by the play of light about his body. *Like my dream.*

Awareness clenched in her abdomen. The jolt radiated outward, curdling her skin and raising the fine hairs of her body in wave after wave of sensation. The man of her dreams was nothing but a figment, something conjured by her loneliness, her need for a lover...wasn't he? The image approaching was not a man, but a shadow, a—a nightmare, not a dream. And she'd promised—she'd promised *him*—she had promised—

By the Dragon, what had she promised?
Anything.

She tried to swallow, to wet her mouth, but her throat wouldn't open. She fought against a sensation of suffocating, of drowning in water she couldn't see. And still he approached, gliding as silently, and as inexorably, as Death.

Chapter Fourteen

The Krad fled in the mad scattering of a terrified horde. It would be hours before the creatures could regroup. To be certain, Durren pursued them into the forest. He returned with the Sword of Drakkonwehr gripped loosely in his hand and the make-shift spear resting across his lap. He flexed his fingers, savoring long-dormant sensations.

Once a warrior, always a warrior, said the Voice in his head.

Durren nodded. He marveled at how easily his body recalled its training. How the scent emanating from his tunic refreshed his nostrils. How the ache in his muscles radiated confidence, pride. Ghost, as if sensing his thoughts, arched his neck and pranced. Durren chuckled and patted the stallion's shoulder.

It had been ages, too, since he'd laughed...for pleasure.

Ages, he thought, since he'd deserved to.

The smoky meadow dotted with Krad carcasses seemed suddenly all too familiar. Drakkonwehr had smoked, too. And carcasses had littered its courtyard. But there had been no triumph in his passage through it then.

Durren closed his eyes as a wave of humiliation washed over him. *Warrior, hah! What kind of warrior lets everything he's supposed to defend be destroyed?*

What kind of warrior fails not only his mission, but his best friend, his family, and his heritage? And what kind of warrior—Damn him!—doesn't even pay for his failures with his own worthless life!

The same kind of warrior, said the Voice in his head, *who lives day after day with the memories.*

And night after night with the dreams. Durren squeezed his eyelids together until purple and yellow rioted behind them. It was a mockery, this being condemned to life. Cursed by Syryk's spell with a physical being too horrible for any human to survive the sight of. Damned to never age, but to watch, alone, while everything around him grew...and died. Gall rose, bitter and searing, at the base of Durren's throat.

Oh, he could die. But not by natural means. And not by the hand of a man. To surrender to a Krad knife, though, would be beneath any man who lived by the blade.

Raising the Sword of Drakkonwehr, Durren considered the broken blade. Directly after the collapse of the Stone Dam at Herrok-Eneth, he should have gathered his wits and gone deep into Beggeth, hunting mage-spawn. With this damaged weapon, doing so would have been tantamount to suicide, but no one would have blamed him for that when they had the fall of the whole world to lay on his head. Instead—his fist tightened on the hilt—he had not acted with honor. Rather, some dim force he even now couldn't identify had drawn his shocked mind and battered body out of the tumult and led him like a homing bird to Drakkonwehr. There he'd stayed, a captive of honor and pride, until the desire to sustain life, however wretched, had driven him out once a year to trade in Ar-

Deneth.

Durren slapped the flat of the blade against his thigh. If only he'd run the whole length of it through Syryk's black heart when he'd had the chance!

'If only' is an illusion, a worthless conceit, said the Voice in his head. *There are no second chances. A 'warrior' should know that.*

Be still!

Why? So you can wallow in self-pity and forget the woman?

The woman.

Durren's spine stiffened. He lifted his gaze and saw her standing above the haze, the rock ledge an island in a sea of mist. "Illusion," he said, trying to tear his eyes from her flushed cheeks and riotous hair.

Promise.

The word shuddered through Durren. His groin quivered with it. Even his heartbeat stumbled. He forced a deep breath. She'd promised, hadn't she? And he'd made her say it twice, to be sure.

But what could she do against Syryk's curse?

Perhaps nothing, said the Voice in his head. *Perhaps...everything.*

"Dear Koronolan," Durren breathed. His chest ached, his legs trembled, his hands shook. Black dots swam on the fringes of his vision, obscuring everything but her face, her body, her uncanny resemblance to the woman haunting his dreams.

What did it matter where she'd come from, or who had sent her and why or how? All that mattered as he rode slowly toward her was that she'd promised.

Anything.

****

The Imposter of Nolar withdrew early into his private chambers. He'd passed a vexing day. First, negotiations with the father of his intended bride, always a delicate matter, had suffered a minor setback. He was sure it was nothing an offer of more gold wouldn't overcome. Second, there had arisen some sort of crisis in the vineyards. He deferred that to the steward, ordering the man not to bother him with such trivialities. The directive earned him looks askance from the steward and attendant vinedressers. No cause for concern, however. While Master Brandelmore evidently was a close and careful manager of his properties, his underlings could hardly blame the man if his impending marriage absorbed an inordinate amount of his energies. Finally, the crystal had hung heavy and restless about his neck all day, but he'd had no chance to examine its multifaceted surface.

Sinking into the chair before his dressing table, he shoved thick fingers through his hair and grimaced at his image in the glass. Not a bad specimen of manhood, but it still disconcerted him to see a stranger's face looking back. He bared even, white teeth. One in limbo could hardly expect to choose. How fortunate he hadn't thrust himself into a woman's body.

He chuckled at the choice of image and considered which of the females among his household servants would be tonight's recipient of his 'thrusts.' Pity he'd been such an ascetic in his previous incarnation. Such activity, which he'd quickly discovered was expected from the Master, always soothed his nerves. Afterward, he would dream of mounting his bloodstone-draped, virginal bride on the table anointed with the Dragon Chant and raising, with the force of their union, the Last

Dragon. The thought of all that primal power at his fingertips always brought him to climax again, and he would bask until dawn in the glory of his prowess.

But for now the crystal burned hot against his naked chest. He extracted the pouch from beneath elegant Colanthian lace and finely woven, Bedian linen. He tugged the laces open, and the broken column seemed to leap into his palm. Even though he had ample warning of its heat, the abrupt sear upon contact made him suck in a hiss. He dropped the crystal to the tabletop and licked his stung palm.

A kaleidoscope of colors ran rampant over the table's polished surface. He breathed a word, and the color shifts slowed. Another word and the crystal's glow receded, withdrawing into the column itself. It pulsed first red, then amber, then red again, and dimmed entirely before throbbing with renewed fire.

He rubbed a thumb over the singed spot on his palm. The amber puzzled him until, reviewing the sequence, he realized the color wasn't the honey of true amber but a raw yellow-orange. "Fire." He sat up straight. "And Krad too."

What in Beggeth?

He bent again and cupped his hands around the column, taking care not to touch it. Red light illuminated his palms, showing dark as blood in the creases and whorls. Red—*this* red—could mean only one thing: Rees and his pot-bellied partner had the bloodstone!

Stricken with pleasure, he almost clasped the crystal to his lips, but another flash of yellow-orange reminded him of the folly of touching the stone. Instead, he spread his hands, palm down, on either side of the column and slid them together until thumb met thumb and forefingers touched. Closing his eyes, he inhaled deeply, held the breath, and blew it slowly out. He could think now, although just barely.

Leaning forward, he peered at the column fragment contained within the triangle of his fingers. There was no mistake. Red light oozed over the backs of his hands and glistened on his nails. His heart whipped at his throat. Years, years of waiting and the stones were practically within his grasp.

Enough of this running about in the Wehrland with old gem-cutters and their nubile daughters. Enough of this gaming with Krad and fire. "Bring the stones to me, Rees," he breathed onto the pulsing crystal column. "Bring them to me now."

****

Mirianna shivered despite piles of brush still smoldering nearby, despite the fire-flush engorging her cheeks. The Shadow Man's steady regard tripped wave after wave of gooseflesh, chilling her like a frigid wind that finds its way through the snuggest stone-and-mortar wall. It was foolish to think he'd forgotten her promise, or to hope he put so little store by it that he would demand nothing in return. Foolish, clearly, in the face of his unerring approach.

He halted the gray stallion directly before her, and time itself seemed to pause, as though only she and the shadow before her existed in this moment, this space. Disturbed by the intimacy of that thought, Mirianna ordered her gaze away, down, anywhere else but fixed on the formless cloth that should have been face, but her body refused any command contrary to the summons issued from beneath the black hood.

"You made me a promise. I've fulfilled my part. Do you intend to keep yours?"

She forced air into her lungs. "Do I—do I have a choice?"

His scrutiny lay like a weight on her shoulders, pressing her steadily into the ground. "Only that which you allow yourself."

To fulfill or not fulfill, as her conscience would permit. Could she deny and live with herself? Could she fulfill and survive? He'd agreed to save them from the Krad. He would not now harm her, would he? Shivers cavorted in her stomach, making her words come out raw and faint. "What—what do you wish from me?"

A black gloved hand unclenched from the sapling lying across his lap, the fingers unfurling like petals opening to the sun. The palm, clad in leather as finely creased as the skin it purported to cover, glided toward her. Two fingertips, their ebony second skin radiating the musky scent of long and intimate union, hung suspended a breath from her chin.

Her mind registered the catch and fall of the tunic covering his chest and the minute corresponding ruffle of his face-covering, but it was her body that recognized the cue. Of their own accord, her lips parted and her lids drifted down.

With an imperceptible movement, his fingertips contacted the sensitive underside of her jaw. Her body stilled, breath bated, all nerve endings focused on two small ovals of heat that trailed as delicately as butterfly wings along her skin.

"What do I wish from you?" murmured the voice that spread like dark liquor through her veins. "Only your presence. Your companionship. At Drakkonwehr."

She responded like one spellbound, her words thick and distant. "M—my companionship?"

The fingertips reached the edge of her chin, and one drifted off. Her body reacted automatically, rising on toes and leaning forward to sustain contact. There was no ground beneath her feet, Mirianna thought vaguely, only this sensation of floating, of suspension by one exquisite, gossamer thread.

"Come," the voice said.

—*Come*—

The single word poured into her like warm honey. It flowed outward, spreading a satiny gloss over her reason, her inhibitions, her conscious self. Once before—was it only last night?—a voice had called her thus, summoning her out of fear to tranquility, and she'd gone without hesitation. Nor would she hesitate now, although this voice offered something far from tranquil, something, instead, that wound the fibers of her being into a taut, breathless cord of anticipation.

She raised her head, and of its own accord her hand rose to meet the open black one. How his fingertip departed her chin, she didn't know. She knew only the sharp, tingling sweetness of its lingering imprint. And then her hand crossed a black leather palm, and her thumb locked with a shadow of itself.

"Stop! Don't touch him!"

"By all that's holy!"

"Mirianna, no!"

She started like a dreamer shaken awake. She would have fallen, but iron fingers banded around her hand and spun her instead in a half circle. Before she could regain her balance, an arm swooped and snagged her about the waist. Breath gushed from her lungs, her feet flew from the ground, and her vision careened past her father's white look of shock.

By the time she planted her hands and shook the hair from her face, her mind had registered several significant details. She was perched sideways half upon the stallion's bony withers and half upon a rock-hard thigh, held in place by an inflexible black-clad arm. Pumble lay sprawled on his back, his own sword jammed into the ground inches from his ear. Above him, Rees held an empty bow, fingers beside his cheek poised in the attitude of release. Beside her shoulder quivered an arrow driven to the feathers through the wrist-thick sapling the Shadow Man had raised to meet it.

Mirianna squeaked an exclamation.

Pumble gaped over his belly. "You missed!"

A milk-white Rees stared through the notch of his bow. "That should've gone through his heart!"

Tolbert, whose fingertips left bloodless spots on his cheeks, dropped to his knees on the rocky ground. "Dragon's blood—"

"Fools!" The Shadow Man lowered the impaled sapling-lance and, with a kick of his boot, snapped the arrow shaft like a stick of kindling. "What made you think you could take me on? I'm invulnerable. A phantom." The hood tilted back and emitted a laugh.

Loud, harsh, and humorless, the sound rippled outward across the smoky clearing and bounced off trees. It rolled back like a hundred reverberant echoes, each one raising the hair on Mirianna's nape, each one a hammer beat driving home the final significant detail: She was trapped, a prisoner of the very darkness that had threatened to overwhelm her in Ar-Deneth. Instead of fleeing this time, she'd given her hand to it...*of her own free will!* She pushed wildly against the arm compressing her diaphragm.

Ignoring her struggles, the Shadow Man rolled the make-shift lance to his right and jabbed the point at Pumble's boot. "Be off, all of you, before I leave your carcasses for the Krad."

Pumble scrambled to his feet and launched himself at Rees's stirrup. "Let me up! Let me up!"

Rees rammed an elbow into the fat man's head. "Quit bleating like a stuck pig and get the old man!"

With a dark look at Rees, Pumble rubbed his cheekbone and turned. "Come on!" He grabbed Tolbert under the arms. "Get your feet under you. We aren't making an all-day stew, here."

Tolbert unfolded stiffly. He allowed himself to be lifted, but once upright, he twisted out of Pumble's hands and spun toward the Shadow Man. His skin stretched like parchment, dry and tight, over the hollows of his face, and his hands trembled, but his voice did not. "No. Not without my daughter."

"Papa—" Mirianna bit her lip, fending off a little girl's cry for the father who'd always protected her. She was grown now, and he was old, and it was her turn to save him—no matter what the cost. "Papa, please, don't—"

Tolbert stumbled toward the gray horse and shook his fist. "You put her down, you black-hearted mage-spawn!"

The stallion snorted and tossed his head. The Shadow Man's fingers adjusted their grip on the make-shift spear. Mirianna's heart wedged in her throat. She flung a panicked glance at Pumble. "Stop him, please!"

Sweat poured down the fat man's face. His gaze skittered from Rees to the Shadow Man's lance hovering only a lunge away. "Come on!" He grabbed Tolbert's arms. "Don't be a fool. Do you want to end up in a Krad pot?"

"No!" Tolbert shoved at the heavier man. "I told you! I'm not—!"

"Take the old bastard," Rees barked, "before he gets us all killed."

With another glance from Rees to the Shadow Man, Pumble bent and caught Tolbert by the waist. Heaving the older man over his shoulder with as much ease as he heaved camp supplies, he trotted to Rees's side.

"Mirianna!" Tolbert raised himself over Pumble's shoulder and broke into a spasm of coughing. When Pumble levered him onto the horse behind Rees, he collapsed like a rag.

"Papa!" But there was nothing he could do, nothing any of them could do unless—

She turned to Rees, opening her hand, pleading with the Master of Nolar's man one last time, but the look he returned was stony. Shouldering his bow, he shifted his gaze from Mirianna to the Shadow Man to the lance, the knife-point of which had flowed unerringly in his direction.

With a sinking heart, Mirianna read his thoughts. His duty required him to deliver her father and the bloodstone. Any obligation he felt to defend her, an incidental participant, extended only so far, and this crossed the line. Tight-lipped, Rees turned his heavily laden horse and heeled it toward the trees while Pumble ran to catch his own horse.

Desperate, she flailed out with elbows and feet. "Let me go! You can't—I won't—" The effort earned her a grunt and a sharp tightening of the arm around her ribs. Air squeezed from her lungs, precious air she couldn't reclaim. She threw her head back, gasping, but it was a mistake. The Shadow Man trapped her up-tilted chin with his head, pressing what should have been cheekbone and mouth against the line of her throat.

Mirianna's heart stopped. Part of her being screamed panic at her utter vulnerability, at his complete and total dominance over her body, her very life. The other, that traitorous part that had been lured by the pleasure offered in her dreams, tripped a maelstrom of involuntary responses. Blood evaporated from her extremities. It condensed in her breasts, where it radiated toward the nipples in a prickling cascade of warmth, and in the hidden depths of her femininity, where it uncoiled in long ribbons of sensation.

The Shadow Man shifted his head, bringing what should have been mouth into direct alignment with the wildly beating pulse below Mirianna's ear. "No, I won't let you go." The words set his coarse face-covering vibrating against her sensitized skin. "Yes, I can take what was offered me. And by Koronolan, you *will* fulfill your promise."

He straightened and Mirianna stared up at a featureless black mask, trying to withstand his regard. He was nothing but darkness and nightmare in the semblance of a man's shadow. There was no substance under that fabric skin, nothing physical that could harm her, only a voice and a presence.

But the torso jammed tight against her shoulder, hip and thigh belied her hopes. It and the cloth sleeve into which she dug her fingers were filled to capacity with something every bit as solid as a tree trunk. And what flexed under those fingers and alongside her left breast was unmistakably hot, blood-fed flesh.

The fine hairs of Mirianna's body stood up. Her breath sucked in on a hiss.

The Shadow Man leaned down and his face-covering fluttered against the pulse at her temple. "Yes, my beauty," he murmured, "I am everything you fear, both shadow *and* substance."

And then, as abruptly as he'd seized her, he let go. With a squeak of surprise, she slid to the ground. Her knees buckled, and she pitched forward into hummocks and blue aster.

"Before you consider doing anything foolish," the Shadow Man said while the gray stallion danced around her prone form, "remember that it's not my *intention* to harm you." He laid the make-shift lance across the horse's withers. "Now, go help Gareth pack while I fetch the other horses."

He wheeled away and, like the fabled horseman Kiros, dangled one-handed from the stallion's mane to scoop up the sword embedded where Pumble had fallen. Thus armed, he galloped toward the woods.

Mirianna stared after him until her eyes burned, then dropped her head onto her arms. Her limbs quivered like new pudding and she could muster no resistance to the shivers wracking her torso. A sob hiccupped from her lips. She sank her teeth into her sleeve to prevent another, but it bubbled through the gag. Others followed, accompanied by the hot sting of tears. She lay, utterly bereft as the full import of her situation sank in. By the Dragon, she'd traded her life to a fiend! He could do with her as he pleased, and no one could prevent it. No one!

Something ghosted across her hair. Mirianna froze, stifling a sob. The contact returned, the touch hesitant, like the flutter of a bird's wing. Terrified, she jerked upright, and the blind boy's hand grazed her wet cheek.

He squatted beside her, a look of consternation on his face. "Please don't cry."

She dragged the backs of her hands across her cheeks. "Why shouldn't I?"

He rotated his thumb across his fingertips, seemingly mesmerized by the texture of her tears. "Well, because I wouldn't mind a bit of help...finding everything, I mean. I can pack. I'm good at that, but—well—I'm not sure where everything is...anymore." He wiped his hand on his tunic and offered it.

Mirianna looked at the hand extended toward her left ear. She inhaled a shaky breath. At least she wouldn't be alone with the Shadow Man. And the boy seemed kind-hearted. Besides, she'd made her choice, however foolish. She might as well begin living with the consequences. Drying her cheeks on her sleeve, she accepted the offer of a hand up.

****

Durren slowed Ghost just inside the shelter of the trees. He forced deep breaths into his lungs, willing his heartbeat to moderate, to cease its rampage against the walls of his chest. By Kiros, those fools never should have tried him while the battle blood still ran hot in his veins. After dispatching an army of Krad, fending off two poor excuses for soldiers and one doddering old man served only to fire in him a raging sense of indignation.

You have every right to be angry, said the Voice in his head. *After all, those pathetic fools thought they could take away your prize of battle, your plunder.*

"Be still! The woman's not a prize." He'd fought the Krad in exchange for her promise. It was a contract, pure and simple, and their clasped hands had sealed it. Those fools should never have tried to interfere. He would have been perfectly within his rights to kill them.

And he almost had. He stared at the sword he'd yanked from the ground, remembering how he'd nearly turned it into the fat man's belly. For one blind moment, his body—*this damned body*—had ruled, and he'd almost broken his oath to her.

With a snarl, Durren flung the captured sword into the ground. He'd wanted to kill—damn him!—and once he'd snatched the woman from the earth, his body and his blood had indeed roared that she was his prize, his possession.

By Kiros, he could still smell the heated lilac of her skin! His groin ached, remembering the tantalizing friction of her bucking and writhing hips. It had taken all his willpower to hang onto the lance when her struggles bared her leg to the knee. It would have been so easy to catch that sleek, alabaster flesh and pull her astride Ghost. So easy, then, to follow the line of her thigh upward to the cradle of her femininity. So sweetly easy to lift her hips and let his fingers lay claim to the hot, satiny recesses he knew in his dreams existed there.

Sweat popped out on Durren's face, gluing the soft, inner fold of cloth to it. He dragged air into his lungs, forced a swallow, and inhaled again. A vision of her tumble from Ghost stabbed at him. He hoped he hadn't hurt her, but if she'd moved against him once more, he was certain, instead of merely dropping her like a hot coal, he would have hauled her to the ground and thrown himself between her legs. By Koronolan, the last thing he wanted was to frighten her, or to issue threats, but he'd clearly done both. And all because of this damned body!

He slid off Ghost, draped an arm over the stallion's withers and leaned against the big animal. His muscles trembled, a sign—at last—of his blood cooling. He peeled the tunic away from his skin, allowing a faint breeze to slip between fabric and flesh, speeding the process. Ghost lowered his head and nuzzled Durren's leg, lipping the cloth over his knee. Dropping the lance, Durren pushed the gray head away, but his hand lingered on the horse's throat. He stroked upward, found an ear and massaged it gently.

I am everything you fear, both shadow and substance.

Durren winced. Why in Beggeth had he told her that?

Perhaps, said the Voice in his head, *because it's true.*

"It's not—" But it was. In a moment of shattering clarity, Durren realized he'd grown weary of denying the Shadow's influence. They were not one, could never be one, but he understood, now, his substance somehow was inextricably conjoined to it. His fingers twisted in Ghost's forelock, mimicking the pain twisting his heart, his soul.

Better that she knows now, don't you think?

Durren inhaled deeply. Perhaps it was better this way. Now that the beads were cast, she knew which were hers to play. And he knew his next casts would have to prove what he sought from her was no more than he'd asked: her presence, her companionship. Considering how he'd frightened her, that task would be difficult enough, but if she touched him again...

Scowling, he shook himself out of his reverie and drew in another long breath. They were not safe here. The Krad could return at any moment. Afternoon shadows already pooled on the forest floor, thickening the shade. It would be well past midnight when they made Drakkonwehr, if nothing else delayed their progress.

And that progress would be possible only if he could find all of the missing horses. Snatching up his lance and the fat man's sword, Durren swung aboard Ghost. Soon, he would be at Drakkonwehr, and for once, he would not be alone there. The realization sent a little frisson of anticipation along his nerves.

Finally, he thought as he heeled the stallion, he might be able to exorcise at least one of his demons.

Chapter Fifteen

Within minutes, Durren had found the pack mare and the woman's gelding, but the boy's mount seemed to have vanished. He could have tracked the animal, but that required time.

Durren snorted at the paradox. Time was something Syryk had given him far too much of, yet he wasn't prepared to waste it on a fruitless search in Krad territory. Especially not now, not when he had two time-bound creatures under his care.

Glancing back at them, Durren noted how the starlight silvered the hood and shoulders of the woman's cloak. She rode with her arms around the boy, who slumped forward with the solidity of one dead asleep.

For the ninth time since the mist had begun to curl wraith-like under the horses' bellies, the thought stabbed Durren that he should've taken the boy instead of burdening her. After all, it was his own desire to reach Drakkonwehr that had driven the boy to this state. But, for the ninth time, he reminded himself he'd burdened the woman precisely to limit her means of escape.

Besides, even he felt the fist of exhaustion grinding into the small of his back. The Krad rock, no more than a flying nuisance hours ago, had left an impact site on his rib cage. Sometime after nightfall, the injury had begun to ache. Now every thud of Ghost's right foreleg sent pinpricks through his side. Durren slipped a hand inside his cloak and pressed it to the tender spot, soothing it with chilled fingers.

He looked back at the woman again, but the shelf of her hood hid her face except for her mouth and the tip of her nose. The compressed line of her lips, however, told him she clung as grimly to wakefulness as she did to the boy.

He wondered for perhaps the thirtieth time what she was thinking. Not in general, although he did wonder what a woman in her situation would think about. Rather, Durren very specifically wondered whether, while in his arms, she'd noticed the ardent response of his body to her nearness.

The sudden darkening of her pupils when he'd raised his head from her throat told him her body had understood the cues. But did the simultaneous widening of her eyes signify a conscious terror of the Shadow Man? Or did it indicate a more general fear induced by turmoil and confusion?

He looked back again, wishing he could scrutinize her hidden face. Did she truly loathe the bargain she'd made, or was she simply afraid of the unknown? All his hopes depended on the second possibility. He couldn't afford to consider the first.

The trail they'd been riding crossed the talus beneath a granite face. The traverse afforded a wide view of their back trail, but it also exposed them like foxes caught in an early snow. So far, nothing stirred below. Even so, he nudged Ghost with a heel.

The pack mare, feeling the tug on the line that connected her halter and the bridle of the woman's horse to Ghost's saddle, neighed a complaint. Durren winced. If he'd wanted to announce their presence, he couldn't have chosen a better medium than the amplifying backdrop of granite. He heeled Ghost into a trot, forcing the gelding and the pack mare to match the gait.

"What's the matter?" the woman said as the boy stirred with the jostling. "Why are we running?"

Durren kept his gaze fixed on the end of the rock cut. "We're not running. We're just getting out of the open." A few more strides and they would disappear into the shadow between the rock face and a massive, towering boulder. Once they did so, they would be within the boundaries of Drakkonwehr.

Ages ago, after Koronolan had imprisoned the Last Dragon, the hero had established a guard post on the rock. All the heirs to Drakkonwehr had kept it manned. Or they had, Durren amended, until the great Stone Dam at Herrok-Eneth split on *his* watch, unleashing a flood of Krad. He glanced up, noting where a spill of rock marked the remains of a wall. When he'd made his way home after the disaster, he'd found his guardsmen near the breach, their flesh eaten and their bones scattered among the stones. Even now, the memory made his skin crawl.

He turned Ghost into the ink pocket between rock face and guardian stone, letting the horse pick its way. The narrow passage was studded with boulders, some as big as horses. A wagon or war engine could pass, but only if the driver knew the way through the maze.

The Krad had rampaged through it once. The full force unleashed from Beggeth had rushed straight to Drakkonwehr, smashed through the walls and destroyed everything within them, massacring every living thing. Even the rats!

Durren steeled himself against the memory of torn human limbs rotting among half-devoured horse heads, ox quarters, rat feet, and bits of chicken, feathers still fluttering in the least breeze, but it was too late. The scene came to him as if it were only yesterday. Still spell-shocked himself, he'd stumbled through the broken gate, and everywhere scenes of horror confronted him. A profound stillness enveloped the fortress, broken only by his ragged breathing. Not even the crows spoke, so thoroughly had the onrushing Krad scourged the land. His warrior's nostrils recognized the heavy, sweet scent of spilled blood and the pungent odor of decomposing flesh. They were battle smells, and he'd often reveled in them. But this was not battle; this was raw, brute savagery.

When he'd retched himself to the gall, he'd done the only logical thing for a man confronted with the shredded remains of friends, servants, pets. He'd taken a torch and burned it all.

The Sword of Drakkonwehr drew his hand to its presence at his belt. He fingered the scrolled hand guard, the crosspiece, the bloodstone as he rode out of the boulder's shadow into the starlight. Today, for the first time since the weapon had broken, he'd felt like a warrior again. He'd killed Krad, and he'd done it well. In some small measure, Durren, the Master of Drakkonwehr, had finally truly returned. And he'd begun to pay his debts.

****

Mirianna's arms had long ago gone numb. Her shoulders and back vied for the honor of paining her more, but she'd ceased to care. She'd made a deal with a creature of darkness, and she was following him higher and higher into the Wehrland, probably to the very walls of Beggeth itself, but even that didn't inspire a reaction.

Every aspect of her being concentrated on the belief each plodding step brought them closer to a point at which they would finally stop. If she could just hang on—to wakefulness, the boy, her perch behind the saddle—she would be rewarded with the knowledge she'd survived the longest night of her life.

On the traverse she'd noticed a sudden quickening of their pace. The jostling had wrung protests from both her body and the boy. It had spoiled her concentration, awakening her mind to the scream of her muscles. Deciding she would rather die than be tortured further, she'd opened her mouth to plead for a rest when the horses stopped.

For several heartbeats, she sat in stupefaction, too fatigued to summon a response. The Shadow Man's silhouette was an ink blot on the night sky, showing his position by the absence of stars. The trail curved down from the ledge on which they stood, and it overlooked a valley bounded on the far side by cliffs so high and sheer, they gleamed even in the starlight.

"Where are we?" Mirianna said through lips that seemed inordinately slow to pronounce her thought.

"Drakkonwehr."

"Drakkonwehr?" The name sounded significant, but her exhausted mind refused to dredge up the meaning.

"Dragon Keep. My home."

She followed the direction of the Shadow Man's

nod and found, clinging to the near side of the mountain, a massive dark shape that, even at this distance, dwarfed the Master of Nolar's fortress. In the dimness, she could discern the outlines of an array of towers, turrets, and walls.

"Dragon Keep?" A frisson of awareness, of comprehension skimmed the back of her neck. "You mean, this is—?"

"Sur-Drakkoneth, the Valley of the Dragon."

Mirianna's memory clicked, supplying from its depths the story she'd been taught to recite as a child:

"*When dawn returned, Koronolan hurled the Last Dragon deep into the earth, and the land heaved over it, and the Wehrland was formed beside the walls of Beggeth. Dragon's blood, raining from the sky, became stone, and Dragontime became Dragon's End. The people rejoiced while Koronolan mounted a bloodstone on the Sword of Drakkonwehr and passed it to his sons and their sons ever after who...*"

Her voice trailed off as her mind absorbed the import of the broken sword, the sheer cliffs, and the human-shaped tower of darkness who sat only feet away astride a ghost of a horse and watched her.

"*—his sons and their sons ever after,*" the Shadow Man continued the litany, enunciating each word, "*who would watch forever the resting place of the Last Dragon.*"

Mirianna stared, mind reeling, but he turned his horse back to the trail, forcing her gelding to follow. If what he said were true, she'd indeed found herself at the walls of Beggeth. And the mist that gleamed yellow as it crept across the trail ahead of them had to be the very breath of the entombed Dragon. It even smelled faintly sulfurous.

She gave herself a mental shake. This whole train of thought was absurd, and she would prove it. She shifted the sleeping boy to her left shoulder and clucked to the gelding, urging the horse alongside the gray stallion.

The black hood turned in her direction and she sensed his regard. She cleared her throat. "Are you—are you telling me that you're a Drakkonwehr?"

"I am the Dragonkeeper, yes."

"You can't be. Ulerroth said the last Drakkonwehr died when Herrok-Eneth fell."

The horses stopped, but she wasn't sure if the decision to rein in had been hers or the Shadow Man's. Either way, his scrutiny made her stomach clench.

"I believe," he said softly, "that the story's proper wording suggests none of the participants were ever seen again. And so I have not been...seen."

Mirianna's nerves hummed a warning. He had only to show himself to her and she would die. But her questions seemed unfazed by the danger her body sensed. "You're Durren of Drakkonwehr, *and* you're the Shadow Man?"

The hood dipped in a gracious nod.

She rubbed her temple. "Then the Shadow Man *is* Durren of Drakkonwehr."

"No."

"What?" Her head pounded and she closed her eyes against the pain. "That doesn't—"

"That needn't concern you now. We need to get inside the fortress." He clucked to the horses, and Mirianna gritted her teeth and hung on to the boy.

Chapter Sixteen

Mirianna threw her arm over her eyes. The sun had no business waking her this early. Her head had barely touched the bedding, and now it was already day? Nearly noon by the height of the sun bouncing off rocks and stone walls and penetrating the sleeve she'd thrown over her face. Groaning, she uncovered one eye and realized she'd slept for hours on no more than a blanket thrown down upon paving stones. Every joint in her body ached as she sat up and took in soaring granite walls, pitted and broken in places as though something huge had swung a club through them. What seemed in starlight like intact towers and turrets were in the clarity of day the shattered remains of a once great fortress.

Drakkonwehr.

Had the Shadow Man really told her that, or had she dreamed it? In full daylight, the idea he should claim kinship with—much less the identity of—the presumed dead Durren of Drakkonwehr seemed something her exhausted mind had created, but there was yet the undeniable reality of this fortress. The incongruity made Mirianna's head ache. She lay down and covered her eyes, seeking to return to the sweet oblivion of sleep.

The smell of roasting meat teased her nostrils and, stomach rumbling, she turned to look for the source. A fire with a spitted rabbit suspended over it smoked within a circle of stones. Nearby, she saw a well with a bucket sitting on its rim and a trough beside it. Realizing she'd eaten and drunk nothing for the better part of a day, Mirianna rallied stiff muscles and tottered to her feet.

The chill water she splashed on her face shocked her mind and body into full wakefulness. She drank deeply, then undid her hair and refastened it, shoving loose curls away from her face with hands that shook. *Don't think about Papa. He's safe with Rees and Pumble. That's all that matters.*

Inhaling a steadying breath, she surveyed the courtyard. In the shade of one wall, the horses lounged, nose to tail. They'd been hobbled and their tack removed but not organized. She suspected she'd helped pile the gear against the wall, but she could remember nothing beyond lowering the boy into the Shadow Man's arms and sliding off the gelding herself.

Of the Shadow Man she could see no sign, but clearly he'd set the rabbit to roasting. The boy still slept, tangled in his blankets, frowning against the sun. His cheeks looked flushed, so Mirianna knelt to lay her hand on his forehead. During the night, the bandage around his head had come askew and she pulled it off, revealing a puckered, reddened gash. She bit her lip, not liking the look of the wound or the dry heat of his skin.

He stirred, mumbling something like "Right away, sir."

"Good morning, Gareth," she said, remembering what the Shadow Man had called him, and remembering he couldn't see her. "How do you feel?"

He yawned, stretched—and winced. "Sore, miss." He sat up and she put his staff into his hand.

"I'll take you to the well so you can wash."

"Where are we?"

"At Drakkonwehr. Your master's home." *Or so he says.* Recalling the boy's self-sufficiency during the Krad battle, Mirianna resisted the urge to help him while he rose stiffly and tapped the paving stones with his staff. "Do you remember anything of last night?"

"Rotten eggs." He wrinkled his nose as he followed her to the well. "Something smelled of rotten eggs." Setting aside his stick, he splashed water on his face, then drained the cup she placed in his hands. "Ugh. The water tastes of it, too."

Now that he mentioned it, she recognized the sulfurous taste lingering on her tongue. "Get used to it." She refilled his cup. "You'll be drinking a lot of it until your fever is gone."

Later, Mirianna rooted in the pile of baggage and found a pot, some dry-cake and an assortment of dried herbs. She cut a haunch of rabbit and gave it to the boy with a piece of dry-cake and a cup of warm water steeped with willow bark and chamomile. If she could just remember all the ingredients, she could make a paste to spread on his gashes, but although she'd watched the Nolar herbalist prepare the recipe many times while collecting her father's teas, her thoughts refused to settle. Instead, she paced, rubbing her hands up and down her arms, and watched the boy eat. At least he had an appetite. When Gareth, despite yawning, suggested they unpack, she refused and made him lie on a blanket in the shade where he promptly fell asleep.

Mirianna hoped she hadn't been too brusque, but she truly didn't have the presence of mind to attempt unpacking things she had no idea where to put, and she especially didn't want the boy to know how her insides quaked every time she thought about where she was and with whom. In the bright light of day, her situation looked no less terrifying than it had when the Shadow Man had clutched her to his chest.

She was indentured to a nightmare. Whatever name he chose to call himself, he certainly was *not* human. And this sprawling ruin was his home. Did he live among the stones, a shadow melding into shadows? Or did he thrive in the dark recesses that lurked behind fragmented doors hanging on blackened frames? Where in the name of the Dragon was he? And just where did he expect this poor blind boy to take up residence?

Perhaps if she roused enough indignation at Gareth's situation, it would keep fear of her own tamped down. She ate a haunch of rabbit without tasting it, chewed dry-cake, and washed both down with sulfur-flavored water, then stood. If the Shadow Man wouldn't show himself, she'd just have to find him.

****

Beneath the fortress, in a pool where one of the tunnels opened into a chamber, Durren floated, arms spread, eyes closed, the water gently bearing him up. All his aches had drained into it, even the bruise from the Krad-thrown rock. When he finished soaking, he would be clean again, purified from the temptations he'd faced down in Ar-Deneth. He opened his eyes, sighed, and touched bottom. A phosphorescent swirl showed where he'd stirred the water, but no other light touched his eyes.

He didn't need light to know precisely where he was, how far from the bottomless part of the pool where the hot water welled up, how near the ledge where his clothes lay, in what direction the tunnel led upward to the broken ruin that was Drakkonwehr. If he'd slept, he was not aware. A man could float asleep in the warm, salty water and open his eyes hours later to see nothing but darkness. It should be full day above ground. He'd left the rabbit slowly roasting. The woman and boy should be capable of caring for themselves while he eased his soul.

He splashed water over his face, watching phosphorescence swirl between his hands. He'd once more purged the effects of Ar-Deneth, but he couldn't so easily purge himself of what had happened since. Not while a flesh-and-blood reminder waited for him above ground. At the thought of the woman, his body tightened. With an oath, he dove, pulling himself hand-over-hand along stones at the bottom until his lungs burned and he broke the surface. He sucked in air, then swam to the ledge and climbed out. This *flesh* had brought her here. Or was it the Shadow?

Perhaps both, said the Voice in his head.

Throughout these fourteen long years, after each necessary foray into the world of men, the pool had never failed to restore his equanimity. Until now. Durren cast a glance upward, as if he could see through solid rock. *She* was up there, most likely walking among the ruins in that homespun riding skirt he'd seen flowing about her ankles when she'd begged him to save her—and the men with her—from the Krad. He'd glimpsed her bare thigh when he held her astride his hip, and that image had burned into his brain. She smelled of lilacs, wood smoke, and...woman.

Durren broke out in a sweat. This body—*his* damned body!—knew what it wanted, what it thought it needed after he'd once more refused to slake its appetite in Ar-Deneth.

It was your choice to punish yourself again, the Voice in his head said. *And for what—to atone for one night of selfish pleasure years ago? How do you know a few hours' delay made the difference? Who's to say Errek wouldn't have died anyway? The mage was expecting you.*

Go to Beggeth! He had enough on his mind without the damned voice adding to it. Somehow, he would have to find a way to deal with her presence. Grabbing his clothes, he threw them on, letting them dry his skin. With the Sword of Drakkonwehr in his belt, he followed the tunnel upward.

He should've guessed he'd find the woman already in the passage. She'd gone as far as the last glimmer of outside light penetrated, and there she stood as if stymied, hand clutching the hewn-rock wall, face white enough to illuminate his way to her.

"What are you doing here?" Durren said, making her start.

Don't be harsh, the Voice in his head said. *She doesn't know any better.*

She still shouldn't have come into the darkness alone. Not here. Not so close to the heart of Drakkonwehr.

"Why did you just go off and leave us?" she said as her gaze located him among the tunnel shadows.

Her question irked him. He had every right to do as he pleased in his own home, to attend to his own compelling needs. "I left you food." Durren strode past her, indicating she should follow. "Did you eat?"

"Thank you, yes, but—"

"Where's the boy?"

"Sleeping. He has a fever—"

He stopped and she stumbled to a halt beside him.

See. He's ill already. You should never have brought him.

Though his gut clenched, Durren ignored the voice in his head and focused on the woman. He saw the flash of her look before her gaze skittered to the rubble littering the floor.

You're scaring her. Is that what you want?

They'd come out into an anteroom. Through the archway ahead, long rays of afternoon sun beat down into the roofless Great Hall and illuminated their feet. Rock scuffs and pine pitch speckled her boots, and over one toe dangled a narrow strip of fabric rent from her skirt. Wondering if he'd been responsible for that, and hoping he hadn't, he modified his tone. "What have you done for him?"

"I found your herbs and made him some tea."

She'd attempted to tame her hair into a knot, but thick curls still spiraled alongside her face, drawing his attention to the delicate shell of her ear and the turquoise earring studding the lobe. Durren braced himself against the rush of desire scorching his skin, but all he could think was how that lobe would feel on his tongue, the fine fuzz of her skin and the cool satin of the stone. *By Kiros!*

Over the hum of his blood, he realized she was speaking. "I trust you have someplace better than an open courtyard for him to sleep in tonight."

Willing his mind into the present time and place, he recognized she'd said nothing of herself, of the fear clearly written on her face moments ago. No, she'd raised her chin and focused on the boy's needs.

You admire that in her, don't you? said the Voice in his head.

What if I do? To the woman, he said, "You'll have better accommodations tonight, if you'll help prepare them."

"Gladly." Head high, she strode across the rubble of the Great Hall, through the broken double door into the courtyard—and froze.

With an oath, Durren sprang, shoving her behind his body and drawing the Sword while spinning to face whatever caused the blood to drain from her face.

In the shade near the pile of gear, the she-lion lay stretched out alongside the sleeping boy, head raised over the boy's head, twin yellow-green eyes fixed on them. Blood stained her muzzle, and her tongue slid over it.

Durren's fingers convulsed on the Sword before he saw the fresh carcass of a deer lying near the fire. "Don't make any sudden moves," he told the woman. "I don't think the lion means to harm Gareth, but I'm not sure what she'll do to us." He stole a glance at the bloodstone embedded in the Sword, but it showed him nothing.

"You mean...you didn't send her?" Despite its pallor, the woman's face in the full sun looked more confused than frightened.

"What do you mean?" he said.

"She brought me to you. She saved me from the Krad. And from Rees. I thought..."

She saved you, too, the Voice in his head said.

Be still!

"If you didn't send her," the woman said, "then

who did?"

Yes, who? the Voice in his head said.

Durren clenched his jaw so tight his teeth ached. "No one! She's just a Wehrland lion, nothing more."

The lion licked the last of the blood from her muzzle with a rasp that jittered his nerves. The yellow-green gaze pulled at him, but he focused between the woman and the cat so he could watch both of them.

Hands on hips, the woman said, "She spoke to me. Twice. I saw myself through her eyes. If that's not magic, I don't know—"

"You *don't* know! How could you? You're just—"

"What? A woman? Is that what you were about to say?" Her chin thrust out, but her lips trembled. "Fine! Keep your bloody Wehrland, and your big black cloak, and your disappearances in the night, and those filthy, disgusting Krad and—and...think what you want! I don't know what in the Dragon's name is going on or why in the world I'm here, but I know one thing. That lion spoke to me. She may want to do you harm, but she's not going to do the least bit of harm to me!" She spun away and, head high, strode toward the she-cat before he could stop her.

Frozen in place, he watched while the lion rose, stretched, and exposed long, curving claws. Then the big cat sauntered to the woman, who'd faltered to a stop by the fire-pit, and twined its sinuous body around the woman's legs like a housecat asking for cream. After the second turn, the lion paused and, with half-lidded eyes, *smiled* at Durren.

****

Despite her bravado, Mirianna quivered every time the she-lion yawned, stretched, or even twitched an ear.

Up close, the creature was huge, longer from whiskered snout to the black tip of her tail than Gareth was tall, and undoubtedly heavier. Even though Mirianna's heart told her she was safe in the cat's presence, her mind couldn't quite wrap itself around the idea, and she understood why the Shadow Man kept his distance. While the lion oozed tranquility and confidence, the Shadow Man regarded the beast with suspicion and something like animosity. The conflicting auras pulled at her all afternoon until she thought her nerves would fray.

Helping the Shadow Man skin the deer carcass, cut it up, and set it to smoking in a stone hut he apparently kept for the purpose, left her jangling with his unease as he constantly looked across the courtyard at the lion. When Mirianna returned to check Gareth, who continued to sleep while the lion watched over him, the lion's deep-throated purr soothed her. Later the Shadow Man took her into the main building and showed her a chamber with an intact roof and door where she and Gareth could lay their bedding.

When she'd been looking for the Shadow Man earlier, she'd found another such door nearby, but it refused to open. She'd thought it merely blocked or jammed, but now she wondered if behind that door was a chamber where he lodged. Clearly, he hadn't spent the night on the paving stones with her and the boy.

While she wondered whether he lodged above ground or below, Mirianna uncovered a broom behind the chamber door and shook cobwebs from it. She was sweeping when the Shadow Man brought her two short benches and a table with uneven legs.

"I hadn't planned on company," he said as she

rocked the table under her hand.

Flattening her palm on the scarred surface, she digested his unspoken message. He'd lived for more than a dozen years, alone, in this wreck of a fortress. By necessity he avoided people. Something had changed that, and he'd acquired the blind boy, a useful servant for a being who couldn't be looked upon without consequence. Then, for reasons she preferred not to consider just yet, he had *acquired* her. Was the Shadow Man implying he'd made these *acquisitions* on impulse? That he had no clear idea how to deal with either or both of them? The idea shook her although the evidence had been building all day. Did that mean he wasn't quite the creature she'd imagined?

When she raised her head to look askance at the Shadow Man, he said, "You're welcome to comb through the buildings for anything you can use, but be careful where you walk. Not everything is as stable as it might appear."

"You do realize—" She cleared dust from her throat and collected her wits. "Gareth won't be able to see the dangers."

He nodded, the movement stirring the fabric of his hood. "I'll mark pathways for him. For now, keep the boy close to you. And stay out of the tunnels."

Mirianna was gratified he took her concern seriously, but his warning about the tunnels sounded as if he didn't want her intruding on his privacy—as if she actually *wished* to go farther into pitch darkness than she already had—and the high-handed way he'd dismissed her faith in the lion still rankled. "How do you know the lion won't harm him?"

The Shadow Man gave no indication of being

startled by her question, but he said nothing for so long, she bent to look for a bit of flat stone to level the table. "She saved him from some Krad. Shortly before you arrived."

Straightening, she watched him out of the corner of her eye. Framed in the late afternoon glow of the doorway, he looked less like shadow and more like silhouetted substance. In the close quarters, Mirianna was acutely aware of sun-warmed wool, of the faint, oily scent of human hair, of the raw, clean smell of masculine exertion. Emboldened, she ventured, "The Krad don't seem to fear you."

"The Krad aren't human. You are. Remember that."

He hadn't moved, yet everything had somehow shifted and she was more aware than ever of the blank hood where his face should have been. She swallowed and forced herself to speak anyway. "And the lion? What is she? Why are you afraid of her?"

When his gloved hand curled around the hilt of the broken sword in his belt, and his thumb rubbed the stone in the crosspiece, Mirianna worried she'd pressed too much. Yet the gesture didn't seem threatening, and she thought she'd seen him perform it before. She was wondering about its significance when he crossed his arms and startled her with the force of his scrutiny. "You said the lion spoke to you. What did she say?"

"I—she said 'Come,' and—and 'Not all of the beasts.' Twice."

"'Not all of the beasts'? When did she say that?"

Mirianna flushed. Enduring Rees's assault had been humiliating enough without having to relive it for this cold column of blackness bent on interrogating her.

She wished she hadn't started the process by trying to get answers from him. Answers he hadn't yet deigned to give. Scowling, she muttered, "Rees—uh—one night Rees tried to—he wanted—"

"The bastard forced himself on you?" She detected anger in the harsh, clipped words. "And the lion attacked him?"

"No—I mean—yes, Rees tried, but the lion didn't attack. She screamed. And then I saw her eyes. And she spoke to me."

"'Not all of the beasts.' And you took it to mean...?"

She shrugged. "Rees. The Krad. Anything living in the Wehrland. Rees had just said our fire would keep the beasts at bay, but she seemed to be telling me..."

"That there are beasts in the Wehrland that aren't afraid of fire? Beasts, perhaps, like me?"

Her gaze shot to his hood, then dodged the empty blackness. She trusted the lion, and the lion had brought her to the Shadow Man, so she ought to trust him—whatever he was—if the lion did so. "No. She brought me *to* you. She saved me from the Krad and brought me straight to you." Mirianna licked her lips. "Who or what is she?"

She thought he wouldn't answer as he stood with arms crossed and hood tilted toward the floor while dust motes her broom had stirred floated on the air.

Finally, he sucked in a breath that pulled at the fabric of his hood. "My sister. Perhaps." And he walked out.

Chapter Seventeen

When Durren returned to the courtyard, the lion was sauntering toward the outer gate. The beast paused at the sound of his boot kicking a pebble and looked over her shoulder.

What do you want from me? his mind messaged.

What I've always wanted, Durren. But you're not ready to give it. Yet. She flicked her tail, and the black-lined lips curved. *Enjoy my gifts. Both of them.* Then she faded into thickening shadows.

Durren kicked another, bigger stone. He wanted to throw it, but he knew the lion would evade his best effort, and an emphatic kick at least gave him the satisfaction of thumping something. Besides, in the unlikely probability the lion were truly Ayliss, she would do as she damned well pleased regardless of what he thought, wanted, or said. Just as she'd always done since they were children and she'd watched his training with cool emerald eyes...

"That sword should be mine," Ayliss was saying as she looked over the top of the scroll she'd been studying. "I'm the firstborn by more than a year."

"Don't be daft." Durren hefted the Sword of Drakkonwehr once more, enjoying a balance so perfect he could imagine himself easily fending off the mage-spawn of Beggeth even though the weapon wouldn't come to him until his sixteenth birthday. Four long

217

years. He sighed and replaced the weapon in its sheath over the mantel. "Koronolan gave it to his sons. His sons, Ayliss."

"Can you recite the Deeds of Kiros? In Shadowspeech? I can."

"I'll know it when I have to. I need to learn the ways of a warrior first. I can't spend all day reading Owender's History—"

"No," she said with a look he couldn't decipher, "you've better things to do, training to protect the world and all that."

"Look, I didn't choose when to be born, and I don't make the rules—"

"Rules? Or traditions?" Ayliss tossed aside the scroll and stood. At thirteen, she was already as tall as a young willow, and he had to look up at her. Durren couldn't wait for the growth spurt his feet promised was coming. Then she would see what it felt like to look up to him *for a change. But Ayliss was already speaking. "Did you ever think—isn't it possible that one person can't possibly know everything? I mean, have you any idea what's in these scrolls? There are spells and chants here and—"*

"Father will teach me everything."

Her eyes flashed with more heat than he'd ever seen in them. "Yes, everything he *knows. Listen, I could help you. We could work together and—"*

"You?" He stared at her, aghast at the idea she could have any part in his training. She was just jealous, as always, wishing she hadn't been born a woman.

Her face shut down, the animation gone like the flicker of a firefly, vanished before the viewer realizes

what he's seen. "Forget I said anything." Scooping up
her scroll, she swept from the room...

She never broached the subject with him again but
buried her nose in the scrolls stuffed into chests and
stored in the crannies of chambers deep beneath
Drakkonwehr. At some point she must have uncovered
the Dragon Chant, deciphered it, and realized its
significance. And then she'd sought out the mage. Or
Syryk had sought her. Sinking down onto a fallen
granite block, Durren ground bits of rubble under his
heel. Who had sought whom didn't matter. Either way,
she'd betrayed them all: her heritage, her very own
brother, even Errek—the lovesick fool!

Pain twisted in Durren's chest, as sharp and breath-
stealing as the first time—every time!—he relived his
best friend's death at his own hand. With a shuddering
effort, he bundled up the misery and flung it at his
sister. *Why did you do it, Ayliss? To 'ride the Dragon'?*
What in Beggeth did you mean by that? The Dragon
was the tool of evil, of the Black Mages. She knew as
well as he that it had to stay buried or the world would
come to ruin.

The ache always concentrated itself just below the
arch of his ribs, and he pushed there against it, holding
it in so it couldn't rip him apart. But his memories
refused to be contained. Whatever it was Ayliss wanted,
she hadn't succeeded because she'd died when she
closed her hand on the bloodstones. With his own eyes
Durren had seen her die.

Hadn't he?

Illusion.

The idea seared like acid through his
consciousness, burning holes in what he'd thought to be

truth, shredding great gaps in what he'd believed for all these years to be reality, dissolving—at last—the fundamental belief he'd been stubbornly clinging to despite the jarring events of the past few days. His hand fell into his lap, and the pain in his chest rushed out, firing along all of his nerves. He could barely breathe, but the pain was secondary to what swept through him on its heels, the shock of letting go, of seeing—now—how he just might have been...wrong.

If Ayliss didn't die...if she were in fact still alive...still living...then that changed...*everything.*

Durren reeled, staggered by the earthquake-like shift in what he knew, what he thought, what he thought he knew. If Ayliss didn't die, if he'd been wrong about that, what else had he been wrong about? Was it possible...could it be...was her betrayal some kind of...illusion?

He gripped his head while questions buzzed like a nest of stirred wasps inside it. He tried to hold them in before they overwhelmed him, but they squeezed out in a rush. If Ayliss didn't die, what had happened to her after he interrupted the Dragon Chant and broke the mage's crystal column? The blast of spell energy had thrown him leagues away and rendered him what he was now. Had it thrust her into the form of a lion? Was she now trapped in the body of the beast? And why hadn't she appeared to him before? Fourteen years had passed—why the demon hadn't she appeared? Why had he been left all alone for so damned long!

He must have made some sound, for the boy sat up and yawned. With a mighty effort, Durren tamped down his frustration and misery. "Feel ready to work, Gareth?" he said when he could control his voice.

"Oh yes, sir." The boy grabbed his staff, and Durren let him struggle to his feet.

"The horses need grooming. Can you manage that?"

"If you'll show me the gear, I'll get right to it, sir."

While he led the boy to the packs beside the wall, Durren shoved the maelstrom of his thoughts about his sister to the back of his mind and forced himself to assess the boy's condition. Gareth looked rested, not so pale, and the gash on his forehead seemed to be healing. The woman had done well to feed him and dose him with the herbs.

She's resourceful. You should trust her.

Ignoring the voice in his head, he wondered instead if he should ask the boy about the lion, whether Gareth knew the beast had been practically cradling him all afternoon. Since the boy's face seemed unconcerned, Durren decided not to disturb his equanimity. If the lion were truly Ayliss, she would be back. This was her home, after all.

And if the lion isn't Ayliss?

The idea raised chills along his backbone. He wanted to believe she was alive, that she had returned, that—*by Koronolan!*—she wasn't the traitor he'd believed she was, but the skeptic in him had been wary too long of illusions, however appealing.

He stared at the gate through which the lion had vanished, seeing nothing there but shadows. If she were not Ayliss, she would most likely be back, too—whatever her reason might be.

****

Tired as she was, Mirianna couldn't sleep. Even though her throat caught every time she thought of her father—and she thought of him hourly—she refused to worry about him. He was with Pumble and Rees, who were pledged to bring him and the gems safely to the Master of Nolar. Besides, if they failed, what could she do? How could she even know? He could be lying in a bramble thicket right now and—

She choked back a sob, then turned on her pallet and listened to see if she'd disturbed Gareth. Although the boy insisted he wasn't tired, he'd fallen asleep almost instantly. She didn't begrudge him the rest, knowing he would heal faster the more he slept, but in the confines of the room, she could hear the precise moment when the boy's breathing pattern shifted and she knew he was dreaming. He wasn't dreaming now, but breathing regularly.

Nonetheless, she decided she couldn't sleep until she'd dealt with at least some of the concerns milling in her mind. Throwing off her blanket, she pulled on her boots and slipped out into the night.

Near the dark peaks soaring above the fortress, the stars looked as if a giant hand had sown them there like fine seed. Mirianna had never seen so many, nor felt so close to them. If she climbed up to the tower, she fancied she could reach out and pick them like a handful of ripe berries. But she hadn't come out to admire the stars. Drawing her cloak about her shoulders, she told her eyes to look for something blacker than the sky, darker than the night itself. Did the Shadow Man sleep? She thought he must, but she suspected he would be no more able to rest this night than she.

She found him on the wall, looking down into the valley, his braced arms spreading his cloak like the wings of a great bat. She'd come up the tower stairs with care, knowing the steps would be broken in places. Still, her boots crunched enough rubble he must have heard her although he made no sign when she stepped onto the rampart. Wondering what so absorbed him about the view, she glanced over the side.

The rocky outcrop underpinning the fortress plunged so precipitously that, when her heart beat again, Mirianna realized she'd hooked her fingers like talons into the stone. She had no fear of falling, rather an unsettling sense that if she weren't anchored, she might simply float off over the narrow valley whose depths were as black as spilled ink.

While she searched for a glimmer of something, anything that would mark the limits of the plunge, out of the impenetrable gloom rose wisps of sulfurous mist. They drifted toward one another, forming pale yellow ribbons that wove themselves snake-like among the treetops visible below. One lifted like a thread of smoke and she watched it dance, curling in and upon itself, until she realized the thin fingertip, ever rising, had come inexorably closer to where she stood on the wall. With a shudder, she tore her gaze from the view and stared at her hands, at the starlight glinting from the pitted granite where her fingernails had scored it.

She shivered again, trying to cast off a gathering sense of dread, and turned her gaze into the courtyard from which she'd climbed. Whatever inner rail had prevented guardsmen from falling off the rampart was long gone, and the rubble piles below seemed knife-edged as they stretched upward. She'd crossed that courtyard moments ago and thought nothing of the darkness, but from here it looked black as pitch. Feeling as if she teetered on the brink of something menacing no matter which way she stepped, Mirianna pulled her hand inside her cloak and forced herself to turn toward the Shadow Man.

"What do you intend to do with us?" She'd meant to speak with confidence, but in the stillness her voice sounded shrill.

He leaned farther over the wall as if he meant to take flight and soar over the spear-pointed pines and spruces piercing the darkness below. At the last moment his head lowered, his shoulders hunched, and his hood seemed to press itself into the very stone between his hands. "Do you have any idea how it feels to be alone? Completely and thoroughly alone?"

His response startled her, not for the question alone, but because of how the words sounded ripped from his soul—if a being like the Shadow Man had a soul. Mirianna put out her hand again, seeking the support of the wall. If this was truly Durren of Drakkonwehr, and he'd lived in this place since the fall of the Stone Dam at Herrok-Eneth, he had indeed been alone for a very long time. "I—"

"Do you have any idea what it's like to know everyone is terrified of you? That they deal with you only because they have to? To know that if you dare show yourself to anyone, you'll kill that person?"

She sought something to say that would offer comfort to a being clearly in misery, but before she could form words, he pushed away from the wall and turned so sharply she thought his cloak slapped her even though Gareth could have laid his length between the Shadow Man's body and hers.

"Isn't it enough that I can't show *my* face? Why

must everyone else refuse to show me theirs? You with your glorious hair and shining eyes men can't stop staring at—you can't possibly know how that feels."

Mirianna flushed, heat rushing from her face through her torso to her toes. That a creature as dark as he, with the powers she'd witnessed, could suffer such apparent misery had taken her by surprise. Nonetheless, her heart had been reaching out to him, seeking some way to ease his pain, until he had said that. Too many gazes in Nolar—and since—had been directed at her in ways he couldn't possibly imagine for her to let his comment go without reproach.

She drew herself up and faced him, trying not to blink while she fixed her gaze on the blank hood. "I know how it feels to be looked on with lust, if that's what you mean. And I know how it feels to be looked on with eyes that covet me like an object to be collected." Her voice shook, but she forced herself to finish, to confront the core of her fear. "Isn't that exactly how you look at me from behind that mask?"

She sensed an alteration in the Shadow Man's posture. Where before she'd felt barraged by his emotions, now she perceived he'd regained control although his energy still sizzled in the air around her.

"Yesterday," he said, his voice faintly hoarse, "when I drove off the Krad, you were my prize. I admit it. But understand me when I say this—much of me is still a warrior. And a man. And you are...beautiful."

Mirianna shivered. At least he was being honest—somehow she was sure of that—even if his reply confirmed her worst fears. Which part of him coveted her—the man or the fiend? She drew her cloak tighter around her body with fingers that shook and wondered if the gesture was futile. He'd seen her body already—part of it—if he were indeed the shadowy figure in her dreams. That waking dream in the chamber that had been his in Ar-Deneth, she'd let him touch her and—

She flushed to the roots of her hair. He couldn't possibly be her dream lover. He was a nightmare, a creature of dark magic. Biting her lip, she shoved those thoughts out of her head and focused on what had brought her up broken stone steps in the middle of the night.

"And now? I believe you didn't plan to waylay us and carry me off, that what you did was an impulse and that...now...you may be wondering if you may have made a mistake." She glanced at the stretch of stone beneath her feet and tried to draw strength from it before she made her final plea. "As for me, what I said—what I promised..."

"Was prompted by fear—I know."

His voice sounded so gentle, so human, she looked up with a fluttering heart. "Then, can you release me from it?"

"No."

She should have expected his answer, but the finality of the single syllable left her stunned, especially after the barely perceptible pause preceding it. "I—" She took a step back, crunched pebbles under her heel, and ought not to have lost her balance, but the rampart swayed under her feet and she stumbled dangerously close to a gap in the wall. All around her, the night groaned like a great birthing beast. A shower of mortar rained from the lintel of the tower door and she stared at it before she realized everything was silent and still again, but for a rapid, heavy thudding against her shoulder.

The Shadow Man's cloak enveloped her, as did his arm about her ribs. She'd dug fingers into his sleeve, fingers that didn't immediately obey her order to uncurl from a solid, bunched bicep. "Wait," he said when she stirred in his grasp. "There's often a second tremor."

His breath brushed the hood against her forehead, each puff a separate caress that tingled along the nerves at the side of her face. "What—what was that?" A delicious languor stole through her limbs, holding her still. She ought not to be enjoying this. She was terrified. He was a fiend. Something was shaking the very rocks she stood upon.

Mirianna gasped. Something was indeed shaking the wall, and the fortress around her, making the stones grind and groan while the Shadow Man held her tight, his free hand locked onto a huge iron ring set into the wall.

"Is it over?" she said when the earth stilled again.

"For now." He relinquished his grip on the iron ring. His arm remained, and her breasts prickled against the pressure of his muscles compressing them.

She bit her lip and trembled, as much from the shock of the strange motion as from the continued contact. "I—what about Gareth?" She pushed at his arm. "He's probably terrified. I should check—"

"I suspect he's slept through it. The shaking is more pronounced up here, and the noise echoes in the valley."

"But the chamber—"

"It's held up this long. It won't collapse when the Dragon makes a turn."

"The Dragon?" She pushed at his arm, and this

time he let her go so she could spin and face him. "You mean, it really *is* alive?"

"Sleeping."

Mirianna's legs quivered. She needed to sit down, but nothing seemed handy on the open rampart, so she turned toward the tower, intending to sit on a stair, but the Shadow Man caught her before she could move two steps and pulled her back against his chest.

"You dream of me, don't you?" he said as her breath hitched in her throat and that strange languor that contact with his body seemed to induce spread through her limbs.

She nodded, and from somewhere deep inside rose the question her conscious mind had been too terrified to ask. "And you dream of me, too,...don't you?"

"For ages, it seems." His hood caressed her cheek like a warm breath. "Have I touched you?"

Touched me? Her womanly core clenched, shooting little pulses of fire along all the nerves hidden there. *By the Dragon, you know you have.* All her bones dissolved, and she melted into him, her flesh spreading across the heated solidity of the body that supported her. Her ribs merged with muscle-corded ribs, her head pressed into sinew-wrapped collarbones, her thighs spread themselves across rock-hard legs, her hips molded themselves around a solid shaft of aroused manhood.

Heart pounding, she tried to turn in his arms, to open her cloak, to offer her throat, her shoulders, even her breasts to his caress, but his free hand on her abdomen held her firmly in place. She moaned in protest until his gloved fingers spread across her belly, scorching her skin beneath layers of skirt and tunic. The fingertips kneaded gently, mere inches from the apex of her thighs. Mirianna breathed with thready gasps, her body an aching, throbbing mass of sensation focused on five pinpoints of delicious pressure moving slowly, deliberately closer to the recesses of her body that yearned, pleaded for their touch.

"Please..." she whispered.

He stilled.

She held her breath, waiting for the delicious sensations to resume, yet sensing a change in him. Finally, she reached for his hand—to do what, she had no idea—but he spun her out of his arms and she stood, swaying like a sapling in the wind, beside the door to the tower steps while he strode—leagues, it seemed—away from her. When he turned, he said, "Go back to the boy."

"But—"

"You don't know what you're asking."

As the night air chilled her skin, it came to Mirianna very clearly just what she'd been asking. Mortified, she backed against the tower wall and sat down with a thud on the step she'd been seeking moments—hours?—ago. The dead, dry, bone-deep cold of the stone drove the fire-flush from her body, leaving her quaking almost as wildly as the stones had done only moments—hours?—ago.

When she gathered enough wit to stand, she rushed down the tower stairs and didn't stop running until she closed the chamber door behind her and barred it with as many of the rickety pieces of furniture she could lay her hands on in the dark. Panting, she dove under her blankets, knowing full well her barricade was useless. If the Shadow Man wanted to come to her, he had only to enter her dreams.

****

Durren strode along broken ramparts, leaping gaps and clambering across rubble. By Kiros, he would traverse the entire wall ten times—a thousand!—if it would cool the fire in his blood. Dear Koronolan, he could have had her right there on the crumbling rampart, on the cold stone, up against the tower wall if he'd chosen. She'd lain against his body not like a sacrificial victim but like a woman offering herself to her lover. Freely.

But he'd known full well her offer was not truly free. This was magic, this linked dreaming. She was awake now—finally—and so was he, and neither of them needed to act while entranced. If she were to give herself, he wanted her awake, aware, and willing—not spellbound or even—damn it all!—obligated.

That promise she'd made—*by Kiros, she should never have offered that much! He* would never have asked it of her, but the Shadow—the damned Shadow!—had coerced it from her. And now *he* had to hold her to it, at least until he could figure out why the she-lion had brought her to him. What possible role could this woman have in whatever magic appeared to be unfolding? How could the she-lion—Ayliss—know about the woman he'd been dreaming of for almost as long as he'd been confined here? Hadn't the lion appeared only days before he first encountered the woman? And this woman was human, as limited in years as the boy. She couldn't be more than twenty. Why her? Why now? What could possibly have set in motion these events?

Durren ran at another gap in the wall and leaped,

his cloak snapping in the breeze he made, but the toe of his boot caught on something, and he landed in a sprawl. Breathing hard, he pulled his legs out of the void and leaned into the solidity of what had once been a guard tower, now roofless against the sparkling stars. He sat, absorbing the chill reality of stone, the clamminess of sweat sticking his tunic and hood to his skin.

You can't escape if you run in a circle, the Voice in his head said.

He wished he could reach into his skull and silence the voice once and for all, but the damned thing that had awakened with him after the spell-blast was right. Blowing out a breath, he looked down into the courtyard. Deep shadow hid most of the rubble, and starlight gilded the walls, making them look whole where he knew full well they were not. Just as he knew full well the terms of the promise he'd brokered with the woman—her company, her presence, her companionship. Not one word of her body open beneath his, not one word of coupling, though—*by Kiros!*—he could think of almost nothing else. Not when every fiber of his being was trained on the chamber whose location he knew with the same surety a homing bird knows the location of its roost.

Chapter Eighteen

A clatter and a muffled "Ow!" brought Mirianna bolt upright and blinking in the dimness. She had the blanket clutched to her chin when she realized it wasn't the Shadow Man but Gareth who'd toppled her barricade and sat on the floor holding his shins.

She threw back the covers. "Are you hurt?"

"No." He rubbed his face across drawn-up knees. "But I thought for sure I knew where the door was."

"You did—you do know." Crawling to him, she ran her hands over his shins and found, to her relief, nothing worse than bumps that would likely bruise. "It's my fault. I blocked the door."

"Why?"

"Um..." She sat back on her heels. Why indeed? What could she possibly tell him that he would understand? His cheeks were still unmarred by stubble, and his voice had yet to deepen. What did he know about the desires that drove men and women? "I—it doesn't lock, and I was afraid..."

"My master will protect us. He drove off the Krad, didn't he?"

"Yes, of course." She wanted to hug the boy to her, to shelter his innocence from all the evil in the world that lay in wait for him, for anyone who lived long enough to encounter it.

"Well, then..." He pulled his feet under him and

232

prepared to rise, but his eyes searched for her in the dimness. She could see a hint of fear, of doubt lurking behind his bravado. Had she put it there?

She remembered how the Shadow Man had thrown himself between her and the lion, how he'd kept her from harm on the ramparts, how he'd risked himself for her, for the boy, for all of them with the Krad. Although his power overwhelmed Rees and Pumble, she suspected he wasn't invulnerable. "You're right. Your master is very brave. I guess I was just scared in the dark."

Gareth grinned. "Good thing you're not blind."

Despite herself, despite all the turmoil of the night and the sleeplessness scratching at her eyes, she laughed. "You're absolutely right." Rising, she cleared away the furniture and opened the door. "Do you remember the way to the privy?"

"I could walk it with my eyes closed."

Her heart lurched with tenderness, with admiration, but she covered the ache with another laugh. Ruffling his hair would probably embarrass the boy. And that would embarrass her.

Gareth was still grinning when he set off, tapping his way across the courtyard.

Mirianna watched him slowly but surely navigate the obstacles until the weariness of a sleepless night made her drop onto a bench and drag both hands over her face. Who was this creature who kept them here? The Shadow Man, Durren Drakkonwehr, or whoever he was, could have had her last night. She flushed, remembering how willingly she had—there was no other word for her behavior—*offered* herself. She'd had no rationality, no reason, no control whatsoever, and he could have taken her right there on the rampart.

Shuddering, she ran her hands up and down her arms. He'd had the perfect opportunity, but he'd inexplicably turned her away. He could have crept into her mind, into this very chamber, but he'd stayed outside. True, she'd tried to ward him off from her dreams by staying awake, but she remembered now, in the brittle morning light, that she hadn't been sleeping in Ar-Deneth when he'd come to her in the room that had been his. Goosebumps prickled her body.

Mirianna shoved her hands into her hair and fastened it away from her face. Somehow, some way, the Shadow Man, Durren Drakkonwehr—whatever he was—had been part of her dreams for as long as she could remember dreaming. The realization raised another wave of gooseflesh, but she could no longer deny the connection between them. What she needed to do now was find out why it existed. And that would require another round of confrontation with a Shadow. Standing, she squared her shoulders. This time she would tackle him in the daylight. With Gareth around.

Stepping out into the courtyard, she wondered where the Shadow Man had spent the night and if he'd spent it in any more comfort than she. By the Dragon, she hoped he felt just as bedraggled this morning. *It would serve him right!*

****

When Durren entered the courtyard, the woman at the well started, dropping her bucket. Water splashed her legs, but she ignored it, regarding him as warily as a sheep regards a wolf. She was still afraid, he noted, but her look had become more direct, and her chin rose in an attitude of defiance.

The thought lifted a corner of his dark mood, but he had no idea why. His head throbbed from too many hours without sleep, his eyes burned, his joints ached from a night surrounded by cold stone. Whatever solace a soak in the pool had given him yesterday had drained away entirely. He eyed the woman, noting she looked pale and drawn, her mouth pinched.

She looks as bad as you feel, said the Voice in his head.

Good! Serves her right. Sitting by the cook fire, he poured himself a cup of heated water and greeted the boy, who replied around a mouthful of porridge. All the while she watched from the well. He lifted his hood just enough to slip the cup under it.

About time she sees how you live.

Hah! If SHE weren't here, I wouldn't have to be so careful about keeping my face covered. The test in Ar-Deneth had proved the boy was safe, but she—she had perfect vision.

Just whose decision was it to bring her here? the Voice in his head said. *And when was the last time you unveiled in broad daylight—by choice?*

Durren choked on a swallow of water, coughed, and cleared his throat. After the first shock of the spell damage, he'd refused to look upon himself, using the pool to bathe and the tunnels to dress. Scowling, he drained the cup and removed it from his hood. *That doesn't mean I want to give up my choices.*

The woman still hadn't moved, even to pick up the bucket. Using a spoon he found lying near the cook fire, he scooped out porridge into his empty cup. The smell of the oats, plain and humble, teased at his nostrils like a king's banquet and he remembered he hadn't eaten since yesterday morning. Just then, his stomach growled long and loud.

The boy clapped a hand over his mouth, and Durren heard a sound he hadn't heard in years. Giggling. He sat, stunned, while the boy coughed, flushed, and hung his head.

"I'm sorry, sir. I didn't think—I mean, I didn't know..."

"That my stomach growls just like yours when it's hungry?"

The boy nodded tentatively.

"Well, it does." Durren set down his bowl uneaten. Amid the stress of the flight to Drakkonwehr, the Krad attack, and his preoccupation with the woman, he hadn't given any thought to how the boy perceived him. What kind of stories had Ulerroth and the others in Ar-Deneth told him? Reaching out, he touched the boy's knee. "Listen, Gareth, in many—most ways, I'm no different from you. You have nothing to fear from me. If my stomach makes funny noises, feel free to laugh."

"You won't mind?"

Durren considered; this was Gareth, not anyone else. He picked up his porridge. "I might laugh with you."

The boy's grin lit up his face.

A strange sensation stretched Durren's lips and he paused, wondering what it was. It was a smile, he realized, a genuine, happy smile, not the bitter, twisted smile he'd grown so used to over the years. Only Ghost, in a periodic coltish mood, could elicit such a smile from him, and he couldn't remember how long ago that had occurred. He ate in bemused silence, his mood lightening with the day.

Only when the boy laid aside his empty bowl and rose did Durren notice a pensive expression had replaced his grin. Once again, Durren wondered if he should have brought a blind boy into a place fraught with so many dangers, but with the Krad active so close to Drakkonwehr, the beads had been cast: there could be no turning back now. "How are you settling in, Gareth? Finding your way around?"

"I've a good memory, sir. Once or twice and I've got the lay of things. With a bit more time, I'll be no trouble at all to you, sir. It's just..."

Durren gave thanks the boy had never learned to guard his expressions. "Tell me what's troubling you. I'm not a mind-reader, whatever you may have heard." He hadn't meant to sound gruff, but the boy stirred in him odd, vaguely...*protective* urges. The sensations were unsettling at the least—irksome even.

The boy chewed his lower lip, pinking the skin with faint teeth marks. "Well, I know it's not my place to say, but...are you really going to make her stay?"

After a moment of perplexity, Durren realized *her* referred to the woman and not the she-lion. The boy— *Kiros be thanked!*—remained blissfully unaware of the lion's existence. Frowning, he reviewed his memories of the woman and boy together. He would wager the stones he'd traded to Ulerroth the two seemed well suited. "Why? Has she been disagreeable to you?"

"Oh no, sir! She's nicer than Freth and Nell together. And she smells sort of...sweet. Not like mutton and ale, but like sunshine and—and flowers."

Like lilacs and wood smoke and...woman, said the Voice in his head.

Blood rushed to his groin, and he fancied he could

detect her scent even though his consciousness told him she still stood by the well halfway across the courtyard. By Kiros, he needed to think, not react. With a deep breath, Durren willed his eyes to open and his heartbeat to slow enough he could grasp what the boy was saying.

"...took care of me, but..." The boy swung the top of his staff in a circle, grinding pebbles under its foot. "She thinks I don't know, but she was crying last night." Cocking his head in Durren's direction, he scratched at the puckered scab over one eyebrow. "Did you know?"

No, he did not.

He must have said something appropriate because Gareth left to tend the horses, leaving Durren alone and feeling as if a boulder had fallen from the wall and flattened him.

While he sat thus stupefied, the woman refilled the water pot on the coals, set aside the bucket, and sat across from him, tucking her skirt about her legs. When she raised her gaze to his hood, he realized he hadn't even asked her name.

Mirianna, the Voice in his head supplied. *That's what the old man called her.*

Her father. With a twist of his gut, he realized she hadn't said anything about the old man although he suspected—now he took the time to think about it—she must miss her father terribly. Hadn't she offered herself—made that damned promise—just to save him? Durren put down his bowl, ashamed of how he'd overlooked far too many details for far too long. "Last night," he said, "I'm afraid I didn't explain myself very well."

She sat primly on the rock Gareth had vacated, hands clasping her knees, the sole of one boot scuffing the toe of the other in a motion Durren found oddly mesmerizing. "You haven't answered all of my questions."

"I don't know all the answers." The words had slipped out, startling him from his trance. While he'd intended to be forthcoming, he hadn't thought to admit that much.

Tell the truth—you haven't thought about anything except as it affects you, said the Voice in his head. *Not since Herrok-Eneth fell.*

Be still! But it was the truth, and the knife of shame twisted again in his gut. For years he'd wallowed in self-absorbed misery, blaming Syryk and Ayliss for his condition and caring for nothing except Ghost. Now the earth had shifted and everything he knew seemed to be transforming before his eyes—and not all of it pleasing to look upon.

Face aflame, Durren made an effort to step outside himself, to look at the woman and see if he could divine her reaction.

She chewed her lower lip but hadn't looked away although her face paled.

She has a warrior's heart. She's scared to death of you, but she won't back down, said the Voice in his head.

She's braver than I am, going unarmed into something completely unknown. Having admitted that, Durren cleared his throat. "Ask, and I'll tell you what I can."

"Last night..." It was her turn to look away, to clasp her hands so tightly the knuckles whitened. "What exactly do you want from me?"

That was easy. He'd thought of nothing else all night. "Your presence. Your companionship. Your company."

He watched a swallow work its way down her throat. Somehow she didn't seem as reassured as he'd expected. Didn't she understand what that excluded? He opened his mouth, but she was already saying in a strained voice, "To live here? With you?"

"And Gareth." Mentioning the boy seemed important, as if his presence might somehow mitigate the situation, her fear of it.

"For how long?"

"I don't know." Something was unfolding, and she was as much a part of it as he. They had to see it through.

"To what end? For what purpose?"

Freedom from the spell that bound him? Death? Even that would be a release of sorts. Dare he hope for redemption? "I don't know."

When her gaze shot to his face, he held it through the fabric of his hood. Her eyes were rimmed with white, and he thought she might bolt if he couldn't find some way to anchor her. "Mirianna..." He tasted the name on his lips. The syllables rolled gently off his tongue, like soothing music. "Mirianna," he tried the name again now he had her attention, "I've been here a long time, living as you see, with no change—until now. Tell me why you're here, what brought you to the Wehrland."

"Are you really Durren of Drakkonwehr?"

He took a deep breath, schooling himself to patience. She had as much to wrap her mind around as he had, if not more. "Yes."

"Can you really—does looking at you—can I die if I look at you?"

He sighed. He'd spent fourteen years waiting; why should a few more moments seem so unendurable? "Mirianna, I don't lie."

She shivered and rocked in her hunched position. "What happened back then? Why didn't you die when the Stone Dam broke at Herrok-Eneth? And why do you think a lion is your sister?"

Durren rubbed his gloved hands over his thighs and glanced at Gareth, hoping the boy hadn't heard the note of hysteria in her voice. He seemed engrossed in grooming the horses, so Durren returned his attention to the woman. "I tried to stop a mage from raising the Dragon. When I broke his crystal, the spell—" He cast around for a better word, but couldn't find one. "The spell exploded, blowing out these walls. I woke up leagues away, like this." He raised black-clad arms, lowering them when her expression told him she grasped his meaning. "The Krad destroyed everything in their path, every living thing that was left." He stared at the ground between his boots. "From Koronolan on, the Drakkonwehrs have been charged with protecting the world from the evils of Beggeth. I failed, so I stayed here where I wouldn't inflict harm on anyone."

"Except when you go to Ar-Deneth."

Something about the place, or her memory of it, made her shudder so violently she almost lost her perch on the rock. Puzzled, he made his reply as gentle, as reassuring as he could. "Even a creature like me has to eat."

"Can you die?"

"Not by your hand or I wouldn't have left you that knife you carry under your skirt."

Her flush shot much needed color into her cheeks.

He wondered what discomfited her more, shame at having been caught thinking of harming him or embarrassment at knowing he'd seen so much of her bare leg. The sudden image of a long alabaster thigh sent a rush of blood to his groin, and he squirmed on the stone. *By Kiros!* He had all he could do to keep her from bolting as it was.

"Believe me, Mirianna, I've often thought the world would be better off if I had died. But I didn't, and now I'm beginning to think there may be a reason why after all."

"Because something's changed? Is that why you think the lion is your sister?"

She keeps her head, the Voice in his head said. *She's scared, but she's still thinking.*

Yes, she's smart.

Smart and brave. Not your typical woman.

Yes! Now, be still! Durren focused on the woman, on how she watched him with those wary turquoise eyes. "The lion first appeared to me a few days before I visited Ar-Deneth. Nothing has been the same since."

She licked her lips, looked down at her boot toes, rocked them up and down before glancing up under her lashes. "Even...the dream?" She flushed scarlet and balled her skirt in her fists, but she kept her gaze on him.

"Even the dream." He dug his fingers into his knees to steady himself against the roaring of his blood. "Especially the dream."

She shivered, a delicate motion of shoulders. "I

first saw the lion after we'd been in the Wehrland a few days. After Rees tried...after he tried..."

"Yes," he said, to spare her the memory. The effort earned him a quick glance and the briefest lift of her lips. He swallowed, thinking about how those lips would feel pressed to his—his anything! For once he was grateful for the hood, for how it hid his thoughts from her. He cleared his throat. "What brought you to Ar-Deneth? You said something about bloodstone."

She released the crumpled homespun and locked her hands together while her lip trembled. "My father...the Master of Nolar wanted my father to make all of his wedding jewelry. That's my father's trade, gem-cutting." She dabbed at her nose, lifted her head and stared at the top of the walls. "We had to go to Ar-Deneth because Master Brandelmore insisted he had to have bloodstone in every piece. Ulerroth didn't have enough."

"So you came after me."

"Not exactly. Rees got us thrown out of Ar-Deneth because of you." When he stared at her with a cocked head, she added, "He called Ulerroth a demon-trader for dealing with you."

Durren expelled a breath. No wonder Ulerroth had thrown them out, after an insult like that. "So you followed me."

"We tried, but the Krad made my horse bolt. And then the lion led me to you."

"And the others followed."

She nodded. "Does any of that help? Do you know now what's changed?"

He studied his hands, wondering how he could explain something magical to one who had no knowledge of it. Especially when he, who should've known all there was to know about magic, had failed so miserably in his studies. The Sword had been his calling, always, but that was no excuse—not then and not now. He drew in a breath and let it out slowly. "A spell is like...weaving. If you make a mistake, or change something before the spell is complete, all someone has to do is pull the right thread and the whole thing will unravel. I just don't know what thread has been pulled."

"Or what mistake was made." She must have sensed his sudden, sharp regard because she said with a shrug, "Well, if it's a mistake, then nothing really is changing, is it? It's just...a weak spot that's wearing out. Sometimes that's why a hole wears where it shouldn't...for no apparent reason." When he continued to stare at her, she flushed. "You said you broke the spell—"

"The crystal. The mage was using the crystal to make the spell."

She scowled—there was no other word for the look she shot him from under her brows. He resisted the impulse to recoil. No one had regarded him with such ferocity in years, but now he understood how she'd survived the Wehrland accompanied only by an aged father, a fat man, and one randy cock.

"The point is," she was saying, "you broke something. Wouldn't that create a mistake? Like when my father cuts a stone and it crumbles because it had a flaw he couldn't see." Her eyes brimmed, and she dropped her head, hiding her face under a fall of curls. Slow, fat tears splashed one after another on her knuckles.

With each glistening droplet, acid leaked into

Durren's stomach. He had no experience with tears. He'd had little enough experience with women before Syryk had changed him into a nightmare. He was a warrior. And a Drakkonwehr. Those had guaranteed him plenty of experience in bed, but other than his sister and mother, he'd never had to deal with a woman on any other terms. His life had been filled with the Sword. Women had no place in it. His mother understood that, but Ayliss never—

The woman sniffled and wiped her hand on her skirt.

Durren glared at her bent head. He'd be damned if he'd let a few tears manipulate him into pitying her. He'd taken her away from her father, true enough, but the old man was a fool to have brought her across the Wehrland for a handful of gems. Even she had to admit that. Look how they'd blundered about, stirring up the Krad. They'd been lucky to escape with their lives. If he hadn't helped them, they'd all be dead. And she couldn't deny she was safer now than she'd been with the man called Rees.

Are you sure she knows that? said the Voice in his head.

She damned well should after last night! But the voice was likely right—in some small way. Perhaps she didn't realize how safe she was, how protected—

Whistling penetrated Durren's consciousness, and he realized Gareth had finished his chores. "Stop your weeping. You'll frighten the boy."

Liar, the Voice in his head said. *The boy already knows.*

He can still be frightened! I have to stop her somehow.

For your own comfort, you mean.

Shame stabbed at him again, but he shook it off and stood.

Her breath hitched, but she dashed both hands over her face. "I'm sorry."

The boy stopped a few feet away and faced their general direction. "I was wondering, sir, if you spend all winter here, you must have a better place to keep the horses, don't you?"

Durren expelled a long breath. "You're quite right. There's some pasture and a garden within the outer wall. And part of the stable is intact. I was planning to show it to you once you got to know your way around." He breathed again while the muscles about his jaw unclenched. "Would you like to see it now?"

****

Gareth had dawdled over grooming the horses as long as he could to give them time to talk. Even though he couldn't pick out the words, he had a fair idea what they were saying from the tone of their voices. His master's was sometimes kindly, sometimes gruff—sort of like Ulerroth if he could imagine the innkeeper as someone who hadn't had a lot of practice talking. Hers sounded scared and sometimes sad.

Gareth wished he could comfort her, tell her it was all right to be sad and frightened when they were far away from everything they knew, that he'd only told the Shadow Man because he wanted to help her. He didn't think the Shadow Man wanted her to be scared. His master was just a bit...awkward around people.

He and his master were two of a kind, really. He lacked sight, but the Shadow Man lacked touch. Gareth didn't know what Mirianna lacked—maybe her father.

She was sad about that, but he understood. He would have to find a way to tell her the pain faded with time, and he mostly didn't notice the ache until something made him think about his mother. Mirianna was a little older than he, and her father wasn't actually dead like his mother was, so maybe it would go easier for her, but then she was a girl, and that could change things. Freth's mood could change in a moment, for no apparent reason, and he'd always felt uncomfortable around Nell. Mirianna wasn't like either of them, but she was still a puzzle.

She and the Shadow Man had made some sort of agreement when the Krad attacked, and now they both seemed unhappy about it, so he wasn't sure why his master was so determined to make her stay. For his part, Gareth didn't want her to leave. She was sort of like a mother and sort of like an older sister—like Freth but nicer, like his mother but younger. And it was nice to have her to talk to and to keep him company at night, even if she did cry.

He would probably have cried too, if he'd been alone here. From the courtyard, Gareth could sense the sheer size and dimensions of the place by the way sounds vibrated, resounded or echoed. In the enclosed spaces, the shadows sucked all warmth from his skin, their chill deep-seated, as though the sun hadn't touched them in ages. When he laid a hand on their walls, he could feel frost beneath the gritty surface, sense the winter freeze lying close to the bones of the place. Yet other walls radiated heat, and on one part of the path to the privy, waves of warmth rose from the stones he trod. He'd paused there more than once, wondering if his senses were misleading him, but it was always the same place and always the same temperature, day or dark.

He'd have to ask his master about that, but for now he was glad to learn this place his master called home had pasture enough for the horses as well as a garden of sorts, chickens, and a couple of kid goats who nibbled on his tunic every time he turned around or butted him gently. He'd have to set them straight about how to treat him, but maybe Mirianna could help with milking the doe, at least until the goats knew him better.

She'd followed along, leading her gelding while Gareth took the pack horse and his master led the stallion. While they loosed the animals in the pasture and explored the garden and tumble-down stable, she'd said nothing, staying just close enough Gareth could sense her presence or smell her scent, but showing no particular interest. Sadness hung about her like a heavy cloak, making her preoccupation so thick the air currents parted to flow around it. The Shadow Man, too, seemed preoccupied, answering questions, but not immediately, as if he had to be recalled to the present.

Gareth stood between them and puzzled over the auras radiating from both. They seemed to be thinking awfully hard, and now and then something passed between them, something prickly that stirred the fine hairs on his arms and made his nostrils tingle. The scent teased, never staying long enough for him to identify. He wondered if they knew what they were saying to each other, but he was afraid to ask in case they didn't. People never seemed to understand how he could know what he knew.

****

The she-lion reappeared after dusk, materializing

out of the shadow of the gate. Before Durren could form a word of warning, she sauntered to Gareth where he sat by the fire and laid her large head in his lap. The boy started violently, but the weight of her head held him trapped in place.

"Don't be afraid," Durren said, half-rising, hand closing on the Sword of Drakkonwehr. "It's a lion, but it's friendly." *Don't you dare harm him!* his mind messaged the cat.

—Trust me, Durren. For once.—

He sat down, but his hand remained on his weapon.

With half-lidded eyes, the lion butted the boy in the chest and purred. His hands, which had flown up by a face gone white, lowered by increments until one grazed her fur. She purred louder and pushed her head against his palm before he could pull it away. His fingers tentatively flexed behind one black-tipped ear.

"She saved you from the Krad. Do you remember any of that?" Durren tried to make his voice neutral, to project calm in a situation that seemed to skirt disaster. If this was Ayliss, how much of the lion was in her? Was she as much lion as he was Shadow? By Koronolan, he wished he knew.

At right angles to all of them, the woman looked as shocked as Durren felt, digging her fingers into her skirt and sitting absolutely still. Whatever she claimed about the lion, she was clearly not yet at ease with the beast. Koronolan be praised that Gareth couldn't see their faces at this particular moment.

The boy lowered his other hand and skimmed it over the lion's shoulder. "I—I thought I heard my mother...humming then." He swallowed, hard. "Are you sure the lion won't..."

"You're safe, Gareth," Durren said with more conviction than he felt. "She obviously likes you." *Did you summon her?* But he dismissed the notion. The lion had appeared to him before he'd gone to Ar-Deneth, days before he'd met the boy. Something else must have brought her.

The lion peered at him through half-lidded eyes, and then raised her head for the boy to scratch her chin.

"She's so soft," Gareth said. The color had returned to his cheeks, but his touch remained tentative. Against the lion's massive head and shoulders, the boy's limbs looked as thin and fragile as kindling.

"And so loud," the woman ventured, licking her lips while her gaze flicked from Durren to the lion.

Durren's nerves strained against his control. He ought to do something, but what could he do? There was no danger he could see—if he accepted the outrageous notion that a Wehrland lion could behave like a tame cat—but his whole being still hummed with warning.

Ghost's neigh from the hidden pasture, and an answering neigh from the darkness outside the gate brought him surging to his feet, Sword drawn. "Get back out of the light!" He kicked a pot of water onto the fire, dimming it, before he spun, intending to grab the woman, but she'd already bolted past him, running not away from the intruders, but toward them!

"Papa!" she cried.

Chapter Nineteen

The old man teetered over the neck of the single horse, and his weight would've taken the woman down to the paving stones if Durren hadn't broken his fall. He lowered the old man to the ground where, with an anguished sound, the woman gathered her father into an embrace. The old man lay there limp, an unconscious bag of bones and fever.

All this registered in the back of Durren's mind while he scanned the gate, the walls, the sounds of nightfall, trying to determine if the two men were alone before he confronted the fat man perched behind the horse's saddle. Previous glances had shown the man weaponless but for a knife, and his eyes had the glazed look of one either spell-struck or frightened out of his wits.

You took his sword two days ago, the Voice in Durren's head said.

I remember. Rubbing the bloodstone in the Sword, he muttered, "*Bluet drakkenoth, ominor ay rhoenon pek,*" but the stone remained dull and dark. No magic here; nothing to fear, yet more than enough to set all his senses on alert.

"Where's your companion?" he demanded. "Where's the other one?"

The fat man blinked once. The horse stood with its forelegs braced apart and its nose nearly touching the ground. Sweat crusted its neck and flanks, telling Durren it had carried its double burden a long way.

"Get down." He pulled at the fat man's sleeve. "Gareth, come and tend to this horse."

"Yes, sir, if you think the lion will let me."

Durren looked back at the dimmed fire. *Let him up,* he messaged to the cat. *He has work to do.*

The she-lion yawned and lifted her head from the boy's lap, rolling onto her side as if she had every intention of relaxing by the fire.

You brought them, didn't you? But she only yawned again, showing a curling pink tongue and gleaming teeth.

"What's the matter with you, Papa?" The woman brushed sparse hair from the old man's face and rocked him. "Talk to me, please." She cast Durren a panicked look. "He's burning up."

The fat man finally slid to the ground, and Durren shook him again. "What are you doing here? Where's the other one?"

"Pumble, what's happened to my father?"

At the woman's voice, the fat man stirred, mopping his face with a tunic sleeve. "Krad," he said, and regarded the soaked sleeve as if he'd never seen it before.

"Krad?" she breathed.

"He got cut...back in the fire circle, I guess. Doesn't take much, just a nick. He couldn't stay in the saddle. Rees was all for leaving him, but..." He shook his head and blinked as if trying to bring his surroundings into focus.

"But what?" Durren prodded. "Where's this Rees?"

Squinting like a mole, the fat man turned, gaped,

and dropped with a thump to the paving stones, the impact raising clouds of fine dust around his posterior. Grabbing a charm at his neck, he kissed it and muttered over it in a voice that squeaked.

Durren resisted the urge to slap him. Coming out of a trance was disorienting enough without the added consternation of finding oneself in an unfamiliar place, but only the fat man could know what—if anything—might have followed them up the mountain. "Stop whimpering. You're safe as long as you tell us what we want to know. Understand?"

The fat man's gaze skittered from the woman to the boy holding his horse and back past Durren's knees to the woman again. "Do as he says," she told him.

Her voice must have sounded calm, reassuring to the fat man, but Durren heard the fear in it. She clutched her father so tightly, he could see her whitened knuckles. He gave her a little nod, to show his gratitude, and addressed the fat man again. "Start at the beginning. After you left us, what happened?"

The fat man mopped his face with the other sleeve. "Rees—he wanted to make distance, so after we found my horse, we rode till the old man fell off. I didn't drop him, miss, but he couldn't hang on anymore."

"Where was he cut?" Durren said.

"A scratch, that's all. Didn't even bleed." He licked his lips. "Just there, above the boot."

The woman grabbed at her father's legs, baring both to the knees. Even in the dimness the swollen, reddened area, large as a man's fist, glared at them from his right calf.

Two days gone. Durren's stomach contracted, tightening the knot that had formed there when the old man fell from the horse. If the old man had been stabbed outright, he would've died within hours. Died *out there,* where no one would find the bones for weeks, even years. But this—this was just as deadly, and it had come *inside.*

Muscles tensed along Durren's jaw as his memory played the messy details of death and its aftermath in the courtyard, walls, and chambers of Drakkonwehr. Even now, he could detect the stench of old blood rising with the day's heat from the paving stones. He'd tried to put the carnage behind him. By Kiros, he'd kept the place *clean!* And now these fools had brought Death back inside!

He was still trembling when he noticed the woman looking at him, her pinched face full of questions. Once again, he gave thanks for the hood's ability to hide his thoughts. "Krad poison," he told her. "It works by paralyzing the limbs."

The fat man nodded. "Rees—I don't know what's gotten into him. He yelled and took the gem pouch and told me to mount up and leave the old beggar—sorry, miss, but that's what he called him. He was going to die anyway, see? And he'd just slow us down. That's what Rees said. He was all hot for getting back to Nolar, but I didn't think it was right, leaving the old man like that." He cradled his cheek with a plump, dirty hand and sniffled.

"So he hit you and took off by himself."

The fat man hung his head. "He used to be my best friend."

"And then what happened?"

"We got on the horse, the old man and me. I thought maybe I could find the way back to Ar-Deneth, but it got dark and I got lost and..." He trailed off and sat staring into space.

Durren's senses screamed at him to load the two men onto the horse and send the animal with its burden of Death staggering back into the Wehrland. To let the Krad finish what they'd begun. The beast-men were likely trailing them anyway, scenting weakness. If the Krad slaked their appetites with these two, maybe the creatures would retreat down the mountain instead of lurking in the valley so close to Drakkonwehr. His own trail, and the boy's and woman's, was too cold for them to follow now, the tantalizing scent of the boy's wound dissipated.

What's more, he hadn't invited this gelatinous bag and his passenger into Drakkonwehr. They were trespassers, and—hospitality be damned!—he owed them nothing.

That's right, said the Voice in his head. *The Shadow Man doesn't owe them a thing.*

The remark stung like cold steel. *But I do—is that what you're saying?*

Depends on whose home this is.

Acid churned in Durren's stomach. Although the woman was only whispering, "Papa, please," and he'd tried to shut his ears to the sound and balled his fists at his sides, the keening penetrated his hood, slicing at his nerves. The Shadow Man could turn them out into the Wehrland, but Durren Drakkonwehr—*Damn this body!*—could do no such thing.

"Gareth, tend to the horse. Get up, fat man, you can't sleep here." Kneeling, he scooped the old man out of his daughter's arms and carried him to the fire. *Thank you so very much,* his mind messaged the she-lion, but she merely stretched one huge paw, showing pearlescent talons before retracting them.

****

Mirianna sponged her father all night, trying to revive him, to bring the fever down. He couldn't die. Not from something as innocuous as a tiny scratch. She wouldn't let him.

She rummaged again and again in the Shadow Man's herb supply, racking her brain for recipes she'd seen the herbalist in Nolar make. She'd already spooned a bit of willow bark tea into her father's mouth, and he swallowed it. That and the sponging made his skin fractionally cooler. She made a poultice for the welt on his leg, hoping it would draw out the poison, but she couldn't be sure she mixed the ingredients in the right proportions.

Hours ago, the boy had fallen asleep where he sat, and she was dimly aware of the she-lion curving her huge body around the boy and pillowing his head on her shoulder. The rasp of her purr had become for Mirianna a barely noticed hum in the background, mingling with the music of Pumble's snores. He'd sat where the Shadow Man directed him to sit, eaten a bit of dry-cake, and promptly fallen into a deep sleep.

The Shadow Man had been gone for hours. He'd slipped off after Pumble fell asleep, and she hadn't noted his absence until now, when her eyes burned and her back cracked as if it would break into pieces. She hiccupped a sob, biting her lip to keep it from trembling. Tears would do no good, neither for her nor her father. Pushing wisps of hair from her face, she sat back on her heels and wrung out another cloth.

"You're only prolonging his suffering. And yours."

The Shadow Man's words bludgeoned her heart, but Mirianna tightened her lips and blinked droplets from her lashes. She wouldn't look up with her misery stamped on her face. She wouldn't give him the satisfaction.

He lowered himself to a seat opposite. The hood that had terrified her for so long tilted and seemed to be assessing her father's sunken features and flushed skin.

She faced the hood with her chin up. "Where have you been?" Her words accused, but what did that matter? To look upon him could kill her, but what did that matter now? Her father was dying. *Dying!* And the Shadow Man didn't care.

He rested elbows on knees and clasped gloved fingers. The hood shifted in her direction. "I was doing what I could to bar the gate. In case they were followed."

The firelight revealed fresh scuff marks on his boots. A shred of fabric dangled as if torn from the hem of his hood. He'd likely slept as little as she these last few days, but she hardened her heart against the thought. Anyone who'd survived the devastation of this fortress couldn't possibly have such mundane, human needs as sleep and solace and simple decency.

"You mean, you were doing what you could to protect yourself," she threw at him, "in case someone disturbs your precious privacy! Admit it—you'd have barred the gate against them if you could have guessed they'd come."

He sighed. She detected in the sound and the slope of his shoulders not only weariness but a deep resignation, as if she spoke a truth he already knew. With an economical movement, he produced a pail of fresh water and exchanged it for the one she'd nearly emptied.

The gesture made tears burn her throat, but she swallowed them down before speaking. "He's cooler. He'll make it."

"If he should wake, make your peace with him. You'll not have another chance." He stood and turned toward the deep well of darkness that was the ruin of Drakkonwehr.

Mirianna bit back another sob. He was leaving her, just like that, to deal with her misery and her pain and her grief. Alone. He would simply fade into the darkness out of which he'd come and in which he lived and moved and had his being, and she would be left by this meager fire with nothing but her two hands and a little knowledge of healing to save her father. And that after—after...

Her head snapped up and words jumped out of her mouth, words her mind hadn't considered but arrowed straight up from the panic choking her heart. "You promised to *save* him! Remember?"

The black hood turned a fraction, and she could see it profiled dimly against the ink of the shadows beyond. A thread of unease stirred in her stomach, but she focused all of her attention on his response. He couldn't ignore her now.

"I did save him. And you. All of you. Remember?"

"No!" She pushed upright before he finished speaking, stiff knees and numbed feet making her stagger while outrage burned white hot along her nerves. "He was hurt *then,* in that Krad attack! You *didn't* save him!"

There, she'd given voice to the thing eating at her

all night, the thing that threatened whatever hope she'd clung to that her sacrifice had succeeded and her father was safe. That he would go home to Nolar and sleep out his nights in the cottage with the little garden in the back and the herb beds along the front wall. That her world—and her life—had not ended in a smoke-filled clearing in the Wehrland.

Stiff and straight, she faced the blank hood while he turned so slowly she had to tell herself to breathe. Sparks dotted her vision. Her face tingled as if the lips she moved were not her own, but she forced them to enunciate each syllable of the one weapon that could possibly make him suffer as she suffered, make him *feel*...anything. "If he dies, my promise is void. Do you understand? If he dies, there is *no promise* between us!"

The tall column of blackness stood square across the fire. What light the embers threw upon his figure seemed absorbed by it, as though his being sucked up all that was light, all that was good, all that was life and locked it away in a pit of darkness, of nothing. She shivered, chilled now she no longer held her father's fevered body. That was the reason for the shaking, not any terror caused by confronting a shadow, a fiend, a nightmare. What would—could—he do? The terms of the promise had been broken. She owed him nothing. He had failed her.

After an interminable time, the Shadow Man turned away as slowly as he'd faced her. Without a word, he walked into the darkness, vanishing even as she tried to hold onto his shape, his essence—all the while wondering why she should want to cling to terror and failure and—

"You promised!" she shouted, but all that returned

was a shrill echo. She strode around the fire and kicked the empty bucket, sending it clattering over paving stones. The sound mocked her loneliness, her powerlessness. Choking on a sob, she stumbled back toward her father, to do what little she could, to pour herself out for him. He was all she had. If he died, what was left for her, a woman alone?

As she knelt, she glimpsed the lion's slitted yellow-green eyes. The lion had comforted her before. Even saved her. She was magic, wasn't she? "Can you heal him? Please?" she whispered.

The she-lion's ribs rose and fell gently under the boy's head. *Trust,* echoed in Mirianna's mind.

"Trust who? What? You?"

The yellow-green eyes closed and the purr intensified, enveloping Mirianna in a warmth that soaked into her bones, liquefying each one in turn. Her head hummed with the gentle sound, and the firelight faded to a glow. She was tired. So tired. If she could just close her eyes for one moment, she could lift that cloth again and wring it out. If she could just lie down next to her father for one moment, she could make more tea. If she could just...

****

Durren stood with his hands braced on the wall, staring out at the valley, seeing nothing but the deep well of darkness below. Nothing stirred but the fine threads of sulfurous mist, and nothing sounded, not even the night birds.

He'd put the courtyard with its feeble circle of light behind his back. The woman was wrong. He'd done everything he could. He *had* saved them. *All* of them. He'd kept his promise. She was just trying to get out of her part of the bargain.

You didn't want her here this morning, said the Voice in his head.

I don't want THEM here. She's supposed to stay. She promised.

This is her father. Her family. She loves him.

Love, hah! Pain and misery, you mean. She's better off without it.

Like you are?

Splinters of granite bit through the gloves into Durren's fingers. He flexed his hands, easing his grip on the stone, but the ache in his chest refused to abate. *Time—time heals.*

Then why does it still hurt like your heart's just been ripped out?

Durren ground his teeth together. He didn't have a heart. Errek's death had carved it out in huge chunks. The fall of Drakkonwehr and the Stone Dam at Herrok-Eneth had finished the amputation. What remained kept this damned body alive, bleeding and aching in stubborn echo. Enough to drive a man mad—if he would only let himself go.

He broke off a stone and hurled it into the darkness.

Pebbles aren't much good against demons. And your demons aren't out there anyway.

Durren flung another, larger stone whizzing into the valley. *Go to Beggeth!*

Why? So you can forget the woman?

Her father's dying, remember? I'm leaving her—

To suffer alone?

In peace, damn you!

Coward.

Durren broke off another piece of wall, but it crumbled in his clenched fist. Breathing hard, he watched the last grains of mortar dribble between his gloved fingers. His anger drained out with it, along with the strength in his legs. He slid down the wall until he sat on the rampart with his knees drawn up and his back pressed against the rough-hewn stone. The cold stole into his bones, but he welcomed the numbness it brought. If he could sit here long enough, perhaps it would fill him entirely. Every fiber, every muscle, every tissue in his body ached as if in these few days his body had aged every one of those suspended years.

I'm tired of the pain. I want it to end.

Then help her.

How? There's no antidote for Krad poison. He wished he could shed everything, every accumulated feeling and regret. His life was a litany of failures. Now he'd added another. The woman—Mirianna—was right about that. He was a fool to have hoped their bargain would hold, would change anything. He'd doomed himself years ago when he'd failed to learn the secrets of the scrolls.

After her ordeal was over, he would put her on her horse and send her down the mountain with the fat man. Pumble—*Was that his name?*—had proved himself decent. With adequate directions, he should be able to get them to Ar-Deneth.

So you'll wash your hands of them. Clean your conscience in the pool, just as you always do.

I'm doing the honorable thing! What more do you want? But an idea ignited in his mind. Startled by it, by the sheer, glittering possibility of a solution where there couldn't—shouldn't—be one, he sat up, separating himself from the wall. After a moment, his shoulders slumped. *It won't work.*

Doing nothing is certain failure. Warriors take risks.

So do fools. He wrapped his arms around his knees and stared at the courtyard below. The woman's fire had died to embers. He saw nothing but the reddish glow of it and, outside the circle, two disembodied pinpoints of yellow-green light that no longer sent chills down his back.

"It's time to act, Durren," said the she-lion.

"It's not that simple." He knew her now, as well as he'd known her before, but that hadn't been well enough, had it? What was she up to? Once more he wished he'd spent time studying the scrolls. Maybe they could tell him why his hair bristled at what he was about to do, why his better sense told him it couldn't possibly work, why his gut overrode every other thought, insisting he had to do whatever it took to hold the woman to that damned promise.

"Doing what's right is always simple. Not easy, perhaps, but simple."

He rose slowly, dusting his gloves and shaking kinks from his joints. "You have a lot to explain, Ayliss."

"Whenever you're ready to listen."

"Wake the boy. I'll need him."

Chapter Twenty

Mirianna woke when the first pale fingers of dawn reached into the courtyard. She rubbed both hands over her face, her limbs stiff with cold, her mind muzzy with half-remembered dreams. She'd been holding her father. He was sick, and she'd been trying to cool his fever.

She sat up, saw the fire had died, and wondered why she'd been sleeping in the courtyard when her bedding lay in the chamber the Shadow Man had found for her and the boy.

Wait! Where was the boy?

She spun, raking the courtyard, seeing nothing stirring but one large, cloth-clad lump that seemed to be...breathing. *Pumble!* She jumped up, stumbled on stiff legs, and whirled around as the events of the night rushed into her memory. "Gareth!" she screamed. "Papa!"

"Wha—?" Pumble sat up with a snort, then promptly flopped onto his back and commenced snoring.

Mirianna fought a wild urge to kick him. Instead, she spun once more, noticing the lion was gone too. Had she really been here? But Pumble was here— Mirianna could smell him now, so she wasn't dreaming. "Papa! Gareth!" Echoes amplified her cries, sending them booming off walls and turrets.

A movement caught her eye, and she spun, seeing the Shadow Man emerge from the roofless Great Hall where she'd tracked him that first morning. Was it only two days ago? She had found him down a tunnel leading from one of the chambers, and he'd warned her to stay out of such tunnels. Now, in the washed out light of early morning, the blot of his form strode unerringly around the rubble piles, followed with equal ease by the boy. Both carried bundles. Gareth's fit neatly in his arms. The Shadow Man's blanket-wrapped bundle had legs and a head.

"Papa..." Her heart wanted to rush to him; her feet kept her rooted. In the harsh morning light her father's uncovered head rested like a child's on the Shadow Man's shoulder. His face looked ashen and the wrapping—*Please let it not be so!*—looked like burial cloths. Her legs wobbled, but she stiffened them and waited while the grim party strode inexorably on.

The Shadow Man had already deposited her father on his bedding and begun speaking before her mind could attend to anything more than her father breathed! She knelt beside him and ran trembling hands over his colorless face. She touched him twice, three times before she could believe what her fingertips told her— his skin was damp but cool; the fever had abated.

"I lanced the wound to drain it. You'll need to put a poultice on it."

She looked up at the being standing across the cold fire pit. Something about the Shadow Man's chest and arms looked different, darker if that were possible. While she puzzled over that, she touched her father's shoulder. The blanket enclosing his body was wet.

Something low in her belly snapped taut, sending

out tiny waves of sensation and sucking all the moisture from her mouth. Licking her lips, she slanted another glance up at the Shadow Man. Every contour of the muscles she'd sensed under her fingertips and along the length of her back two nights ago showed where the damp blanket had molded the Shadow Man's tunic to his body. Once again she knew with heart-stopping certainty this was no hollow specter. Flesh and blood lived under that shroud. Before she could ponder the significance, he spoke.

"I've done all I can. The Krad poison had two days to work on him. If he lives, he may never be the same." He circled as if looking for something, then strode a few steps to pick up a bucket lying on its side.

Mirianna flushed, remembering how she'd kicked it into the night when he'd left her. She'd challenged him then, heaped upon him all her misery and scorn, dared him to deliver on his promise no matter how impossible, how absurd. Now he'd returned, having answered yet another of her challenges. Amid gratitude and overwhelming relief at having her father alive and seemingly improved, simmered a growing shame at what she'd said, how she'd behaved toward the Shadow Man.

"Gareth will bring you some water for your father to drink." The Shadow Man handed the bucket to the boy, who'd laid his bundle—her father's clothing—on the ground. "No one but your father drinks this water. Do you understand?"

Mirianna nodded. Her fingers clenched so hard in the blanket over her father's shoulder, liquid welled between her knuckles. "Why?" she said before she could stop herself.

The blank hood regarded some spot halfway between her and the boy. A gloved hand gripped the sword hilt at his belt while she waited for him to decide how he would answer, or if. "Because I don't know what effect drinking the water will have. There's a chance it will help his body fight off the poison."

"How much of a chance?"

"Enough that I'm willing to offer it to you. To fulfill my promise."

The emphasis on the last word set off shivers low in her belly, but she tried to quell them. She was merely cold. Worried. Exhausted.

He turned a fraction, and the regard of the unseen eyes fell on her with a palpable weight. "The choice is yours, Mirianna. If you don't want to try the water, Gareth can bring it back." He said something to the boy, and they both walked toward the roofless Great Hall.

He'd said her name. The Shadow Man—Durren Drakkonwehr—had said her name. Again. Each time the syllables reverberated within her like the tiny tuning fork her father struck to test the quality of crystals. Still quivering with something oddly like pleasure, Mirianna watched the broad black shoulders meld into the shadows. *About time he used my name.* She ignored the little voice reminding her she hadn't once called him by name. *Any* name.

****

Gareth hunkered down beside the fire pit and broke apart a dry-cake he found among the Shadow Man's stores. He hadn't eaten since yesterday's supper, and the intense general glow told him the sun was directly overhead. No wonder he was so hungry. They'd been underground for hours, what with running down to the pool again for the Shadow Man to fill the bucket.

He munched a small piece, chewing it thoroughly because Freth always said he wasn't an animal and shouldn't bolt his food. While he ate, he listened to movements around the fire pit.

Mirianna was too busy nursing her father to think of food, so he'd fended for himself. She seemed surprised at what he could do, even if she didn't say so, but she wasn't used to him yet. His mother had told him, because they were alone in the world, he had to do for himself as much as possible so she could be free to earn the coin they needed to survive. Then, when he was old enough, she taught him to earn his own coin. He snuffled and wiped his nose on his sleeve.

The smelly man still slept. According to the snoring, he hadn't stirred from that spot. The horse he and the old man had ridden had been so spent, it could hardly put one hoof in front of the other to reach the trough. Gareth had groomed the worst of the grit from its coat and poured it a measure of grain, but the animal seemed content just to stand. He'd have to check it when he finished eating. All that weight could have left it lame.

The Shadow Man had stayed down in the tunnel after filling the bucket for him. Together, they'd already gone down twice and back once, and Gareth had memorized the turnings before he had to come back alone. Besides, if he got off track, he had only to sniff the air. The rotten-eggs smell was strongest by the pool.

Gareth sniffed his hands and made a face. He would have to wash in well water to get rid of the stink and a sliminess that clung to his fingers after helping his master hold the old man in place at the pool's edge. The blanket had gotten a bit wet under the old man's head, but they'd needed the cushion because the edge was nothing but rough and ragged rock. More lumps and pebbles littered the ledge where they knelt. Even though he shifted as many as he could from under his knees and backside whenever the Shadow Man told him to stretch, the stones had poked him everywhere.

One stone, though, had smooth sides, as if something had cut it cleanly from whatever it had been part of. He'd rubbed his thumb over it, made to toss it after the others, then tucked it into the pouch of his sleeve. The stone wasn't big, about the size of a green walnut but shaped so it fit neatly into the curl of his fingers. Maybe the Shadow Man could look at it later and tell him why it was different. Or the old man, if he lived. He was some kind of gem hunter, wasn't he?

Breaking off another piece of dry-cake, Gareth shivered. His tunic was drying in the sun, but the breeze licked up the sweaty spots. Even the hair at his nape was still damp. When they'd gone into the tunnel, he'd expected the bone-chilling cold of those enclosed spaces off the courtyard, not stinking, sweltering heat.

"Forgive me," Mirianna's voice startled him. "You're hungry, and I haven't given you a thought."

"Got food," Gareth mumbled around a mouthful. "Want some?"

"You finish it. I don't think I could eat right now." Cool fingers closed around his wrist and she put a cup into his hand. "Here. You probably need something to wash that down."

He drank gratefully. "How is he—your father?"

"Resting." She exhaled, a long, deep breath that

told him some of her panic had eased. "Tell me—where did your master take him? What did he do? He didn't say much of anything...and then he left." Cloth rustled as if something refused to settle in it.

"We went down. Inside the mountain, I think. There's a pool of hot water down there, and my master wanted to soak your father in it. My master needed me to hold him when he cut the wound open. I don't think your father felt it, miss." He reached toward the sound of the fabric, hoping to find her hand and comfort her.

She grasped his instead, a quick pressure of cold fingers, before she let go. "Thank you. You were gone a long time."

He shrugged. "Did you give him the water?"

"I haven't made up my mind about it yet."

"It stinks something awful, and it's slimy."

"It leaves brown stains, too." She tugged on his sleeve.

He sniffed the fabric and made a face. "I wondered why my hands smelled so bad."

She blew out another breath, and in the ensuing silence, he worked up the nerve to ask what had been troubling him since he'd come back to the courtyard. "That lion—is she gone?"

Mirianna didn't reply for so long, he worried she didn't know what he meant. Maybe it was all a dream...but her father was real, and so were the tired horse and the smelly man.

"She comes and goes as she pleases," she said at last. "I didn't know until you looked so shocked last night that you had no idea she existed. Sometimes I find it hard to believe, too."

"My master said she saved me from the Krad. Did

she help you too?"

"Twice. And she led me to your master."

"So that's how you found us. I wondered."

They sat in silence broken only by the smelly man's snores until she said, "How much do you know about your master?"

He cocked his head, wishing he could hear more in her voice, sense more from her breathing than the vague impression her mood had shifted. She wanted something or something was troubling her. He couldn't tell which, so he thought a bit before he spoke. "I know he's the Shadow Man, and he wanted me to serve him because I can't see so he can't kill me with a look." He flushed, recalling how he'd been just as terrified of the Shadow Man as anyone in Ar-Deneth, until his attitude changed. "He took care of me when I got hurt, and he doesn't mind if I laugh when his stomach growls. He lets me do what I'm able to do, and he trusts me."

Ulerroth had been a good master, reasonably patient, and he took care Gareth had enough food, clothing, and a warm place to sleep. The Shadow Man was doing the same, but there was something more between them, something Gareth couldn't put his finger on. He sensed she needed to know about that something, but he couldn't find words.

"Why?" he said instead. "Is there something else I should know?"

Tension leaked out from her, stirring the air with the short, bated pattern of her breathing. She intended to tell him something, but she exhaled and stood. "No. That seems to be enough."

Wiping his mouth on his sleeve, he stood too. "I was thinking I should tend to the horses since I didn't get to it this morning, but if you need me, I'll stay."

"I'll be fine. Thank you."

He took his staff and headed off. Part of his mind counted the steps and paid attention to the turnings while another part wondered whether he should've asked her more about the lion and the strange sensation of comfort the creature brought.

****

Mirianna sat beside her father and inspected the water Gareth had delivered. In the bucket, it looked like well water but smelled much worse, as though sulfur were concentrated in it. Even though the water appeared clear, stains scalloped the boy's cuffs and the blanket's hem, pale rust-brown stains that materialized as the cloth dried. The liquid oozed through her fingers with a slippery, oily sensation, but she could detect nothing like the scent of lamp oil.

Should she take the risk and give her father this water? Did he need it? Whatever the Shadow Man had done with him in the tunnel, it had broken his fever. The lancing of the wound had drained away more than half the swelling and the redness. Soaking in the pool, the source of this water, had performed this miracle, according to the boy.

Raising her head, she saw Gareth across the courtyard just as he disappeared into the passage they'd taken yesterday to stable the horses. Should she have told him what she knew about his master, about the lion, about the Dragon? He didn't seem to know, but how could he not? Once more her heart ached for him, but wasn't he properly the Shadow Man's responsibility? She wasn't Gareth's mother or even his sister, and she had her own father to look after. Now they were together, nothing—*nothing!*—would separate them again. She would make sure of it. Even if that meant taking a chance on this water.

She picked up a cup and prepared to dip it into the bucket. Her silhouette stared back at her, the water glittering around the shadow she cast on its surface.

I look like him.

At the thought, she shivered and lost her nerve. Something in those rocky depths where this water came from had created the Shadow Man, had fused...*darkness* with the essence, the being of Durren Drakkonwehr. The last warrior in an ancient line and the thing of night, two not quite happily in one form. She'd encountered them both, yet she trusted... Whom did she trust? Did she have to choose? Hadn't they—together— delivered on every promise?

She regarded the cup in her hand. If she followed through on the "promise" of this water and her father lived, she would be bound to the Shadow Man—to Durren Drakkonwehr—for as long as he thought fit. Her mouth went dry at the thought of how he might want her bound to him. She'd seen enough that night on the rampart despite what he'd said the next day about "company" and "companionship." Besides, her own treacherous body seemed determined to respond to him as if he were her dream lover. Her flesh curdled at the idea, but she reined her mind back to the matter at hand.

If she passed up the water and her father died, she would be free of her promise. The Shadow Man would have to let her go, but where would she go? She would be a woman alone, far from everything she knew and without anything—anyone—to live for.

On the other hand, her father might live without

drinking the water. That was possible, but something other than logic told her there was power in the water and she needed all the water's power to save her father. If she loved him, she would do this, just as she'd made that promise in the beginning because she loved him and would do anything for him. Just as he would do anything for her.

This time, though, she would make sure the Shadow Man didn't send her father away. There was no need for him to return to Nolar. Rees already had the stones, and someone else could design the pieces. She and her father could stay here as long as the Shadow Man wanted her to stay—or at least as long as it took her father to recover.

Steeling herself, she dipped the cup and let water run into its bowl. Her hand shook, making little ripples that lapped the bucket. By the Dragon, sealing the bargain was no easier the second time—knowing more yet somehow knowing even less. What did he really want from her? Was it truly something she could give? She'd have to do her best because her father's life depended on it.

Bending, she touched the cup to her father's lips. "Papa? Here's something to drink."

His eyelids fluttered. "Mirianna, lamb, is—is that you?"

She bit her lip to stave off its quaver. He sounded so weak, his voice barely a whisper, but his eyes focused on her and recognition lit his gray face. "Yes, Papa, I'm here. Take a drink, will you?"

He sipped obediently. "Ugh! That—that's..."

"Foul, I know. Everything here tastes of sulfur. Take a little more and then you can rest."

He swallowed and then let her lay him back. His hand twitched as though he wanted to lift it but couldn't.

Her chest constricted, squeezing her heart. The Shadow Man had warned he might not be himself, that the poison paralyzed limbs. She prayed only weakness and dehydration plagued her father, that the poison was gone, but she had no way of knowing. The only surety was the water. If it had the power she'd already seen, it would save him.

Lifting his shoulders again, she put the cup to his lips. "Take a little more, Papa, please. It'll make you stronger."

****

Durren sat on a boulder at the edge of the pool with his knees up, stretching out the ache in the small of his back. In the absolute dark, only the phosphorescence of occasional bubbles rising from the depths lit the chamber. He and the boy had let the old man soak in the pool for hours. He could've undressed and supported the old man from the water. That would've been easier on the boy and his own back, but Durren couldn't bring himself to enter the pool while the wound drained into it. Nor could he do so now, though his body screamed with need.

He didn't fear the Krad poison. That was by now diluted, even purged as the water continuously freshened from below. He knew by heart the pattern of circulation and where it flowed out under the rock to join, perhaps, the source of the well water, explaining the faint sulfur taste. Nor did he fear the boy, who now knew the location of the pool and must've guessed at its power. At some point Gareth would come down unbidden and disturb him, but he hoped the boy had sense enough to come only when necessary. So far, Gareth had proved trustworthy.

He could come down when you're not here, said the Voice in his head. *To test the water for himself.*

That was a risk, true enough, but he counted on the boy's open, expressive face to betray such notions before he had a chance to act on them.

Durren clenched and unclenched his fists, tired of the way his mind danced around the real issue—this place that had been his only solace for fourteen years had hosted a *stranger.* Last night his hair had bristled at the mere thought, but he'd listened instead to his gut without considering the consequences.

The pool had shared itself willingly enough. It was a pool, after all. It didn't think, didn't react, simply healed all manner of ills he brought to it. Koronolan be praised he'd found the pool so soon after discovering the havoc the Krad had wreaked on the fortress. How would he have survived if the spell blast hadn't opened the passage to it? He couldn't remember how he'd thought to follow the tunnel down after seeking shelter in the upper chamber. Something had spoken to his spell-shocked mind, and he'd lain here in the water until he recovered enough to deal with what awaited him above ground.

That was well and good, but he needed the pool *now,* just as much if not more. There were *people* in Drakkonwehr, people he had not invited in, more people than he knew how to deal with. For more than a dozen years, he'd lived alone, interacting only with animals and hearing no human voice but his own. Visiting Ar-Deneth for a few days caused him so much consternation, he made the trip no more than once a year, if possible.

Wherever he went, people were always pushing him, testing him, trying to see if what they'd heard about the Shadow Man was true, and then treating him like a pariah when he proved their fears. Once he discovered the effect seeing him caused, he dared not unveil to anyone.

Except for those would-be robbers, the Voice in his head said.

They deserved what they got. They'd goaded him, ignored his warnings and forced the Shadow upon themselves. He thanked Kiros at least Ulerroth understood the Shadow Man's needs, providing a haven where he could trade in peace. But Ar-Deneth was of no concern here, now. He needed to deal with the problems at hand—a fat man and a sick old fool who understood nothing about where they were or how they should behave.

And the sick old fool had lain in his pool.

By your own choice, the Voice in his head said.

I don't recall having much of a choice. But the damned voice was right, as usual, and what he'd done terrified him. The woman—Mirianna—thought he'd saved her father, but none of them were truly safe. One slip, one provocation, and the Shadow could assert itself again. He'd been thinking like Durren for—what? Three days? The Shadow had owned him for more than a dozen years. It could afford to lie in wait.

Sweat ran into the corner of his mouth and he licked it away. If he stripped off his clothes, he could wash all that grit away, all that fear and loathing, suspend this misery, this frustration. For a few hours he could lie with his mind blissfully blank and just drift...

****

Gareth returned with a couple of eggs and some vegetables cradled in his tunic. He flushed when Mirianna thanked him, but his offering reminded her they all needed to eat, she as much as the others. She found the pot and filled it with water while Gareth cleaned the vegetables. She remembered the venison from the lion's kill, and he fetched slices to add to the stew while she set the eggs to boil.

The smells woke both Pumble and her father. Pumble devoured the stew Mirianna put before him. She spooned a bit of the broth into her father's mouth and washed it down with more of the Shadow Man's water. He smiled at her and his voice seemed less raspy. He lifted his hand, too. His fingers couldn't close around the cup, but they skimmed her cheek, and the touch brought tears to her eyes. While she blinked them away, Pumble let out a belch.

"Freth always says that's a compliment to the cook." Gareth had kept pace with Pumble, and he burped too.

Pumble laughed, but his eyes darted around the courtyard while he drained his cup. "What is this place?"

"He calls it Drakkonwehr." Mirianna glanced at the boy and wondered if he knew that.

"Drakkonwehr? But that's—that's practically at the gates of Beggeth!" Pumble pressed his charm to his lips. "I wish somebody would tell me how I got here."

She could tell him a Wehrland lion had led him, but he'd already blanched on learning the name of the place. Instead, she said, "What do you know about this place?"

"It's the Dragon Keep. Every child knows that."

"I don't," Gareth said. "What dragon?"

Pumble stared across the fire at the boy. "Why, the Last Dragon. Don't you know the tales?"

Gareth shook his head.

"Well then." Pumble released his charm to rub his hands together. "Rees always gets in first with telling the story, but I know it just as well. Let me see..." Chin on fist, he pondered, then his voice deepened, and he looked not like a pear-shaped man in floppy hat and stained tunic, but a master of the art as words Mirianna had heard from every storyteller who'd ever come to Nolar wove their timeless spell...

"*In Shadowtime the world was dark and violent, and the Krad ravaged the land. The people clung together for comfort and protection, until Kiros and his sword cleared the fertile bottom land, the forests—even the broad, high plain—of the beast-men, destroying their camps and hovels. He set in place the Stone Dam at Herrok-Eneth, separating the good land from the evils of Beggeth and bringing forth Dawntime.*

"*For many ages of man, the plains and the valleys and their waters lay at peace. Then the Dragons came, and the Black Mages with them, and together they plunged the land into Dragontime. The winged lizards breathed upon the grain in the fields, the pastures, the forests, and the land burned with a creeping flame while magic crackled like lightning in the summer sky.*

"*It was a time of horror and fear, and the people despaired. At last, Koronolan raised the Sword of Drakkonwehr and the Hero Mages rallied to its shining. They drove the Black Mages against the walls of Beggeth and smote them with magic and sword until the earth quaked and smoke covered the sun and night lay on the land for a full cycle of seasons.*

"When dawn returned, Koronolan hurled the Last Dragon deep into the earth, and the land heaved over it, and the Wehrland was born beside the walls of Beggeth. Dragon's blood, raining from the sky, became stone, and Dragontime became Dragon's End. The people rejoiced while Koronolan mounted a bloodstone on the Sword of Drakkonwehr and passed it to his sons and their sons ever after them, who would watch forever the resting place of the Last Dragon.

"And that resting place, my boy," Pumble said, spreading his arms to encompass the courtyard, "is under the fortress Drakkonwehr, the Dragon Keep."

Gareth had sat enthralled while his people's history unfolded, but now the brows showing dark through his shaggy hair drew together. "If this is Drakkonwehr, as my master says, and it's the powerful place you say it is, why is it a ruin?"

Pumble lowered his arms and looked around in the twilight. "Um...so it is." Then he brightened and leaned forward. "Well, there's another story about that, you see."

"It's about Durren Drakkonwehr." When man and boy turned to her with expectant faces, Mirianna wished she'd kept her mouth shut. She didn't want to participate in a story-telling session, but she couldn't sit still and let Pumble tell the boy a version that might've been perverted by Rees's imagination. She'd already seen in Ar-Deneth how he'd twisted the tale.

"He..." She rearranged her skirt over her knees while she tried to remember what Ulerroth had told her, what Durren himself had told her. "He's the last Drakkonwehr. Years ago—before you were born, most likely—a mage came and tried to raise the Dragon he was guarding. He stopped the mage, but something went wrong and the Stone Dam at Herrok-Eneth broke and released the Krad into the Wehrland. They—they destroyed this place and everything in it."

Although she gazed up at a sky streaked with purple and gold, she saw none of its beauty. Instead, she imagined the horror Durren found in this courtyard at the end of that awful day. The closest she'd come to that kind of carnage had been their battle against the Krad days ago. She tried to compound that image, but her mind refused to comply. Even her attempt raised shudders from the pit of her stomach. How could he have endured? He was a warrior, but this was a massacre of unspeakable proportions.

"But the dragon—" Gareth's voice recalled her to the present. "He stopped the mage from raising it, didn't he?"

"Yes. He did that." The Shadow Man—Durren Drakkonwehr—had told her he'd failed, but that wasn't true. He'd done what he'd been charged to do. At least part of it.

"So it's still here." The boy tapped the earth with his staff. "Somewhere below us?"

Pumble nodded. Then with a chagrinned expression he thumped his forehead and spoke. "That's right. It's sleeping."

Gareth's hair obscured his face as he seemed to study the paving stones. Mirianna itched to cut it for him. While the strands dangling in his eyes had to be uncomfortable, what troubled her more was when he bent, she couldn't read his expression under the mop. Dealing with one being whose face she couldn't see was difficult enough.

"I suppose that's why it's so hot down there," the boy said.

Pumble raised an eyebrow. "Down where?"

"In the deeper chambers," she said before Gareth could elaborate. "They're full of rubble and not safe. Especially when the Dragon takes a turn."

The two gaped at her. Mirianna uncurled her fingers from her skirt, hoping she'd diverted their attention. Somehow she didn't think the Shadow Man wanted Pumble to know about the tunnels.

"Don't tell me it *moves*!" Pumble said.

"Why haven't I felt anything?" The boy frowned.

Now what do I tell them? She licked her lips. "It happened when you were asleep. Besides, you don't really notice the motion unless you're up on the wall, but it shakes the whole place. That's why it's not safe to go deep into any chambers." She wondered if her warning would penetrate the shock showing on Pumble's face. He'd pulled his charm from his tunic and was mouthing words over it.

Gareth, meanwhile, sat with forearms on knees and staff grasped before him. He rotated his staff between his palms, making a faint grinding sound on the pavement.

She held her breath, suspecting he was about to ask another difficult question. Pumble proved easy enough to divert, but Gareth hung onto an idea like a dog with so few bones he was determined to chew every bit.

"If Durren Drakkonwehr was the last of the Drakkonwehrs, why does my master call this place his home?"

"Because..." Mirianna didn't know why she felt compelled to explain. Perhaps to clarify her own mind, to come to terms with what she'd learned, to try to comprehend what had only days ago seemed incomprehensible, but now...

They both turned in her direction, Pumble's face white and glistening, Gareth's head tilted in a sign of close attention.

She gripped her knees. "Because it is...his. Home, I mean."

Pumble expelled a breath. His eyes expanded to the size of cups. "The Sword! That—that's the Sword—" He gripped his charm in both hands and panted as if he couldn't breathe.

Mirianna watched him in alarm. When blue tinged his lips, she reached over and pushed his head between his knees. "Stay down until your head stops spinning."

"What sword? You mean that short sword in the pack?"

"That—that one must be mine," Pumble wheezed, stirring dust between his feet. "He's...the Shadow Man is..."

"Durren Drakkonwehr," she said, hoping to stop his talking. If he keeled over too close to the fire, she and the boy together couldn't shift him out of harm's way.

"But...if he was the last, and everything was destroyed, didn't he die?" the boy said.

She plucked at her skirt, wondering how to explain what any sane person, who understood nothing of magic, would say was impossible. "He didn't die, like everyone thinks, but he got...damaged when he stopped the mage."

"Cursed—that's what magic does, curses people." Sticking out a hand, Pumble flashed his charm. "You need protection."

She wanted to point out his little charm hadn't protected him from being attacked by Krad or magically led to this place reeking with its own magic, but she held her tongue. "Anyway, now he has to cover himself and he stays away from people because—"

"Because he can kill them with a look." Gareth seemed pleased to supply an answer. "But if he's really Durren Drakkonwehr, why does he call himself the Shadow Man?"

"He doesn't." She remembered the moment she'd first glimpsed the fortress and learned the identity of the being who held her by a promise. "Other people call him that."

"Why does he let them? I wouldn't want anyone to call me by some other name."

"I'll tell you why." Pumble heaved himself to an upright position and mopped his face, now mottled a somewhat healthier pink and red. "Because it's easier, that's why. If some mage blasted you with a curse that made you what, immortal?—who'd believe you?"

"Oh," Gareth said as if Pumble's words made perfect sense.

They did, Mirianna thought, but they didn't go far enough to explain why a being who couldn't die was hiding out in a ruined fortress. Wouldn't such a being be tempted to flaunt his powers? He could lead armies and suffer no ill effects while slaying countless enemies with a mere look. No one could stand against him if he desired to rule. If Durren Drakkonwehr had come down out of the Wehrland in his changed form, she could barely comprehend how her world might have changed.

Why hadn't he done all that and more? Why had he chosen to essentially crawl into a hole and withdraw from the world? Because he hadn't died and was convinced he should have? Because he was no longer himself and was ashamed of, even afraid of, what he'd become? Because he didn't want to be associated with a name, a reputation he'd failed to uphold? Because he held himself responsible for destruction he somehow should've been able to prevent? Which of these was true?

Everything he'd told her suggested all were reasons he'd give her, if she asked. She wondered if the real reason was simpler. He was a warrior with a broken sword, but he carried that broken weapon with more grace than any man she'd seen. He had great power to do harm—he could've killed them all with a look when they happened upon him the first time—yet he'd hidden himself rather than confront them. And then he'd helped them find their way, even kept her horse from shying, when he could've remained hidden. And he kept the boy, not as a slave but safe, and the boy trusted him.

She saw his shame, his pride, his heart-wrenching loneliness, and she understood at last why she'd been permitted to sit by a fire in a ruined courtyard with her father restored to her while the being, the man who was responsible, hid himself in the dark depths of the place. And she understood, at least a little, what he sought from her promise—*Only your presence. Your companionship. At Drakkonwehr.*

He'd delivered on every part of his promise, but

she'd given so little in return. She tried to swallow the lump filling her throat. Just because the idea terrified her was no reason to withhold what he asked, what she knew he needed more than anything.

Chapter Twenty-One

Standing up, Mirianna smoothed her hair from her face with shaking fingers. "I—I'm going to take a walk. If my father wakes, give him more broth and this water. As much as he wants. And remember, no one but my father is to drink this water."

"Why?" Pumble leaned over the bucket and sniffed. "Dragon's Blood! That's foul!"

Gareth chuckled. "That's why."

She pocketed the cooled eggs. She was bringing them to him because the Shadow Man needed sustenance—that's what she'd say if her nerve failed when he demanded why she'd come. Before she could change her mind, she walked away from the firelight and the voices of man and boy.

Within steps, Mirianna found herself in a different world, one where night creatures sang and shadows pooled in doorways and arches. A few bright stars speckled the indigo claiming the sky like a slow tide. In concert, darkness crept into the courtyard, deepening in such increments she couldn't detect the change until it settled like a gossamer veil around her shoulders.

By then she'd entered the Great Hall where rafters arched into the night sky, casting jagged bars of black over the shadowy rubble underfoot. Between the bars, bits of mica in the tumbled granite glimmered like miniature stars to light her way.

Mirianna crossed the open area, heading toward the chamber she'd found days before. She thought she knew the way, but a wall of unrelieved blackness faced her. Chewing her lip, she wished she'd brought a torch or candle, but she knew very well why she hadn't. He lived in the dark, in the shadows she feared. To bring light would be to bring an enemy into his domain. If she meant to go to the Shadow Man, she'd have to go on his terms.

She trod a few steps, feeling with her toes, probing the darkness with outstretched arms, fingers. Was this how it was for Gareth? This complete absence of sight? This blind fear of falling, of colliding with the unknown, of danger lurking a mere breath away? Her teeth chattered, but she clamped her jaw and planted her boot. Stones crunched under the sole, rolling her off balance, forcing her to step one foot across the other.

When she righted herself, panic seized her. What if she'd turned herself around? Without something to touch, to trail her hand along, how could she know? She'd heard of lost travelers who'd gone in circles— and those poor souls had possessed their sight! How did Gareth manage?

By the Dragon, she couldn't make herself go another step into this...*nothingness,* yet she knew a wall stood here with an arch broken out of it. Her memory of the chamber was so clear, she could count every mouse bone and bit of fur scattered on the rubble below an owl's nest. In the dark, though, everything seemed bigger, longer, farther away. She could go back outside, wait till morning, and have light for at least a little way into the tunnel. How much beyond the point where light vanished would she find him? The journey wouldn't seem as terrible then, starting so much closer to the end. But that meant waiting hours yet, and going backward when she'd already come so far.

So far? She'd come no more than a few steps into the chamber. She could easily go back and try again in the morning.

When Mirianna looked over her shoulder for the glow of starlight that should be visible outside the chamber, she saw nothing. Warm air feathered her eyeballs, telling her she'd stretched wide her lids, but thick darkness enclosed her like a muffling cloak. She could see nothing, hear nothing, feel nothing except the internal quaking that had begun before she left the company of men and since spread to her limbs. To hold herself together, she made fists, but her body shook so, she feared she would shatter.

Her nails bit into her palms, and the pain brought her a measure of control. After a moment, she managed to slide her right foot forward. Her boot sole flexed, but not on the level paving stones of the chamber, rather on the uneven pitch of a rough-hewn floor.

The tunnel. She almost collapsed with relief. Somehow she'd passed through the arch without knowing, but at least this space was narrow. She and the Shadow Man hadn't been able to walk side by side here. If she raised her arms outward, she should be able to contact wall. When her fingers touched nothing but air, she inched to the right. If she could just touch stone and not some disgusting tunnel creature, she could control the gasps sawing in and out of her mouth, keep her heart locked in her chest, stop the sobs that bubbled just behind her teeth. Screaming would do no good. She was just—

There! She clawed the rocks with both hands and hung on, panting. The tunnel went only two ways—back up or down to her goal. There was nothing to fear. She'd come this far already. If she turned back, she'd have to cover the same ground in the morning. And she would cover it, wouldn't she? She wouldn't find a reason to hesitate, to put off doing what was necessary, what was right. Would she?

She inhaled a steadying breath, but the clarity it brought raised gooseflesh along her entire body. No matter how her better sense pushed her to turn back, to take advantage of the morning light, she knew entering the darkness had committed her. She had to find the Shadow Man—or lose herself trying. Paralyzed with fear, she choked out a sob and dug her fingers into the wall.

Trust.

She recognized the soothing reassurance of the sound echoing in her mind. She'd followed that voice before, and it had led her to safety.

No! It had led her into danger, to this terrifying place reeking of death and grief. If she hadn't followed the voice, trusted the voice, she wouldn't have walked into something that felt remarkably like the stone bowels of a hideous beast!

Trust.

The voice wrapped itself around her like comforting arms. A hint of lavender teased her nostrils. When she tried to breathe it, the scent dissipated, but her mind cleared. She stood on a threshold, at the brink of something she needed to cross, someplace she needed to enter. But to do so would be to step blind into utter darkness.

I'm afraid. Can't you show me the way?
Trust your heart.

****

The smelly man had fallen asleep after feeding Mirianna's father more broth and water, but Gareth stayed awake, waiting. He laid his staff by his side and passed from hand to hand the stone he'd found. While his fingers stroked idly over its smooth sides, he concentrated on listening. Within minutes, the night creatures in the direction of the gate fell silent. He cocked his head, wondering if lion feet made more or less noise than the squirrels that hopped about where trees had grown up through tumbled rock. He heard a pebble rattle, and then caught a whiff of the scent that had filled his nostrils most of the previous night, the scent of warm fur.

The air stirred, caressing his face with faint pressure as she glided through it—much more silently than squirrels—and butted his shoulder. Her whiskers tickled his nose, her purr vibrated along his skin, and he put an arm around her neck, nestling into her throat. She sat on her haunches, cradling him against her tall body while she washed his ear.

Giggling, he twisted away from the rough tongue. "I knew you'd wait to come until Pumble was asleep. You wouldn't want to scare him or the old man." She turned her tongue on his hair, and he let her, enjoying the gentle pulling, like when his mother combed the strands with her fingers. The she-lion smelled of pine and lavender, like fresh-cut logs and the herb his mother laid beside his pillow when he had trouble sleeping. With a yawn, he relaxed between the she-lion's forelegs. "Mirianna said you saved her too. That

291

was good of you."

The lion licked across his forehead, scraping the hair from it. Her action let him see, like a ghostly image, the faint red glow of the banked fire. Sighing, he rubbed the stone between his palms. "I found this today. It has six...seven smooth sides and these rough edges. But I'm careful. I won't let it cut me."

Her tongue washed the back of his neck with long strokes, the sensation so soothing, his head lolled forward onto his chest. His eyes may have drifted shut, but he couldn't say for sure since that faint glow still played around the edges of his consciousness even as words filled it. The words rose up in his mind like a long-dead memory and tumbled off his lips. He could no more stop them than he could comprehend them, but his mouth seemed to know how to form the strange syllables as over and over they rolled from his tongue:

"Beggeth beggedon tyrannor mott.
Ominoth peurinon cauldor keth.
Beggeth rappanon drakkonnor tor.
Tyrannoth drakkon ominor et!"

When the last word faded into the silence, the she-lion lowered herself to a reclining position. Feeling suddenly exhausted, Gareth snuggled into her shoulder. Before he fell asleep, her tongue licked across the fingers still gripping the stone. He had the strangest feeling she was smiling.

****

Durren heard the rattle of pebbles in time to drop out of his float and spin toward the tunnel mouth. Just in time for the impact that plunged him, open mouthed, nearly to the rocks below. Amid a maelstrom of phosphorescent bubbles, he surfaced, coughing and tearing at what enmeshed his limbs.

Something—a hand maybe—raked his shoulder.

He kicked free, turned toward thrashing sounds, and seized something loose and flowing.

"Ow!"

Kiros! He had her by the hair! Well, that couldn't be helped. From the gasping and sputtering, the woman was tangled in her garments. He kicked toward the rock ledge, towing her. She came too fast, bumped his chest, and clamped onto him like a leech. They sank together, her skirt enveloping his body. He yanked his legs free, kicked to the surface, and pried with one hand at the shoulder digging into his throat while scraping her hair from his face with the other. "Don't...choke me!"

"I'm sorry." Her voice sounded hoarse, frightened, but her grip on his neck eased.

He treaded water, trying to orient himself. He knew every inch of the pool, every rock and eddy, yet at this precise moment, he had no idea where the shallow end was.

Her torso was pressed full length to his. Her legs—Kiros help him!—were locked around his hips with heels digging into his buttocks. For all the protection her clothes afforded her when dry, soaked they clung like skin to every female contour. Her breasts made tantalizing circles of malleable pressure on his chest, the nipples beading just above his own. Her belly was concave, a taut, tight abdomen narrowing to a mound, the contour of which he could trace through her skirt. That mound rode below his navel, and the thought of it, of what lay hidden under the cushion of curls adorning it, made blood rush to his groin. If she meant to ride him, she couldn't have mounted him better.

She squeaked. He'd clenched her ribs, so he forced his hold to loosen. Her hands shifted to his shoulders, and her fingers flexed, the tips tentative as they slid across his skin. Her eyes reflected a phosphorescent mass drifting a few feet away. Her skirt, or part of it, he was thinking when one thigh, bare and slick, slipped down his hip and chased all logic from his brain. *Dear Koronolan!* If he pulled her down, he could have her. His body was stiff and ready. He had only to tear away any remaining fabric and thrust himself home.

At that moment, she gasped, "You—you're naked!" Then she catapulted backward.

When Durren broke the surface again, he heard nothing but the echo of his own gasps and the slapping of waves against the sides of the pool. By Kiros, where was she? A swirl of phosphorescence in the depths caught his eye. Not her skirt; that had snagged on stones in the shallows. Gulping in air, he dove toward the glimmer. It was sinking, slowly, sinuously, into the bottomless hole where the hot water welled up.

He plunged toward the trail of bubbles, grabbed at it, found something solid and pulled. She came limply, a tangle of clothing and limbs. He seized her torso, kicked upward, and kicked and kicked until he exploded into air. Panting, he dragged her head out of the water and ripped apart the garment plastered over her face. Then he towed her to the shallows, bent her over his arm, and thumped her between the shoulder blades.

After she coughed and gasped, Durren let out the breath he'd been holding. His head spun, and a shower of red and green stars erupted behind his eyes. When darkness returned and his heartbeat slowed, he hauled her onto the ledge and rolled her to her side while she coughed out the rest of the water she'd swallowed. Despite the heat, he shivered, but not from cold. His muscles always shook after such intense exertion, after they'd responded to a demand for immediate action. This had nothing to do with fear, with the possibility she might've drowned and he would've lost her.

****

After the coughing spasms eased, Mirianna tried to breathe in through her nose and out her mouth. Maybe that way she could keep her insides—stomach, lungs, whatever else felt lodged in her throat—from heaving out of her body. But the stink wasn't helping. No matter how she breathed, the air reeked of rotten eggs. She coughed again and tried to push over onto her back.

"Easy," said a voice, at once familiar and yet not. Hands gripped her shoulders and lowered her gently. "You almost drowned. You may have injured yourself on the rocks, too."

Mirianna frowned while those hands, their touch equally familiar yet oddly not so, glided across her face, the fingertips pushing aside soggy strings of her hair. They moved, business-like, over her shoulders, and then followed each arm to the hand, working the wrist and fingers together and singly. Her limbs lay like lead weights in those exploring hands, pliant but completely without strength. When the hands touched her ribs, her senses awoke with a rush. She sucked in a gasp, and the fingers stilled.

"Does that hurt?"

Hurt? Her heart rattled against her ribcage. How could the sweet, wild thrill triggered by the touch of fingertips—*naked* fingertips!—on her bare flesh be could considered painful? If that were the case, she ached all over for more of the same! She sucked in another breath, head spinning with ecstasy. Somehow, she'd navigated that tunnel in total darkness and found him! Only he'd been—a flush swept her from head to toe—he'd been *naked* and she'd nearly drowned them. And now—her flush intensified—she'd lost her clothing, at least part of it. And he—he was still—!

"Am I hurting you?" he repeated, fingertips pushing ever so gently on rib after rib.

Despite the water she'd swallowed, her mouth lost all moisture. Her pulse throbbed at her throat, making her ears resound with it. The fingertips, ten points of delicious pressure, shot fire along her veins. "I—no."

If she didn't discourage him, didn't move a muscle, those wonderful fingers would glide on down her torso. She bit her lip, wondering how long she could endure the incredible torture of his touch without crying out. Did he realize he was touching bare skin? How much of her flesh was exposed? The air was so thick and hot, she could be wearing nothing but the sodden garments clinging to her arms and not know the difference.

Yet none of that mattered. What mattered was he was touching her, like in her dream, and the sweet pain of the contact coursed through her body, setting off spasms in her womanly core, drawing her hands into fists while his palms grazed her hip bones.

And stopped.

Heartbeats later, he transferred his palms to her knees, and she remembered to breathe. Disappointment stabbed at her. She resented those hands, so impersonal as they avoided her hips and thighs and instead slid down each shin, lifted each foot in succession and pulled off the boot. Water sloshed out of each boot, a spatter of droplets neither hot nor cold but thick, and wetting her skin.

Like blood.

What in the name of the Dragon made her think her foot was bleeding? Just because her pulse hammered there like a smithy was no reason to—to—!

Her mouth opened to gasp, but her lungs seemed paralyzed, unable to draw breath to sustain the sudden wild thunder of her heart. Dots cavorted before her eyes, bright colors illuminating the darkness, but she saw none of them. Every particle of her focus concentrated on the ankle still enclosed by his fingers, on the tiny patch of skin under which her lifeblood drummed against his thumb.

He was shaking.

Tremor after minute tremor vibrated from his hands to the ankle suspended within them. His breathing had intensified too. She heard the rasp of it over the pulse pounding in her ears. A thrill ran through her, a jolt of feminine power. Touching *her,* skin to skin, had done this to him. She reveled in the thought, in knowing he was as affected by the contact as she.

She licked dry lips while his thumb traced feather-light circles over her ankle bone. Although her eyes searched for him in the absolute dark, following the whisper of his breathing, she could detect nothing but a faint glow, like a banked fire, that vanished when she stared at it.

"Mirianna," he said, lowering her foot gently to the ground, "you seem to be uninjured." His fingers loosened on her ankle.

"Don't—!"

He stilled. "Does that hurt?"

"No—I mean, don't stop."

"What?"

"Don't stop touching me...Durren." There, she'd spoken it. Named him for herself. Chosen the identity, the entity she trusted.

"Mirianna..." His voice was hoarse, a plea.

She understood he might be afraid. It had been a long time since he'd been the man he once was. She had to help him remember how to be that man. That required her courage, all of the courage trembling inside where she'd gathered it to speak what needed to be spoken. "I want you to...touch me."

He drew back with the hiss of an indrawn breath, and his fingers left her ankle. "If this is about that promise..."

The separation, the latent prints of his fingers, stung her flesh like a burn. She flinched with a hiss of her own, then summoned her courage again. "It is...but it isn't." The promise had bound her to him, had brought her on this journey she would otherwise never have taken, but that was the extent of its power. Obligation couldn't compel her to act. To take the steps she meant to take required something else entirely. "I know who you are now."

He groaned. "A shadow. A hollow creature. A failure."

His misery cut at her. She sat up, intent on her purpose, intent on easing his pain. "You're Durren Drakkonwehr and you're the man in my dream."

"Illusion, Mirianna. Nothing but damned illusion! You only see what you want to see. I learned that a long time ago."

She heard the muffling of his voice, sensed that inches from her, a hand-span or so, ran the curve of the back he'd turned toward her. She imagined that curve running uninterrupted from the crown of his head down the full length of his spine. When she clung to him in the water, she'd been thinking only of survival, but the musculature of that naked torso had imprinted itself on her arms, palms, thighs, breasts. Those places sizzled now with the memory.

She cleared her throat. "I don't see any illusions. I don't see anything at all. But that's not important. What's important is the dream. *Our* dream."

He shifted, the movement ghosting air across her cheek, and his breathing altered, but when he spoke, his voice was flat, dull. "Dreams are illusions, too."

"Illusions are meant to deceive." Startled by the words springing from her lips, she took a breath. She knew nothing of magic, of spells, yet she knew this as truth. He'd forgotten that somehow, or lost faith, and she had to convince him, make him believe again.

"Dreams are...s*hared* dreams like ours are foretellings. Premonitions. They tell us the future. We don't always understand them, not at first. When my dream showed me a shadow of a man, a figure outlined against the light, I thought—I thought that when I met the right man..."

She trailed off, face aflame. Said aloud, her girlish dream of a lover, her childhood conviction the man in her dream was her destiny sounded so foolish. People fell in and out of love all around her in Nolar, madly passionate one year and yelling curses at each other the next. Why did she think she was different? Was it because in her meager twenty winters, she hadn't seen a single man who even in some small way matched the man in her dreams? Or was it because when this one man spoke to her, when his voice echoed out of those Wehrland trees, her heart leaped? It knew him. It had always known him, his true nature, even while her mind refused to believe.

She ran her tongue over dry lips, inhaled deeply, and leaned toward him, toward where her heart tracked the great, tender, aching thing that beat within his breast. It drew her, always, like iron to a magnet. "I thought when I met the right man, his face would appear on my dream-lover, but I was wrong. What I didn't understand then is I've always seen *you,* Durren, just as you are...inside. It's not your face that matters; it's your heart, your touch. No one can ever touch me as you do." She reached out and laid a hand on that lovely curving spine.

For a moment, they could have been statues— living, breathless statues. Then, in a faint reddish blur that registered only after the motion, he caught her hand, shifted his grip, and held her away by the wrist. "Mirianna!" His anguish reverberated from the chamber walls. "You can't just...*touch* me! I'm not—"

His flesh was warm, the fingertips separate and defined as his grip encompassed the fine bones of her wrist. Her pulse beat against the pressure, sending a drumbeat of echoes along her nerves. Along his, too, or the words wouldn't have died in his throat. The contact linked them, communicating the tension of sinew and muscle, the heat of blood, the imprint of flesh on flesh. And this—this was the certainty.

"I *have* touched you, Durren. More than once." Quiet and sure, her voice filled the chamber without echoing. "I know you're not empty, not a hollow specter sheathed in black. In the water, I felt your skin. And the pulse at your throat. Your fingers have nails. Your limbs have muscles, bones, flesh to cover them. You're substance, not shadow, Durren. And I want to touch you again. I've always wanted to touch you."

"Do you know what you're asking?" he said on a ragged breath.

"Oh yes." This time, she knew exactly what she was asking. It was the thing she was most sure of. "Make love to me. Please."

He groaned and his hand captured her head, fingers snagging wet strands of her hair. She gasped—into his mouth. At first there was nothing but the overwhelming tang of sulfur and a sensation of pressure, wetness, and heat. Then he breathed, and the taste of him filled her mouth with rapture. Her lips awoke beneath his, opening to the invitation of his tongue sliding along her teeth. She fisted her hand in his hair, long, thick hair that wrapped around her wrist and slid like wet silk between her fingers.

He broke the kiss, their gulping breath echoing in the chamber as he pulled her full length against his body. "Mirianna ...sweet, sweet Mirianna..." whispered along her throat while his mouth trailed wetly down its curve. "You don't know how long I've dreamed of this. Of you...like this." His hand brushed her breast, the contact expelling air from her lungs. His hand returned, trembling, while their gasps mingled. "Dear Koronolan, I want you so badly...but not here."

Panicked, she clutched at his neck when he pulled away. "Don't...stop, please."

His breath rushed over her face. His hand returned

to her breast, cupping it, exploring its fullness and limits before stroking a fingertip over the nipple. She convulsed and cried out. His fingers dug into her flesh. "I'm not...stopping, sweet. But not here, not on these rocks. There's a better place, and you can lie on my clothes."

Then he was lifting her and she was pressed to his chest, to the wide expanse of skin and muscle rippling under her palm and fingertips. He kissed her while he walked, and she lost herself in the taste and texture of his lips, teeth, tongue, so beguiled she noticed nothing until he drew back and she saw his head and shoulders outlined in a faint red glow, like a stenciled silhouette, before he bent and closed his lips over her breast.

With a cry, she arched upward, raking her fingers across his shoulders. He suckled, pulling at the nipple, taking a mouthful of her breast between his teeth until she whimpered and bucked in his grasp. When he shifted his mouth to her other breast, she seized his hair, convinced she'd die of the pleasure. Somehow, what remained of her garments disappeared. She knew they were gone when he lifted his mouth from her breast and trailed scorching kisses down her belly.

"Open for me, sweet," he murmured, sliding a hand up her thigh. When it grazed her mound, lightning shot through her nerves and exploded stars behind her eyelids.

"What—what did you do?" she panted.

"Did you like that?" He trailed his tongue along the soft inner side of her thigh. She shivered, and gooseflesh ran along her skin, but she wasn't cold. Her skin burned, and the heat of his mouth intensified the fire. While she panted, he stroked down her abdomen, increasing the pressure as he approached her mound.

"What—what are you doing now?"

"I'm going to touch you. Here." His palm slid over her mound and cupped it. She jumped, but he pressed her down, holding her body captive as his finger touched her. She sucked in a breath. Her body hummed with tension, all her attention focused on one tiny spot that waited for a single fingertip to touch it again and slay her with its magic. Pain, pleasure, agony—and then he was touching her, sliding his finger, slick with her own wetness, between the folds, probing the tight inner space where no man had entered.

"Durren!" she gasped, and his mouth came down on hers as he pushed his finger deep. She felt as though lightning struck. Shot through every nerve with pulsing fire and light, convulsing around that hot, hard touch that pushed with her, pulled with her, teased every last quiver from her body until she fell back and exhaled into his mouth and he released her lips.

"That was...that was...incredible," she breathed while her body spiraled down into a sweet, nerveless lethargy.

"Not as incredible as you, Mirianna." He placed kisses on the corners of her mouth, her chin, the base of her throat where her blood beat just beneath the skin. "So soft, so...delicious ..."

Even in her dreamy state, all the tension gone out of every muscle and nerve—or because of it—she heard the edge in his voice, the unfilled need. She reached up and tunneled her fingers into his hair. "You've done it again, Durren. Given of yourself. I came here to give to *you*."

He touched his forehead to hers, and his breath

flowed sweetly across her face. "My darling Mirianna, you don't know how much you've already given me." His hand skated the length of her arm, circling the fine bones of her wrist before his fingers spread over the backs of hers. Turning his head, he pressed slow, tender kisses to her palm and each fingertip. "Just your being here, in my arms like this, is a gift." With a sigh that seemed to come from the depths of his soul, he bent and kissed her with the utmost care.

She could barely breathe past the ache in her throat, past the swell of unshed tears burning there at the thought of his loneliness, the years he'd spent alone without a single soul to touch him, to hold him. Intent on rectifying that need, she wrapped her arms around his body and set about caressing every inch of skin she could reach. The rumble issuing from his throat startled her, but she took it to signify pleasure when he cupped her face with both hands and deepened the kiss.

Sighing, she stroked her hands over his face. As her caressing fingertips took their time, she discovered something she hadn't noticed in the first mad rush of passion—a tracery of fine ridges scoring his skin. As she widened her explorations, she encountered more of them, at irregular intervals, cross-hatching his shoulders, arms, back and chest. Scars, she thought, thin and faded, like old memories. She stroked over his brows, finding across one a ridge like a knotted rope. *Another scar.* Her heart thudded, hard and heavy, at the evidence of his suffering, at the truth of what he'd endured.

Framing his face with her hands, she pushed gently until his lips released hers. "I want to give you more." A breath apart, she held him at bay and spoke past the lump in her throat. "I want you to take me...as I am. I want you to take pleasure in me, Durren, not just give me pleasure."

He chuckled, a gentle, tender sound, and kissed the tip of her nose. "I intend to, sweet, but you're untouched, and I don't want to hurt you. Now that you're properly relaxed, however..." He laid the full length of his torso along hers, sliding his thighs one by one between hers, pressing her legs apart.

She sucked in a breath. How his body could feel hotter than the air in this chamber, she had no idea, but his skin burned everywhere it touched hers, and the long shaft of his desire scorched her belly with its silken thickness. "Oh, so you planned this?" she said, but the words came out breathy rather than bold.

"Um-hmm. This is *my* part of our dream." She felt his smile against her cheekbone before he clasped her earlobe between his teeth. With his tongue, he flicked the lobe, then laved wet fire around the earring there. "Mmm...just as I imagined. Only sweeter." Shuddering, he raised himself a little. He slid his hand into the space where their bodies slowly separated, stroking over her breast, touching the nipple with a fingertip, caressing each rib before flattening his palm on her belly and sliding the fingers into the curls covering her mound. With a shaky breath that told her he was reaching the limits of his control, he nudged her legs wider apart. "I want you. Kiros knows I want you, Mirianna. Do you trust me?" His fingers stroked through her curls and massaged her folds.

Just when she thought she had to be sated, freed of all desire, it roared into life again. Squeezing her eyes shut, she panted, knowing this time, it would not be only his fingers that found her pulsing hidden places, but that part of him that would mate with her, would claim her irrevocably as his, that part of him that would spill his seed within her. This, then, was what she'd been waiting for—all those lonely days and nights, those wistful thoughts, unfulfilled yearnings. This was the moment. This was the man.

Opening her eyes, she traced his lips with her fingertips. "I've always trusted you, Durren. Even when I didn't believe."

He was trembling again. The tremors and his whispered, "Mirianna, love!" cracked her heart so wide she opened her arms and legs and took all of him in, body and soul.

Chapter Twenty-Two

"Imposter! Imposter! I tell you, he's an imposter!"

The man pretending to be the Master of Nolar jerked wide-awake at the ruckus in the corridor. Between the bed curtains, he saw the door to his chamber, which he'd bolted from the inside upon retiring, had been thrown open. A naked man rushed into that aperture and gestured toward the bed. "There he is! Seize him!"

The imposter stared at the face he'd grown used to seeing in the mirror, a face now worn by the man in the doorway. *What in Beggeth?* Vaulting from the bed, he clutched the pouch at his neck and shouted, "*Immenor!*"

A sequence of thuds told him all the bodies near the door had fallen. He wasted no time wondering how Master Brandelmore had escaped his transference spell but threw on whatever clothing came to hand.

A glimpse in the mirror as he snatched a cloak from a nearby peg showed him a face he hadn't seen in more than a dozen years. He grinned. "Hello, Syryk, glad to see you haven't changed a bit."

Throwing up the hood, he dashed out the room and down a servants' stairwell before the effects of his immobilizing spell could wear off.

He'd barely reached the stables when shouts rang out from the living quarters. With an oath, Syryk ducked into a vacant stall while soldiers and groomsmen rushed past. *Moments, damn it!* He'd been able to make that spell last twice as long before.

Crouching behind the stall door, he pulled out his pouch and tumbled the chunk of crystal into his hand. Clear as water, the flat surfaces magnified his palm, showing his lifeline as unusually long and confirming what he already knew—nothing, absolutely nothing, remained trapped inside the crystal. He caressed it with fingertips, gauging the broken column's power, wondering if he dared work a confounding spell. The pouch limited his access. Maybe now, with his skin pressed to the seven planes, he could summon enough—

No. This wasn't the time or place for a test. Besides, now he'd overcome the surprise of seeing his own face again, he was convinced something—or someone—had broken the transference spell. If the spell had merely weakened, he would've noticed a transient shifting of features days ago, but this shift had occurred in the blink of an eye—or rather in the moments just before he'd awakened to the shouting. By all rights, he should have awakened *inside* the crystal! But here he crouched in his own skin, in the body he'd forsaken fourteen years ago when that idiot Drakkonwehr interrupted the Dragon Chant and spell-blasted everyone to Beggeth. Scowling, he slid the crystal into the pouch and tucked it under his tunic. He needed time to think, to probe the crystal for clues, and a place to do so in safety.

Rising from his crouch, he peered between the stall door's slats. What he needed at this precise moment was a fast horse. Spotting the captain of the guard's horse already saddled just outside the stable, Syryk applauded his impulse days ago to decamp court to Master Brandelmore's rarely used "summer home" abutting the Wehrland. He'd risked stirring the staff's suspicions to bring himself that much closer to Rees and the bloodstones, but his instincts, as usual, proved correct.

He leaped into the saddle and gathered the reins, glad to see he still wore the seal of Nolar. He could flash it at the ill-trained yokels manning the gate in case they tried to bar his way. Just to make sure they wouldn't think of it, he clutched his pouch and muttered, "*Dymoneseth fyannador!*"

A geyser roared from the courtyard well, turning all heads. Syryk heeled the horse. Outside the gates, he made directly for the Wehrland. Let the fools follow him if they dared. In less than a day, he would have the bloodstones. And then his destiny would be within easy reach.

****

Durren held her as she slept sprawled across him. He may have slept too; he couldn't tell. She'd cried out when he filled her, but she refused to let him withdraw, digging her fingers into his flesh, scoring him with her nails. "Stay!" she said so fiercely he'd nearly come there and then without giving her the pleasure she deserved for taking him in so deeply, for opening her very heart.

So he'd kissed away her tears, kissed the mouth she offered him. And when she sighed, and the hot, tight sheath that gripped him so deliciously opened a little, he pushed into it, making her forget pain, forget daylight, forget everything but the pleasure, the satisfaction he and he alone could give her. She came in a crescendo, and he rushed after her, emptying himself so thoroughly that for moments—hours, perhaps—he could remember nothing but the sweet bliss of their union.

When she stirred, he coaxed her to bathe in the pool with him, to let the water ease her discomfort, heal the aches caused by his intrusion. He kissed her while he massaged her limbs, and she turned into him, touching his lips with her tongue.

She wrapped herself around him, and he held her up while she explored his mouth until her sweet, tentative caresses turned his blood molten and his fingers dug into her buttocks. She squeaked, and he gasped, "Forgive me! I didn't mean—"

"Yes, you did," she panted. Then she slid down his torso. "Is it easier...in the water?"

Dear Koronolan, she was trying to mount him! As that sweet spot opened over him, he thrust into her and nearly drowned them. They came up gasping. He latched onto the rocky ledge with one hand while his arm around her hips pulled her all the way down, hard, so their bones ground into each other. When he sucked her whole breast into his mouth, she came with a wild cry. He spilled himself into her, shuddering until he was empty, so empty there was nothing more to give. Then, somehow, they crawled onto the ledge, onto the bed of his clothing, and collapsed.

Now he lay, replete, sated, and loved her.

You can't stay here forever, the Voice in his head said.

Fury shot through him, lighting up the darkness behind his eyes. *Go away, damn you!*

For how long? Till you get hungry? Do you know

how long you've been down here?

No! And I don't care! They were safe here, cocooned in the darkness that had let them become one. Up there—up there was daylight. He would have to cover himself again, and she would be as a stranger to him, a touch through the barrier of clothing, thin leather as impermeable as a stone wall, cutting him off from her. Here, only here, could they be as they were meant to be, as the dream fulfilled.

You can't stay here forever, the Voice in his head repeated. *You tried that before. It didn't work.*

It would have! But hunger had driven him out of the tunnel then. Hunger and a dogged determination to survive, to somehow defeat Syryk by *living* in the face of death. If what he'd been doing counted as living, that is.

She came to you, you know, because you waited. Because you lived.

The words shook him. The years he'd railed at for passing so slowly, the interminable seasons that changed without changing what mattered had finally brought him...change. If that instrument of change weren't pressed skin-to-skin to the full length of his body, if her soft breath didn't tickle his ear and her heart beat solid and steady against his ribs, he would imagine himself dreaming. She chose that moment to stir, to run her hand down his ribs and under his shoulder, snuggling closer.

Dear Koronolan, he loved her! Every move, every sound she made punctured him, drilled holes into him, cut and sliced him into tiny fragments of yearning, bleeding love so great, he ached with the overwhelming pain of it.

He pressed a kiss to her curls, savoring their springiness. He visualized the cloud haloing her head as he'd seen it last in the thin light of dawn. Kiros, he couldn't have guessed then that his dream of running his bare fingers through their fine silk would at last come true.

Nor could he have guessed she'd come to him, offering herself fearlessly, with no regard for the consequences.

Ah, consequences. So noble of you to consider them—now.

Go to Beggeth! And take your consequences with you! But the voice was right again. Durren fought the bitterness threatening to swamp him, to overwhelm the newborn joy still so fragile in his heart. He would keep that joy as safe as he would keep her and damn the consequences! She'd given herself to him, purely and innocently. If nothing else, he would cherish that forever.

Sweet sentiments, said the Voice in his head. *How long will you be satisfied with meeting her here in the dark? How long before you want to "see" her? Like in the dream?*

The words punched like a fist to the gut, taking his breath away. Of course he wanted to see her in the light of day. Just once, to see her true body, to replace the dream vision with the glory of her flesh in the radiant sunlight. Her beauty under his fingertips already took his breath away, and he knew—*knew*—she was lovelier than the vision, but he wanted to see, just once...

And when you see her, you'll want her, then and there.

And then he would kill her.

Ice water poured into Durren's veins, raising goose flesh over his body. She would see him, revealed, and the sight would kill her. With a groan, he pinched his eyes shut and buried his face in her hair.

She stirred, snuggling against his throat. The gesture, so trusting, cut him in two.

"Mirianna, sweet, we should—" He cleared his throat. "Aren't you hungry?"

"Mmm. For you?"

He sucked in a breath as her hand trailed down his abdomen. "Um, I meant food, love."

"I brought eggs."

He felt inordinately dimwitted as her finger played with his navel. "Eggs?"

She nodded against his chest. "I thought you might be hungry after—after being down here so long."

That she'd thought of his basic human need for food, for sustenance, stirred something inside of him, not the passion that still roared in his blood, but something that arrowed straight to his heart. "Thank you...for the eggs, Mirianna."

She sat up, and he flinched, the separation of her skin from his like a ripping of flesh. He ground his teeth at the fiery pain, but she'd already moved away, and he heard her picking up and discarding clothing. "Where's my skirt?"

He sat up as the chill of her absence seared the burning parts of his body, making him gasp again. Dear Koronolan, was this how it would be every time she left him after their lovemaking?

Pleasure? Pain? Sounds like love, said the Voice in his head. *Are you man enough to take it? Or will you let the Shadow run away with you again?*

Go to Beggeth!
Can't be worse than this place. Without her.

Durren hugged his belly, trying to catch his breath, to master the pain before it swamped him. She was inching farther away, rummaging in the dark. "Love, please, you'll fall in the pool. Or cut yourself on the rocks."

"Then help me."

"Put on your clothes. I'll look in the pool." He stood, but he couldn't straighten up. He bent again, gathering her clothes, handing them to her as he passed, moving as fast as he dared, as fast as the stabbing pain would let him. The water would stop the misery, would relieve the pain, and he'd be able to breathe again. He slid into the pool, moving toward the shallows where he'd seen part of her skirt snagged on the rocks, but the garment was gone. "It's lost," he said, wincing as another spasm struck.

She made a noise of frustration. "We'll have to go up, then, and I'll make you some more. The others will probably be hungry too. I wonder how long we've been here."

Hearing the rustle of fabric, the sounds of movement as she dressed, he remembered he'd torn whatever garment had covered her face in the pool. "Love," he said, measuring his breath, "do you have enough clothing to cover yourself?"

"I think so." She coughed out a laugh. "They'll know what we've been doing, won't they?"

In his mind's eye, he saw a beguiling sweep of color filling her cheeks. "Does that trouble you?"

Her boot scuffed a rock. "No," she said, and then with more force, "I'm not afraid, Durren. I love you."

Her declaration ought to have eased the knife-blade between his ribs, but instead it twisted the hilt. He hunched in the water, begging the pool for relief, for the healing magic to begin. The pain was like a fire burning him from the inside out, so fiery he imagined he could see the glow through his skin.

"Durren?"

"I—I'm coming, love. Go back to the wall, face it, and follow it left to the tunnel. Go slowly."

"I will if you want me to, but...is there something...*red* in the pool?"

Durren's eyes snapped wide open. *By Kiros!* His body radiated a faint red light, like a banked fire seen through a grate. The glow followed his limbs as he moved them, glimmering in the water. Dear Koronolan, it was as though he leaked fire! It had to be the pain, flowing out of him as the water took it and eased it ever so slightly.

"It's...it's just phosphorescence, love. A trick of the eyes." Kiros, she couldn't be allowed to look at him! What if light cracked open the black blot of his body like flame through stirred coals, and she saw him for what he was? No, he had to divert her attention and leave the pool. The sooner he covered himself, the better. "Go on, find the wall. I need to dress."

Holding his breath, teeth gritted, he listened for her movements away from him and toward the wall. Then he staggered to the edge and hauled himself out. Dear Koronolan, he could see the bones in his hand now! They stood out black as if his hand were illuminated from within. And the pain, while modified, made him pant against it. *What in Beggeth is happening?*

****

They didn't talk as they climbed the tunnel, but Durren held her hand, guiding her, waiting for her to plant her feet before moving on. Although he didn't hurry her, Mirianna sensed a core of tension in him. Did he want to be out of the tunnel or did he, like she, want to remain in that sheltered place where they could make love in peace? She'd told him she loved him. He'd called her "love" as if it meant the same. Yet as the air freshened, his fingers tightened and she realized as she caught his arm when she stumbled over loose stones, he was both sweating and burning up.

"You needn't worry about my father," she said, thinking that troubled him. "You saved his life."

He turned. She blundered into his body, only his grip on her arms keeping her from falling. "Mirianna, love..." With shaking hands, he captured her hand and pressed it to his chest. "Please, don't ask to see me...as I am. Promise me you won't ask that."

Beneath his tunic, under her five spread fingers and palm, his heart throbbed as though it might shake free of the bones encasing it. Those bones expanded and contracted like a bellows, the top of the arch pushing at the heel of her hand. The rasp of his breath, the thunder of his heartbeat filled the tunnel, echoing around her while, under her fingertips, his muscles stretched taut, waiting for her answer, her promise.

"I'm not afraid, Durren."

He thrust a hand into her hair as if he meant to pull her to him, to kiss her through the hood he'd replaced before leaving the pool, but he only held her there, leather-clad thumb stroking her cheekbone. "You're as brave as the bravest warrior, Mirianna, but this isn't about courage. This is about...trust. Can you trust that I

316

know how dangerous it would be for you to look upon me? Can I trust you not to ask, not to try to see...what lies under this cloth?"

"I know you have scars, Durren. I've felt them and—"

"Scars aren't—it's not just the scars. Please, Mirianna, promise me you won't ask, you won't try...to see me. I couldn't bear it if I hurt you."

Under the heat oozing from his hand, her cheek tingled like winter-chilled skin before a fire. She stroked his hand, turning her lips into his gloved palm. The contact sizzled. "If it matters that much to you, I won't ask. You can trust me, Durren."

He exhaled as though a great weight had lifted from his shoulders. "Thank you." Touching his thumb to her lips, he took her hand in his again and started to climb.

"Are you—you're burning up. You know that, don't you?"

His fingers twitched in hers. "I—it's the pool. I was down there too long. You're hot, too."

She hadn't noticed, but since every part of her body had gone boneless hours ago, the sensation of heaviness in her feet and fingers must be due to soaking in hot water. Besides, now he mentioned it, the steadily freshening air snaked down the back of her neck and made her shiver.

The setting sun burnished the pillars of the Great Hall and hazed golden light into the courtyard as, still hand-in-hand, they entered it. Her father saw her at once, and a smile lit his face. His cheeks, so pale and sunken mere days ago, shone pink and his cry of "Mirianna, lamb!" sounded twice as strong.

"Go to him," Durren said, releasing her hand.

She looked at the hood, black as night despite the golden glow glazing everything else. She'd touched the face behind that hood. Her fingers had memorized every detail of his skin. She knew intimately the body under the garments that sucked light into them and gave none of it back. She knew him. She loved him. He was hers. She smiled, and her eyes welled. "Thank you...for giving me back my father."

****

The radiance of her smile still beaming down upon him, Durren watched Mirianna run to the fire and throw her arms around the old man. He saw the old man's face scrunch up into tears of joy and the old hands fumble with her hair. She drew back, and he watched her try to smooth her father's wispy hair into some kind of order.

The pain Durren had been holding at bay twisted again in his side, just between the ribs. Something had pierced him there after he'd broken the mage's crystal and all Beggeth broke loose. That wound had taken the longest to heal, longer even than the burns. Now it raged anew in his side, turning like a corkscrew until he wanted to groan with it.

"Ah," said a voice, all too familiar and yet not so. "I thought there might be consequences."

The voice had come from his left. He turned, holding himself stiffly upright, hiding the pain beneath his garments, his covered head concealing the clench of his teeth and the sweat running down his face.

A woman stood illuminated by the last slanting rays of the sun. She wore Mirianna's cloak tied at the throat and belted at the waist. Her slender arms had

318

been thrust through slits cut into the cloak's sides, and her feet peeking from under the hem were bare. Her hair, long and straight, shone like polished amber, and her eyes gleamed like twin emeralds.

"Ayliss..." Durren said, and crumpled.

Chapter Twenty-Three

The pain hit Mirianna like a stab in the ribs. She winced, holding her side, waiting for the stitch to pass, while her father cooed over her. He must have sensed her discomfort because his face paled and his brows knit together. "Mirianna, lamb, you're so warm." He touched her cheek.

"It's nothing. It was a bit close in the tunnel," she was saying when she heard the thud of a body falling.

Turning her head, she saw Durren sprawled on the paving stones and a woman standing over him. Without thinking, she seized the nearest object at hand, a pot, and rushed the stranger.

The woman fixed yellow-green eyes on her.

Mirianna froze, pot half-raised, as the woman shimmered around the edges the way heat shimmers a horizon, but this shimmering made her see, for the briefest of glimpses, a lion. "You're—"

"Ayliss," the woman said. "His sister."

She knew. But she didn't know. The lion—the woman—had guided her here. She trusted her—the lion. Should she trust the woman? Durren lay crumpled at the woman's bare feet. Mirianna flushed, hot again, pain stabbing at her side. She dropped the pot, made to go to Durren's side, but Ayliss stepped in front of her.

"Mirianna, wait. He's shadow still. Let Gareth take care of him." Closing the distance between them, Ayliss took her hands.

At the contact, calm spread throughout her body. Durren would be all right. So would she. She breathed, and her side hurt again, but not as much.

Ayliss's brow wrinkled, one small line in an otherwise perfect forehead. She called for Gareth, but kept her gaze fixed on Mirianna while the boy stood up by the fire pit. He came as if he understood the need without instruction, tapping his way to Durren's side and kneeling there.

Mirianna wondered how much he knew and what had transpired when he discovered the lion wasn't a lion. One part of her mind wondered what Ayliss had told him, and what in the name of the Dragon had Ayliss told her father? And Pumble? But Ayliss was looking at her intently, and her mind couldn't settle on those thoughts. They were of a height, Mirianna observed, of similar slender build, but Ayliss's skin shone like polished porcelain, and her hair, a honey gold parted in the middle, fell smooth and straight to her elbows. "What are you?" Mirianna said. "Are you…human?"

"More so than you think." Ayliss's grip tightened. "You have pain?"

"It's nothing. A stitch in my side."

Ayliss cocked her head, and for a moment Mirianna glimpsed the lion in the gesture. "I see." She released one hand and turned Mirianna toward the fire pit. "Awaken your portly friend. We need to move Durren."

Mirianna hesitated. "Things are changing, aren't they?"

"Yes." Ayliss smiled and squeezed her hand. "But

not entirely at random."

****

The crystal guided Syryk directly to the blond man who sat on a stone, holding his head in his hands, a moon-in-miniature slice of crystal suspended by a thong around his neck. That slice of crystal gleamed in the late afternoon sun like a homing beacon. Syryk dragged his exhausted horse to a halt and tumbled out of the saddle. Finding Rees had been easy, if riding for hours over rugged land on a horse whose gait varied from a bone-jarring trot to a swaying, pick-a-careful-path walk could be considered easy. *Damn, but this body hurt!* The Master of Nolar was a fit man and used to riding. *His* body would've been the better choice for such an escapade, but such were the choices one made when spells fell apart. He cracked his back straight and ordered his feet to walk.

The man sitting on the stone could've been made of stone for all the attention he paid to the skidding horse and whirl of dust it raised. Disconcerted, Syryk paused. Where were the others? There was but one horse and one man, and he looked spell struck. Syryk's stomach crawled with more than hunger pangs from missing the first and second meals of the day. Rees's saddlebags looked thick. More than likely there was something to eat in them. He would see for himself, once he dealt with the problem at hand. Reaching out, he cuffed Rees on the shoulder.

Rees stirred as if from sleep and tilted his head up. He blinked. "Who are you and where in Beggeth did you come from?"

Resisting the urge to roll his eyes, Syryk grabbed the crystal around Rees's neck and touched his own pouch. "I'm your master, fool. Now, where the Demon are the old man and the stones?" Rees stared at him for so long, Syryk added, "I was in disguise before."

He asked the crystal for more power, wondering again what had gone wrong and whether losing his captive had depleted some of the crystal's power. It was only a piece of the original whole, but it was a significant piece, and he knew how to use it.

Rees blinked again and sense came into his eyes. "The old man's dead by now. Krad cut. That fool Pumble stayed with him when he fell off the horse. I've got the stones here." He reached for another thong around his neck and pulled a pouch from his tunic.

Syryk licked his lips. He seized the pouch and yanked it over the blond man's head. "And the girl?" he said as he weighed his destiny in his hand.

"Gone. The Shadow Man took her."

Syryk froze. "The Shadow Man?"

Rees shuddered and rose from the stone. "Black mage spawn. Creature of Beggeth. He may have saved us from the Krad, but he damned well did it to get the girl. Who knows what he's done to her by now. Filthy pervert!"

More perverted than your creative imagination? Syryk put aside that thought and assessed Rees's information. Losing the girl was a blow. She was an important part of the spell. Where would he find another virgin in this wasteland? As for this Shadow Man…he could be none other than the Dragonkeeper. If he had the girl— Well, the Dragonkeeper didn't have the stones, and the stones were all that truly mattered. Pulling the thong strings apart, Syryk dumped the contents into his palm.

Five small round stones and a larger oval one rolled out. They sat like dull gray lumps in the sunlight caressing his hand. Syryk waited. His palm warmed. The stones sat, a shadow pooled under each piece. The long beams of the late afternoon sun shot sparks off flecks of mica and quartzite on each surface. Syryk waited while his stomach clenched and acid dripped into it.

"Aren't they supposed to glow?" Rees said, cocking his head.

They were.

These did not.

"Damn you to Beggeth, you half-brained bastard son of a Krad!" Syryk flung down the stones and seized Rees's throat. "Where are my bloodstones? Where in the name of the Demon Master are my bloodstones?"

Rees was bigger. He was fit and armed, but before he could raise hands to defend himself, Syryk drew on the power of the crystal and made himself into a huge, raging bear. Rees dropped in terror of the beast, and Syryk froze him where he cowered. He returned to his own form—no point in risking being trapped again—and forced his mind to clear. Someone still had the stones, most likely the old man—apparently not the doddering old fool he'd seemed. He was dead—somewhere. They would find him, find the body, and recover the stones.

"Backtrack," he said, and Rees snapped out of his trance.

"What?"

"Find the old man!"

****

When Durren came to, he lay in a dark room.

324

Gareth leaned over him and sponged his face. A bit of twilight seeped through chinks in the front wall, and he recognized the chamber he'd given Mirianna and the boy. "Stop." His mouth was so dry the word came out as a rasp.

"You're burning up, sir. I have to bring the fever down."

"I'm...not...ill." He pushed up onto his elbows. A haze of colored lights dipped and whirled before his eyes, making him fall back again.

"You need to drink something, sir. I don't think you've had anything to drink or eat in two or three days, have you?"

The scolding tone in the boy's voice made Durren want to laugh but even breathing hurt. "I had...porridge...with you."

"Well, there you are. That was days ago. Here. Drink this broth." With surprisingly strong hands, the boy lifted Durren's head and managed to find his lips with the cup. Most of the liquid made it into his mouth, and he swallowed. When the cup was empty, Gareth made a satisfied sound.

"Who...put me in here?"

"Pumble's very strong, sir. After Mirianna told him to stop kissing his charm and get on with it, he picked you right up. She wanted to come in here and help, but I told her she better not. After all, this is what you chose me for—to help you when no one else should."

The boy had managed to remove Durren's hood, unlace his tunic, open the cuffs and push up the sleeves. The cloth he'd stopped Gareth from swabbing over his face, sloshed now onto his bare chest. Durren flinched, but he did feel marginally cooler. "I'll...drink some more."

With a grunt of assent, Gareth spread the cloth and left it on Durren's chest. In the dimness, he could just make out Gareth's form as the boy poured and turned. "Here you are, sir."

When he'd drunk a fourth cup, Durren made another attempt to rise onto his elbows. Gareth protested, and Durren's head swam again, but he had to know—did his skin still glow?

Dear Koronolan, it did! But the quick glance before he fell back again told him two things. The glow had dimmed, but the brightest gleam came from his side, from the old wound that still throbbed with fire.

"I can't wait any longer. I have to know what's wrong." Mirianna's voice, breathy with fear, sounded from the other side of the door. "Durren? Can you hear me?"

"Don—don't come in, love!"

"Cover him, Gareth," said another woman's voice. "We need to talk to him."

He had not hallucinated his sister; Ayliss stood right outside that door, restored to her own form. He didn't know whether to laugh, curse or cry. His eyes responded first, leaking from lids he'd clenched shut.

"They ought to wait till morning," the boy grumbled. "You're still too hot, but I guess if I soak your blanket, that should keep you cooler and covered." After some sloshing sounds, Gareth spread the wet fabric over Durren's upper body.

Durren sucked in a breath, but the cool shock revived him enough to open his eyes.

"I'm going to put a compress on your forehead," the boy said as he wrung out another cloth. "You have to promise me you'll keep it on or you'll heat right up again under that hood."

"There's...an inner cloth. Just...cover me...with that."

With some fumbling, Gareth managed to locate the cloth and position it. The muffling weave was open enough Durren could make out the boy bending and smoothing the blanket and hood drape, checking for any exposed flesh, but it stifled the fresher air, filling Durren's nostrils with the sulfurous scent he'd lived with all too long. His stomach roiled at it. Dear Koronolan, he could hardly breathe!

"Loosen it...could you?"

Gareth plucked the fabric away from Durren's nose and mouth. "That better?" He straightened. "I have to say, sir, I didn't expect to wake up this morning to a lady who used to be a lion asking me to find her something to wear, but as this is the Wehrland, I guess I shouldn't be surprised."

"You're...a good lad, Gareth." He wanted to touch the boy's arm to show his appreciation, but all Durren had strength for was speech, and he needed to conserve that. Ayliss had a lot to answer for.

The chamber door banged open, and Mirianna dropped to her knees at his side. "Durren!" She plunged her hand under the blanket before he could stop her, but she made no move to uncover him, only laced her fingers into his. "Thank goodness you're cooler." Her eyes glimmered in the light of a single candle flickering from the doorway. When she turned toward the boy opposite, a tear track sparkled on her cheek. "You've done wonders, Gareth. Thank you."

"He needs more to drink," Gareth grumbled.

The candle and its bearer moved into Durren's line of sight. Ayliss laid a hand on the boy's shoulder, and the look she gave him was full of tenderness. "We won't keep him long." When the boy made a move to rise, she held him in place. "You need to hear this too, Gareth. You're as much a part of it as we are."

"What about Pumble?" the boy said.

"Our portly friend needs to watch over Mirianna's father." With a graceful adjustment of her cloak, Ayliss placed the candle next to the wash basin and settled herself on the bench beside the boy. Gareth leaned into her, and she draped a slender arm around his shoulders.

They made a pretty picture, and she looked not a bit altered from when Durren had last seen her despite the years and the spell blast, but he'd long since passed the relief stage. "What... consequences?" he demanded through his teeth.

"Patient as ever, I see."

"Fourteen years, Ayliss..."

Her brows dipped into a V. "Try counting that in lion years."

There you go, thinking about no one but yourself again, said the Voice in his head.

Be still! It's time she explained herself. "Where were you...all that time?"

"Watching. And waiting." With the back of her hand, she flipped her hair over her shoulder.

The gesture, so truly Ayliss, made Durren's throat swell. Dear Koronolan, she was his flesh and blood, and despite everything, he loved her. "What for?"

"Her, for one. I had to wait for your dream woman."

Mirianna flushed, her already high color

deepening. "I can accept that you're Durren's sister and you've been trapped in a lion's form just as he's been trapped in the Shadow Man's form all these years." She paused, rolled her eyes skyward and blew out a breath. "Two weeks ago I wouldn't have believed any of this, and here I am talking as if I know something of magic."

"You do," Ayliss said. "Or you wouldn't be here."

Mirianna quirked an eyebrow. "It's the dream, that's all that's magic about me. Anyway, how do you know about the dream? And how did you speak to me from your lion form? Can you read minds?"

Good questions. Durren squeezed her hand to tell her, and she cast him a brief smile before refocusing on Ayliss.

His sister sat up straighter and carefully rearranged the drape of her cloak over her legs. "I know about the dream because I put it there." When they gaped at her, she said, "Not the particulars. I didn't know precisely who your 'dream woman' would be, Durren, or when she would come, but you needed to recognize each other, so I gave you both the dream. It was all I had time for after you burst into Drakkonwehr and fell for Syryk's illusions."

"Wait—" Mirianna put up her free hand. "You knew I was coming—even back then?"

Ayliss tilted her head. "More or less."

"No. Not more or less." Mirianna's eyes narrowed and Durren recognized the fierce expression that had jolted him only days ago. "I want to know—just *what* are you? A…mage?"

He read in his sister's eyes the same struggle for patience he'd undergone days earlier and squeezed Mirianna's fingers. *Keep pressing, love. Make her tell us.*

Ayliss smoothed the fabric over her knees. "All of us have power. Even your portly friend outside. We're born with it. Some of us have more gifts than others. And some of us are better at using the powers we have. I happen to be rather good at reading Shadow Speech and unlocking ancient mysteries, both of which told me a woman—who turned out to be you—was coming."

Mirianna's hand lowered to her lap. She chewed her lower lip. "So…you're not a mage?"

"If a mage is someone who has knowledge and power, then, yes, I suppose I could be called a mage." She gently brushed hair from Gareth's face. "But I would much rather be known as a Drakkonwehr because everything I am and do comes from that lineage."

"You…betrayed us!" Durren spat out.

"*You* weren't supposed to be there for the Chant!" Her eyes flashed green fire. "Contrary to what you seem to think, I was trying to protect you by keeping you out of Drakkonwehr. I knew Syryk would try to kill you if you came, and what I meant to do required all my concentration, but somehow you managed to get inside the chamber anyway. When he went for you, I intended to stop his spell, to shield you, but then you broke his crystal in the middle of the Chant and"—she shrugged one shoulder—"well, the spell energy rearranged everything. I tried to cast both of us out of the chamber, to safety, but I must have taken some of Syryk's curse because I came to in the body of a lion, and I couldn't change back. You had disappeared. Syryk had vanished. The fortress was a smoking ruin."

"And…Errek?" He hadn't wanted to know, but the

words were out before he could stop them.

Ayliss contemplated the hand she'd turned palm up in her lap. When she raised her eyes, they were dark and full. "That was no illusion, Durren. But you knew that anyway."

He did. He'd known as soon as the knife left his hand. But the acknowledgment intensified the shame, the guilt, the sorrow. If only his heart would stop beating so he could lay down the pain and simply die.

He must have clenched Mirianna's hand, for he became aware of the gentle stroke of her thumb across his knuckles. There was such tenderness in her look the iron band around his heart loosened a little and he breathed again.

"Who's—?" said Gareth, but Ayliss touched her finger to his lips, and the boy leaned into her shoulder once more.

"When I finally found you again, months later," she continued, "you'd become this Shadow being and I couldn't reach you. Not until something changed. I could feel it coming, but I couldn't reach into your mind until that day the Krad attacked you at the stream. And you," she said to Mirianna, "you had to enter the Wehrland."

"That was—that was two weeks ago," Durren said, recalling the matter at hand. "What happened…last night?"

With a cat-like smile, Ayliss glanced at Mirianna, who blushed bright red but met her gaze. "Apparently, with the spell energy unraveling, a great many things," Ayliss said, "most of which were exactly as I'd hoped when I used the piece of crystal Gareth found down by the pool to return to my own form."

"You…made us—I mean—we were enchanted…" Mirianna trailed off, looking aghast.

"Hardly." Ayliss smiled and patted her hand. "You simply did what your hearts had already chosen to do. No spell can change true hearts."

'True hearts and no fear, against a mage's power, hold dear.' The words from Owender echoed in Durren's mind.

Ayliss looked directly at him, meeting his eyes through the weave of his face covering, and he knew she'd heard his thoughts. "All I ever asked of you was to trust me, Durren, to let me help you, but you wouldn't hear of it."

"You were jealous…"

"For a time. Who wouldn't be? Especially since you kept flaunting it." She looked at Mirianna and explained, "The Sword of Drakkonwehr, which Durren has and which has always been intended for him. It's his destiny, and I've never disputed that."

Durren sucked in air, struggling for speech.

Ayliss's gaze drilled into the hood, finding his eyes as easily as if there were no barrier. "Yes, I know I needled you about it. I'm the elder child," she told Mirianna, "and the Sword always passed to the firstborn—"

"Son!" Durren rasped.

"The firstborn, which just so happened to be sons until my birth." She looked down her nose at him, so much the thirteen-year-old of his memories again his eyes welled. "Despite what you may have thought, I've always known my destiny lay in the scrolls. No one seemed to realize their significance. Grandfather may have read some of them—once—but I don't think

Father ever did more than poke around."

"Like me."

"Yes, like you. The dust was that thick. Anyway, I started reading, realized they were in a jumble, and spent weeks putting them in order."

"Dragon Chant...you weren't supposed to—"

"Find it? Yes, I was. You had the Sword, Durren. I had the Chant. That's why there were two of us, and why I was the firstborn, not you. I was meant to find that Chant."

"Not to—to give it away!"

"All I've ever asked of you, Durren, was to trust me, just once, and to let me help you."

"Giving Syryk the Chant was...helping me?"

"If you'd read the scrolls, you wouldn't be asking that now."

"Syryk?" Mirianna said. "Is that—?"

"The mage," Ayliss said. "He came to me because he'd been chasing the Chant. Some of his ancestors were Black Mages, and he'd found bits and pieces of their scrolls, enough to know that what he wanted had to be buried in that dustbin deep in Drakkonwehr."

"Syryk is evil—"

"Syryk is selfish. He wants to control the Dragon for his own purposes. Don't you think I know that?"

"Why...did you help him?"

"Because he had something I needed, a power source. Crystal columns concentrate great spell energy in the hands of the user, but they're very rare, and rarer still are those who know how to work them."

She paused, looked off in the distance and seemed to compose herself. When her focus returned, the emerald eyes gleamed like twin beams, as if some power shone through them. "There's more to being the Dragon*keeper* than you think, Durren. More to it than everyone since Koronolan knew about how to *keep* the Dragon. There's been an unbroken line of sons who needed to know only the Sword, because all they had to do was make sure the Dragon stayed entombed, so that's all they read about, all they spoke about. But the Dragon wasn't meant to be entombed forever.

"The Black Mages used the dragons, enslaved them. Koronolan didn't know this until he defeated the Black Mages and broke the spell. By then there was only one dragon left. Koronolan didn't want to kill the beast since it and its brethren hadn't participated willingly in the carnage, but he knew his people wouldn't accept giving the beast its freedom without some penalty."

"Like…going to sleep?" Gareth asked.

"Yes, going to sleep until there would come a time when his people would accept the return of the dragon. Koronolan wrote it all down, so that those who came after him would know of the bargain he made with the Last Dragon, but his sons were afraid. Memories of the Black Mages' treachery and the dragons' destruction were too vivid in their minds, so they hid the scrolls of Koronolan, and soon those scrolls—and Koronolan's promise—were forgotten."

She leaned forward and her eyes intensified. "Tell me, Durren, you hear a voice, don't you? Ever since that night you broke the crystal, you've heard a voice?"

She means me, the Voice in his head said.

Durren swallowed, hard. *You're not—*

Oh, but I am. And I have been patient a very, very long time.

Chapter Twenty-Four

Syryk drew his cloak tighter around his shoulders. It was an expensive cloak, well made, befitting the Master of Nolar's status and fortune. Such a cloak kept out both the cold and damp that came with the twilight pressing in on him from all sides as the horses plodded ever upward into rougher and rockier terrain. Pity it couldn't ward off the growing sense of dread that pooled in the pit of his stomach and turned the dry-cake he'd demanded from Rees into a burning lump in his stomach. He shifted again in his saddle, attempting to find a position that hurt less, but nothing availed. With each bone-jarring, stone-crunching step, they came inexorably closer to the truth: the old man and his fat companion were headed to Drakkonwehr.

What could possibly be drawing them there? The Dragonkeeper had no such power. With the girl and the bloodstones, though— No, the fool had no idea how to use them. Syryk had the only crystal. He'd banked on it, the bloodstones, and Master Brandelmore's bride being enough to complete the Chant and raise the Dragon wherever he wished. There was no need to go back to the gatehouse of Beggeth. No need to traverse this place that reeked of sulfur and—he sniffed—urine?

Rees halted and stood in his stirrups, head turned like a hound scenting the wind. "Krad," he said. "There've been Krad through here."

An unearthly howl rent the air. Stones cascaded down from above, pelting the ground, the horses, Syryk's head. He reeled in his saddle and saw stars before Rees grabbed his reins and shouted, "Ride!"

****

There was a rumble, and the floor of the chamber heaved. Mortar showered from the lintel over the door. Mirianna leaned over Durren, covering him, and Ayliss sheltered the boy. The paving stones rolled like a gigantic mole passed beneath them, raising and shifting years of dust. The groan seemed to well up from the depths, a great creaking of earth and stone as the fortress swayed all around them.

"I am awake!" said the Voice, and it seemed to have gained power. It reverberated in Durren's head and even, he fancied, echoed in the chamber, but that was impossible. It was his own thoughts he heard, wasn't it? It was his conscience. The Shadow Man and Durren had split. The Shadow Man had been overthrown and Durren had reasserted himself, and the voice should have vanished, been beaten into submission by the will of the warrior, but here it was and louder, and—*by Kiros!*—not his voice at all.

"The time has come. You must keep your bargain, Drakkonwehr. For I willingly laid down to sleep for your ancestor. The Chant awoke me, my mind, before you broke the spell. Now you must finish what was started. Raise me and mine."

Mirianna shuddered beside him, but her gaze darted into the shadows, as if seeking the voice she, too, could hear. Even Gareth's eyes widened, but Ayliss smiled the cat's smile he'd come to thoroughly detest.

"Ayliss," Durren demanded, reaching out his free

hand and seizing her ankle. "What in the name of Kiros is happening?"

She looked down her nose at the contact, the first between them in years. She'd made no previous move to touch him, either as lion or woman, and he wondered why until he saw the red glow shining between his black-gloved fingers as if the leather could barely contain it. Shocked, he let go, looked at where he held Mirianna's hand under the blanket. The glow through the weave had intensified, no longer like banked coals but a log about to burst. And not just there— everywhere his skin had been bared for Gareth's sponging pulsed anew with red fire, matching the beat of his heart. *Dear Koronolan!*

"You're fulfilling your destiny, Durren," his sister said. "All these years you've been *keeping* the Dragon in the only way possible since you interrupted the Chant. Its consciousness has been living inside you."

"No!" Durren gasped.

"Yes! You broke your sword in my flesh, and now it resides in your own side. You eased your wounds in the pool wherein my blood from that wound seeps. Your blood is mine, Drakkonwehr, and mine is yours. Now, set me free!"

The voice echoed off the chamber's walls, and within Durren's skull. His head pounded and he wanted to hold the voice inside where it had at least been contained. But now the voice was out and filling the air, it had a hiss he hadn't noticed before, an ancient thickness of the tongue that caressed soft sounds. By Koronolan, this could not be happening! He could not now be sharing a body with a beast—the Beast!—he'd vowed to keep entombed. And yet here was the creature demanding release according to some ancient 'bargain.' And here was his sister telling him he had to give it what it wanted.

"Syryk's spell is nearly unraveled, and we must complete the Chant," Ayliss said. "If we don't, you'll die because the only thing that saved you when the spell exploded is being bound to the Dragon, and that connection won't last much longer."

He heard her but faintly, as if she spoke from the surface above the whirlpool he was drowning in. Was nothing true? Had his whole heritage been a lie perpetrated by fearful sons of Koronolan? Had he been so thoroughly wrong in his beliefs, his decisions that his life meant nothing? Amid the crush of incongruities and impossibilities, his mind grasped the one salient point that might still matter. "Then…kill me! I'd rather be…dead. At least I'll have…discharged my one duty as a Drakkonwehr—keep the Dragon bound!"

Ayliss kicked him. With her bare heel, she hauled back and kicked him in the thigh. Her eyes flashed green fire as she thrust her chin forward. "You bloody, stubborn knucklehead! No one is going to die. Do you hear me? We are going to live through this, every last one of us. *That* is our destiny, Durren—to complete Koronolan's promise and restore the world he once knew when dragons and the People lived in peace. I've been trying for years to get you to see the truth, but you had eyes for nothing but that Sword! Yes, we need the damned thing, and it has yet a purpose to serve, but right now what we need is for you to trust me, to believe what I've learned from the scrolls is going to help us—all of us. Can you do that? Or are you going to lie there and bleed fire until you die from the inside out?"

Always so cool, so calm, Ayliss hadn't lost her temper in his presence for...for longer than Durren could remember. He'd always envied that control, but her loss of it now, here, showed him more than anything she'd so far said that she loved him, needed him, and meant to save them.

"'True hearts and no fear, against a mage's power, hold dear,'" Ayliss said, her gaze full of the passion he'd once glimpsed so many years ago. "Have you seen my 'true heart,' Durren? Or do you need more proof?"

I've seen YOUR heart, said the Dragon, this time inside Durren's head. *Your 'demons' have cast a long shadow over your soul, but your heart is still intact— much as you've wanted to rip it out for the pain it's caused you.*

Be still! All these years he'd resented the interfering voice in his head, and now he knew why. It was not his conscience. Not even *his* at all! *Hold your tongue!*

Why? Because now you know it's forked?

Treacherous beast! Get out of my head!

'Treacherous beast,' hah! Let me remind you, Dragonkeeper, this 'treacherous beast' is the very one who's lived inside you for more than a dozen of your paltry human years, who's listened to you endlessly bemoan your fate, who's kept you sane those countless days and nights when you had no one else to talk to, who let you soothe your body in my pool—

"Trust her, please." Mirianna's entreaty penetrated his skull and overrode the Dragon, silencing both of them. "Trust her, Durren," she said when she had his attention. "I do."

"So do I." Gareth held out his hand, palm up, and Ayliss grasped it. Her lip trembled, and she dropped her gaze before Mirianna reached across Durren's body and covered both of their hands with hers.

"We trust both of you." Mirianna shared a long look with Ayliss before she let go and laid her hand on Durren's heart. She looked deep into the eyes she couldn't possibly see in the dimness and through his face covering. "Do you trust us?"

The tenderness of her touch, the love radiating through the blanket's weave to Durren's skin, penetrated to his heart. He looked from Mirianna to the boy and responded with his heart before his head could process the reasons, "I…trust you."

"If you die…if you give up and let go and take the Dragon with you," Mirianna said, "everything you've worked for, everything you've worked to preserve will go too. The Shadow Man will win, and Durren Drakkonwehr, the man you once were and were becoming again, the man I love, will disappear too."

He knew in his bones she was right. He loved her, had committed his heart to her, but he realized he loved the boy too, as a man loves a younger brother or— even—a son. They and his sister were his family, and he had to take care of them as best he could. Even the old man and the fat fool were his charges now. He'd been shadow too long; he'd almost forgotten how to be a man. It had taken a motley bunch of humans and their bumbling hearts to make him care again. He would give his life, but not in the name of Drakkonwehr. He would give it to save them, the people he loved, and that was as it should be.

"What…do we do now?" he said.

Mirianna's eyes shone. He saw unshed tears, but also pride, love and fear.

Ayliss swallowed and cleared her throat. "You complete the change that the broken spell set in motion. I'll do my best to weave the spell, but I have to warn you, with this small piece of crystal, I'm only buying us time. Neither of you will be...entirely whole. The Dragon will take your body, Durren, but you'll be within the Dragon. It will keep you alive until we can find enough crystal to complete the Chant and, hopefully, separate the two of you."

"Hopefully?" Mirianna said on a whisper.

Ayliss leaned forward and covered her hand where it lay atop Durren's heart. "'True hearts and no fear,' Mirianna. That's older magic than crystals and spells. Remember that." Gripping Gareth's hand, she stood. "I'll give you a moment," she said, taking the boy with her out of the chamber.

Mirianna's hand on his chest trembled.

"You're not...going to lose me," Durren said as she blew out the candle.

"I know. The dream—we'll always have the dream." She turned and took in the glow radiating everywhere from his body.

She was terrified. He understood. His heart would be as cold as the stones of Drakkonwehr right now if it weren't burning so hot with dragon flame. "No more...time, love."

"I said I would do anything, Durren, and I meant it. I love you." She raised shaking hands to his face covering. "I want to kiss you, and then I'll go."

"Close...eyes...please."

"For now. But you'll be back, and the spell will be

broken and you'll be yourself again."

Would he? Dear Koronolan, that would be as wonderful as the fresh air caressing his face before her lips, cool, touched his so sweetly, so tenderly, he sensed more than felt the kiss. Then she stood and rushed from the chamber, leaving him alone in the dark—but not alone as the pain in his side intensified and the glow grew and the beast inside him stretched and the world shifted, wrenched itself inside out, and went dark…

****

Mirianna tramped along the path back to the fire in the courtyard. Full darkness hid the tears she wiped from her eyes, and she had her voice mostly under control when she met Ayliss and Gareth at the edge of the firelight. "I'm going down to the pool. If Gareth found one piece of crystal, there should be more to be found."

Gareth blocked her with his staff. "She wants you to wait."

Ayliss stood with her arms outstretched, palms up, eyes closed. Firelight shifted across her face, sparkling the sweat beading her forehead as she mumbled in a language Mirianna didn't know, but seemed somehow familiar.

Shadow Speech, she guessed, remembering Durren's gesture days ago—was it only days?—when he'd rubbed the stone, a bloodstone, in his broken sword. It had power too, the sword or the stone—or both. The Sword of Drakkonwehr, Pumble had called it. Where was it? Still with Durren in that chamber or—no, she couldn't think about that now, what might be happening in that darkened room. 'True hearts,' Ayliss had told her, and she sensed there was power in that or

342

she wouldn't have left Durren alone to face whatever was going to happen to him. *By the Dragon!* Mirianna jammed her fist to her chin to stop its tremble. She needed strength now, not tears.

Ayliss stopped speaking. She opened her eyes, but recognition came into them slowly, as if her thoughts returned from a great distance. She reached out for the boy, who took her arm over his shoulder.

Mirianna needed no further evidence of a connection between the two. Every touch, every unspoken communication since the she-lion had made herself known to Gareth told her Ayliss had secrets yet to tell. She would push her, but not just yet. Durren came first. "Well?"

Breathing deeply, Ayliss spoke. "Going down to the pool is a good idea, and we may yet have to do that, but do you remember Syryk?"

"The mage? You said he died in the spell."

"Disappeared," Gareth corrected.

Ayliss smiled at the boy. When hoof beats sounded in the courtyard, she nodded toward the clatter. "Well, I think he's found us. As the spell unravels, it seems to be drawing all who survived back to its wellspring. The circle should be complete now."

****

Rees rode like the demons of Beggeth were after them while Syryk clung to the saddle pommel with both hands. His head throbbed and blood dripped into his eyes, but he dared not release his grip to wipe it away. The demons of Beggeth were indeed on their trail, and though the Krad had no horses, they could climb like goats in pursuit of a blood-smell far less fresh than his. Behind, he could still hear distant howls despite the twists of the narrow rock passage they followed ever upward. At last Rees rode through what seemed like a gate, and ahead Syryk glimpsed a fire.

"Don't come any closer!" A squat, round shape in a floppy hat stood silhouetted in front of the fire, sword drawn.

"Pumble!" Rees leaped out of the saddle. "How in Beggeth did you get here?"

"He came with my father, you bastard!" said a woman's voice.

Syryk slid off his horse and wiped blood from his eyes. Yes, it was most definitely a woman. And she held a long wooden stick in front of her like a pike or halberd. She was garbed like a warrior woman he'd once seen depicted on an ancient scroll, her skirt sheared off at mid-knee and split over one leg, exposing a length of alabaster thigh. If this was the old man's daughter, his luck had definitely turned. But he had a more immediate problem. Rees had stepped forward with a look of befuddlement on his face.

"Mirianna! I..." Rees trailed off, lowering his sword.

She lunged. The stick caught him square in the chest, knocking him on his back. "That's for leaving my father to die!" She loomed over Rees, pole jammed into his throat as if she dared him to resist, to give her an excuse to ram it home, but the otherwise competent warrior lay at her feet, apparently stunned.

The fat man rushed up to snatch Rees's sword. "You should never have done that, Rees. That's not like you."

"Take his knife, too, Pumble. And any other weapons you know he carries."

344

"I'm sorry, Rees." The fat man relieved Rees of a knife in his belt and one in his boot. "But you really made her—and me—mad."

The woman backed a step, raised the stick, and rotated it toward Syryk's chest. He thought, being behind Rees in the darkness, he might have escaped her notice, but no—she'd merely prioritized her attack. "You! Drop your weapons and come out of the shadows."

Syryk stared. He'd never seen anything fiercer, or more breathtaking, but he grasped his pouch and closed his fingers around the crystal within because someone had to take control of the situation. While she was making an admirable attempt, he much preferred playing his own game. Taking a deep breath, he drew on the power of the crystal.

"Who in Beggeth are you?" The fat man's question broke his concentration.

Syryk glared down his nose at the miscreant despite the fact they were of a height. "I'm your master, fool!"

The fat man shook his head. "That's the Master of Nolar, and you're not him."

Syryk clenched his fingers on the crystal and projected its power, sending it to Rees, who still lay like a lump on the ground, to the fat fool staring at him as if he'd emerged from the cracked Stone Dam at Herrok-Eneth, to the woman warrior who set her feet and prepared to level him with her stick. Why were none of them responding? Why did the woman glow with a red aura? Why did another woman's voice speak his name from somewhere in the darkness behind him? And why in the name of the Dragon did she sound like the one woman he'd never expected to hear again?

He turned. And she was there, coming into the reach of the firelight, her hair a fall of gold on either side of her face, her eyes as green-gold as he remembered, her face, if possible, even more beautiful. "Ayliss," he said.

"Hello, Syryk."

"You…you're dead."

"So are you."

"But…we're not."

"So it would seem."

Chapter Twenty-Five

When the clatter arose, Gareth moved as he'd been instructed. How Ayliss—he still thought of her as the she-lion—told him what to do, he had no idea since she didn't speak it. He simply knew he had to follow Mirianna toward the intruders and hand her his staff. The man who spoke first he recognized as the loud one who'd frightened him when Mirianna and the others had first come upon the Shadow Man's camp.

When she knocked the man down, Gareth's blood ran hot. He wanted her to hit the man again, wished he'd struck the blow himself, but this was her fight and whatever she chose would have to do. The other man smelled of fresh blood, cold sweat, and the tangy spice of some herb-and-oil mix he'd once smelled on a guest who arrived at the inn with an armed escort. Coin had flowed freely, but so had the demands. Gareth frowned. This stranger spoke in that same sneering way. He wished Mirianna would level him too, but Ayliss intervened, drawing the newcomers' attention.

Mirianna pressed the staff back into his hands. "I have his sword now," she whispered.

"Do you know how to use it?"

She blew out a breath. "I used to try the blades in my father's workshop. Maybe now I know why." She squeezed his shoulder. "Go. Do whatever it is she told you to do. I'll be fine."

Helen C. Johannes

Waves of energy flowed from her. Gareth's heart pounded in response, and his breath quickened with it, but this energy didn't prompt chills. Instead, all his senses sharpened—if possible—and he wanted to act on what they reported. He gripped his staff, wishing once more he could strike a blow against the menace the strange man projected, but the she-lion—Ayliss—was depending on him. Backing away from the glow of the fire, he headed for the shadows.

****

"Ayliss..." Syryk stretched out a hand, took a tentative step in her direction. He hadn't until this moment given a thought to regrets, to the consequences of any of his actions, his decisions. He'd always been forward focused, on finding his ancestors' scrolls, on locating the Chant, on raising the Dragon. When all Beggeth broke loose in the chamber, he'd naturally acted in self-preservation, saving himself, never once thinking—in all those years he'd been trapped in the crystal, waiting for someone to find it and shed blood on it—about what he might have lost in that moment, what he'd risked in the pursuit of his dream, his destiny. Yet here she was, alive, against all odds, all expectations. If only he'd taken the time, at the time, to see what he saw at this moment. "I never meant..."

Her face, that beautiful, perfectly unchanged face, hardened. "Of course you did. And so did I. The time for lies is over. You used me to get the Chant. I used you to get the power of the crystal. The arrangement was mutually beneficial—until everything went wrong."

She hadn't touched him, not advanced even an inch, yet her words hit him like a body blow. Evidently

348

she hadn't been suspended as he had for all those intervening years. He swayed, stunned, while he wondered where she'd been and what she'd endured and why in the name of the Demon Master she looked at him as though he were a piece of Krad dung. A thought worked its way through the haze of his mind. By all the Demons in Beggeth, this was an illusion! Either that or a hallucination brought on by the Krad rock he'd taken to the head. Well, he would deal with it as he had everything else that interfered with his plans. He tightened his fingers around the pouch and focused on the crystal inside.

She did not disappear. Nor did she fade. Nor did anything else surrounding him alter. If he squeezed the crystal any harder, he would slice open the leather and his fingers. Panicked, Syryk tore the pouch from his neck, yanked open the thong, and tumbled the crystal into his hand, murmuring all the time.

The illusion had the effrontery to roll her eyes. When he stared at her, Ayliss extended a hand and opened it. Something shimmered on her palm, shifted colors, and glowed. "You can't work your crystal because I have a piece of it. Now our pieces are together, they cancel each other's power—unless we work together."

Syryk flushed. He should've thought of that. After all, he was the only one who could work illusions. *He* was the mage, not she. She hadn't studied through all her youth, pored over all those musty scrolls, spent all those years learning crystal craft. Besides, she'd foolishly shown him her power source. He smirked, covering his own between his palms. "My piece is bigger."

"Yes, and you know the secrets of working it."

His eyes narrowed. Why would she so readily acknowledge the truth? He would never yield the slightest advantage to an opponent. Yet she seemed not the least cowed. He surreptitiously stroked his crystal, and power tugged at his fingertips. Not as much as usual, to be sure, but power nonetheless. She would expect him to use it against her. He sent it to Rees instead, to the disk suspended around the man's neck—just enough to regain control.

The shard on her palm pulsed. Her already stony expression hardened. "Did you not *read* the scrolls?"

Of course he had—once—when he'd sorted them. Most contained unimportant, irrelevant drivel. The ones that held what nuggets he needed, those he'd memorized—down to the random droplets of ink on the page. A bead of sweat—or maybe blood, he couldn't be sure which—trickled into his eyebrow, tickling as it went. He'd read everything. Everything! What was she so sure he'd missed? She raised her gaze, and her eyes burned with a strange green fire. He sensed power, and not crystal power. Where in the name of the Demon Master had she found that power?

"You're standing on Drakkonwehr ground, Syryk. Your spell has completely unraveled, and your power source is shattered. What you began is undone, but what you set in motion…"

That ground heaved, tilting the giant paving stones and opening crevices between them. The fortress groaned, and the walls shifted, swaying in the dark around them as if an earthquake shook the place. The movement went on and on, filling the night with the agony of stone on stone, the thud of falling rock, the screech of wooden beams straining to hold against massive pressure. Syryk stumbled, flailed for his horse. The beast shied and blundered into Rees's mount. Both animals bolted into the shadows beyond the courtyard.

Rees scrambled to his feet, face pale. "What in Beggeth—?"

The fat man, mouth agape, pointed at the ramparts.

Above, lightning sparked. But not earth-shattering bolts of blue-white, Syryk realized with a growing sense of awe and horror, but strings—whiplashes, really—of snapping, snaking red-yellow fire. Silhouetted against a billowing cloud of smoke was an enormous shape he'd beheld only in scrolls. He swallowed. The scrolls had not done it justice.

The Beast roared, and the foundations rattled again. Lightning flashed. Even the stars shook in the night sky. Then the massive head, yellow smoke curling from nostrils large as cauldrons, lowered, and two iridescent eyes with foot-tall slits for pupils focused on him. "Hello, little mage. Should I thank you, do you think? Or would you rather I did your bidding, little one?"

Syryk trembled, but he summoned voice and tried once more to pull power from the crystal. "Beast, behold your master! I raised you. I broke the enchantment. I—"

The Dragon laughed, a hoarse, hissing sound that filled all the corners of the fortress and licked chills up Syryk's spine. "Your ancestors bound me and mine to do their bidding. They led us to slaughter! Now I am free, I will do naught for you, spawn of the black arts!" A jet of flame shot into the earth at Syryk's feet.

His recoil landed him within inches of Ayliss. "What..? But the Chant—"

"Drakkonwehr ground," she repeated, sparing him a glance. "Your boots are smoking."

With a yelp, Syryk kicked dirt over the smoldering spots. As fast as the embers died, his rage flared, overriding fear and stampeding directly to certainty. *She*'d given him the Chant. The Dragon had arisen. But the Beast was not his to command. "You bitch! What did you leave out?"

"Nothing you couldn't have figured out yourself— if you were as clever as you thought you were." Her retort stung nearly as much as the fact she hadn't even glanced at him. "Now pay attention and focus on something other than your miserable self for once. It's going to take all of us to get through this." She held out her hand to him, the one with the shard of crystal lying on the upturned palm. "Drakkonwehr ground," she said for the third time, through gritted teeth, with one fierce glance full of green fire that drove from his mind all— *nearly* all—thought of snatching the shard from her grip.

Ayliss thought he was selfish, did she? She thought he was a fool? He would show her how much he retained of the scrolls, the history, the spells. He shifted his crystal to his left hand and slapped it into her palm, wrapping his fingers around hers, jamming the two shards together.

The contact blew Syryk back on his heels. His hair stood on end and power coursed through his entire body. Their joined hands vibrated. Sparks flew between their fingers.

She smiled, and her face shone like the sun before she turned it toward the Beast. "Koronolan bound you!" Her voice rang out, strong and sure. "Koronolan binds you still. To this ground, to this blood."

The Dragon lashed its tail, and flame crackled from its mouth. Stones tumbled from the parapet as it beat its wings. "Free me! I have kept my bargain!"

Despite the rushing in Syryk's ears, despite the energy lighting up every nerve in his brain, bits of scroll lore clicked into place like the last pieces of a particularly ingenious puzzle. Her power was as elemental as the ancestral blood flowing in her veins, as solid as the unique ground under her feet. He needed her—Ayliss—as much as she needed him. They could only raise the Dragon here, together, but to *control* it…

"Where are the bloodstones?" Syryk whispered. There was one last chance he could still salvage this.

"What…bloodstones?" Ayliss hissed.

Ah-hah! Satisfaction surged through him. The energy spike pulled their joined power in his direction long enough for him to divert one small burst. He sent it to Rees. *Find the old man!*

Chapter Twenty-Six

Durren breathed. The ache in his side had subsided, and he felt surprisingly…weightless, as though he floated in the pool, but there was light in this darkness. Sparks and streaks of it, and a roaring noise in his head, and underneath that a regular *ka-thud, ka-thud*, like the beat of a heart—a very large heart. He gasped.

Drakkonwehr, the Beast hissed. *So you have survived once more.*

He must have passed out. Or passed on. Was this what dying felt like? Losing all bodily sensation and simply floating? But he was not dead. His mind, his soul, his consciousness still existed, trapped in a burning, leathery, glowing red body. But not just a body, a mind too—a mind surging with rapid-fire thoughts, ancient memories, strange, inhuman desires. By Kiros, he was *inside* the Beast—and privy to its intentions! *All those times I wished myself dead…you convinced me to live—for your own purposes, Beast!*

My life is worth a hundred of your paltry lives, my age beyond your measure. If you value the petty spark that is your life, pray that I keep mine. There is much danger yet to be faced, son of Koronolan.

Durren had no more—in fact even less—reason to trust the Beast, but the urgency in its words was sincere. Now his consciousness had awakened, he realized the light was more than flashes of mind-light such as would shimmer behind closed eyelids. The darkness he perceived was outside where full night had descended on the fortress, and the flashes flared from the Dragon's mouth as he saw through the Beast's eyes. Everything looked distorted, elongated, yellow, and tiny. The figures he took to be humans were standing down in the courtyard, and—*Dear Koronolan!*—the Beast must be perched on the ramparts. As his eyes adjusted to the Dragon's vision, he searched the figures for Mirianna, the boy, his sister—found Ayliss and, at her side, not Gareth but a face he hadn't seen since he'd broken the bastard's crystal.

Syryk!

Durren's vision hazed. At least he thought it was his vision, but he couldn't be sure now he and the Dragon were one. The rage pulsing through his consciousness, however, *that* was most certainly his. His hands itched for his Sword. Broken or not, he would plunge it to the hilt into the scheming bastard's heart. But he had no hands, no Sword. Only an all-consuming desire to remove from the face of the earth the one person who had wrecked his life—No, by Kiros!—had wrecked the world! *Blast him! Step on him! Eat him!*

Patience, son of Koronolan. A chuckle rumbled in the Dragon's throat. *I have already given him a taste of my power.*

A taste! Damn you, Beast, there stands the bastard who put you inside of me!

No. That was as much your doing as his. He wove the spell; you broke it. That is the first demon you must face if you would be yourself again.

Though he had no body to absorb the blow,

Durren's consciousness reeled as if he'd been struck from behind. *What demon?* Yes, he'd broken the crystal column. Doing so was necessary to break the spell, to stop the mage from raising the Dragon. That was his duty as a Drakkonwehr. He'd done all he could to fulfill his pledge, even after his sister had—

But she hadn't betrayed him or their heritage. He knew that now, had accepted it. That was why he was here in the Dragon's body. Koronolan's promise overrode the keeper of the Sword's pledge. They had to raise the Dragon, to free it as promised. There was no demon in that. But Syryk—the mage deserved to die for his part!

The little mage has big dreams, Drakkonwehr, but you and I yet require his services. Your blood-kin and I understand this far better than you do.

Durren steamed. The Dragon's heat had pushed his temperature beyond what his humanly body could bear. He wondered briefly where the shell that once housed his soul lay, wondering if this Beastly heat had consumed it, leaving an outline of ash for Ayliss to work her charms over. How could she make him whole again? Was it even possible? Yet here was the Beast holding out just such hope while rage made sparks sizzle around the edges of his vision. Demons, hah! He'd done no more than his duty, had acted because Syryk was going to win.

Was he? Or did you merely think he was?

"Illusion, Drakkonwehr..." Syryk's sibilant voice came to him like an echo through the threads of memory. The image of the mage gloating over Errek's death—and Durren's own part in it—played in all its vivid, minute, agonizing detail. He'd killed Errek by

believing what he saw was true. Dear Koronolan, had he done the same by taking the Sword to the crystal? Had he intervened when intervention was not necessary? Had he in fact caused—? No! The idea was too outrageous, too mind-altering to consider.

Illusions may flatter us, confuse us, or betray us, Drakkonwehr. Or they may be images we cling to when the truth is too difficult to face.

Too...difficult...to face... If he still possessed eyes, Durren would've closed them. But he had no eyes, and he had no means of stopping the thoughts that rushed up like an enemy horde to assail him. He should've trusted Ayliss. She had studied the scrolls, after all, which was more than he'd done. He'd always envied her knowledge, her quick mind, her mastery of Shadow Speech. But he hadn't trusted her precisely because of how much she knew. His one advantage, which he'd daily thrown in her face, was no more than an accident of gender. He had not *earned* the Sword. He'd been *given* it. Hidden in his heart, etched into his very bones, he'd borne that knowledge, that he deserved nothing on merit. In all ways she was better. And he'd never forgiven her for it, had never stopped trying to prove himself and denigrate her.

There. That was the truth slicing like steel through his defenses. She was the hero and he the jealous fool who'd cracked the gates of Beggeth and let the demon Krad loose in the land. He'd failed, more miserably than anyone but he and the Beast he'd entangled himself with knew.

Good. You have named your demon, son of Koronolan. What will you do now?

He'd lived fourteen years with the knowledge of

his failure, and he'd yet failed to right it. Even, until now, to acknowledge it. Durren wished the Beast would let him go, let him give up whatever life-spark kept him earthbound. Then he could finally put an end to this never-ending misery, could absolve himself of the raw pain of thinking, of caring about the people—Mirianna, Gareth, Ayliss, even the old man and the fat fool—he was now helpless to protect.

You pathetic humans! Flames shot from the Dragon's nostrils with a rumbling roar. *It escapes me how you endure any trial long enough even to breed, yet here you are. And why do your kind persist at all? Because every now and then—once a century, perhaps—ONE of you understands this: Death is what you accept only when you have spent all that you are— to the very last drop of your sweat and blood—in order to save what you love. That, son of Koronolan, is what a hero, a true warrior, would do.*

For far too long the Beast had lectured him. He'd listened before he knew the voice's true identity—after all, the Dragon's words aligned, mostly, with his conscience—but this scathing indictment exceeded all bounds! *How dare you speak of heroes, Beast! How in the Demon's own Name would you know anything of duty, of honor, of sacrifice?*

The Dragon growled, a long, rolling grumble that gathered power and volume and reverberated outward from the Beast's throat until every inch of the Beast shook with it.

Durren recoiled, drew himself into a ball, but the maelstrom he'd triggered rose up and swamped him anyway. Memories slammed into his consciousness. One after another in rapid, red-hot, relentless succession, they bombarded his senses. Flames, searing heat, smoking flesh, explosions in the sky, a soul screaming as it plummeted to the earth, a nest of cracked stones. No, not stones—eggs with sticky, spilled, lizard-like shapes drenched in blood. The smell, the thick tarry blood steaming as it drained. A raging sense of loss, loneliness like a boulder crushing a soul alone, so very alone…

Into the aftermath, the raw silence where Durren's nerve endings jangled with each eddying emotion the flood of memories had unleashed, the Dragon spoke quietly. *Have you seen MY heart now, Drakkonwehr?*

Thoughts, bare fragments of ideas crawled out of his consciousness, yet he had to name the thoughts, not for the Beast, but for himself. *You…lost your mate, your brethren…yet you lived. You gave Koronolan your promise, you surrendered. You laid down to sleep because…because dying was less of a sacrifice than living as a prisoner, buried at the whim of the insignificant human who gave you one last chance to…to save what you love.*

Like a flash of lightning illuminates a space, Durren saw a pool surrounded by rough rock walls and a pebble-strewn ledge. He recognized it as the pool deep below Drakkonwehr although he'd never once seen it lighted by more than phosphorescence. Just below the surface in the corner where the warm water welled up from the depths lay a jumble of five smooth boulders Durren knew as well as he knew the contours of his own body. They were of a size, rounded at one end and…gently pointed at the other. The image faded, but comprehension shuddered through him.

There are…eggs…

The last of my brethren. The future of my kind. Now do you understand, Drakkonwehr?

The Dragon's world had crumbled. Durren had seen it as if he'd lived it in those moments of searing memory. The Beast would do all it could to save the precious last survivors.

You and I are not much different in that, son of Koronolan. You also lived when many times you longed for death. You wish to protect your mate, your blood-kin, your kind from the harm this little mage would unleash.

What do we do?

Now you must face your second demon. Do you know its name, Drakkonwehr?

Trust. The word tasted like gall retched up from an empty stomach, but Durren forced himself to say it. *I have to trust you, Beast.*

And your blood-kin, your chosen mate, and those frail creatures you consider brethren. You must trust their hearts are truly aligned with yours. And you must act as if it were so.

Hearts in alignment? Dear Koronolan, how would he know?

He couldn't. That was the nature of trust. He had to leap, but by Kiros, there was no way of knowing where—or if—he would land. Well, he'd faced the Krad with nothing more than a knife and a torch, and he hadn't known how that would turn out. He had far less to lose then, only the hope—the possibility—that Mirianna could—might—unlock the curse. Now she'd brought back his soul, had restored his heart, why should he fear the risks when so much more was at stake? Knowing the Dragon was waiting, that everything depended on the Beast's powers and their joined knowledge, Durren opened his mind. And then with one last fervent wish he wouldn't fall, he opened his still so fragile heart. *Let's finish this.*

The Dragon laughed, and smoke shot from both sides of the Beast's mouth. *Come, son of Koronolan, let me show you how to fly.* Unfurling giant wings, the Dragon sprang at the stars.

Chapter Twenty-Seven

Mirianna covered her ears, but her palms and fingers did nothing to mute the roaring and rumbling assailing her from all sides. The ground shook. Her body trembled, buffeted by the noise, the quaking earth, the fear engendered by the beast spewing columns of smoke and bolts of flame into the night sky.

She'd only imagined such creatures. They existed in legends, in tales told by traveling bards, written down and rolled up in scrolls like Owender's *History of the People*, but surely not in full, enormous, flaming life. The creature was huge! And Durren—she must remember Durren was trapped inside it somewhere. The terrifying creature had to live because Durren had to live. The beast couldn't possibly mean to harm her because it and Durren were one. While her heart knocked at her throat and her mouth tasted dry as the dust falling from the walls, she told herself all that. And she repeated it, again and again, until her mind opened wide enough to take it all in.

When she collected enough of her wits to reach out for Gareth, he was already gone, had most likely disappeared before the beast showed itself. For that she was glad. What he would make of the noise and sulfurous smell, she had no notion, but she suspected he would recover sense faster than Pumble, who stood transfixed by the sight. The boy was nothing if not resilient.

Ayliss and the man called Syryk had recovered their senses too, joining hands to face the beast. Ayliss called him a mage, but what Mirianna saw beyond the expensive cloak and fine boots—now torn, stained, and scorched—was a pale, thin man not much older or taller than Ayliss. Under close-cropped black hair, he bore the furrowed brow of a scholar. Nothing about him matched the description of the mages of old. Nothing, that is, except his eyes. The one glimpse she'd had as she threatened him with Gareth's staff had shown her eyes of indeterminate gray, as subtle and shifting as quicksilver, under winged black brows. Ayliss had drawn his gaze away then, and Mirianna had been glad of it. There had been power in that look.

She shivered and bent to pick up Rees's sword where she'd dropped it when the Dragon had materialized. Hand on the hilt, she froze. Where in the name of the Dragon was Rees? His knife still lay at her feet, and she picked that up as she made a slow turn away from the mesmerizing scene on the rampart.

After the glare of the Dragon's flame, even the fire pit seemed dim and the shadows around it thicker. Yellow smoke, curling down from the ramparts in long ribbons, further hazed her view, but she was sure, heart-stoppingly certain, where before only her father's shape had lain by the fire, now there were two. And one had pounced on the other.

"The bloodstones! Give me the damned stones, you old bastard!"

Mirianna charged. She had no thought but to save her father, and no idea how, yet somehow the sword hilt in her hand came down like a club on Rees's shoulder.

He grunted, and they broke apart, three bodies scrabbling on the pavement. The sword slid away. The knife she must have dropped, for Rees came up with it in his hand.

He crouched, panting, a feral beast but for the look of consciousness in his eyes. "I don't want to hurt you, Mirianna. Just give me the damned bloodstones."

"What bloodstones?" She needed to buy time, not just to insert more of her body between Rees and her father, who lay still tangled in his bedding, but to understand what was at stake here. "Pumble said you took them when you ran off."

Rees snarled, and her hair stood on end. "The old bastard switched the gems. That pouch had nothing in it but worthless pebbles!" The disk he wore slid out of his tunic and spun on the end of its thong, a glimmering, gleaming slice of crystal moon.

"Papa, what's he talking about?" Her gaze darted between the disk and Rees's face. The mage used a crystal. Durren had broken it. Now the mage was here, with Rees.

Tolbert pushed himself up to a sitting position behind her. He coughed. "I—uh—I never trust anyone, lamb. For just such a reason."

A melee of emotions rushed Mirianna—pride for her father's unexpected cleverness, frustration for his stubborn insistence on keeping the gems in the face of such danger, fear for what the stones must mean to the mage that Rees would threaten their lives and pursue them to the very gates of Beggeth to obtain them.

"Where are they?" Rees waved the knife. Spittle flew from his mouth. "Hand them over!"

"They—they're in my boot."

Rees's gaze flashed to the boots lying alongside her father's bedding. "Get them out and hand them over. Carefully."

Mirianna bent to the boot her father indicated. He caught her eye, and she saw her own fear reflected there, but something else too. She frowned, wondering in what other way she might have underestimated her father, but he only said, "The seam, lamb, above the ankle. There's a hidden pocket."

She found the pocket, but puzzled over how to open it until her probing fingers located a loose thread. What appeared to be stitched was merely tied. She pulled the thread and tipped the stones into her palm.

"Hand them over," Rees demanded, inching closer.

Mirianna stretched out her hand and opened her fingers over his palm. He was sweating. So was she. She wiped her hand on her skirt while he scrutinized the dark shapes.

"They don't glow," Rees said, scowling.

"Not without sunlight," Tolbert said, as if the fact were obvious.

"If you've tricked me again…" He thrust the knifepoint at Mirianna's chin.

She flinched, but her father's hand at her back steadied her.

"No! Of course, I wouldn't. You—you could test it with flame. The heat of the fire would trigger the glow, but I wouldn't—"

Rees flung a stone into the fire-pit.

"—do that," Tolbert finished as the stone shot out spears of scarlet light.

Bathed in red, Rees grinned. "Finally." He lowered the knife. "Now, what were you saying I shouldn't do?"

Her father looked up, face aghast. "Well, it could melt, and then where would you be?"

For a moment, Rees simply stared. Then, with a look of horror, he dove at the fire.

The boot still in her hand, Mirianna pivoted, swinging it with all the force she could muster at Rees's head. When he went down, she clobbered him twice more. Then, tossing the boot aside, she picked up the knife and dropped to her knees on Rees's back. The air whooshed out of his mouth and he gurgled. "How do you like being climbed on for once?" she said, "Not much fun, is it?" Finding the disk under his hair, she cut it free of the thong.

She sat back and turned the slice of crystal in her palm. It shimmered in the fire's glow, fluidly shifting colors like a spill of lamp oil in a puddle. The disk changed the surface, made it beautiful and alluring. But the illusion was as thin as the slice itself. She knew that, yet the crystal whispered to her, promised power. She needed power now, power to save Durren, her father, all of them. The crystal could help her—if she kept it. Used it. Let it use her.

While she rose to her feet, her father poked a stick into the fire and dragged the glowing bloodstone out between the stones of the fire ring. At once, the glow faded. Tolbert sat back on his heels and gasped with the effort. Beside him, Rees moaned. The other bloodstones lay where he'd dropped them, black clots in the powdered mortar dusting the paving stones. Mirianna slid the knife into her belt and one-by-one picked them up.

She'd touched bloodstone just once, in her father's workshop, but only with her fingernail. Nothing had happened then. Now the stones on her palm tingled with little snaps of energy that zipped up her arm, across her shoulders, and down to the crystal disk pressed to her other palm. Everywhere the energy flowed, the fine hairs of her body responded, rising and falling in waves. In her hand, the disk shimmered as if lit from within. The colors shifted, merged, swirled, and she knew she should look away from the strangely hypnotic dance, but the vision was so beautiful and the energy zipping across her shoulders filled her with such a sense of power, she couldn't. Instead, she brought her hands closer together and watched while the bloodstones hummed and the crystal disk pulsed and a red glow enveloped her.

"Mirianna...!" Tolbert gasped and shielded his eyes.

Helen C. Johannes

Chapter Twenty-Eight

Syryk saw stars, orange and green and yellow stars, circling over his head. His brain told him they were not the night stars, and he was lying flat on his back atop paving stones sown with enough pebbles to dig a score of points painfully into his back. He wanted to listen to the rest of his brain's message, but his body screamed for air and his left palm burned as if he'd planted it in hot coals. Beside him, someone groaned. His head wouldn't turn, but he shifted his eyes enough to see Ayliss, her hair flung over her face in a wild frizz as if each strand had been separated by a jolt of some kind of power.

Power...

Syryk sucked in a breath and remembered the bloodstones. Rolling to his right, he saw the red glow he'd glimpsed an instant before...before what? Syryk blinked. One minute he and Ayliss had been holding the Dragon at bay, and he'd sensed Rees put his hand on the bloodstones. There had been a thrill of power in the crystal, and he'd turned a fraction, just a fraction of his attention in that direction. And then...*something* had laid them both flat. Rees didn't have the power to set off the bloodstones. Rees didn't have any power. But someone did.

The warrior woman and her strange red aura...

Syryk swore. He struggled to his hands and knees

368

while his clothes smoked and his muscles trembled. Weeks ago he'd formulated a plan after emerging from the crystal, a beautiful, simple plan using the Master of Nolar's resources to collect gems necessary to complete the Chant while enjoying bodily pleasures he'd previously foregone to pursue crystal craft and scroll lore. *By the Demon Master, this was not how the plan was meant to go!* First Ayliss had surprised him with the power of her blood, her heritage. Now this woman he'd hoped to use for the Chant had some sort of secret power.

He could barely move the fingers of his left hand, but enough sensation remained to tell him he still gripped his own crystal. Or else the skin had melted to it. Shaking off that thought, he cast around and saw Ayliss's hand curled near her head. Between her blackened fingers he spotted the glint of crystal. He reached for it, hesitated, then pried it free of her hand. "Sorry," he said when she moaned, "but I did what you asked, and now it's my turn." His conscience told him that wasn't entirely true, but he would deal with his conscience later—if at all.

Staggering to his feet, a crystal shard in each hand, he spoke to the disk, to Rees.

But it was the warrior woman who turned, and the disk, now in her hand, shone blood red. She faced him, feet set, head erect, hair a cloud of curls about her face. The scarlet aura threw into relief cheekbones, jawline, and eyes that must have been blue before the glow turned them purple. There was a sword at her feet and a knife stuck in her belt.

Once more she held him mesmerized, but he couldn't afford to stay that way. Even if she were as unskilled as he suspected, she had to realize being able to activate the bloodstones without sunlight was a gift nothing in the scrolls had predicted. He shuddered to think what else she could do with the stones if he gave her time to experiment. Drawing on the crystal, he spoke. "I paid for those bloodstones. Yield them to me. The Dragon is mine to command. You can't hope to control it with that tiny piece of crystal."

"Control it?" Her laughter—not at all the reaction he'd expected—broke his concentration. "I need to set it free and save Durren."

The message his brain had been trying to deliver finally arrived. *The Dragonkeeper!* How could he have overlooked the Dragonkeeper in this already nightmarish scenario? That Krad rock was to blame. Clearly, it had done more than merely rattle his thinking processes. While his mind worked to catch up, Syryk's stomach responded to the news, roiling acid into his throat, and his mouth spat out, "Oh, that's just bloody perfect, isn't it? Don't tell me—let me guess. Drakkonwehr is riding that damned Beast of Beggeth, isn't he?"

"No. He's *in* the Dragon. He and the Dragon are one."

Syryk reeled. Could this get any worse? How in the Demon Master's Name had his plan gone so awry?

Wait a minute, I can use this! An idea flashed into his brain, and his consciousness latched onto it like a man tumbling over a cliff grabs a root or vine. He had no clear idea what power the warrior woman had, but she seemed to have even less of a notion. If he kept her off balance long enough, he might be able to find an opening.

From the crystal he drew a slowly increasing flow of power that shifted his features, cleaned up the tatters and focused attention on his soothing, reasonable voice. "So, he's trapped in the Dragon, and you want to save him? You can't do it yourself, you know. Not with that tiny crystal. You need more power. I can help. Just join your crystal with mine, and together we'll add the bloodstones."

When her eyes narrowed, he made himself smaller, his pose non-threatening. "You can even hang onto them if you want. After all, that's a woman's power source. I wouldn't know what to do with it."

He was blathering now, but what he said didn't matter. Everything depended on his voice. Watching her face, he studied his illusion of helpfulness, of safety reflected in her eyes. Even though his hand throbbed and his body ached, the spell was perfect, as usual, and first doubt, then indecision flickered in her eyes. Her hand moved a fraction, and his mouth watered. If he could just get his fingers on one bloodstone…

Chapter Twenty-Nine

Durren and the Dragon flew up and up into the night sky while the fire in the courtyard diminished to a spark. They were soaring in a tight circle, and stars whipped by, no longer sparks of light but streaks in the black void. The Dragon's heart raced and Durren's raced in sync with it. So this was what freedom felt like, this exuberant sensation of breathlessness and speed as earthly bonds fell away and the sky wrapped its velvet blanket around them. When they leveled out, Durren laughed with the pure joy of the moment.

My sentiments exactly, the Dragon said, and Durren understood how long both of them had been bound, he by the curse and the Dragon by the promise. But neither of them was yet fully free. He could tell by the slow looping passes the Dragon was making over the fortress, passes that didn't widen.

You can't fly away from here, can you?

I have been raised, but only blood can free me. One of your kind has brought into this place drops of my blood, and the little mage would lay his hands upon them.

Your blood? You mean bloodstones, don't you? A prickle raised phantom hairs on Durren's nonexistent neck as his memory flashed over events since he'd found the gems. Mirianna's father bought the stones Durren had traded to Ulerroth, but the old man wanted—needed—more. According to the fat man, Rees had taken them, but perhaps not if Rees came all the way to Drakkonwehr and brought Syryk with him. *Then we'll get the bloodstones before Syryk can get his hands on him. Where are they?*

The Dragon angled its head down, and Durren saw with hawk-like clarity an array of figures bathed in a red glow he knew all too well. Three sprawled on the ground. His heart lurched when he recognized Ayliss, but despite the great height, the Dragon's vision showed him she still breathed. Rees lay face-down in the pose of someone unconscious, and the fat man had started toward him while the old man huddled near the fire pit. The boy was nowhere to be seen, and for that Durren gave thanks even as he spat out a bitter oath because that left Syryk and the woman he loved face to face and altogether too close.

Go! Now! Down! Mirianna was alone, facing a master of illusion who must have doubled his crystal supply with Ayliss's, and only Kiros knew how Syryk had gained that advantage. *Go! Stop him! Damn you, Beast! She needs me!*

Yes, but not now. The Dragon continued circling. *Your chosen mate is finding her own power, and you must trust her to use it wisely.*

Her own power? What in Beggeth—? Then he saw. That all-too-familiar glow *centered* on Mirianna, shooting out not just from the bloodstones on her palm but arising from her, *all* of her. He understood, at last, what he'd always known in the deepest way of knowing where the mind cannot comprehend how the heart can know a truth with absolute certainty—she had saved him. She would save them all, if he would just let her.

Good, said the Dragon. *Now send me your warrior skills, for we must face the abomination that would be human if the Demon Master of Beggeth had not turned them to his own needs, and I know little of fighting them.*

The Dragon's gaze shifted, and Durren saw dark shapes, hundreds of them, swarming up the rubble piles near the fortress gates. *Dear Koronolan!* He knew there would be Krad. There was too much blood in the air to hope the beast-men hadn't noticed. But he'd never imagined there would be so many. The last time he had Rees's arrows to back him up and Ghost to ride, but there were fewer Krad. This time he had no body, no horse, no arrows, and no knife—but he had a Dragon and command of the heights.

Are there any limits to your flame, Beast?

My body has just awakened. Until my core is fully warmed, I can make no predictions.

Well, he would just have to make every shot count. But that was nothing new for a warrior who'd trained all his life for the moment to defend everything he lived to protect. Everything he would die for.

There are two things to remember, he told the Dragon. *Krad fear fire, but their weapons are poisoned, so you have to stay out of reach. Now, let me see the wider field.*

****

Gareth moved down the tunnel as quickly as he could despite his burden. The body was surprisingly light, and he'd managed to balance it over one shoulder, but even though he was glad to be carrying it downhill instead of up, he'd already sweated through both tunic and undertunic. His hair, plastered to his face, dripped stinging beads of sweat into his eyes, so he shut them. He maneuvered best by memory and touch anyway, and the increasing temperature and slight leveling of the floor told him he'd nearly reached the pool.

A sensation of airiness, as if the tunnel had widened, stopped him. He secured his burden and felt with the toes of one foot for the edge of the pool. Finding it, Gareth backed a step and turned left. He paced off nine steps and knelt in a flat area he knew had been cleared of rubble. Puffing with effort, he lowered his burden, making sure no part of the body banged into the rock floor. Then, hands on his knees, he paused. He had another task to perform back up at the surface, and the groaning of the bedrock surrounding him meant there must be a battle going on above. He sensed he would be needed there soon, but he couldn't bring himself to leave just yet.

The she-lion—Ayliss—believed she and Mirianna could save his master, and he trusted her—trusted both of them—but just in case this was to be his master's last resting place, Gareth couldn't leave his body as it was. Durren Drakkonwehr had lived in darkness much longer than Gareth had. It was the bond they shared. But in death his master could at least rest uncovered. Reaching out, Gareth removed his master's face covering, folded it, and laid it alongside his master's head.

The Shadow Man—Gareth still thought of him that way—had told him never to try to touch his body. Gareth understood his reasons. Still, someone ought to remember his master for what he was rather than what everyone feared he'd become. After all, Gareth had sponged that face. He knew there was a face there, and it hadn't seemed horrible, but he hadn't been focused on discovery then. Now, however, he wanted to say good-bye, and he wanted to remember. Tentatively, Gareth touched his fingertips to his master's still face.

Chapter Thirty

If they survived this night, Mirianna would have to thank Pumble. He'd shrieked, nothing a man would ever admit to, but his vocal expression of horror penetrated her brain just enough she remembered where she was and with whom. She was in Drakkonwehr fortress, fighting for her life—for all of their lives—and facing the master of the crystal disk she held. Pumble's shriek had made her blink, and in that blink she'd seen through the cotton wool of illusion to the tattered man with the quicksilver eyes who'd spun the fantasy.

She stared, and he stared back as his mask slipped and the disk scorched her palm. Mirianna knew it now for the snake it was, and she flung the crystal to the paving stones. Her heel came down on it with a satisfying crunch. For good measure, she stomped twice more and ground the remnants to powder. It was a lie, that promise of power. All the power she needed was already hers to command. She'd called on it before when she'd gone to Durren in the tunnels. She'd followed her heart then, and she would follow it again.

The mage blanched. He dropped to his knees and gurgled as though she'd stabbed him through the heart. For a moment, Mirianna wondered if breaking the disk had done that much damage, but Pumble shrieked "Krad!" again, and this time she understood what he said.

She ought to have been afraid. Days ago she would've stood paralyzed as dark shapes separated from the deeper darkness of fallen stones and broken walls. She would've watched in open-mouthed horror as more and more of them swarmed through gaps and over rocks. But even as she acknowledged that, she was already bending in one fluid motion to grasp the sword at her feet while turning toward Rees. She recognized her own power now, and it impelled her to act, to tuck the bloodstones she still held into her remaining pocket, shutting off their glow. Or maybe the crushing of the crystal had dimmed them. She would consider that later—if there was a later.

Dropping to one knee, she shoved Rees over onto his back. If she was right, taking the disk freed him from the mage's power. If she was wrong—

"Mirianna..." He blinked up at her, and she knew she'd guessed correctly. "I don't know what in Beggeth made me..."

"You were entranced." She seized his tunic and pulled him up while the beast-men's yips and yowls reverberated from the walls. "I need to know—can I depend on you?"

His gaze followed the noise, and comprehension spread across his face. "To fight Krad? Always!" Climbing to his feet, Rees wobbled. He touched the back of his head, winced, and shot her a glance. "You...hit me...more than once!"

"You deserved it. Now get your bow from Pumble and make him stop screaming, will you?"

He looked at the sword in her hand, his sword, and she wondered if he would demand it back, but when his gaze returned to her face, he said, "Don't let the filthy beasts inside your reach. Use a torch like a shield."

"Thanks...for the advice." He turned and ran to Pumble while she mulled the change in him. Had releasing him from the crystal made him see her that much differently he would trust his life to the sword in *her* hand? Or had she truly changed? Either, or both, could be true, but she had no time to think because the Krad were so close she could smell their stench. She grabbed a burning brand from the fire pit and turned to her father. "Keep the fire going, Papa. We need more flame. Can you do that?"

Tolbert nodded. Planting both fists on the ground, he pushed himself to his feet while sweat popped out on his forehead. "You can count on me, lamb," he said as he stood, white-faced and swaying, before her.

Mirianna's chest ached. Her heart had swelled so, it pressed painfully against her ribs, but she had no time now to tell her father how much she loved him, to apologize for underestimating him all these years, or even to tell Durren how grateful she was for the miracle of the water. Her hands were full of weapons, and she had to go into battle. Somehow, that prospect no longer terrified her. With the bloodstones lying close to her skin, barely weighting down her pocket, she charged the nearest group of Krad.

****

Durren fell. Head over heels and spinning, he tumbled down and down into an inky pit, into a deep black hole darker than absolute darkness. One moment he and the Dragon had lit up the walls with blasts of flame, and Krad shrieks still rang in his ears. He could yet see in his mind's eye the seared-in-place images of beast-men, alight like torches as scores of them fell—or jumped—from walls and debris piles. He and the Dragon had done this, together, and the masses of furry bodies had ebbed away into the darkness outside the walls. Durren had shouted for the sheer joy of routing that threat.

The Dragon had turned to climb for another pass at the beast-men still inside the fortress when Durren was ripped from the body of the Beast. For one long terrifying moment as he fell, he heard nothing. No swish of wind under giant leathery wings, no thunder of a huge heart, no creak of sinew and flesh as joints moved and muscles gathered. There was only this dizzying plunge into the abyss, without warning, without pain, without anything resembling death so that he couldn't believe he was truly dead—at last. Before he could marvel at that, he stopped.

Was that it? The end?

Why am I still thinking?

And then...he breathed.

Dank warm air rushed into lungs that had forgotten how to expand, delivering a kick to the heart they surrounded. Blood surged, and pain fired along every nerve the life-force replenished. In the darkness, Durren howled. His body bucked as if lightning-struck. He plunged once more, this time into something warm, wet, and soothing. As he slid under the surface, he realized where he was. Somehow, he'd come back to himself, to his own body, in the pool deep beneath Drakkonwehr fortress.

His muscles responded to commands, and he broke the surface. Panting, he sucked in air he'd never expected to breathe again. Someone must have moved his body to the pool because a quick hand-search told him everything he remembered was intact, including his clothes. Muscles still quivering from their recent *death*, he pulled himself out of the water and rested.

He would thank Ayliss from the bottom of his heart, but only if Mirianna was safe, and he had no way of knowing that from here. How long had passed since he'd last seen her facing down Syryk? The Dragon had urged him to trust her to use her power, and he did. But that was when he could still help her, could still see how the battle fared. Now, however, there was no more voice in his head to advise him, to show him what he'd overlooked. He ought to rejoice after years of constant interference. Instead, he felt bereft.

But Durren had no time for grief. He poured water out of his boots, pulled them back on and stood. His legs shook, but they would hold. They would have to. He had a long way to run to the surface.

Chapter Thirty-One

"Damn you, woman!" In his mind, Syryk heard thunder in his voice. All this pathetic body could expel was a whisper. He wanted to shake his fist at the warrior woman's departing back, but his hand refused to rise from the grit into which her heel had powdered his last, best weapon. Somehow, she'd seen through his illusion. Even against the power of both crystals, she'd seen. And she'd taken the bloodstones away with her.

Rocks pelted the ground, kicking up dust around him. Syryk raised his head. Nearby, an old man he recognized as the gem cutter limped around a fire pit, tossing sticks onto rising flames. Shrieks filled the air, shrieks Syryk knew all too well. Sweat beaded on his forehead, stinging afresh the cut there, and he staggered to his feet. Krad surged out from every nook and cranny, from every shadow and crevice! Syryk clutched both crystal shards to his chest and shambled in a circle. *We're going to die! We're all going to die!*

His foot caught on something, and he stumbled, recovered his balance—and forgot to breathe. Beside the singed toe of his boot, lay a smooth, round ash-covered stone about as big as his thumb tip. *Was it—? By the Demon Master, it was!* Dizzy, Syryk fell to his knees. His first grab missed. More rocks showered around the fire pit, but he forced himself to take in air, to reach deliberately for the prize, to capture it with blackened fingers screaming with pain.

He sat back on his heels, heart drumming, while the old man tossed more wood on the fire. Its roar echoed the rush of his blood, and the rising heat seared his face, but Syryk took his time bringing his prize closer to the crystal shards in his other hand. The stone flickered, and he breathed more words over it, like a man lost in the snow coaxing a reluctant fire to light. Another glimmer, and another. *By the Demon, yes!* Energized, he surged to his feet and shouted, "*Karachorynth alyminor! Beggedon ominor et!*"

Silence reigned. No more clatter of rocks. No yowls. Only the crackle and pop of the fire continued. Around the fortress the Krad stood frozen in various poses. Now, almost as one, they turned toward him, and dark, feral eyes fixed on him. Syryk swallowed.

"You…idiot!" hissed a voice he'd once thought dear. "What in the name of all that's holy have you done?"

Ayliss stood, teetering, scorch marks streaking the cloak she wore, her bare arms, her face. From the tangle of hair fringing her face, she glared at him.

"I did what you asked," he retorted. "I helped you raise the Dragon. Now it's my turn."

"To call upon the powers of Beggeth?"

"I've got one damned bloodstone! I'll use it however I wish. And right now, I wish to be gone from here! If I have to make a deal with the Demon Master to get my wish, I will!"

"You're a coward and a fool, Syryk."

"Good-bye, Ayliss. I'd hope to meet you again, but I don't think the Krad will let that happen." He shuffled toward the nearest group of beast-men. Even though their stench fried his nostrils, he choked back the urge to gag. The creatures were unpredictable and the bloodstone weaker than he'd expected, but with his two crystal shards, he had enough power to enthrall the weak-minded creatures into effecting his escape. The others, well…

"You have a few moments before the Krad regain their senses," he told Ayliss as the group of beast-men he joined folded in around him. "I suggest you make the most of them."

****

Durren saw flickering lights far ahead, but he lumbered on, breath sawing out of his mouth, before he realized these lights were not caused by his air-deprived blood sparkling behind his eyes. These shone only one color, and they were brightening. The floor of the tunnel leveled, and fresh air chilled his dripping face. His legs ached and his boots felt as if he'd never emptied them, but he dared not pause. The courtyard where he should've heard the screams of battle was eerily silent. And he smelled blood.

****

"Arrgh!" Mirianna swung her sword in an arc, cutting down three Krad. One part of her didn't think it fair to kill them while they stood stunned, but the newly discovered part knew fair play didn't matter against beasts, and there were yet too many of the creatures within the fortress. Nearby, Pumble wielded his sword with surprising dexterity for such a large target, and Rees shot arrow after arrow, moving forward as he retrieved his supply from fallen Krad.

She ignored the blood, ignored the stench, and charged after the vanishing mage, but Ayliss stopped her with an outstretched arm. "He's getting away!" Mirianna yelled. "We need him to save Durren!"

"He's done his part. The rest is up to us." Dirty face grim, she turned and held out her hand. "Gareth, I need a weapon."

Panting and drenched with sweat, the boy materialized out of the shadows of the Great Hall. He held out his staff and the Sword of Drakkonwehr.

"Stand behind me with the Sword," Ayliss said, taking the staff. "We need to hold them off until Durren can get here."

"He's coming?" Mirianna gasped. "But he's in the Dragon."

"Not anymore." Ayliss shoved hair out of her face. "Gareth put him back by the pool. Its healing power should restore him."

Mirianna's heart skittered at the 'should.' She thrust her hand into her pocket, reassuring herself the bloodstones remained next to her skin. They were warm to the touch—or maybe she fancied that. Regardless, her nerves calmed, and she knew she couldn't wait for her hopes—for Durren—to materialize. The Krad were already awakening.

****

Outside the fortress, darkness enveloped Syryk. A small band of Krad padded on nearly silent feet around him. He would barely know they were there but for the stench and the insistent pressure of one or another paw guiding him, not downward into the valley, but upward, toward the gates of Beggeth. Overhead, a shadow passed, and he glanced at it, one last look at the Dragon lit by the distant fires within the walls.

So close…

But this new plan was infinitely better—or would be, if his charms could dampen the smell of his blood long enough for this band of Krad to escort him across the mountain tops to the Demon Master himself.

Chapter Thirty-Two

Gareth gripped the Sword of Drakkonwehr with both hands. He swung it from side to side, protecting the she-lion—Ayliss's—back as she bashed Krad after Krad with his staff. The beast-men's shrieks hammered at his ears, but they told him how many swarmed them and from which direction. He'd struck several with the broken blade, and his hands ran with something slicker than sweat.

He didn't think about killing anymore. This was like fighting off wolves. You did what you had to do to survive. To protect those you loved. And he loved the she-lion—Ayliss. And Mirianna, and the Shadow Man. Even Pumble. He wasn't sure about the man called Rees, but at least that man seemed to be helping them. Not like the traitor Syryk.

"Left!" Ayliss yelled, and he thrust. Matted fur brushed his fingers. Gareth pulled the Sword back, and warm liquid sprayed his arm, his face. He gagged, but resisted the urge to swipe the blood away. He couldn't drop the weapon now. The Shadow Man was coming.

****

Durren's head swam—colors, images, memories, all a blur. The light ahead faded, and he thought he might fall—fail—inches before his goal. Then one image separated from the rest...

He saw himself crouching, as always, in a rock-

387

hewn tunnel, lit by a distant torch, while tendrils of smoke oozed from crevices around a massive oaken door. They spiraled upward, feeding a thick yellow haze overhead. He coughed. Sweat dripped from his hair, stinging his eyes. The sound of rushing footsteps brought him swiveling to his feet, shield up, heart pounding. His fingers gripped the hilt of the ancient double-edged Sword of Drakkonwehr, where the large bloodstone embedded in the intersection of hand guard, blade, and hilt glowed softly, a dark, deep red...

With a gasped, "No!" he shook off the nightmare. He'd lived it long enough. This was the end; he would pay for his mistakes once and for all. If only he had the Sword...

He saw it just as he hurdled boulders nearly blocking the Great Hall door. Gareth and Ayliss, back to back, she swinging the boy's staff and Gareth wielding the broken weapon, surrounded by Krad, alive and dead. Drawing his knife, Durren charged the horde.

He may have screamed some war cry. He had no recollection, and certainly no hearing other than the snick of the blade and the roar of his own blood rushing his ears. But the Krad fell over themselves—and their fallen comrades—fleeing into the shadows.

Ayliss lowered the staff and leaned on it, panting, while Gareth turned to her and said, "Now?"

"Now," Durren's sister replied.

The boy, instead of handing over the weapon, switched his grip on the hilt. Holding the Sword with the blade pointing down, he raised it over his head.

Dear Koronolan, the boy means to kill himself! Horrified, Durren gasped, "Gareth, no!" and threw himself at the boy. *Ayliss, damn you!* his mind messaged, *Gareth's not meant to be a sacrifice!*

No. She smiled that serene cat's smile he hated. *He's meant to do what neither you nor I can do.*

The Sword hilt reached the top of its arc and paused for an agonizingly long moment while Durren willed his muscles to plow through air thick as mud pulling at him. He had to stop this senseless death. While he inched forward, time slowed, contracted, reversed...

He saw himself once more before the oaken door. Rushing footsteps brought him swiveling to his feet, shield up.

His best friend—and second in command—Errek Eolen rounded the corner. "I've bolted the tunnel door. I don't think the guards know we've made it down here."

Durren blew out the breath he'd been holding. "The dragon's stirring. We have to stop the mage first." He nodded toward the door. "Think your axe'll open that?"

"Three strokes—if there's no spell on the wood."

"There won't be." When the big man shot him a questioning look, he stifled a sigh. He hoped he wouldn't have to explain how his whole plan relied on the little he remembered of Owender's History of the People. *He wished—again—he'd paid more attention to the scrolls, but it had always been the Sword that drew his hand and his heart. Gripping it now, he recited, "'True hearts and no fear, against a mage's power, hold dear.'"*

True hearts. The words penetrated the nightmare, and he recognized Ayliss's voice. *Trust me, Durren. For once in your life, think before you act.*

For as much as Ayliss confounded him, they were blood, and his blood told him Ayliss would never hurt Gareth. Twisting in the air, he stopped his forward motion. And time returned.

The Sword flashed. Durren's heart dropped to his stomach, but the boy plunged the broken blade straight down into the stone pavement between his feet.

Sparks flew. The ground shook. A crack split the stone like a tear ripped in the very foundation of the fortress. Rocks tumbled from the walls. Ayliss threw herself over the boy, who had pitched forward as the Sword sank to the hilt. "Don't let go!" she cried.

Above, the Dragon screamed. Durren fell to his knees. Pain like the stab of a red-hot knife stole his breath. He doubled over, gripping his side, feeling the old wound fresh and bleeding under his fingers. *Dear Koronolan!* He dragged himself forward as the Dragon crashed to the paving stones behind him and the fortress shuddered with the impact. "Ayliss! What in Beggeth…?"

Chapter Thirty-Three

Mirianna clung to her sword and torch, but raised her arm against the dirt peppering her face. She dared not close her eyes, lest any of the beast-men shrieking around her recovered sense enough to strike.

From what she could make out, the Dragon had fallen out of the sky and crushed a score or more of Krad. The giant head still snorted flame, and leathery wings beat at the ground like a bird trying to right itself. Over the clatter of falling rocks, she heard Pumble's panicked screams cut short by Rees's barked command. She glimpsed them standing back to back against the remaining horde, who once again had lost focus. No thanks to the mage this time, for the Krad seemed not enchanted but, she hoped, demoralized by their mounting losses. The shadows still crawled with furry bodies, but more fled than entered. If she and the others could keep the momentum they'd gained…

She risked a glance over her shoulder. Amid the settling dust, her father had fallen, but he waved away her concern and, still kneeling, tossed more wood on the fire. Near the Great Hall she spotted three forms sprawled but moving on the pavement, Ayliss, Gareth, and—her heart lurched—the man she loved. She stuttered a step forward, calling, "Durren!"

****

Gareth spat grit. The she-lion—Ayliss's—weight

had flattened his every bone, even his chin, into the stone. His elbows burned, and the fall had likely scraped away both sleeve and skin, but none of that mattered. What mattered was the ground no longer shook. And he still gripped the Sword.

Ayliss lifted herself off him, and he breathed—then coughed. She grasped his shoulders. "Hang on to the hilt, Gareth. You have to get up and pull."

She helped him to his knees. The movement dug knife-edged pebbles into his forearms, and he sucked in a hiss. He hoped the quaking earth hadn't tipped over the bucket of that special water. He would need its healing power when this was over.

Ayliss's arms circled his chest, and her hair brushed his cheeks. Her heart beat against his shoulder blades the way her lion-heart had once soothed and cradled him not so very long ago. "Are you ready?"

He nodded. Dragging first one foot and then the other forward and underneath him, he concentrated on holding tight to the hilt while she balanced him. He took a breath, spat more grit from his mouth, and pulled. For something buried only a hand-span or two deep, the blade stuck fast. Tightening his grip, he pulled harder.

The Sword gave with a sudden shriek of steel. Just as Ayliss stopped his backward stumble, Gareth flinched at twin screams of pain, the Shadow Man's very human one and the Dragon's bellow.

****

One hand pressed to his side, Durren crawled toward his sister and the boy. His head buzzed with pain and the sound of someone shouting a long way off. His name? He couldn't tell. The buckled pavement separating him from his goal rose like a mountain, but he had to know if he could trust the image imprinted on his brain. The Sword should never have penetrated the stone. It should have shattered upon impact. Had it? Were those sparks bits of the blade disintegrating? *By Kiros!*

Mere feet away, Ayliss had wrapped arms around the boy, helping him gain his footing. Gareth's face shone white and pinched under its coat of dirt, but he clung to the buried hilt. Straightening, the boy began to pull.

What in Beggeth...?

Steel sang. Sparks cascaded. Light flashed on a broad, gleaming blade, and before Durren could comprehend what he'd seen, the thing that pierced his side a moment ago, now pulled back, searing a white-hot trail in its wake. He writhed on the ground, screaming, while his nerves vibrated with shock and pain.

And then it was gone, and he collapsed onto his back, spent and boneless. When he opened his eyes, Ayliss and the boy stood over him. "It's over now, Durren," she said, sagging with both hands on the boy's staff. "You're whole again. You and the Dragon and the Sword."

Gareth dropped to his knees at Durren's side. "Are you all right, sir? I've fixed your sword...I think."

Durren sat up. As though in a dream, he grasped the weapon the boy held out. The blade shone in the firelight, the full unmarred, restored length of it. The hilt fit to his hand, just as it always had, and the weight of it balanced perfectly, so light he could be holding nothing but air. Nothing but an illusion...

Staring at Ayliss, he rose. "Nobody but a Drakkonwehr…"

"Can wield the Sword," she finished. "That's right, Durren."

He expected the cat's smile, but none came. Instead, she reached down and helped the boy to his feet, all the while watching him with those green eyes he'd never really known as well as he thought.

He frowned at her, thoroughly confounded, and meant to demand an explanation, but the Dragon bellowed, "Drakkonwehr! The beasts return!"

At the same time he heard what his pain-wracked brain had heard before, but not comprehended, the voice of the woman he loved. He spun.

Across the courtyard littered with Krad bodies, Mirianna was calling, "Durren!" In the firelight, her hair billowed like a cloud about her face, and she brandished sword and torch like a warrior of old. He had never loved her more.

Near her, the Dragon gained its feet and blasted flame at a group of Krad slithering down the wall beside the gate. While those shrieked and fled, more Krad poured through other cracks and crevices to the left and right. Rees and Pumble charged in to meet the rightward group. Mirianna dashed off to the left.

"I'm coming!" he shouted, pelting after her.

The Sword whistled as he waded in beside Mirianna. She flashed him a smile that made his heart sing. She swung right, thrust the torch to her left, and spun to catch a Krad behind a rock. *Dear Koronolan, she's magnificent!*

Ayliss said he was whole again. If that explained the surge of energy filling him now, well and good. He needed every ounce of power he could summon. The others had done more damage to the Krad horde in his brief absence than he could've hoped, and this current assault looked to his trained eye to be a last-ditch attempt to overwhelm them. If they could just hold out a bit longer...

Mirianna stumbled. Two Krad leapt to confront her. Durren's heart skittered, but she righted herself and skewered one while scorching the arm of the other. Behind her rushed two more she couldn't possibly see. By Kiros, she'd die if he didn't help her, but he was too far away for the Sword. Durren seized his knife. If he could strike the one in the lead, she'd have time to turn and defend herself. He grasped the blade between fingers and thumb, reared his arm back to throw...and time stopped, the world wrenched itself inside out, and went dark...

He saw himself deep inside Drakkonwehr, this time in the pit, while the words of the Dragon Chant reverberated around him. Above, he heard an anguished cry. "Ayliss!"

"Illusion, Errek!" Durren screamed. "Don't touch her!"

But Errek, still on the pit's rim, lowered his axe and his shield. "Ayliss," he said to the shimmering woman in white who ascended a narrow staircase and held out her arms to him.

Durren blinked, stared at her outstretched hands and blinked again. An image flickered in and out of view, an image of something held in one slender hand— no!—one large, heavy-wristed hand.

"Errek!" he screamed. "It's the—"

"Ayliss," Errek said, and embraced her.

395

The hand moved—in a quick, thrusting motion.

Durren seized his knife and flung it at the woman in white.

There was a moment when time seemed suspended, when the knife, rotating gracefully hilt over tip, floated through the air while nothing else moved. Even his hand couldn't complete its downward arc. Nor could sound, rolling like thunder, form into more than slow reverberation. Only the woman in white could glide onward, shimmering, through Errek's embrace.

"Illusion, Drakkonwehr," purred the mage's voice in his ear. "How kind of you to fall for it."

Powerless, Durren could do nothing but stare in horror as the knife, continuing its uninterrupted motion, slid smoothly into Errek's tunic. It struck a spark from the chain mail covering his friend's chest, a tiny spark that winked out even as the blade penetrated with agonizing leisure, penetrated to the hilt. A fine spray of red droplets punctuated the impact, hazing into the air.

"No!" he cried as Errek's body, ever so slowly, rounded over the antler-handled hilt, now spotted with blood.

The big man staggered and his hand came up to his chest. "Durren—" Errek raised his head, a look of shock in his eyes. "Your knife—" And he crumpled, slowly, to the ground...

Drenched in a cold sweat, Durren gripped that same antler-handled knife by fingers and thumb while the memory dissolved and the courtyard took shape. He could throw now and save the woman he loved from the threat he perceived, but two words echoed in his mind as time hung as delicately suspended as his knife—*trust* and *illusion*. The Dragon told him to trust Mirianna, that she had power and knew how to use it. He'd lived all these years knowing he killed Errek by falling for an illusion. The guilt had nearly crushed him. But what if he held back now and failed to save her? By Kiros, he had to throw now and save the woman he loved!

Didn't he?

"Damn you to Beggeth, you demon-spawned Beast!" Durren shouted at the Dragon, but he held the knife suspended.

Time returned in a blur of Mirianna spinning at just the moment he would've let the knife fly. She stepped in front of the Krad he'd targeted and thrust her torch. Durren's heart stopped. If he'd thrown when he intended, he would've killed her just as he'd killed Errek. Instead, the burned Krad backpedaled into the second one, and both fell down. Mirianna finished them with two strokes of her sword.

She straightened and threw her hair back. In the light of her torch, her face glistened through the dirt smudging it, but she paused only long enough to adjust her grip on her weapons before charging at another Krad.

Durren's knees shook. He steadied himself by leaning on the Sword. *Dear Koronolan!* Would his heart ever recover? Life was simpler when he trusted no one.

Simpler, yes, his heart replied, *but nowhere near as satisfying as living for a purpose again.*

By Kiros, yes! He had people to live for. People he loved. And one of those people was calling for help right now. He spun toward the center of the courtyard and saw Mirianna's father brandishing a firebrand at two Krad. The old man could barely hold the stick with two hands, and he shuffled backwards under their assault. The rest of the horde was fading into the shadows, pursued by the Dragon, Mirianna, and the two men, but these Krad seemed intent on taking down at least one of the defenders. Power surged through Durren's body and rushed into his arms and legs. The Sword leaped to his hand, and he charged. No one was going to harm Mirianna's father. Not while Durren could stop them.

He should've seen the third Krad, the one that rushed him out of the shadows, but the glare of the fire and the old man's torch concealed the beast-man until it was almost too late. Durren pulled back the Sword of Drakkonwehr, and the Krad crumpled at his feet, joining the other two bodies. Around the fortress, the rest of the Krad had gone silent, melting away into the darkness outside. He heard the roar of the Dragon and the shouts of Mirianna and the two men as they pursued the stragglers. They had won. At last.

He took a step back.

Two steps.

His knees trembled, but not the way muscles shook with the depletion of adrenalin. No, this was shock, and it spread with the burn of poison. All these years he'd considered stepping into a Krad blade to end it all, but when he no longer wished to die, when he finally had found his way to redemption, he'd failed to see—and stop—the flint knife lying at his feet, coated in his blood. Odd that it looked no different from the Krad blood coating the Sword. Odd that it smelled the same—strangely sweet—but the realization tasted bitter as gall.

He fell to his knees, and the Sword and knife

clattered from his hands. Well, he'd done all he could. He'd spent himself to the utmost of his ability. If only he'd had another moment with Mirianna, a moment to tell her once more that he loved her, that she'd saved his soul, redeemed him when nothing and no one else could. It was better this way. He would've killed her sooner or later when she asked to see him unveiled. And he couldn't have lived with that.

Hands gripped his shoulders, Ayliss's hands. Through the mist clouding his senses, he heard Gareth speak. Someone laid him down. Shivers racked his body, small ones at first, but he knew what was to come. Dear Koronolan, it would be a relief to finally die.

If only he still wanted to.

Chapter Thirty-Four

Mirianna stopped short. Her side burned as though she'd been stabbed, but no Krad had touched her. They'd fled into the night, melted away into the shadows beyond the fortress. They could regroup, but her newfound instincts told her the battle was over. She panted, holding her ribs, while she wondered if this was what victory felt like. She didn't think so. Not with every breath paining her more. Something was wrong. This pain had first come to her when Durren had collapsed at Ayliss's feet—was it only yesterday? So much had happened since.

But this—she and Durren were linked by it, just as they'd been linked by the dream. And this was bad. Filled with dread, and despite the pain, she ran back to the courtyard. She saw the others huddled around the fire, some bending, some kneeling, and one sprawled on the stone.

"Durren!" She flung herself between her father and Pumble, and stood while the breath sawed in and out of a throat so tight, her breath whistled. "Durren," she gasped again, and dropped to her knees to gather his hooded head into her lap. "What happened?"

"Krad knife," her father said. "He saved me from them."

She saw the furry bodies, the bloody flint blade, and met her father's eyes. He'd come back from that kind of death, but barely. And his wound had been a mere nick. The damp patch of cloth above Durren's belt already fed a red pool on the pavement beneath. This wound was worse, much worse, and they both knew it.

She cast her gaze, and her hopes, at Ayliss, the only person who might have answers. "What about the water? We still have some, don't we? It saved my father—"

"He needs more than a bucketful," Ayliss cried, "but the pool is too far. He won't last long enough for you to take him there or bring up more water." A tear wet a path down her dirty cheek. Even though her lips trembled, she drew first one deep breath, then another. When she reached across Durren and covered Mirianna's hand with both of hers, the green eyes shone once more with the certainty Mirianna had followed through a dark night and a forest of shadows—was it only days ago? "But there is another way," Ayliss said. "Do you have the bloodstones?"

Mirianna nodded. Those eyes and that voice had led her to safety. And to love. She would follow Ayliss again, if only she understood how. "But they're to raise the Dragon."

"To control it. But there's more to their power than that. The Dragon knows." Rising, Ayliss addressed the Beast, who stood with lowered head, listening, just outside the group. "I used bloodstones once before to set in motion the spell to make you whole again. With these stones, you and your kin may go free from here. Or Mirianna can use them to save the man she loves, the man who kept your soul and consciousness alive while the spell worked its way out."

In Mirianna's arms, Durren shuddered. His

breathing rasped beneath the hood still covering his face. Mirianna clutched him to her chest. "I don't know what you want," she said to the great Beast, "but you've helped us thus far. Durren gave himself to help you." Freeing a hand, she dug into her pocket and pulled out the stones.

The Dragon snorted, and the huge nostrils glowed. This close, the Beast radiated more heat than a forge, and it could destroy them all with one blast of flame. From the way the foot-tall eye slits gleamed at the sight of the stones on her palm, she suspected the Beast was considering it.

Then, the great head rose to its full height, and the luminous gaze regarded all of them. "Your brief lifespan gives your kind little true perspective. At least the two children of Koronolan can see with long eyes, and I have learned much of your kind from my imprisonment in a human body—as you no doubt intended, daughter of Koronolan."

With a pointed look at Ayliss, the Dragon huffed, and smoke curled out of both sides of its mouth, a warning, Mirianna was sure, of its power—as if they could've forgotten with the Beast itself standing so near amid the carnage it had wreaked on the Krad. Across from her, Pumble edged behind her father, and Rees sidled behind Pumble as all three watched the Beast with wide eyes. Once more her heart ached for her father, for facing a dragon as bravely as he'd faced an enchanted Rees. But it was Durren who needed her now, and everything hinged on the Dragon, who spoke again.

"Your kind slaughtered mine, and my heart aches when I think of it, but I have come to trust the children of Koronolan to keep his promise. The blood of my kin lies scattered all over this land. Finding stones to replace these will, sadly, not be impossible. Therefore, I say to you, these few stones may be replaced and the spell completed well before my kin awaken, but the son of Koronolan needs them now, for his life-spark wanes."

In her arms, Durren's body bucked so violently, Mirianna had to wrap both arms around him until the spasm passed. "What do I need to do? Tell me, please."

"Bare the wound and hold the stones over it," the Dragon said.

"Here, let me help." Ayliss knelt and ripped open Durren's garments just above his belt. Under the dark red glistening around a ragged puncture, his skin shone like alabaster in the firelight. With each breath, more blood oozed out and painted Ayliss's hands.

Mirianna had never seen skin so white, but she had no time to marvel at a body not touched by sunlight for years. Durren would never see the sun again if she didn't act now. While her hand shook over his wound, she opened her palm.

The stones glowed again, as they had the first time she'd held them. Power tingled along her arms and up across her shoulders, little zips of energy she recognized. This was life-blood, solid and ancient, but potent still. "You mean to give him your blood," she said, understanding at last. "How is that possible?"

"Blood answers blood, especially that given for the sake of others," the Dragon said. "He has already bathed in my blood, as have you, in the pool where the wound he and I shared fed into the waters. Squeeze the stones and you will replenish what we share that has been lost."

She looked from the Dragon to Ayliss, who nodded. With a deep breath, Mirianna closed her fist. For heartbeats, her hand glowed as if lit from within, the fine bones silhouetted against a warm red light. Then…darkness, like a light extinguished.

Panicked, she squeezed harder. Her knuckles whitened and her muscles shook with the effort. Her side burned, specks swam before her eyes, and darkness tugged at her consciousness, beckoning her to peace, to oblivion, to a soothing nothingness where her heart would be at rest. Forever.

She saw the vision for what it was—not her own but Durren's soul poised on the brink between life and death, between a world that had been filled for too long with more than its share of pain and an end to that suffering. If she let him go, he would find peace.

If he still wanted it…

From the blackness that surrounded her, her heart spoke to her again as it had in the tunnel when she'd chosen Durren over the Shadow Man and gone to him in the depths of Drakkonwehr. *He wants life. He wants to live. Save him.*

At once, the stones collapsed inside her hand. She opened her eyes to black-red blood squirting between her clenched fingers. Fine streams trickled down her hand and dripped from her wrist. While she watched, entranced, drop by precious drop landed on Durren's wound, where each one sizzled and soaked in.

When the flow stopped, she laid her hand on the puncture and smeared what remained on her palm into the cut. If she could do nothing else, she could at least give every last possible drop to the man she loved.

****

Durren had passed into that blessed nothingness again, that free fall into oblivion, when something yanked him back. *Dear Koronolan, would this pain never end?* And then it did—except for the all too familiar searing sensation of a blade being withdrawn, of a fire burning from the inside out. He coughed, sucked a mouthful of something, and gasped, "I…can't breathe…"

"Yes, you can, or you wouldn't be telling us."

He heard relief in his sister's voice, but those were not her arms cradling his body. He spat fabric from his mouth and breathed again, this time inhaling the scent, the essence of the woman he loved. "Mirianna…" he whispered.

"Oh Durren, you're back!" Under his cheek, her heart beat with solid, life-affirming thuds.

He'd been cold but, oddly enough, warmth flooded him as the burning receded. His muscles responded, and he reached up to touch her. Her fingers laced into his gloved hand, but darkness persisted before his eyes. "Where are you, love? I can't see you."

"Maybe it's time you took that hood off," Ayliss said.

"What?" Mirianna's voice echoed his, and she gripped him as hard as he gripped her.

"You know I can't," he said to Ayliss.

"Is that possible?" Mirianna breathed.

"You're whole again, Durren. You and the Dragon and the Sword," Ayliss said. "You saw the Sword."

"Yes, but…" *Was it possible? Did he dare?* He'd lived so long in the dark, under the curse, he could barely conceive of anything else.

"I've touched you, Durren. I've seen you with my fingers," said Mirianna, her voice taut with the sound of hope. "I know I have nothing to fear."

"Trust in yourself, son of Koronolan," said the Dragon. "Trust that you have become again what was always best about you."

If he truly was redeemed, if Mirianna had in fact saved him, perhaps he could…trust. *Dear Koronolan!* He could see a little now through the weave of the fabric he'd lived under for so long. Always it had obscured his vision, darkening and limiting his world. He'd done that to himself, but now he was free. *Wasn't he? Did he dare?*

"I need to stand," he said. Mirianna and Ayliss helped him up, and he told them, "You have to let me go," when he found his balance, shaky though it was. "You've brought me this far. I have to do this part on my own." After they stepped back, he reached up under his hood and felt for the cloth that always covered his face. But it wasn't there.

"I—uh—took off your face cloth, sir," Gareth said. "I know I wasn't supposed to touch you, but I figured since I'd already sponged you once, and I was afraid you were going to die, I wanted to—you know—remember you, sir."

Durren swallowed past the lump in his throat. Anyone could've seen him during the battle if his hood had shifted. He could've killed them all—if he still bore the curse. Only the fabric he'd lived so long beneath separated him from a life he hadn't known in years.

Was he worthy?

With trembling hands he held his breath and pulled back his hood.

At first he could barely see for the brightness of the fire. It shone like the sun into eyes not used to direct light of any kind. Still, no one gasped. No one fell down in shock, so he slowly raised his head.

Ayliss smiled at him, and Gareth peered in his general direction. The old man tilted his head like a curious bird. Rees stood with crossed arms and glowered from the edge of the group. The fat man kissed his charm, gaze darting between the Dragon and Durren as though unsure what posed more of a threat. Not one of them died—or screamed—so the curse must truly be lifted.

What in Beggeth did he look like now? He could barely remember the image he'd paid so little attention to in the mirror so long ago. He'd thought it passable then, but now… *Dear Koronolan!* Baring his face to the judgment of the woman he loved was more terrifying than anything he'd ever done. Heart rattling his ribs, he turned toward Mirianna.

****

Mirianna dreamed the same dream again, just before morning. Her lover leaned over her, as he always did, with his strong shoulders blocking the light and his face nothing but a glimmer of eyes. Sometimes he touched her lips, but when she woke to the contact, it was her own fingers tracing the shape of her mouth, as they did now, while she looked at the man of her dreams.

All these years she'd searched for him among the men she'd met, waited for him to come, and here he was, standing before her in the firelight, his form, his figure everything she'd come to know over the last days. But his face? In all the times she'd feared seeing him unveiled, in all the nightmares and daydreams, she'd never once considered what he might look like other than being appealing to look upon. Down in the pool, her fingers had told her he had a straight nose, thick brows, strong cheekbones, and fine scars crisscrossing his skin with a deeper one scoring one eyebrow. And his hair? Thick, like hers. Straight, not like hers. And definitely in need of a trim.

She saw his eyes first, eyes she'd longed to see, to read, to understand the soul behind them. They glimmered, she realized, as they always had, the same green as his sister's, and she breathed. So that was why her heart knew that color, and trusted it.

"Do you—do you find me...pleasing, Mirianna?" Durren asked.

Cocking her head, she stepped closer. From here she could discern the straight nose, the strong cheekbones, the thick brows. And his hair, loose—and definitely too long—framing his pale face with a surprising ebony contrast. She'd never expected dark hair, but perhaps she should have, considering her dream image.

She took another step, and the particulars of his face took shape. The scars, fine silver lines her fingers had discovered, gleamed subtly everywhere, and the bigger one ran down from his hairline like a silver cord to split one raven eyebrow. He was whole now, and these fine scars showed her how his once broken body and soul had been knit back together, piece by tiny piece. She'd helped with that, she and Ayliss and Gareth and the Beast that had lived inside him. But he'd taken this last step himself, throwing off his fears, his burdens, all that he'd been for so long, to open himself to her.

"Do I find you pleasing, Durren?" she said as he looked at her with hope in his eyes. "How could I ever find you otherwise? I've loved you since I first met you—in our dream." She flung herself into his arms and rained kisses on his face.

Chapter Thirty-Five

When they'd piled the Krad bodies on a pyre outside the fortress gates, the Dragon blasted the heap with flame. A fresh breeze arose with the dawn and blew the stinking black smoke away into the Wehrland.

"That should warn off the rest of the Krad," Rees proclaimed. He untied his horse from the well's trough while sunlight warmed the courtyard. "We should have safe passage all the way to Nolar."

Mirianna handed him his sword. "I'm not going back."

He eyed Durren, standing beside her. "I thought as much."

"I'm not going either," said Tolbert from where he sat sipping hot water beside the coals of the fire he'd tended all through the night.

"Are you sure, Papa?" Mirianna said, even as her heart swelled. "What about our house? Your tools?"

He waved his hand. "We have all summer to think about settling our affairs and fetching our goods. The point is you need me here now. This place is a wreck. You and the Sha—Durren need someone with an eye for how things fit together." He flushed when Mirianna bent to kiss the top of his head.

"I'm not going either," said Pumble. He drew himself up to all the height he could manage. "I know I'm not good with a bow like Rees, but you're going to need someone to go for supplies to rebuild this place, and I know the way through the Wehrland as well as anybody." He scuffed a toe through the dirt. "Besides, this is the greatest story to come out of the land in two lifetimes, and I'd like to be the one to tell it."

Rees shook his head. "You can have your stories. And that Beast of Beggeth, too." He nodded at the Dragon perched on the highest rampart, sunning its wings. "There's too much darkness here for my taste."

"Perhaps it feeds your own shadows," Durren said.

Rees snorted. "Spoken by the man of shadows himself." He handed the sword back to Mirianna. "Keep it. You're good with it, and I like my bow better anyway. Besides, something tells me you're going to need it. This place is too damned close to Beggeth, and you've stirred the nest over there."

"You could stay, too," Pumble said. "Who knows what's happened in Nolar since that mage gave up our master's shape. You could be in trouble."

"I'll take my chances. I can handle anything human." He swung into the saddle and turned his horse toward the gate. "Good luck. If I see any of you again, it'll be too soon."

As Rees rode out of sight, Pumble wiped his nose. "He'll be back. Did you see how he looked at the lion lady?"

Mirianna nodded. If she correctly read the muscle twitching in Durren's jaw, his feelings on that possibility matched hers. "I don't think Ayliss shares his interest."

Pumble shrugged and sat down beside Tolbert. "Just as well. I don't think he knows she used to be a lion."

Helen C. Johannes

Tolbert chuckled and Gareth grinned while he polished the Sword of Drakkonwehr, but Ayliss sat half-turned toward the ramparts with a faraway look in her eyes.

Mirianna glanced at Durren. The thick brows she was beginning to know with her eyes as well as her hands knit into a frown. Understanding the direction of his thoughts, she laced her fingers through his, flesh to flesh in the open at last. "She'll tell us when she's ready."

"Perhaps." He exhaled. "Syryk can wait, for now. There's something else that can't." Walking around the fire pit, he drew Mirianna to a stop before Ayliss and the boy. "I need to know," he said to Ayliss, "about the Sword."

She turned and the green eyes focused on the here and now. "You mean, why Gareth could wield what only a Drakkonwehr can wield?"

"He's my son, isn't he?"

Ayliss smiled, a full blooming smile. "You've known it from the moment you saw him, didn't you? Your heart told you. You just didn't think it possible you could've conceived a child with the woman you visited at Ulerroth's that night before everything fell apart."

"I—but…my mother had a husband…" Gareth gaped at them.

Ayliss hugged him. "Your mother wed the first kind man who offered to take her away from Ulerroth's. In my lion form I followed her when she left Ar-Deneth, and I watched you grow after he died. I knew who you were from the moment you were conceived."

"You mean…I'm part of your family?"

412

"Oh, Gareth!" Mirianna said as his face lit up. She wanted to clasp him to her heart, but this move was not hers. This was between Durren and Gareth, and what the man she loved said next was all that mattered.

"You *are* our family." Durren reached toward the boy's shoulder, but Gareth dropped the Sword with a clatter, leaped to his feet, and flung his arms around the man who used to be a shadow.

****

Durren's arms crept around the boy as Gareth's hair tickled his cheek. He stood, shivering, while his gut burned as it had one night not so very long ago, when he'd been someone else entirely. That someone had longed for the tunnels, the caves, the deep silent blackness beneath Drakkonwehr. That someone feared his own Shadow, the darkness and guilt staining his soul. He'd almost lost himself to that Shadow, but now he knew it for what it was, the part of him that taught him what was truly worth living for, what he dared not lose again.

The Shadow Man had no knowledge of how it felt to touch and be touched, yet here he was, Durren at last, hugging his son. "My son," he choked.

He threaded fingers through the boy's hair, savoring the fine strands between his bare fingers, absorbing the warmth flowing from Gareth's body into his own, holding close what he'd never dreamed to have. He reached out and seized Mirianna, drawing her into the embrace. "Ayliss thinks she made the magic, but you're the one who really broke the curse. You loved me when I wasn't worth loving."

"You were always worth loving," she said, smiling through glistening eyes. "You just forgot that for a while. And I didn't break the curse, our hearts did."

Durren planted a kiss on her lips. Maybe the little he'd remembered of Owender's *History* had been enough after all.

A word about the author...

Helen C. Johannes lives in the Midwest with her husband and grown children. Growing up, she read fairy tales, Tolkien, *The Scarlet Pimpernel*, Agatha Christie, Shakespeare, and Ayn Rand, an unusual mix that undoubtedly explains why the themes, characters, and locales in her writing play out in tales of love and adventure.

A member of Romance Writers of America, she credits the friends she has made and the critiques she's received from her chapter members for encouraging her to achieve her dream of publication.

When not working on her next writing project, she teaches English, reads all kinds of fiction, enjoys walks, and travels as often as possible.

Helen is the author of *The Prince of Val-Feyridge*, also published by The Wild Rose Press, Inc.

Thank you for purchasing
this publication of The Wild Rose Press, Inc.
For other wonderful stories of romance,
please visit our on-line bookstore at
www.thewildrosepress.com.

For questions or more information
contact us at
info@thewildrosepress.com.

The Wild Rose Press, Inc.
www.thewildrosepress.com

To visit with authors of
The Wild Rose Press, Inc.
join our yahoo loop at
http://groups.yahoo.com/group/thewildrosepres
s/